Praise for *Maya's Dance*

'If there is one thing you learn from *Maya's Dance*, it is that art sets
us free. An unforgettable and moving love story in the midst
of one of the darkest and most terrible times of humanity.
A book that from the first page you can't stop reading.'
Armando Lucas Correa, bestselling author of *The German Girl*

'*Maya's Dance* combines the perfect blend of tragic heartache and
enduring hope. Helen Signy's voice is true to the times, and in Maya
and Jan she has created characters that leap from the page. This is
a book that any lover of Holocaust fiction will cherish.'
Anita Abriel, bestselling author of *The Light After the War*

'This novel, based on the true story of a Holocaust survivor, resonates
with the horrors of these terrible times. Helen Signy portrays the
horrors of a slave labour camp, the kindness of a Polish guard,
and a love story that spanned decades.'
Maya Lee, bestselling author of *The Nazis Knew My Name*

MAYA'S
DANCE

Dear Uncle John

MAYA'S DANCE

All my love

HELEN SIGNY

Helen Signy

SIMON &
SCHUSTER

London · New York · Sydney · Toronto · New Delhi

MAYA'S DANCE
First published in Australia in 2024 by
Simon & Schuster (Australia) Pty Limited
Suite 19A, Level 1, Building C, 450 Miller Street, Cammeray, NSW 2062

10 9 8 7 6 5 4 3 2 1

Simon & Schuster: Celebrating 100 Years of Publishing in 2024.
Sydney New York London Toronto New Delhi
Visit our website at www.simonandschuster.com.au

NATIONAL
LIBRARY
OF AUSTRALIA

A catalogue record for this
book is available from the
National Library of Australia

ISBN: 9781761421419

Quote from *Man's Search for Meaning* by Viktor E. Frankl
Copyright ©1959, 1962, 1984, 1992, 2006 by Viktor E. Frankl
Reprinted by permission of Beacon Press, Boston

Cover design: Christabella Designs
Cover images: Woman dancing © Ildiko Neer / Trevillion Images; Soldiers © Kozlik / Shutterstock
Typeset by Midland Typesetters, Australia
Printed and bound in Australia by Griffin Press

For Lucie

The second way of finding a meaning in life is by experiencing something – such as goodness, truth and beauty – by experiencing nature and culture or, last but not least, by experiencing another human being in his very uniqueness – by loving him.

Viktor E Frankl, *Man's Search for Meaning*

1

My darling Jan

Today I have been dreaming again. I was sitting in my chair, watching the dust motes tumble and curl on the buoyant air. My eyes were heavy, but I swear I did not sleep. I remember feeling the knotted wool of my cardigan beneath my fingers, and watching a cockatoo absent-mindedly chew a gumnut in the tree outside my window.

And then I heard it. The orchestra. I glanced at the television, but it was turned off and the room was still. Yet I could hear the music clearly, each note of each bar. The drums beat first and then the clarinets joined in, jolly, celebratory. The music swelled and grew. Now violins. I shut my eyes and saw a marching band, twirling and stamping through the streets. I could almost smell the roasted chestnuts and feel the sweet shock of ice cream on my tongue.

They were playing the Radetzky March. *Our dance. Do you remember how I spun and twirled? How I became more than a Jewish girl with battered shoes and dirty clothes – I became a part of the air, the trees, the sun. I remember the intensity of your blue eyes as you watched me from the back of the crowd. We did not know then what it would mean, how that dance would change our lives.*

It has been fifty years since then, Jan. Time is losing its direction, both stretching and contracting, playing tricks. This morning is an aeon past, a tiny dot seen through the wrong end of a telescope. It is impossible to distinguish the details. Yet those months with you, they shine large and clear. I can see and hear the camp. Those stolen moments with you, the squeeze of my mother's hand, the sun on the back of my head as I stoop toward the wheelbarrow. The memories envelop every sense. I can smell them.

Here in Sydney, I am a world away from Poland and the Nazis. But you seem to be closer than ever. Space and time mean less to me now. Five long decades are dissolving and there you remain, at the centre of every-thing. You are strong and in focus. My love for you has not diminished. We are still bound together, you and I.

Today, after I heard our dance again, I made a decision. I have thought about it often over the years, but now the time is right. I am alone and my brain won't work for ever. Today I met someone who can help me. I am going to find you again.

Just a little longer, my love. I am coming to you.

For ever

Maya

Sydney, May 1995

Kate tied a double knot in the laces of her sensible shoes and opened the front door. Steadying herself with a deep breath, she paused for a moment before she stepped out of the cool, dark silence of her cluttered hallway into Sydney's buzz and hum. Late autumn filled the street; the weak sun slanted across the rooftops but the clouds were heavy with rain. She opened the gate and headed up the hill. Today would have to be better.

She fixed her eyes on the broken paving stones at her feet as she walked quickly towards the bus stop. She knew them well now, each crack and hole in the pavement. The discordant warbling of currawongs in the treetops reminded her that she was far from home.

Last night she had lain awake, crumpled covers twisting around her legs and her radio alarm clock flashing through the seconds. The time had swelled and spread, dragging her heavy, listless body through alternating stages of wakefulness and sluggish sleep. Peter was gone.

It was a month now since his letter had arrived. Her heart had brightened at the Hong Kong postmark, and at first she did not believe what was written in the familiar black ink of his fountain pen. He had met someone else. Her name was Natasha. They were moving back to the UK – together. He had tried to be faithful, he really had, but his relationship with Kate was never going to work across the distance. He would always remember her with affection.

Kate blotted her eyes with her sleeve and focused on the busy road at the top of the hill. Oxford Street. It was already milling with people: young men in suits, women with freshly shampooed hair and heels they would regret by lunchtime. Some of them were smiling. Kate weaved among them, twenty-eight and all alone, swept along by the crowd in the big, dusty city.

He would have loved it here. In the six months since she had arrived, it was as if each new experience had existed only in order that she could one day relive it with him. Every day had spoken of a shared future. She had assessed her work acquaintances for their potential as his friends. She would run a silent conversation with him in her head as she sat by the sparkling Harbour or scanned a menu in a new café. Eventually it seemed as if he had been here with her all along in this friendless new city. It was unimaginable that through those months he had been living a different, real life in Hong Kong. And she no longer played a part. Her stomach knotted.

She walked past cafés and clubs, sidestepping sleepy restaurateurs as they hosed last night's grime and vomit from the pavement. Past the bookshop, no time to linger, then she slowed as she neared the bridal shop, its window resplendent with cream silk and taffeta. Her reflection stared back at her, ghostly against the wedding dresses and sparkling chandelier. Just a normal young woman, hair pulled back carelessly into a high ponytail, work pants a couple of years out of fashion, cardigan slightly pilled from the wash. A well-bred, intelligent sort of woman, someone you would introduce to your mother. Dependable, no-nonsense, English. The sort of young woman who just yesterday had burst into tears when her GP had asked, 'How are you?'

She held the strap of her handbag against her chest like a protective shield as she climbed onto the heaving, fume-spewing bus. The brakes squealed and she jolted forward as it harrumphed its way towards the terminus. Today, like every day, she would pull herself together. Walk into the newspaper office, nod politely in the lift, sit at her desk and take a moment to still her racing heart. Hold on white-knuckle tight, as if gripping a palm tree in a tsunami.

'Morning.' It was a statement rather than a greeting. The chief-of-staff, Jackson, did not look up.

'Hi.' Her tone sounded unnaturally bright; the small shock of hearing her voice outside her head.

'You will need to go back to the city. There's a fiftieth anniversary memorial for the Holocaust this weekend. They're planning a big do at the Opera House. There's a press conference this morning with a group of survivors. Scully's just finishing off in the darkroom, he'll drive you.'

Jackson held out a piece of paper with printed instructions. His voice softened. 'I know, I know. It's another picture story. I know you're more than capable of covering something bigger than this, with your experience in Asia and everything. That's why I'm asking you to do it.' He studied his hands. 'Go and see what you can find. You never know, this could be your big break.'

⁓

Scully was sullen and hungover. He swore as they waited at the traffic lights, lurching start-stop through the morning traffic. He cursed again when he could not find a parking bay. Kate rested her hands on her lap, occasionally glancing at his strong hands on the steering wheel, his delicate brown fingers, the pale pink of the webbing where the sun and surf had never reached. Was he angry at her? The photographers all knew her assignments were a waste of their time. Her ethnic affairs and religion round usually yielded page ten at best – stories about migrants and church groups. 'We're bound to find a good human-interest angle,' she said brightly, trying to sound convincing.

They were already late when the white sail tips of the Opera House came into view. Scully threw the car backwards and forwards aggressively as he manoeuvred into a parking space, then heaved his heavy camera gear off the back seat. Kate trotted beside him as they made their way back along the road towards the Harbour. Side by side up the steps. To anyone else they could have been mistaken for a couple. She thought of the times she had walked up steps with Peter, grabbing each other's hands, and pushed the image away. Scully shoved through the door in front of her and she followed at his shoulder, trying to keep up as he strode through the echoing foyer.

A small group of journalists had already gathered. They were shuffling their feet and looking at their watches. Scully backslapped a Channel 10 cameraman, his white teeth gleaming and his eyes creased in a greeting. Kate slipped to the side of the crowd, close to the door, and peered into the room where the final touches were being made for the press conference. Trestle tables had been erected at one end, covered in white cloths, a cluster of microphones on top like a bunch of black flowers. A small audience sat fidgeting and coughing, settling into the seats, greeting each other, laughing. The Holocaust survivors.

She sat down quietly and started to observe. She felt calmer now, more of a real person and less one half of a broken couple. Her work, where she was trained to read faces and listen to snatches of conversation – this was what she did best. She took out her notebook ready to find an angle, something new, something interesting.

The organiser was talking about the Holocaust, but she focused on the survivors. An elderly gentleman in the next row smoothed the back of his hair with a sun-spotted hand. As his sleeve rode up, she noticed a neat row of faded numbers tattooed on his forearm. Others held hands or wiped away tears as the speaker recited a few lines of poetry. What must these people have seen? Every one of them would have a story.

But which had *the* story? The story that would prove to her colleagues that she could turn her hand to almost anything.

This was harder than they realised, those other journalists whose only job was to record what was said in parliament or at court. There the story was handed to them on a platter. But here? These people had suffered, they had lived through the Holocaust for God's sake. You couldn't just grab one and ask them what it felt like. This was what took real skill – forming that connection, encouraging them to talk. And then the writing. That had always been her expertise. Capturing a lifetime's experience and trauma in a few hundred carefully chosen words. She would chip away at the sentences until they were right, until the narrative sang. Not everyone could do that. Not as well as she could, anyway.

She glanced down at the still empty page of her notepad. She would find the story. She always did. She was a good journalist; better than they knew.

The organiser finished speaking and placed his hands gently on the lectern. For a moment, a respectful silence echoed around the room until, as if on starter's orders, the journalists stood and moved as one towards the survivors, like seagulls swooping on fish. Kate sat back, watching the television reporters divide their spoils, hiving off interviewees into exclusive corners of the room. Just be patient, she told herself; it's going to happen. The story always found her, she just needed to hold her nerve. Scully was standing in the aisle, arms folded across his chest and the camera hanging loose off his shoulder, waiting for her to make her move. She glanced around. There weren't many survivors left to interview.

An older lady to her right smiled at her – a warm, gentle smile.

'Quite a speech.' Kate smiled back at her, encouragingly.

'Oh yes, he spoke very well.'

The lady's head was bent forward; her grey hair was pulled neatly into a bun at the base of her neck, a style she had probably worn all her life. Her skin was now thin and taut over her high cheekbones and there was a hint of fleshiness about her nose and jowls, but the set of her mouth, the straightness of her back, the scarf elegantly draped around her neck, implied her former beauty.

'What brings you here today?' Kate asked. Keep it fresh and friendly; wait for something significant to be said.

The lady smiled again, perhaps with embarrassment. 'I was in a camp in Poland. I lost my mother and my grandmother. My stepfather, too.'

Kate hesitated for a moment, unsure what to say. 'How awful for you.' She was aware how inadequate she sounded.

The lady extended a thin arm. 'I am Maria. You may call me Maya.'

Kate glanced at the tip of the lady's handkerchief poking out of her sleeve, but there were no tattooed numbers that she could see. A diamond bracelet glinted on her wrist.

'Which camp were you at?' asked Kate.

Maya smoothed her skirt. 'I was in a small labour camp in east Poland. I lived there for more than a year. One of the guards fell in love with me and helped me to escape.'

Kate's stomach clenched with the thrill. What a story! The rush was better than any drug. 'I'd love to hear about it,' she said, taking out her notepad and beckoning Scully with her eyes.

2

Maya was seven years old and she was dancing, twirling, soaring in the living room. Her mother, Rosa, had gone to the shops, just for an hour – 'Stay quiet, Maya, your father's trying to sleep' – but Maya had ignored her. Mutti was too distracted these days to ever administer any real form of punishment. In fact, Maya was being far from quiet. She had snuck into the formal living room, past the volumes of her father's book collection stuffed haphazardly into the heavy wooden bookshelf, past the crystal vases and the Persian rug, to her new possession, a gramophone. She had carefully lifted the needle – not yet brave enough to touch the record itself or pull a new one from its case – and wound the handle.

The room filled with anticipatory crackles until the orchestra's strong, determined notes rang out. The volume was too high – surely they would come for her now. She stood with a straight back, her feet in first position and her hands in *bras bas*, waiting. The music lifted her with gentle hands and her legs started to move. She raised her arms and spun. She became a bird, a butterfly. She flew high above the red roofs of Prague, swooping and diving and feeling the wind with the tips of her fingers. She whirled and whirled. Faster, faster. Her fair hair shone as it flew in front of her eyes. The walls start to blur and her skirt lifted into a circle. She felt free, as light as air. Dizzy. Elated. She could dance for ever.

Sydney, May 1995

Kate woke early the next morning, parched and nauseous after a night with the other journalists in the pub. She had let their chatter and laughter envelop her, the plumes of smoke from their cigarettes, their bragging. She was drinking too much, she knew she was. But the pub after work was the only place she could find company. And with a beer in her hand, she could forget Peter, the last six months, his letter. Maya and the Holocaust had faded into another day's work with each foamy bottle.

The weekend ahead loomed long and empty. In Hong Kong, Peter would have come to her, stroking her head as he offered a glass of water and a paracetamol. They would have mopped up their hangovers with yum cha, then made their way through the hot, heaving crowd back to their little apartment with its dripping air conditioner, high above the steamy street. They would have gone back to bed and, afterwards, she would have rested against his chest as they read the Saturday paper.

'Stop it,' she admonished herself. The voice in her head sounded like her mother's. 'Chin up, you just have to *carry on*. Or you can always go back home . . .' No, that was ridiculous. She had this chance, it was one of the world's great newspapers. She would show them. And today, at least, she'd have a by-line.

She pulled on her clothes, tiptoed quickly along the hall and retrieved the bulky newspaper from the front step. She picked at the cling film to find the seam and spread the paper flat on the floor. There, on page three, Scully's photograph of the old lady stared up at her from the page. She felt a stab of disappointment as she saw that her story had been condensed into a six-line caption: *Holocaust survivor Maria Schulze-Johnson, 69, meets other survivors at the Opera House yesterday ahead of this weekend's Holocaust remembrance celebrations. As a teenager, Mrs Schulze-Johnson lost her entire family in the extermination camps, then escaped from eastern Poland to live undercover in Nazi Germany for two years until the end of the war. Members of the public can meet survivors and hear stories from the Holocaust at this week's memorial exhibition, opening at the Sydney Jewish Museum on 29 May.*

Kate examined the photograph. It was a close-up shot. In the low light, the wrinkles on Maya's cheeks formed dark canyons and rivulets. Her bony hand brushed her chin and her eyes looked straight into the camera, steadfast and bold.

Kate leaned back against the wall, holding the paper at an angle towards the weak light of the frosted glass of the front door, and stared into the eyes of her future.

3

Dear Ms Young

We met two weeks ago at the Holocaust memorial press conference. I would like to thank you for taking the time to speak with me.

It is now fifty years since I last saw the young man who saved my life, a Mr Jan Novak. As I explained to you, we were in love and he risked his life to get me out of the camp. My husband died recently, and I feel that now is the time for me to finally find Jan and thank him in person.

I am writing to ask whether you would consider helping me to find him? In return I am happy to tell you my full story. I think you would find it interesting.

Yours

Maya Schulze-Johnson

Kate re-read the letter, which had sat on her desk for two weeks now. It was marked with a coffee stain and creased where she had accidentally covered it with a heavy file.

It wasn't rare to receive requests from readers. Most were looking for free help to track lost relatives or money; there was nothing in it for a busy journalist whose career depended on the daily uncovering of something new – or something that at least wouldn't be discarded by the chief sub because it was irrelevant to the broader readership of the paper. Losers, he'd call her refugees and 'ethnics'. Boring for our readers, he'd say. Recently, she'd received a rambling letter from a young student who the following weekend had fired a starting pistol at the Governor-General. Thank God she'd kept that letter, which luckily contained a photo of the shooter along with the clearly set out reasons for his attack. It had appeared on page one. His gripe was something about the treatment of Cambodian boat people. To be honest, she understood his frustration; no Australian media would cover the story. Since then, she'd been careful not to throw correspondence away; letters sat crowded in her drawer next to the stapler and paperclips.

Maya's story intrigued her, of course, but it wasn't *news*. She turned the large, crisp pages of today's newspaper and expertly folded it to read page seven. Only an experienced journalist could wrangle a broadsheet page like that. The newsroom buzzed around her – Australian reporters working on stories about politics and the economy. So sure of themselves. Jackson hadn't given her anything to do today, and she was never going to climb the ladder just sitting here, doodling on her notepad.

'Just try *harder*, Kate.' The parental voice in her head again. She had not talked much to her mother before she left, stuffing a few clothes into a battered rucksack and heading for the Far East – 'India? It's just not clean darling' – then years spent on the move, in grimy dormitories and humid alleyways, moving, always moving, searching for who knew what? Her parents' genteel living room in Surrey slowly filled with photos of their only daughter, but it always felt stifling to her.

She realised she had scratched right through the page. Maybe a breath of air would help. She threw the pen onto the desk and took the lift to the roof. Haywood, the deputy foreign editor, greeted her with a wave of his hand. He was smoking a cigarette with purpose and tapping his fingers on his thigh.

'Working on something interesting?' They stood at a convivial distance, gazing across the city towards the hazy blue of the mountains beyond.

'Actually, yes,' she lied, and paused for a moment to think of something to tell him. 'It's a great story about a Holocaust survivor reuniting with the guard who fell in love with her and saved her.'

'Good one.' Wisps of smoke escaped between Haywood's grey teeth as he spoke. 'I reckon if you got that story up we could go big on it for a Saturday. A good pic and we could maybe get page one and a feature inside.' His enthusiasm grew. 'When's the meeting happening? Could we have the story for this weekend? I've got a bloody great hole that I don't know how to fill.'

Kate smiled. 'I'm going to see her this week. I'll let you know how it goes.' She returned to her desk feeling lighter than she had in weeks. She picked up the receiver and dialled the number. 'Mrs Schulze-Johnson? This is Kate Young from the *Times*. I got your letter and I'd love to follow up. Shall we make it tomorrow, say eleven-ish?'

⌒

Kate arrived at Maya's front door promptly at eleven the next day and rang the bell. There was a muffled bump of something falling on carpet, then silence. She waited. Still nothing. She rang the bell again. At last, a shuffling in the hallway. Maya opened the door and peered out in surprise. 'Good morning, can I help you?'

'Hello, Mrs Schulze-Johnson. I'm Kate Young. The journalist from the *Times*? We met the other day at the press conference about the Holocaust memorial, and then you wrote me a letter.'

Maya narrowed her eyes and gazed momentarily into the distance above Kate's head with the effort of remembering, then her face relaxed. There was light in her smile. 'Oh, of course, my *liebe*, I'm so sorry. Please, please, come in.' She moved aside and beckoned Kate into the hallway. 'And please, call me Maya.'

The house was tidy and clean. Dark, polished walnut furniture filled the living room and a large clock ticked loudly on the mantlepiece.

The room smelled of coffee and dill. So, was this what a life looked like after the worst imaginable suffering? Kate wondered what it would take to have survived something like that. How could you rebuild, make it count?

She looked around the room. Dusty books were stacked this way and that on a large bookshelf, so many that the overflow stood on the floor in neat stacks. The titles were in different languages, German, English and French, many of their spines displaying titles that Kate could not read. Maya followed Kate's gaze. 'German is my mother tongue, and I speak five other languages fluently,' she said. 'I love reading in different languages. Each one gives you such a unique perspective on the world. Please, sit down.'

Kate sank into a well-worn armchair. She wished she had paid more attention to her German lessons at school.

Framed photographs covered every available surface. Maya smiled out of them in black and white and colour, laughing with different groups of friends, on her wedding day – an older bride, fifty perhaps – riding a horse, at the ballet.

'You have the most beautiful smile,' Kate said.

'Yes, I have been told that many times. My smile has saved my life in fact, more than once.' Maya placed a tray with china coffee cups and almond biscuits on the table. 'Please, eat something.'

Kate sipped her coffee. It was strong.

'You must be wondering why I wrote to you,' said Maya. 'Let me explain. Six months ago, Glen, my third husband, died. It was very sudden.'

'Oh, I'm so sorry to hear that,' said Kate.

'Thank you, my dear. Now I'm nearly seventy and completely alone again.' Maya's head shook slightly. 'Of course I have been terribly sad, but now at least I have time to think of myself. All my life, I have dreamed of finding Jan, the Polish guard who helped me. And I have realised that time is running out. It is my last chance.'

Kate pulled her reporter's notepad and pen out of her bag. 'I have to be honest with you, I'm not an investigative reporter. But I can certainly give it a go. I've already got interest from the paper. What can you tell me about him?'

Maya rummaged through a stack of letters on the coffee table between them. She pulled out a grey envelope and handed it to Kate. It was softened and stained with age, bent at the corners with frequent handling. Kate took it and gingerly lifted the flap. Inside was a thin letter, almost translucent, folded over a black and white photograph. From it a young man gazed up at her with steady eyes. His head was held stiffly above a high army collar and woollen jacket. His hair was slicked back in the style of the forties, receding a little already over his smooth, high forehead. He had an aquiline nose and full lips, settled into a stern expression but with a hint of an uneasy smile around the corners. He was clearly not comfortable having his photograph taken. Kate turned it over in her hands. The words 'Jan Novak, Chelm, 1943' were written on the back in blue ink.

The letter was in the same hand and addressed from Chelm, Poland. It was dated *Maj 1944*. 'Let me translate it for you.' Maya did not need to look at the words; she recited the letter's contents by heart.

May 1944

Maryska, my love, my dearest

This may be my last letter. The Germans have suffered heavy losses and Chelm will soon be conquered by the Red Army. The Russians have already crossed the River Bug and I can hear the bombardment in the distance. It seems the Third Reich is over, the time is near.

My darling Maya, you must wait for me where you are. For now you are safe at the convent. We do not know what will happen. Soon there will be no mail, no travel, no order. But I will come for you. I promise I will come. Believe in this.

Dance for me, sing for me. Stay strong, my love. This is our final test. I love you.

For ever

Jan

'He must have really loved you.' Kate stifled a quick stab of pain as she pictured Peter's letter, still sitting on her mantlepiece.

'Oh yes. You know, despite the hardship, during the war I also experienced a great deal of happiness.'

The clock ticked. Maya sat forward in her chair, waiting for Kate to say something.

'Okay, if we're going to find him, I'll need as much factual information as you can give me. Basically, I need you to tell me everything you know about him.'

Maya screwed up her eyes to think. 'He was a gentleman, he was courteous and kind.' Kate's pen hovered in the air, but she did not write this down. She let Maya fill the silence between them.

Maya started again. 'Well, his name was Jan Novak. He was nineteen when I met him. He was born in Warsaw, but his family moved to Chelm for his father's job during the war and he lived there with his parents and sister, Danuta. Jan was studying engineering at university and at that time he was working for the Third Reich as part of the *Wasserwirtschafts Inspektion*.'

Kate shook her head, not understanding.

'Water management inspection,' Maya translated. Ah, some tangible information. Kate wrote quickly and turned to a clean page. Perhaps she could do a search of the organisation's records to find him.

'What was his father's job?'

Maya shook her head. She appeared slightly flustered. 'I must tell you that I sometimes have a little trouble with my memory.'

Kate realised she would need to take this slowly.

'Do you know anything about Jan's movements after the war? After he sent you this letter?'

'Well, I heard he may have died in the Warsaw uprising in 1944. But I have never believed that. My intuition has always told me that he survived. Though unless we trace him, I will never know.' Maya looked at Kate expectantly.

'Right.' Kate placed her notepad and pen on her lap. This was not going to be easy. She would need to let Maya talk. It did not actually matter whether or not she could remember the factual details that might eventually lead to Jan. There was a story there, Kate could feel it. She just had to listen and it would come. She glanced at her watch. She had plenty of time.

'Okay, I guess we start at the beginning. Tell me how it all started.'

4

Brno, Czech Republic, March 1939

It was Saturday morning and the first buds were bursting in the chestnut trees outside the bay window. The air was thick and warm. Maya sat in her favourite armchair, her legs curled up beneath her. Her puppy, Antonín, snored softly on her lap. She tickled under his chin with her foot and felt his fur soft between her toes. It was her favourite vantage point, gazing through the bay window onto the busy street.

It was six years since Papa had died. Rosa had diminished after her husband's death; she had seemed to collapse from the inside, unable to get out of bed, relying on Maya to bring her food and water until, after three months, Maya's grandmother had swept them up and brought them here, to her apartment in Brno, far away from home in Prague. Now a teenager, Maya still loved to sit in this spot for hours and watch the new city continue, oblivious, below.

Today the crowd was busy. They seemed to be moving in one direction, towards the other side of the park beyond the square, but Maya was not sure why. Rosa and her new husband, Franz, had been out all morning; something was happening. Last evening, Maya had hung back by the open door as her grandmother, Omi, and Rosa stood around the radio, still, as if waiting for instruction. Omi's mouth had gaped open and Rosa had looked drawn and worried. Maya had listened as the solid wooden beast erupted into a Mozart waltz, then a jitterbug and a

21

snatch of crackling German before settling with a fizz on a newscaster's clipped tones. Maya had heard the word 'Hitler'. She knew what that meant. Last year they had been on summer holiday in Vranov when the Nazis had swept into Austria to a wildly cheering, saluting crowd. Her mother's cousin, Martin, had seen the writing on the wall for the Czech Republic. He had escaped with his wife and the children to Switzerland, from where he had been sending regular reports of the persecution of the Jews in Austria, thousands of whom were besieging foreign embassies for a visa out.

But it wouldn't happen here. That's what Franz said. Her stepfather believed Hitler wouldn't dare. 'We will still go down to the lake and swim this summer, I will make sure of it.' His words were calm and reassuring, but there were so many rumours. Everyone was waiting nervously, dreading this day but expecting a miracle.

Franz and Rosa had been married only a few months, filling Omi's little apartment with laughter again. Maya loved that he had become a part of their lives. He was funny and kind, intelligent. An engineer. He would look after them. Despite the gloomy news from the radio, Maya felt more secure now than at any time since her father's death.

She scanned the distance through the bay window, straining to see the raised arm of a Nazi salute or to hear the stamp of marching boots. She shivered and realised she was thirsty. She slid out of the chair, moving carefully so as not to disturb the sleeping puppy, and padded through the apartment, away from the window and the frenetic energy of the street. She poured herself a glass of milk and took it into the living room, running her free hand across the smooth Steinway piano. Omi had a beautiful apartment, and this piano was definitely its best asset. Maya loved to play, letting the music flow around her like water.

She drank the milk, placed the glass on a small table, then turned to look at her reflection in the dark wood of the piano, holding her head to one side and pulling her fair hair back with her fingers. She could pass for much older than thirteen. Sophisticated – some might say beautiful. She raised her arms above her head and realised how tall she had grown.

The door opened with a gush of air. 'He's arrived. Hitler has arrived in Brno,' Rosa spoke brightly but her jaw was tight. She adjusted her hair in the hall mirror, as if that would make a difference to the Führer. 'Come, let's go and watch. We can buy ice cream on the way home.'

Mother and daughter wandered arm in arm through the park, heading towards their favourite patisserie in the city centre. It was doing a brisk trade today and the baker laughed as he handed out *strudl* and *trdelnik* to the excited crowd. Men were drinking beer; the waiters took their orders with an eye on the street, craning their necks in anticipation. Maya and Rosa positioned themselves in the middle of the throng. A little boy next to them was sitting high on his father's shoulders. Maya smiled at him. People leaned out of the windows above their heads, their Nazi flags rippling slowly in the festive air.

Soon a frisson ran through the crowd. Something was happening. There was clapping in the distance, a soft crackle at first but it quickly swelled into a rhythmic chant, louder and louder along the street until they were enveloped in sound, euphoric cheering, staccato and strong: '*Sieg Heil! Sieg Heil!*' The man with the little boy grabbed his hat and thrust it into the air with his arm held straight in the Nazi salute.

The cavalcade approached. Maya heard the rumbling of the car as it glided over the cobblestones. She could see him now. Hitler was a little man, but his presence filled the street. He stood at the front of the car, his back straight, his right hand raised in a fixed salute, his left holding the windscreen to steady himself. He was smiling. The crowd was wild. The little boy burst into tears.

And then the Führer was gone. Maya realised she had been holding her breath. Rosa grabbed her by the arm and pulled her quickly away, back across the park. Just a few minutes had passed; the benches and the trees were the same, the birds oblivious as they pecked crumbs from the ground. But Maya felt strangely uncomfortable. Was everyone *staring* at them? She held her mother's hand tightly and their pace quickened to nearly a run as they made their way to the sanctuary of the apartment.

～

At 8 am the next day, Rosa's German senior shop assistant, Vilma, arrived at the apartment. She stood up straight before Maya's mother. 'You must give me the keys. The textile shop has now been Aryanised.' She did not look Rosa in the eye.

Maya watched in disbelief. Her mother and Vilma had worked together for years, laughing and chatting as they stacked colourful fabrics and sewing needles onto wooden shelves. They were friends. Vilma had taught Maya to sew; just last week she had hugged Maya goodbye and told her not to worry. Had Maya done something to upset her? She smiled at Vilma; her smile usually worked, it would soften anyone. But Vilma was immutable. She opened her bag and retrieved a paper. The orders, crisp and newly stamped.

'I see.' Rosa tried to smile, but Vilma's face remained stony. 'I will still sew for you. I can serve the customers. They know me, they will buy from me.'

'No one will buy from the likes of you now,' Vilma snorted. She snatched the keys and turned away.

'But Vilma, how will we live?'

'That is not my concern.' Vilma turned to clatter along the corridor in her high heels. She did not look back.

The reason for Vilma's urgency soon became clear. By the end of the week, an edict was issued that all the Jews in Brno were to wear a cloth Star of David. Rosa sewed Maya's onto her coat by lamplight as they listened to the BBC on the radio. 'There are more than 11,000 Jews in Brno. The textile shop will have never been this busy!' laughed Franz, puffing on his pipe.

Maya tried to laugh too. But as she held up her coat to admire her mother's handiwork, she could not ignore a new feeling fluttering deep in her stomach. Fear.

～

Over the next few weeks, the German minority of Brno became louder and more aggressive. They would gather in groups, wearing *lederhosen* and *dirndls*, singing loud German folk songs through a haze of alcohol. Rosa and Omi made enquiries about the *Kindertransport* – rescue missions for children organised by the British. 'You can easily pass for Christian, with your fair hair,' Omi whispered to Maya as she led her by the hand to drop her off at her first Catholic Mass one Sunday. Maya looked down at the long black and white taffeta dress that Omi had insisted she wear. 'The Quakers will happily take you in, but they need you first to be christened. And for that you must start attending church.'

But Omi was wrong – it would not be easy to pass as a Christian. With or without the cloth star, no matter that Maya's mother tongue was German, like all the well-to-do Jewish families for the first time in her life it seemed everyone they passed could tell she was a Jew.

When the service was over, Maya left the church and set off along the tree-lined boulevard for home. People did not look her in the eye anymore – they looked at her star. Her dress crackled with each step. She felt ridiculous. She ducked down a side alley, away from their eyes. It would be a longer route, but it would be quieter.

She was nearly home when she felt the first hit. A sharp sting on her cheek. Before she could raise her hand to touch the growing welt, something else struck the back of her head. They were stones! She spun around. The narrow alley was filled with children, some of whom she recognised from school. She had never seen the others before. They were armed with pebbles and rocks. 'Get out, Jew! Go away, get out!' Their mouths twisted with the ugly words.

A large piece of brick zipped past, narrowly missing Maya's head. She could not move. A stone hit her on her shoulder, another on the side of her foot. They were raining down on her. She had no tears, no breath.

The crowd was nearly upon her; she could see the flecks of spit on their lips, a smear of chalk dust on a boy's shirt. A large rock thudded into her chest. A bolt of adrenaline shot through her and she started to run. They were close on her heels, the stones stinging the back of her head. She reached a road, then turned right into another alley. She sprinted around the corner, back to the main street, where she hoped the passers-by might slow her pursuers.

There was Omi's building, at last. She hurled herself through the gate and flung it shut, pushing against it with all her might, fumbling as she pulled the bolt across. Then up the stairs, two at a time, towards the safety of the apartment.

The higher she ran, the fainter the cries of the crowd became. But still, their words rained down on her, sharper than rocks.

'*Jude, Jude, Jude. Raus, Jude!*'

Sydney, June 1995

Maya rubbed her shoulder. 'I haven't thought about that day for many years; now it is almost as if I can feel the stones again.'

'Let's have a break.' Kate put down her notepad. She thought of the sting of Peter's betrayal. 'I can't understand how people can turn on each other so suddenly,' she said.

'Oh, it was not unusual. Things were very different in those days,' said Maya, shrugging. 'The Jews were scapegoats all over Europe. We behaved differently, we sounded different.'

'How did you go on, after that day?'

'We just had to. There was nothing we could do, there was nowhere for us to go. Everything started to change. Once Hitler arrived, it was too late for me to leave on the *Kindertransport* after all. We took things day by day, clinging to the belief that things would be all right.'

'So you just accepted it? Why didn't you fight back?'

Maya thought for a moment. 'When they started to take everything from us, the only thing we had left was the choice of how to respond. And we chose to respond with dignity. No one could take that.'

Kate looked down at her scrawled notes. 'The only thing left was choice of how to respond.' She circled the words and put a star in the margin, so she could easily find the quote later.

5

Brno, Czech Republic, March 1942

The letter was sitting on the hall table when Maya pushed open the front door and threw her school satchel on the floor. She picked it up; the seal was broken. It had been opened, then the letter had been carefully placed back inside and the flap smoothed down.

'Maya, we have been ordered to report to the school in Šlapanice.' Her mother stood in the hallway, a dishcloth in her hands and an apron tied around her narrow waist. Her red fingernails dug into the fabric, feeding it from hand to hand as she spoke. Her face was pale. 'Don't worry. We can each pack fifty kilos. You need to think about what you're going to take.'

'What if I don't want to go?' Maya thought of the boy Frantisek, how she had caught his eye at youth group, the thrill when he returned her smile. She clenched her hands into annoyed fists. She was sixteen now, just starting to be given some independence. Wasn't this stupid war supposed to be over already?

The letters had started arriving in alphabetical order. First the Benedeks had gone, then the Epsteins. Just last week their neighbour, Mrs Eisner, tried to kill herself by eating soap. Maya imagined her, vomiting and in pain, believing that to be preferable to whatever the Nazis had in store for her. They had heard that Jews were being taken to a centre at Terezín. What happened after that, nobody knew.

Now the Nazis must have reached the letter 's'. Rosa and Franz Schneider. Only a few years married, in love. Maya still bore the surname of her father, Schulze. At least they were keeping the family together.

She sat down angrily on her bed and turned her back. There was no privacy. These days, the four of them were living in just two rooms; two other families were occupying the bedrooms upstairs. Maya's family had been here for more than a year now, since they were forced out of Omi's apartment and into this grimy part of town. Perhaps their new accommodation would be better?

Would she be able to dance where they were taking her? She could not imagine a life without dancing. No one ever called her names when she danced. They just watched her with their mouths slightly open, enthralled.

She wished she was still allowed to go to the ballet. That was banned now, too, for Jews.

She looked at the few possessions she had salvaged from Omi's apartment. Not much, but surely more than fifty kilos? She had no idea what she would need where they would be going. Should she take her tap shoes? No, they were too heavy. She looked at the books lining the walls. How much did a book weigh? She took a pen and her notepad and began to write a list.

$\sim$

Omi stumbled under the weight of her carpet bag as they hauled their luggage off the bus and towards the school hall where they had been instructed to assemble. 'Did you really need to bring that vase?' Rosa tried to smile. Maya was bent low under her own bundle but held out her other hand to relieve Omi of her burden.

The hall was full and noisy. Maya followed Franz towards a small space at the back, stepping over people who had already settled themselves on the floor, looking around with wide eyes. They spread out their belongings and Maya helped Omi to sit down on the floor. The air was stuffy and smelled of sweat. Occasional spikes of temper rose above the low hum of conversation as the afternoon wore on.

'Oh my word, there is Elizabetta!' Omi exclaimed. Maya knelt up to see her grandmother's friend, Mrs Meyer, slowly picking her way distastefully between the seated families like a Persian cat tiptoeing through puddles.

Mrs Meyer was a formidable woman. Maya had feared her since she was a child. She had met her a few days after she and her mother had moved to Omi's house in Brno. Maya had hidden behind Omi as Mrs Meyer flounced up the leaf-strewn steps, tutting, her impressive bosom reaching the front door some considerable time before her immense rear. 'I've come to meet your waifs and strays from Prague,' she had said to Omi, glaring over her pointed nose at Maya, who squeezed closer into the folds of her grandmother's skirt. Omi had pulled her out and proffered her to Mrs Meyer like a new hat. Mrs Meyer had straightened Maya's dress and tutted again.

Mrs Meyer was a frequent visitor to Omi's apartment after that. She would sit in the front room with Omi, sharing coffee and cake, wiping crumbs delicately from the corner of her mouth and always reaching for a second slice. She was impeccably dressed in silk or lace, diamonds glittering from her pudgy fingers and the faint aroma of lavender wafting around her whenever she moved. Maya would sit there in silence, terrified and stiff, listening to their chatter and watching the upholstery of Omi's sofa sag under Mrs Meyer's weight.

She had never said a kind word to Maya, but one day she brought her a puppy. 'I found this pathetic thing in my back garden. Look after it, please, or I shall have to drown it.' Maya could not remember having ever said thank you, even though she had loved that dog Antonín with her whole heart. He was always by her side; he was even there in the new wedding photos, her mother's hand on his head as she looked adoringly into Franz's eyes. Who would feed Antonín now?

It struck Maya that this was the first time she had heard her grandmother utter Mrs Meyer's first name.

Mrs Meyer was tutting as usual. Franz leaped to his feet to help her with her bag and held her arm as she lowered herself heavily to the floor next to Omi. 'It's my back,' she explained as Rosa moved over to allow her to rest against the wall. She looked tired and strands of grey hair had escaped from her filigree silver hair combs. Maya offered her a cup of water. 'You are a good girl, Maya, a good girl,' said Mrs Meyer as she fanned herself with her handkerchief.

There was nothing to do but sit back and wait.

On their fourth day in the school hall, the low hum of conversation was broken by the distant rumbling of approaching buses. Maya stood up for a better view out of the open door. She was stiff after three nights with little sleep; the food they had hastily packed from home was nearly gone. She yearned to run outside in the sun, but armed guards stood at the door.

It was difficult to move around. The hall was crammed with people – Jews from across the city and the surrounding farms, the city intelligentsia mingled with labourers, religious leaders and non-practising businessmen. They were old and young, slim and fat, each with their fifty kilos of luggage and eyes wide with apprehension. When they stood up to visit the amenities, the smell of unwashed bodies was becoming overwhelming.

There was no information. The waiting was unbearable.

Rosa sat stiffly with her legs politely folded to one side. 'Surely, they'll tell us today what's going on?' she said to no one in particular as she divided their last bun into five pieces, taking the smallest for herself.

Franz was still chewing when a German official barked his name from the front of the room. At last! Franz stood up, a trifle too quickly, and strode towards a trestle table by the door like a man who has finally been called from the waiting room by his doctor. A row of clerks sat behind the table, filling forms and placing them in neatly stacked piles. Franz approached. The official had small round glasses at the end of his nose, which was red and dripping with a cold. A ledger was open on the desk in front of him.

'Name?'

'Franz Schneider.'

'Date of birth?'

'15 July 1907.'

'Address?'

The diesel buses chugged and spat outside the doors.

'Occupation?'

'Engineer.'

'Speak up, *Jude*.' For the first time, the clerk lifted his eyes to meet Franz's, like a farmer looking at a pig.

'Engineer.' In truth, it had been many months since Franz had been permitted to work. They had lived off Rosa's earnings from her sewing and knitting.

'May I ask, sir, how long you intend to keep us here?' Franz spoke politely but, watching from a distance, Maya could see from the way he stood that he despised the clerk.

The clerk's pencil scratched across the page.

'Sir, I was just wondering . . . It's just, my wife, she's not strong. And her daughter, too. We reported as instructed. We're wondering what will happen next?'

The clerk slowly placed the pencil on the table and straightened it with his forefinger. He breathed a fragment of a sigh, though Maya could not tell whether it signified boredom or disdain.

'Sit down and await instructions.'

'But, sir, we have been here for more than three days . . .'

The clerk's eyes were fixed back on the ledger with its thousands of neat names, each letter precise and ordered.

He scratched out three more entries at the bottom.

Franz Schneider – Transport AF643 – Brno to Terezín.
Rosa Schneider – Transport AF644 – Brno to Terezín.
Maya Schulze – Transport AF645 – Brno to Terezín.

'Next!' he barked.

6

The weak sun of the Sydney autumn afternoon was fading and Maya stood up to turn on the lamp. 'It is my greatest regret that I do not have a photograph of my parents,' she said. 'These fifty years, I cannot remember my mother's face.'

Kate glanced at her watch. She had been here all day. They would be expecting her back at work, but she literally had nothing to report. It was Friday evening; the Saturday paper would have nearly gone to bed by now and there was no point returning to the office. She thought of the other journalists congregating in the pub. She had not been invited. These Australians and their close-knit social groups were so hard to crack.

'Can I use your phone?' she asked.

'Of course, my dear. It is in the hallway.'

Kate dialled the news desk on the old yellow phone. Like every other surface in Maya's house, the hall table was covered in envelopes and letters. She flicked through them instinctively while she waited for the copy kid to answer. It was such a bad habit of journalists, to read other people's mail. But she looked anyway. One letter in particular caught her attention.

33

Dr Michael Robinson
General Practitioner
St Leonards

RE: Mrs Maya Schulze-Johnson, D.O.B. 25/08/1925

Dear Dr Robinson
Thank you for referring Mrs Schulze-Johnson to me for cognitive assessment.

I saw Mrs Schulze-Johnson on Wednesday 5 April, 1995. Her husband is recently deceased. She described herself as 'happy', but reports difficulties with her short-term memory, and says she misplaces items frequently. Her long-term memory remains good. She is still capable of independent living, and says she has a close circle of friends. She is eating and sleeping well, although she complains of feeling very tired during the day.

On examination, Mrs Schulze-Johnson maintained good eye contact and appropriate behaviour. There was no evidence of a mood disorder or a psychotic disorder. In terms of her cognitive state, she scored 27/30 on mini mental state testing, losing three points in delayed recall. On the Addenbrook cognitive examination she scored 85/100, with impairment in delayed recall and recognition.

In terms of her past medical history, there are no vascular risk factors, but her blood pressure is elevated at 171/96. Of interest, Mrs Schulze-Johnson is a Holocaust survivor and likely suffers the ongoing effects of trauma. I suspect this may be contributing to her cognitive decline.

I have arranged to see Mrs Schulze-Johnson in three months' time and thank you for monitoring her cardiovascular risk factors in the meantime.

Dr Hugh Hanley
Geriatrician

'Kate?' Maya called from the living room.

Kate put the letter down quickly. It made sense now, Maya's desire to find her old boyfriend – before she forgot him altogether.

'Coming.' She joined Maya, who was pulling on her coat. 'Oh, are you going out?'

Friday night, and Maya had somewhere to go when Kate did not. It would be another night at home with nothing on television but the football. She felt a rush of anger at Peter. A month ago, it hadn't mattered so much that she was alone. They were still a couple; he was going to join her eventually. But now she saw a future of walking into bars by herself, of tables for one.

The voice in her head. 'You know nothing about being alone, Kate. Maya lost her whole *family*.'

'I was going to call a cab,' Kate said hurriedly. 'Do you need a lift somewhere?'

'That would be wonderful,' said Maya brightly. 'I'm going dancing. Would you like to come with me?'

⌒

Kate could hear the music before they reached the hall, the beat of drums and the strumming of guitars spilling through the door and into the street. Salsa. Maya hooked her arm through Kate's for support as they unconsciously quickened their steps in time with the rhythm. Kate pulled back, hesitant. 'Come in. You will have fun,' Maya whispered in her ear.

The door was flung wide despite the winter chill, opening onto a large hall where wooden chairs and tables were pushed against the walls and a ghetto blaster pulsated from a Formica table. The space was starting to fill with people. Maya pulled Kate's hand and guided her into the throng. These were her friends. Most of them were middle-aged or older, many in their sixties or seventies, but there were a few teenagers and even some children. A vagrant sat in the corner; Kate could see his toes tapping through a split in his weathered shoe. There were serious dancers too, men dressed in tight black trousers and women with swirling skirts, sweat glistening on their panting chests and their hips swaying provocatively from side to side.

A young woman behind a reception table stood up and hugged Maya warmly. As they chatted, Kate slipped away into the hot, pulsing room and headed for an empty seat at the back. She sat, arms crossed awkwardly across her chest, tensing and releasing her muscles in time to the beat.

Friends were laughing and gossiping everywhere, but Kate was alone. She had been in Sydney for months now and, to be honest, she wasn't sure whether she would *ever* fit in here. Perhaps it was time to give it all up and go somewhere new. Everyone seemed to exist in their little groups, most of them still hanging out with the friends they had known since school. It was not a very friendly city and she'd never thought she would be doing this on her own.

The music paused, then a new song began. Maya glided across the hall, her eyes shining. She was stiffer than the younger dancers, her feet a little heavier and less agile than they had once been, but her limbs still moved with a remembered confidence of once having been strong and lithe. She danced as someone who knew her body, its parameters and possibilities, how it translated music into movement. The rhythm throbbed through her, every note becoming something physical; her legs, her fingertips, were precise and graceful as the music embraced her. She joined the other dancers who moved as one around the room, enveloping her then pulling back, pulsing like a living organ. Kate could not take her eyes off her. No one could.

When the music ended, Kate felt a stab of loss as Maya's body stilled. For a second, just a fraction of a moment, Maya seemed to lose her bearings, then caught Kate's eye and headed across the room to her. She sat down next to her, breathing heavily. Her diamond bracelet sparkled under the flashing lights.

'You dance beautifully,' Kate said.

'I have always loved to dance. Before the war, I spent my whole time going to ballet, jazz and tap lessons. We went regularly to dances in Brno and Prague. I knew all the ballerinas' names. Even in the camp, I danced.'

'I wish I could dance, but it makes me feel so self-conscious.' Kate looked at her feet.

'Oh, for me it is the opposite.'

'What do you mean?'

Maya smiled. 'When I dance, I know I am free.'

7

Terezín, Czechoslovakia, April 1942

Maya was dreaming she was dancing. Earlier that day, Rosa had beckoned her to come and listen to a group of musicians who were practising a collection of chamber works. Terezín was severely overcrowded and there was not enough food, but Maya felt she could endure it as long as there was still music. She had shut her eyes and let the sound of violins and cellos wash over her; when she went to bed that night, she had taken flight out of the camp and back to her home in Brno, swooping through the window and back into her own bed, soothed by the kindly notes of Beethoven.

She awoke to harsh lights and barked orders. Rosa opened her eyes, startled.

'Is it time for us to go?' Maya asked, sitting up.

'Quickly,' said Rosa, 'pack up your things.' A whistle blew in the corridor outside.

Maya stretched and tried to shake off sleep. She was in a tiny dormitory with her mother and thirty other women. Terezín was teeming with Jews, people of different shapes and sizes, languages and accents, crammed into stuffy rooms while they awaited redistribution to the east. Maya and Rosa slept on a thin mattress on the floor, from where they gazed up at the packed bunks above their heads.

They had been here for two weeks, and there was no news of Franz
or Omi. The children and elderly were being dealt with separately.
Maya was flattered when she was selected for a women's barracks with
her mother. She was now taller than Rosa, who seemed to be shrinking
and withering like a peach in the sun.

The weak winter dawn was only just breaking as they were herded
through the gates onto the platform; the grimy walls of the station were
grey in the pale light and the smell of the guards' cigarettes hung heavily
in the air. Rosa gasped with joy when she spotted Franz through the
seething crowd on the platform. He looked thin and tired, but his face
lit up as he walked towards them with open arms. He embraced Rosa
fiercely then set about helping them with the luggage. He marked their
names in large chalk letters on their suitcases and loaded them onto
the hissing train. 'Keep your knapsacks with you,' he said, pulling their
smaller bags from the growing pile of luggage. 'We don't know where
we're headed. We may need them.'

Maya passed the time by practising her ballet steps on the platform.
She pointed her toes and did a few *pliés*. Her legs felt stiff. Rosa smiled
at her and pulled her scarf more tightly around her neck. 'Oh, look
who it is!' She waved with her free hand above the heads of the crowd.
Mrs Meyer stood stock still in the middle of the platform, her large
suitcase by her side and her mighty bosom squeezed into a jacket that
looked two sizes too tight. Her face had taken on a permanent look of
bewilderment ever since their arrival at Terezín, when a German guard
had pushed her roughly on the shoulder after she had politely asked
whether she might have a south-facing room.

Her expression relaxed as she caught sight of Rosa. 'This is prepos-
terous.' She waved a pudgy hand to encompass the platform. 'First they
take us to Terezín and the accommodation has been far from adequate,
let me tell you.' Her neck was red and there was shrillness in her voice,
as if she were complaining to a young shop assistant. 'I have tried to
speak to the officer in charge . . .' Before she could continue, the guards

were behind them with sticks and whistles, hurrying them up the steps
and onto the packed carriage.

Maya was relieved that it was a regular Czech passenger train, rather
than the overcrowded cattle trains that the other inmates at Terezín had
described. She clambered on board. Instead of polite passengers reading
the paper or smoking their pipes, there were hundreds of people,
squashed four to a seat, looking around them nervously as the final
crowds from the platform boarded and tried to find somewhere to sit.
A group of teenagers from the asylum in Prague occupied some seats
in the middle of the carriage. They were grimacing and gesticulating,
clawed hands flying through the air, grunting with fear. Somewhere at
the far end of the carriage, towards the latrine, a baby howled.

Maya's stomach cramped. It was a long time since she had last eaten.
She stood by the window as a whistle screamed and the train slowly
pulled away from the station. It gathered speed and she pressed her
nose against the cool glass to watch Terezín disappear into the distance.

Rosa and Franz had found a space on a bench. They shuffled over
so Maya had room to perch between them. She felt listless and sick.
She closed her eyes, swaying with the rhythm of the carriage, trying
to keep her nausea at bay. The clackety-clack of the train lulled her but
she could not get comfortable on the hard wood. She stretched her
legs and pointed her toes to get the blood moving, imagining her feet
long and graceful in her ballet shoes.

Fences and shrubs sped by, and lines of cold rain streaked across the
dirty window. She had lost sight of Mrs Meyer.

Hours passed. Finally, the train shuddered and hissed to a halt. Bare
trees danced and bent in the biting wind beyond the grey platform.
There was something different about the station. The writing on the
sign looked foreign; they must have crossed a border. Maya made out
the name of the station: Lublin.

'Poland,' Franz said, shaking his head in exasperation as they
watched mounds of suitcases being unloaded from the train. 'They've
brought us to Poland.'

Maya spotted her suitcase to one side of the pile. Would she be allowed to retrieve her sweater? The carriage doors were locked and she was afraid to ask. She sat still, holding her hands tightly in her lap. No one was talking. Three young German officers walked quickly to the pile and started loading the cases onto a carriage marked 'Berlin'. Were they going to Berlin, then?

'Maya, eat something.' Rosa reached into the canvas knapsack at their feet and took out an apple, smuggled from the kitchen where she had worked in Terezín. It had made them laugh when she was assigned to that job; Rosa had never cooked in her life.

Maya studied the apple. It was green and waxy, and a withered brown leaf clung to the stalk. She rubbed it against her coat, but she felt too sick to eat.

The train lurched forward and steam filled the platform for a second. As it faded away, she took a last look at the pile of luggage, the fifty kilos of their possessions so carefully packed in Brno, still lying on the platform. She twisted her neck to watch her suitcase diminish to a dot in the distance as they headed further towards the east.

Franz raised his eyebrows, touching his collar, a forced smile on his face. Rosa had sewn bank notes and jewellery into their coats before they left. They were cleverer than the Germans, his eyes said, they would beat them. Maya settled into her seat. There was nothing they could do. The inevitability was somehow calming.

⁓

They arrived at their destination early the next morning. A white sign with black writing slid into view: Sobibór. 'We're really at the arse end of Poland now,' Franz joked as the train shuddered to a halt. He was not usually so crude. It made Maya smile, despite herself.

The carriage was suddenly full of German SS guards. They shouted and beat the benches with batons. '*Raus! Raus!* Get out! Get out!' Rosa grabbed the arm of an old lady who stumbled in fright; Franz lifted her backpack and guided Maya before him through the door and onto the platform. People were pouring off the train, hundreds of them crowding the station, disoriented and shivering in the April wind. The asylum patients looked confused and afraid; they walked the wrong way or clung to the door. Their helplessness seemed to enrage the guards more. Large dogs snapped and pulled at their leashes, sending the crowd scurrying in a wide arc around them like frightened rabbits.

Before long, the entire load of exhausted human beings had spilled out of the train. They walked and limped, dazed, into a barren field behind the tracks, encircled by barbed wire. Maya hugged her arms around herself for warmth. The SS guards shouted and huffed. They looked impressive in their black uniforms. Some of them were young and, Maya thought, good looking. At the front of the crowd, a senior guard, smart in a long woollen overcoat and polished boots, started arranging people into two rows. Right and left. Behind him, another held a dog. It strained on its short leash, teeth bared yellow against its mane of black hair.

The guard approached Maya and her parents. '*Du rechts, du rechts.* You right, you right,' he barked. They trotted to the row on the right and stood, six abreast in a neat line. Guards swiped at their heels with their batons to ensure they stood straight. Everything was happening so quickly. Maya looked at the others around them. They were strong and sporty, mostly adults, though she could see a couple of teenagers in the distance. The elderly and the young children, the disabled and the woman with the baby were in the other row, to the left.

Hundreds of people, right and left, pale and shocked, cowering from the dogs, disbelieving and cold.

Maya glanced at her mother. Rosa's head was bowed forward, as if she were about to vomit, and her shoulders sagged. Maya grabbed her hand and Franz slid his arm around her waist to support her.

Once the crowd was organised into two long lines, the guards shouted at them to start walking. Maya's backpack already weighed heavily on her shoulders; Franz carried Rosa's as well as his own. They left the field and walked into a sparsely wooded area, pine trees at each side absorbing the sound of their shoes as they trudged along the road. The line stretched back behind them. Too many people for Maya to count. No one was talking, some were crying, but soon they fell into the rhythm of the walk.

The guards set a hard pace. Maya did not mind. It felt good to be walking after the long, cramped journey, to feel her legs move steadily under her and to inhale the cold air into her lungs. It helped her to forget about the hunger. When about ten minutes had passed, the distant clatter of gunfire rang out from the direction of the station. Maya looked back in disbelief but Franz grabbed her arm and pulled her onwards. 'Just keep walking,' he said, his chin jutting strongly forward but his eyes bright with fear.

They emerged at last from the wood. The long, straight road stretched ahead of them, two sandy tracks with a raised hillock of dusty grass in between. Tattered leaves of corn stood high at each side; straight lines spanning into the distance, arrows pointing to an unknown destination. Above them, the clouds swirled grey, the edges ringed with bright light as the sun tried to push through. The air smelled of manure.

The SS guards had remained at the station. Now their captors wore brown uniforms with a black Star of David and white arm bands: Polish Jewish police. They carried sticks and their orders were harsh and insistent, but the prisoners started to relax a little. A few conversations struck up. Someone hummed the jaunty theme from Disney's *Snow White*. Franz suggested a game – 'One point for a wren, two for a rabbit and five for a woodpecker. Let's see who gets to fifty first.' Maya smiled at one of the guards and he smiled back. She felt safer now.

'Excuse me,' she said in German after a few kilometres. 'We are very tired, we haven't eaten and we haven't slept most of the night. Would it be possible for us to rest a little?' To her surprise, the guard nodded and shouted something in Polish to a colleague.

'You speak German?'

'Yes, a little. Do not talk, it will be better for you.' He smiled briefly, a flash of crooked teeth, then strode quickly ahead and out of view.

Soon the convoy slowed and stopped. They dumped their heavy bags on the sandy ground and sat down. Maya embraced her mother then excused herself. She clambered through the corn, pushing aside the stalks, and crouched close to the brown dirt to relieve herself. Away from the crowd, she shut her eyes and listened to the soft trilling and peeping of the birds. The sun had come out and she could feel its weak warmth on her back. Corn stalks rustled above her head, and she examined a tiny blue cornflower between her fingers as she squatted. She breathed deeply, inhaling the smell of the soil and grass. With a start, she realised she was being watched by a little mouse, sitting on his hind legs a few metres away in the safety of the stalks. His fur ruffled a little in the breeze; he was so close she could see his twitching whiskers. Then he turned and bolted, his tail a slither of grey as whistles and shouting started up from the road.

'*Pospieszyć się!* Hurry up!' The Polish guards had already started to shout at them again. Maya quickly pulled up her undergarments and hastened back to her family. The crowd was standing up stiffly, lugging their backpacks onto their shoulders or quickly pulling on shoes and socks over their blistered feet. Rosa was in a state. 'Where have you been? Come quickly! We are going.' The guards' sticks were at their heels again.

They walked for hours. At the top of every rise, Maya hoped they would see their destination, but each time the road stretched ahead. The sun climbed high in the sky. Maya felt dizzy and her feet were sore as they trudged along the sandy track. How far had they walked? Ten kilometres? Fifteen? Twenty?

Around her, others started to fade. They shuffled and limped painfully; some fainted; others vomited. The guards were becoming increasingly aggressive, urging them to go faster, faster. Their urgency increased in proportion to the exhaustion of the prisoners. Maya had lost sight of the kind guard.

Finally, they were called to a halt again. It was clear many of the group could not go on.

'They need us to be strong. They know we cannot keep this up,' Franz whispered.

They sat on the road, a line of desolate humanity as far as Maya could see. She slipped off the straps of her knapsack and massaged her sore shoulders. Franz used his bag as a back rest while Rosa laid her head in his lap. She had found a bar of chocolate in the side pocket of her bag and they shared it, licking it slowly and savouring its decadent richness on their tongues. Behind them, a lady prayed aloud. 'Hear, Israel, the Lord our God, the Lord is one.' There was no singing now.

When it was time to leave, Rosa slumped forward, her head bent low. Her face was grey, her lips white. 'I think I'm going to be sick,' she muttered under her breath. Legs shuffled past them and a guard looked in their direction. Rosa clutched her hands to her stomach and let out a moan. 'I can't walk. They must leave me here.' Maya rubbed her back and Franz knelt at her side. 'Rosa. Come, Rosa, we will help you.' But there was no moving her. They were near the back of the queue now; nearly the entire group had limped into the distance, but Maya and her parents remained at the side of the road. A guard walked towards them. His hand was on his baton.

The first blow hit Maya on her forearm. Then another, aimed at Rosa's back. 'Get up! Quickly, quickly. Get up.' Maya's eyes came back into focus and landed on the Star of David on the guard's uniform. 'Please ...' she cried, throwing her body over her mother as he stood over them, his stick raised high, threatening to beat again. Franz leaped up, shielding the women with his body. He was taller than the guard, older. His nose was just centimetres from the guard's, his arms open wide to hold back the blows.

The guard hesitated and, in that eternal second, Rosa roused herself. She planted her hands in the dirt and pushed herself to stand on unsteady feet. She brushed down her skirt and straightened her headscarf. 'I'm all right, let's go.' She grabbed Maya's hand, the familiar gesture from Maya's childhood, and set off quickly. Maya expected the sting of the stick against her shoulders, but the guard walked away.

⌒

It was dusk when they finally reached a small village. Warm yellow light shone out of the windows of whitewashed farmhouses; they passed a little church and a bakery; there were flowers on the windowsills. The road beneath their dragging feet was muddy and well-trodden. A forest loomed dark in the distance. They trudged through the dusk, heads bent, past the village and beyond. Surely they would stop soon?

Out of the twilight, at last, their destination came into view. A handful of buildings surrounded a large square: permanent stone structures and what looked like newly constructed wooden barracks. The periphery was surrounded by barbed wire. A man in an SS uniform pulled open the heavy gates, a rifle slung across his shoulder. They stumbled through, still in perfect straight lines, into the centre of the square, until all five hundred of them had assembled in neat rows as directed. One of the Polish police pointed directions, but they could not follow his foreign words. Maya stood to attention, desperate to sit down, unsure how long her legs could hold her.

The SS guard strode towards them through the dusk, his shiny black boots prancing across the dirt, a row of silver buttons below his jutting chin. His thinning hair was slicked back and his eyes were narrow slits, grey and cold. Eight harsh electric lights snapped on and lit up the square. The man started to shout at them, but Maya was too tired to listen or to try to understand. 'Commandant Ondyt,' whispered one of the guards at her side, tilting his head towards the man.

The Commandant marched from row to row, counting in rough German words. '*Eins, zwei, drei . . .*' Ten groups, each of fifty men or fifty women. Most of them were in their twenties or thirties, strong and athletic, although, for reasons known only to themselves, the Germans had selected some older women and teenagers too. The guards shepherded each group by turn towards a wooden hut. Franz went first, shuffling with the men, his sporty frame stooping slightly as he hauled the heavy backpack to his shoulders once more. Maya and Rosa were selected for a hut at the opposite side of the square. They marched obediently through the wooden door.

Inside were rows of rough wooden bunks, three rows high. Damp straw was strewn haphazardly on top to serve as both mattress and blanket. A small stove sat in one corner, though there was no wood to fuel it. The windows were held shut with bent nails; gaps in the frames let the wind gush through. The women each claimed a space, clambering heavily up the wooden ladders, scuffing their knees and fidgeting to get comfortable. Row upon row of heads stuck out, like sheep in a pen.

Maya and Rosa chose a top bunk near the door. Rosa climbed up carefully, Maya beneath, ready to catch her. They collapsed onto the straw, pulling their ski jackets closely around them, found each other's hands in the dark, and fell asleep almost immediately.

8

My darling Jan

*Something strange is happening to me. It started with this young lady,
Kate. She is a journalist with kind eyes, she is clever and observant.
From the moment I met her I felt protective towards her, motherly.
I know she is the one who will help me to find you. So far, we have just
talked about the war. But I feel we are making progress. We are getting
to know each other, at least.*

*We meet every Saturday. She comes in the afternoon and we drink
tea. We talk and we talk. I have told you that my mind is failing,
and, indeed, I am losing my keys and forgetting my way. But that's
the thing. As I sit with Kate, the details come back to me more clearly
than they have for years. Long-forgotten memories are surfacing
from the deep.*

*I have an example for you. Today I stood in my bathroom to wash
my hands. All these years, my whole long life, through the many thousands of times that I have lathered soap in my hands, not once have
I done so without a feeling of dread. It's the smell, you see. Before,
I have easily pushed the feeling away, but now it is much stronger,
demanding my attention. I have finally realised what it reminds
me of.*

Soap. The smell. My first day in the camp.

Sawin, April 1942

Maya awoke in the early morning. It was not quite dawn. Her bladder was full. She tried to move her aching body, but her muscles were cold and stiff after yesterday's long walk. The wooden bunk was hard under her elbows as she sat up. Her tongue was swollen and sticky with thirst.

Gingerly, she disengaged herself from her mother and crept towards the ladder. Some of the women were snoring, someone coughed lightly. She descended quickly until she felt the solid ground beneath her feet then padded towards the door. To her surprise, it opened easily. At least it was not locked. Outside, the square was grey and still. The electric lights shone hazily in the dim morning light, and cold, black barbed wire prickled against the dawn. Which building did they say housed the latrines? A few other people were stumbling past in different directions like pale ghosts, disoriented shadows wandering here and there.

Maya walked past the dormitories, beyond the square, and finally found the toilet block. Inside, there was a raised bench with a row of neat, round holes on top. Even in the cold spring morning, the sharp stench of urine tickled her nose. She carefully climbed up onto the bench, pulled down her undergarments and relieved herself, trying not to catch the eye of the few women who came and went. She was glad to get back to the hard wooden bunk and the soft warmth of her mother, who was still sleeping an exhausted sleep.

She lay awake until the birds started to chirp outside. Suddenly, the dormitory door burst open and the guards flooded in, shouting and banging the floor. Their whistles pierced the morning stillness. 'Szybko, szybko – quickly, quickly! Get up! Go!'

The women stumbled out of the hut and into the square, adjusting yesterday's crumpled clothes and picking straw out of their hair, turning their collars up against the cold. Five hundred men and women blinked in the light, not quite believing their new reality. They assembled into neat lines and watched, barely daring to move, as two Jewish prisoners strained to pull a wooden cart topped with a massive barrel of water into the centre of the square. Each prisoner was issued with a small aluminium bowl and instructed to form a queue by the barrel. They shuffled forwards, one by one.

Maya clutched her bowl tightly and shivered. When she reached the front of the queue, she lowered her eyes and held it out to a large Polish woman, who splashed two ladles of cold water into it. Maya drank thirstily and felt a little better. Others had moved to the edges of the square and were dipping cloths into their water, using it to wash their faces. Maya and Rosa walked back to their hut, found their toiletry bag in the knapsack and took out a soap box. Maya had had a moment of indecision over which soap to bring; she had chosen rose over lavender and had given the other to her grandmother. Where was Omi now?

She lathered the suds in her hands and watched the bubbles burst between her fingers. The soap smelled of home.

She started to feel more human once her face was clean and her teeth brushed with her own toothbrush. The guards bullied the prisoners into the large square in the centre of the camp, the 'Appellplatz'. They assembled into neat lines, women to one side, men to the other, their heads bowed and arms hanging limp at their sides. A Polish Jewish guard addressed them in halting German. His men were in charge of their daily lives, he said. 'Do not think because we are Jewish that we will make your life easy. We answer to the SS.' He explained that the prisoners had been brought here to work for the Third Reich, who were building a drainage system. This would be overseen by a group of Polish engineers. The prisoners were to do exactly as they were told. They were to meet here for twice-daily roll calls. Those who did not arrive in time for these 'Appells' would be beaten. But obey the rules, and they would have a good life.

There was nothing they could do other than obey. Around Maya, the prisoners relaxed in their helplessness.

In the daylight, they could see that the camp was constructed inside the Jewish ghetto of Sawin. Along two sides of the square were the timber dormitories from which they had spilled earlier; the other two sides were bordered by the stone buildings of the village, looming cold and white in the morning light as if they had turned their backs on the Jews. The front wall had been removed from one of these buildings and a wooden platform added, with three steps leading to the ground. Inside, Maya could see steaming vats on top of two stoves, stirred by a solid Polish woman with red, pudgy arms. That must be the kitchen. Her stomach rumbled. She was hungry after nearly two days without a proper meal and their long walk from Sobibór.

They were to form orderly lines, two by two, and queue for their breakfast. Maya scanned the men for Franz, but she could not see him in the crowd. When their turn came, she climbed with her mother up the wooden steps and held out her bowl. The Polish woman dispensed a small ladle of thin, brown liquid. 'Coffee,' she said, defensively. She handed each of them a single slice of black bread. It was hard and heavy, more like a chunk of earth than something edible. The woman gestured towards an earthenware jar, which contained a thin, orange substance. Apricot jam! They were allowed a small spoonful each before they were hurried back to the square to find a spot on one of the wooden benches to eat their meal.

Maya sipped the liquid and felt its burn in her gullet. Then she tried the bread – more of a gnaw than a bite. 'Look, it's made of potato peelings!' said Rosa, pulling a hard, brown sliver from her portion.

Franz found them after a few minutes. They bunched up along their bench so he could sit down. 'They give us the finest food in Poland!' he joked. Now they were together, Maya could almost see the funny side. She took a mouthful of weak liquid to wash down the stale bread. Franz rubbed Rosa's back and winked at Maya. It was going to be all right.

Once breakfast was over, the Polish Jewish police used their batons to usher them into ten rows of fifty. Why were they always in such a rush, screaming at them like animals? Franz stood near the back with the other men. He shrugged his shoulders and grinned. Two guards walked along each row, one knocking their feet with his stick and the other dispensing shovels. When he came to Maya, he thrust the shovel hard against her chest, making her stumble backwards. She fixed her eyes on her feet, her cheeks warm with indignation.

She had seen shovels – the street cleaners used them to remove the autumn leaves in Brno – but she had never used one before. It was heavy and cold. Rosa wavered slightly as she lifted hers onto her shoulder. The wooden handle looked offensively rough against her soft, white skin.

It was time to go. The guards' whistles pierced the morning air as they hurried them row by row through the open gates and towards the fields. It was apparently important to the guards that they march in time, right, left, but it was harder than it looked. Maya's blisters were burning from yesterday's long walk and she could not find the right rhythm. 'Like this,' said one of the prisoners, showing Maya how to time her steps against the feet in front. 'I was an officer in the Austrian army, fought for my country, and now this,' he mumbled. Maya adjusted the handle of the shovel to a more comfortable position on her shoulder and concentrated on the beat of her shoes on the road.

The sun came out and she felt a hint of warmth in the breeze. The sweet smell of earth wafted from the fields as they passed. They kept up their pace, leaving Sawin behind and marching across the muddy fields. A group of Polish farmworkers looked up at them. An old man in sagging trousers stood with his feet planted each side of a ditch; he straightened stiffly from his digging and raised a hand in greeting. But the rest turned their backs.

At last, they reached their workplace. It was a wide, brown swamp. Sticky mud stretched before them, pools of dark water reflecting the chestnut trees to their right. A trench cut through the middle like an incision; stumps and roots stuck out at odd angles from the murk. A neat row of wheelbarrows stood to one side.

In broken German, the Polish guards gave the prisoners their orders. They were to extend the trench. Get to work. Hurry. Dig.

Maya carefully clambered down the steep bank into the trench. Immediately, cold water trickled inside her shoes and seeped, freezing, between her toes. The shovel was heavy in her hands, awkward to manoeuvre. She took a deep breath and attacked the side of the trench. With a clang like metal on metal, the shovel bounced off the hard earth and fell into the grey-brown sludge at her feet. She smiled in embarrassment, glanced up at the guard, and quickly picked up the shovel again. Next to her, Rosa was having trouble too, weakly chipping away at the side of the trench as if she were painting rather than digging.

This was ridiculous. Maya grabbed the handle, now slimy from the mud, and fiercely jammed it into the trench wall. To her satisfaction, a clod of earth fell away and sloshed into the water. She watched it disintegrate as she stepped on it heavily with her sodden shoe, imagining it was the guard's head. She sliced her shovel into the water once more, retrieved a wad of sodden earth, and heaved it into the wheelbarrow. Then again – another clod of earth, another shovelful. Her feet were burning with cold but her forehead prickled with sweat.

When the barrow was full, she set off to push it to the edge of the field. Its wheel careened and squirmed in the unforgiving mud that sucked at her shoes. But she soon got the hang of it, using the strength of her shoulders and back to steady the weight. By the time she returned to the trench, Rosa had managed to shovel a few loads of her own. Elegant Rosa, knee-deep in Polish mud. The guards patrolled up and down, calmer now. Maya set to work again, alternating shovel loads between Rosa's wheelbarrow and her own. It would not do for her mother to fall behind.

They dug all day. They were allowed a break at lunchtime, but there was no food or water. Maya stretched her screaming, stiff shoulders, but her body felt vital and strong. She was upbeat on the march back to the camp, humming a folk song, remarking on the view. Rosa limped at her side. The journey back seemed shorter, and Maya was almost looking forward to being home. Surely it must be time for dinner.

Later that evening, the prisoners were again called to form orderly lines in front of the kitchen. A vegetable smell wafted from the steaming copper vats. Not bad. It was soup, a pale and murky concoction with a piece of potato and a cabbage leaf swirling at the bottom. At least it was warm; Maya pretended that it was filling her aching stomach and nibbled on the potato slowly to make it last. Around her, the meal was raising the spirits of the other prisoners. Soon their chatter floated on the air; there was a snatch of laughter from the men. At the end of the evening, Maya climbed into her wooden bunk, using her upturned bowl for a pillow, and slept more soundly than she had since they had left home.

                                    ⌒

By the time the green leaves of the chestnut trees were starting to burst and unfurl beyond the barbed-wire fence, it seemed as if they had always been here.

Each bunk had become unique to its occupant, with its own distinct pattern in the straw, the clothes hanging a certain way, shoes drying on the floor. Mrs Meyer huffed and puffed as she clambered into her lower bunk. They could hear her complaining from the moment she woke until late into the evening; during the night, she filled the room with indignant snores.

Rosa tried to make their bunk their own, a haven from the noise and stench of the camp. Each morning she brushed the straw evenly over the wood, making it neat and tidy. She stacked their few possessions in a corner: their jackets, knapsacks and aluminium bowls. Their whole world.

Maya lay there, thinking of home. She longed for her own mattress and feather pillow. She shut her eyes and thought of the piano in Brno, tapping out an imaginary melody with her fingers on the hard wood of the bunk. She had not changed her clothes all week and she felt a louse wriggle its way underneath her armpit. She retrieved it and squashed it with her thumbnail. What had she done to deserve this?

When she could wait no more, she hauled her tired body down the wooden ladder and walked into the Appellplatz. She moved without thought or feeling, her feet marching blindly and obediently to the new routine. She did not look up as she made her way to the latrine, past rows of clothes strung like sad bunting from the eaves. Afterwards, she joined the queue for water and bread. She quickly hid half in her pocket for lunch. During the morning, she would touch it occasionally, reminding herself it was there, counting down the minutes until she could chew and swallow. The rest she ate slowly, without tasting it.

Her hunger was constant. The rumbling of her stomach that had bothered her for the first few days had gone now. In its place was a permanent dull ache, as if the walls of her intestines were closing in and sticking together, twisting. Sometimes, she doubled over with the pain. But hunger was more than a physical sensation: it had become the whole of her. Emptiness radiated through every part of her body – through every strand of hair, her fingernails, her little toe. All were crying out for food. The guards seemed to know how far they could starve them. Just when she thought the only option was to lie down, when it felt as if the shovel was just impossibly heavy today, she would arrive home from the fields to the smell of cooking meat. The prisoners would swirl their evening soup to find the precious chunks, pull them apart with their teeth and savour every morsel as if it were a steak prepared for them by a chef in Prague. Just a little sustenance was enough; the next day she would march again, the shovel a little lighter on her shoulder and her legs somehow strong enough to carry her towards the swamp.

This morning, the prisoners assembled as usual in neat rows, standing to attention as best they could. The smell of freshly baked bread wafted across the camp, as it did every morning. A bakery was just beyond the perimeter, a daily sensual assault to add to their torture.

Maya automatically found her place. In only a few weeks, she had learned how to stand silently, eyes firmly fixed on the muddy ground and shoulders hunched, subservient. They were still dressed in their clothes from home, tweeds and wool, thick jackets and leather shoes. Resignation hovered over them like a heavy cloud. It stuck to their skin and caught in their throats.

They had seen little of Commandant Ondyt at first. They merely sensed his presence, a vague marauding danger, an occasional barked order from his quarters beyond the gate. This morning he appeared for the first time, newly bathed, his hair slicked back and his uniform starched and clean. His rifle was slung over his shoulder as if it were a part of his body. They watched as he strode towards them. There was a cold sense of purpose in his step. His steely eyes scanned the crowd.

'*Du, du* . . . You, you.'

He pointed to people at random. They stepped forward, exposed and miserable. Silence hung over the square. He began to shout, something about plans for escape, about undermining his authority. A blob of spittle gathered on his lower lip. The prisoners were confused and shocked; one middle-aged lady at the edge of the group looked as if she were going to faint. '*Ich schiess euch in den bauch hinein,*' the Commandant screamed, pointing his gun. 'I'll shoot you in the stomach for this insubordination!' Maya watched in terror, appalled at the arbitrariness of it. He aimed his rifle. No, surely no? Seconds passed, unbearable anticipation. But he lowered his gun and his thin grey lips twisted into an ugly smirk. He was playing with them, a cat among the mice.

The Commandant started to walk among the rows of prisoners, slowly inspecting them, one by one. The barrel of his rifle passed inches from Maya's nose. She fixed her eyes on a stone at her feet. *Keep invisible.* His boots creaked as he went.

He turned and came back to stop in front of her. Her bowels clenched; the stone at her feet blurred. *Stand still, stand still.* He was staring at her, right in her face. Studying her features. He lifted a strand of her fair hair with his gloved hand, examining it like a specimen in a museum.

'*Wie ist dein Name?*' he said quietly. 'What is your name?'

'I am Maya,' she replied. Her voice was hoarse. She did not look him in the eye.

An imperceptible snort and he moved on. Maya breathed out. She thought she might be sick.

The whistle blew: it was time for work. As they filed away, Maya darted a last look at the group the Commandant had singled out, still standing forlornly in the square. They were gone by dusk. She never saw them again.

The next day was Sunday. Maya had always loved Sundays. The air was thicker somehow, slower. A day to sit by the window, to listen to the clatter of Omi baking in the kitchen while a jitterbug played on the radio. In the camp it meant a day of rest from labour. The prisoners sat on benches or strolled around the Appellplatz in the weak sunshine, stretching tired arms, rubbing feet, scrubbing caked mud from their woollen trousers and curling their hair around their fingers to coax it into a style from home.

Maya sat with Rosa and a group of women outside the dormitory door. Her clothes were already looser; it felt like she was diminishing within them and would one day disappear completely. The women were talking about food. It was always the same, every morning and evening as they lay back on the straw, pulling their jackets over their tired bodies and wriggling to find some comfort on the hard wood. They would spend hours recounting their favourite recipes, arguing over the best way to make potato cakes with stewed apples or *rosol*, chicken soup. 'I always put two carrots in my broth, it makes it sweeter,' said Mrs Kolman, an artist from Prague who shut her eyes and smacked her lips at the memory. At other times they would share recommendations for cafés and restaurants where they would meet when this was over. Maya would fall asleep, drifting into a fantasy of white bean soup, convincing herself that she could smell parsnips in the musty hay.

Her lips were dry and flaking and her head throbbed. She scratched a mosquito bite on her arm and watched a perfect, round spot of blood bloom from beneath her skin. She licked it away. It tasted of metal and salt; it made her think of her last full meal. She wished she had eaten it more slowly, appreciated it more. Who knew when she would next taste proper food?

A sharp whistle cut through the low chatter. It was the Commandant. He was standing by the kitchen in front of a huge wicker basket stacked high with bread. Not the black, gritty bread of their daily rations, but real, freshly baked loaves, straight from the neighbouring bakery. Maya's mouth filled with saliva at the smell of them.

He blew the whistle again. Hesitantly, fearfully, a few prisoners stood up. Maya stood too. The world squirmed momentarily until her dizziness subsided. Everything seemed disconnected, like she was not herself, not real.

No one knew what to do. The Commandant slowly placed his rifle at his feet. He was smirking, his eyes glinting, humourless. Watching the prisoners intently, he reached into the basket, picked a loaf and held it there. The prisoners were transfixed, suspended in uncertainty, their eyes locked on the bread. He flung it into the air. They watched, stunned, as it landed with a soft thud. Then another.

Suddenly there was a scuffle as a young man dived forward, grabbed one of the muddy loaves and fled, his eyes wild, clutching his prize to his chest. Maya went to move towards the bread, but Rosa grabbed her arm and shook her head.

The Commandant laughed. He grabbed two more loaves, one in each hand, and threw them high. They arched over the crowd. This time, two prisoners leaped into the Appellplatz, catching the bread before it touched the ground. He threw another and another. The bread rained into the square. Like a pack of dogs, the prisoners fell on the ground, pushing and trampling each other, crawling on all fours, colliding with each other in mid-air, tearing at the bread with their teeth before it was snatched from their hands.

Maya stared numb and disbelieving as Mrs Meyer – who so recently was feasting in Brno's best restaurants, diamonds in her ears and her fox fur around her shoulders – fought like a dog, just for a loaf of bread.

9

Sydney, June 1995

Kate went to bed at half past midnight. She could not sleep; her imagination took her to Sawin, the barbed wire of the camp, the desperate need for food. She opened her novel, but her eyes skipped over the words without grasping their meaning. She gave up, set her alarm, and turned off the light. It was chilly in her bedroom, and she regretted having left her warmest winter clothes in the UK. Why didn't Sydney houses have proper heating?

The minty green digits of her alarm clock pulsed relentlessly. Kate had the feeling that something important had happened today, though she was not sure what. She sat up to take a sip of water then lay back down and forced her eyes to close, trying to think about something nice, something restful, like her childhood bed at home in England. It was a foolish choice. She pictured her eighteen-year-old self, sitting on that bed, opening her university offers. Life had held so much potential then. These days, she felt she was moving through treacle.

At about two, she decided to count the men of her past, like sheep. She imagined herself in a room, the boyfriends standing in a semicircle. There was Gareth, her first love, the boy who had taken her virginity on her parent's hearthside rug while they were out at the theatre. She had broken his heart, left him within a term of going up to university. He was married now, with two daughters. There was Andrew, her university flatmate, who had never thought of himself as anything more than a friend, until that dreadful day when she confessed her love for him and he slept with her out of pity. He moved out soon afterwards. Her stomach squirmed.

The others were less distinct, lovers whose paths she had crossed on the steamy beaches or beery pubs of Asia. And then there he was. Peter. She had met him a few weeks after she'd arrived in Hong Kong, a young cadet journalist bluffing her way into a job she didn't know how to do. He was English, a senior correspondent; he'd covered Tiananmen and was now writing analyses of the upcoming handover of Hong Kong to China. Soon they had moved in together, as you do in a foreign country, shared bills and recipes, hosted dinner parties and adopted a stray cat. They had had so much sex, every day until their cheap bed had creaked and listed. How they had laughed. When she landed the job in Sydney, he had been genuinely pleased for her. They had packed up the flat together, joking.

And then, a month ago, she had received his letter.

Why hadn't he wanted her? Why wasn't she good enough?

She groaned out loud and felt a tear wind its way hesitantly down the side of her face, then speed up and pool in her ear.

The voice in her head again. 'What are you afraid of? Your life is good, you're young and healthy. You're privileged, Kate. Snap out of it. You have absolutely *nothing* to complain about.'

Some time after four, she descended into blackness. Monsters reached out in the dark, floating and amorphous. They sang of a desolate future, of husbands she would never have and babies she would never know. She felt both hot and cold. She was hungry. She got up and went to the toilet, then turned on the light and started to read. Her eyes felt scratchy and her legs were heavy with fatigue.

She pictured Maya. They had sat together in the dance hall until almost everyone had gone. Kate had shivered as they walked out onto the street. She had turned, awkwardly, to shake Maya's hand. Maya had smiled at her. 'But I will see you next Saturday,' she said. 'We are only just starting. There is much more for me to tell you.'

Was it that obvious that Kate had nothing else to do with her weekends? 'I'll be in touch,' she said evasively, waved to finalise the conversation and turned to walk back to the bus stop.

'Kate!' She had turned to see Maya smiling her beautiful smile. She had walked towards Kate and wrapped her arms around her in a tight hug, just long enough for Kate to relax and feel the calm. 'It will be all right,' Maya said, pulling back and looking her directly in the eye. 'You will not always be alone.'

Kate sighed at the memory of the embrace. Her whole body was heavy and her head was swimming. At last, sleep. She drifted away to the rasping *caah* of a crow and the distant clang of a garbage truck as it made its way up Oxford Street.

Sawin, May 1942

Maya stood in the queue waiting for their evening meal. She tried to stand *en pointe*, stretching her toes in her leather boots, remembering what it felt like to move to music. But there could be no dancing here.

Her shoulders ached from the digging and she felt weak and tired. The rations were becoming more meagre every day. This evening, there were just three oats floating at the bottom of her bowl of soup. Hard bread, a cabbage leaf, a hunk of potato – how could they be expected to work all day on this? Her cheekbones were protruding, her skin was sallow, and her trousers were held up with string. Yet she knew not to complain. She must not falter, no matter how hungry and sick she felt, how sore her feet or infected her blisters. The weak were the ones who disappeared.

She drained the last dregs of her soup and watched the others milling lethargically through the Appellplatz. Beyond the fence, the shadows of local Polish farmers emerged phantom-like from the fields. They unfurled paper packages to display hunks of bread and slices of meat. These they would barter for whatever the prisoners could offer – silk stockings, US dollars, a piece of jewellery – valuables they had brought with them, sewn into the seams of their clothes or hidden in the bottom of their canvas bags. The trade was strictly forbidden; both Jews and farmers were beaten if they were caught. But nearly everyone took part. Last week, Franz had bought potatoes.

There was a stir as Irena, a young woman from Maya's dormitory, walked quickly towards them. 'Look, I have sugar!' She could not believe her luck; it was the most precious possession of all.

'I have an egg,' Rosa said, sitting up brightly. Someone else had flour, another milk and butter. 'We can make pancakes!'

Behind the dormitory, amid scrappy weeds and sharp pebbles, Irena's husband gathered some spare bricks and stacked them into a lopsided square. He took a sheet of iron discarded at the perimeter fence and placed it on top, brushing the mud away with the cuff of his jacket. Rosa and Maya fetched sticks the women had stored by the stove in their dormitory; it was still cool in the evenings, but pancakes would be more precious than heat tonight. They carried the wood furtively under their jackets, their hearts pounding with the thrill, the anticipation. The prisoners squatted on their haunches and watched as Irena's husband stoked a fire, their stomachs rumbling as the comforting crackling took hold. Irena spat on the iron to check it was hot. She tipped the flour and sugar into her aluminium bowl, made a well in the centre and broke the egg into it. She added milk, little by little, and stirred the mixture vigorously with a stick.

A tiny knob of butter danced and disappeared into a pool of yellow bubbles. The first pancake sizzled on the iron, small and round. The smell of it! Saliva spurted into Maya's mouth; it was all she could do to prevent herself from lunging forward and grabbing the pancake with her fingers. Its glistening surface faded to opaque as it cooked. Little holes sputtered open and Irena moved it around with the stick, preventing it from catching on the metal. She carefully turned it over. It was golden brown, perfect.

A small crowd had gathered now. All fixed their eyes on the makeshift stove. The Polish guards were watching, but they did not intervene. Irena waved a hand in the air, not shifting her eyes from her task. 'Bowl?'

One of the women handed her an empty bowl, into which Irena carefully lifted the cooked pancake. The crowd hesitated, then a ripple of applause broke out. 'Eat, eat, before it gets cold! I think I will have enough for all of you.'

Irena poured two more rounds of mixture onto the iron. The pancakes seemed to be cooking so slowly; Maya swallowed, imagining the tickle of sugar on her tongue.

At first, she did not see the Commandant appear around the corner. No one did. The guards melted into the distance. Maya felt an urgent hand on her shoulder and leaped up with the others, scattering away. But Irena did not notice. She was humming softly to herself, her cheeks flushed and dark curls clinging to her shining forehead as she concentrated.

The Commandant strode up behind her and shoved her roughly to one side. She stumbled and fell onto her knees. He kicked the stove over, scattering bricks and blackened wood, stamping on the flames. The iron clattered onto the dirt and knocked over the bowl. The last thing Maya saw before she fled was the creamy pancake mixture soaking into the dirt.

~

The next morning, Maya stood listlessly in line, hungry and despondent, when her gaze fell on the soft brown eyes of a young woman three rows in front of her. She was in her early twenties, and pretty. She smiled. Maya was immediately drawn to her; there was a softness and innocence about her, a need to put one's arms around her and protect her. As soon as roll call was over, they headed for each other through the crowd and embraced. It felt as if Maya was reconnecting with someone she had known all her life.

Her name was Erna. She grabbed Maya's hand and joined the breakfast queue with her. By the time they sat down, they were giddy and giggling.

'Maya, I'm so happy to have met you. I know we shall be friends. Please, will you share my bread with me?'

Maya glanced at her own breakfast, half eaten, then at Erna's bread, untouched. A priceless offering. Tears pricked her eyes. Erna must also be hungry, but she was willing to share with a stranger.

'Thank you, thank you. But let me share mine with you also.'

They broke the bread into small pieces and pooled them into a pile. They shared them equally, smearing each morsel with jam before dipping it into their bowls of dark, steaming liquid. A feast. Maya relaxed into the warmth of Erna's shoulder and thigh as they pressed against her own on the crowded bench. She already felt as though Erna were a dear friend. How strange to make such an immediate connection, in a place like this.

'I have something exciting to tell you,' Erna said when they had finished. 'A group of us have been talking about putting on a concert for the camp. Would you be interested in joining us?'

Maya could not speak. She could not picture music and dancing in this barren, hungry place. For a moment, her mouth gaped wide in astonishment, until she remembered she was in company and clamped it shut.

'You're surely not serious? A concert?'

'Yes, yes, it's true.' Erna was jubilant. 'Even the Commandant knows about it, and he actually approves – so it's happening, later this week. Please say you will take part? You can surely dance, Maya, no? I can see it in the way you move. You're a dancer, aren't you?'

Maya saw herself at the barre at the ballet school, her arms drawing a graceful arc through the air. That was before the ballet teacher had been forbidden from delivering lessons to Jewish girls, of course.

'But what about music? Costumes? I can't believe it would be possible to put on a concert in here.' Her mind raced and her words tripped over each other in excitement.

'One of the Polish technicians has a gramophone, and some records. He'll let us borrow them. And there are some planks left from building that bridge over the channel. My husband Pavel knows a carpenter in the men's dormitory. He has nails and a hammer, and he's happy to make a stage for us. Oh, here's Pavel now.'

Erna's husband was walking towards them, brandishing his break-fast before him like a waiter with a cloche in an expensive restaurant. He smiled. His coffee jiggled as he pretended to trip, eyebrows raised, then he placed it on the table with a flourish. Maya laughed. He spread his arms wide in an extravagant greeting and leaned over to kiss his wife tenderly. His black curls quivered as they brushed her forehead. They looked too young to be married, little older than children, really.

'Pavel, Maya is going to dance for us in the show.' It was decided.

Before Pavel could speak, the high-pitched whistle broke the mood and ordered them to work.

⁓

Two days later, Maya was granted permission to leave the camp with Erna to choose music for the concert. She still could not believe that this was happening with the Commandant's support.

'He's not going to shoot us all while we perform?' she whispered to Erna nervously as they walked out freely through the gates.

'Pavel says it's to keep our minds off our stinking work.' Erna laughed. 'Don't worry, there are guards involved too. It's really going to happen.'

They had been fantasising about the concert all day. They had plotted it in their heads as they shovelled the wet, brown earth. The line-up changed constantly, a mix of comedy and burlesque, Czech folk songs to raise the crowd's spirits, a violin solo from a young man who had left everything behind other than his instrument and, incredibly, had managed to keep it unscathed. But they needed music; something happy and buoyant to cheer them up.

The engineer's house was less than fifty metres from the wood and straw of Maya's bunk, but it was as if it were in a different world. A world of music and hope.

'The selection's not huge, but there's enough I think?' Erna's eyes were shining as she leafed through the gramophone records. Maya sat on the stone floor opposite her. They could have been teenagers on a Saturday afternoon, cranking the battered gramophone.

A memory popped into Maya's head. She was young, maybe six or seven, and she was waiting on the stairs of the house in Prague for her darling Uncle Emil to arrive. The memory always started with her shoes, white patent leather with hard little buttons and scuffs on the toes. She could see herself gazing up at his towering body, his massive, twirled moustache wide like an elephant's tusks and his great hands reaching out to her with a large package wrapped in brown paper.

'They say we Czechs are born with violins under our pillows, but you will have a gramophone instead, my little *Mayalein*.' Uncle Emil had laughed, wrapping her in his huge arms. How she had loved that gramophone, playing it through the years in her little bedroom, gazing at the dusty pink flowers of her wallpaper as the music rang out. The thought gave her comfort now.

'What's this one?' Erna cranked the handle and the first notes billowed out, cold and blue. Bruckner's eighth symphony. Too slow and sombre. Not right at all. Erna removed the needle with a ripping scratch. They sat in horrified silence for a second, afraid that the engineer would smash into the room and accuse them of damaging his possessions, but there was no sound other than a busy fly at the window.

The next record was a Polish military song. It was rousing and upbeat, its slurring Polish syllables neatly fitting between trumpets and a rhythmic beating drum. They caught each other's eyes. They could not follow the words, but they knew without speaking that this music spoke of the partisans in the woods. The SS would not approve. Erna quickly stopped the gramophone, put the record back in its sleeve and buried it quietly at the bottom of the pile.

'Try this.' Maya held out the *Radetzky March* by Johann Strauss. She had listened to it many times at Omi's house. It was nothing special, but maybe it would work.

The needle tick-ticked at the edge of the record. Slow applause rippled from the gramophone's horn, then silence, almost unbearable. Maya could hear the musicians lifting their instruments to their lips, their shoulders. Then the familiar first notes exploded. It was as if the entire orchestra burst into the room. Violins and clarinets, clashing cymbals, fairgrounds and streamers flying through the air. She thought of stamping feet and thunderous applause. She saw the line of prisoners marching in time, smiles on their faces and their eyes lifted to the bright sky. She realised she was smiling.

'Can you dance to this?' Erna was nodding her head in time. It was almost impossible to refrain from tapping along.

Maya thought for a moment. It was not the sort of music she normally danced to, but nothing was normal now. Besides, it was rousing and happy. It spoke of life, of a future. A tap dance. Yes, a tap dance might work. She mapped out some steps in her mind.

'Yes,' she turned to Erna. 'Yes, I think I can.'

Sydney, June 1995

'From the moment we met each other, Erna and I had a special friendship,' said Maya. She settled her hands in her lap like a teacher addressing a classroom of small children.

This was Kate's third session with Maya, and she was realising that her stories were often long and complex. They would meander down winding rabbit holes as she described in detail conversations she recalled, lurching from one scene to the next, her feelings bubbling along and then immediately forgotten. Kate faithfully recorded them, knowing that much of the transcript could not be used.

This time she listened patiently, her pen held in the air above the empty page.

'She was a little taller than me, slender, and she had a lovely clear olive complexion and dark hair. It is her eyes I remember. They were soft and brown, like an angel's.'

Kate smiled to herself. *Dark hair, dark eyes*, she wrote in shorthand.

'You know, love was the only way you could survive in the camp. And Erna, she loved someone. That is how she kept alive.' Maya looked at Kate intently as the thought occurred to her. 'This is what I learned, and it is the most important thing for you to remember. The greatest thing in life is to love another.'

10

My darling Jan

The doctor wants me to take some new pills. They are to help with my memory, he says.

I asked Kate to come to the appointment with me. She is very good at taking notes, and I cannot remember what people say from one moment to the next. I feel a strong connection to her already, as if she is part of my family. And she seemed pleased to have a job to do.

She ordered a cab and helped me inside. As if I needed help! It is my mind that's going, not my legs. But the thought was there.

The doctor made me perform some tricks. 'What is the year, the month and the day? Count backwards by sevens. What was the name of those three objects I showed you earlier?' I do not think I did very well. Kate and the doctor exchanged looks. I saw them but I pretended not to notice.

I am not stupid, it's just that there is so much going on. I am too busy to concentrate. My thoughts are like birds, fluttering just beyond my grasp. They settle into focus eventually, shimmering with the gentle beating of silent wings. It is so hard to catch them.

And all the time the orchestra is in my head. Today it was Tchaikovsky, the Manfred Symphony. The clarinets floated up, the violins, then the oboes and horns. How could I answer his questions when they were playing so loudly? I smiled at him, but I must have forgotten to speak out loud.

Kate shook my arm. 'Are you okay, Maya?' she asked me.
And then I remembered how to talk. 'Ich bin,' I said, smiling.
I am what I am, Jan.
I am.

Sydney, July 1995

'Today let's talk about the concert,' Kate said, pulling a fresh notebook from her bag. She knew she was onto something. Maya's memories were pouring from her now. 'How did you get permission?'

'Oh, the Commandant supported it. I also could not believe it. But it was part of his sick game. Keep us happy, we would work harder, we would not question their intentions for a little longer . . .'

'But it seems so unlikely for a labour camp. You were all starving and exhausted. I just can't imagine that you would want to sing and laugh?'

'Oh yes! There was always laughter. We were human, after all. Laughing made us remember that.' Maya's hands began to move to a silent melody. 'That music, that dance . . .' She looked at Kate, and her face lit up. 'You would do the same, wouldn't you?'

Sawin, May 1942

Hammering filled the air. The incessant *thwack, thwack* lifted Maya's spirits with every beat. The prisoners were busy, more purposeful than usual as they strode around the camp in the evening dusk, each of them playing their role, doing their part to bring the show to life.

To one side of the Appellplatz, near the kitchen, a stage was starting to take shape. The men had hauled wooden planks from the fields and a small group of prisoners was working through the evening to secure them with improvised nails fashioned from fence posts. They did not have a saw, so the edges of the construction were rough and uneven. But it was a stage, most definitely a stage, about three metres square with rough-hewn steps at the rear leading to a makeshift corridor through which the performers could hurry to and from the kitchen, their dressing room.

Maya stood with her back to the wall, watching, trying to quell her nerves. One of the men emerged from underneath the stage with a hammer in his hand. He had taken his shirt off and his muscles undulated across his protruding ribs as he lifted a plank onto his shoulder and shifted it into place. He had been working all day in the swamp; like all of them, he was exhausted. But he had energy and life as he went about his task. Would they all be beaten for this?

'There you are!' Erna emerged from the kitchen carrying a clutch of goose feathers and a hessian bag. 'I saw these on the march home from the swamp this evening, I think we can do something with them in our hair? Have you decided what you're going to wear?'

Maya did not have a costume. She gazed over the bustling camp, hoping for inspiration. Everything was brown and grey; the prisoners' faces were pale, even their eyes were dull and dark.

'Well, now then, let me see.' Erna was teasing her. 'Let's start with these.' She brandished the bag and thrust it into Maya's hands. It was heavy. She assumed at first that it contained food, but whatever was inside it felt solid, almost metallic, under the fabric. She undid the string and peered inside.

It was a pair of tap shoes. Tap shoes! 'How in the world did you find these?' She blinked at Erna in disbelief. Erna shrugged, laughing, shuffling on the spot with excitement.

Maya turned the shoes over in her hands. They were deflated and tired. The metal taps on the soles were worn and the leather, once smooth, was crossed all over with tiny lines. But they were intact. The stitching was strong and the laces long enough; the scuffed metal taps felt cold and solid under her fingertips. She raised the shoes to her nose, breathing them in. They still had the dance shop smell she knew so well.

She pulled off her limp woollen socks. Her feet were dirty and bruised. The skin on her heel was thick and her toenails were long and cracked. She balanced against the rough edge of the stage and squeezed into the shoes. They squashed her toes a little, but they would do. Yes, they would absolutely do. She turned her heels this way and that to admire the transformation of her legs, then spread her arms wide, her calloused fingers moving as delicately as tiny feathers.

‎ *~*

It was not until later that night that she was struck with the reality of it. She woke, nauseous and sweating, trying to focus on a strand of cobweb above her head. All evening, she had ignored the twinges in the pit of her stomach as she and Erna hopscotched together back to the dormitory, arm in arm. She stifled her fear as she drank her soup and rehearsed the dance in her head, planning, humming the tune with toes twitching to the imaginary steps. But now, as she lay on the straw next to her deeply breathing mother, the pain exploded into silent sobs.

‘Maya, my darling, shush, you’ll wake up the others,’ Rosa whispered urgently.

‘I can’t do it, I can’t.’ Maya’s entire body was heaving. She could barely breathe. ‘How can I dance? I do not have a costume. And what about make-up? I have nothing, just nothing.’

‘Shh, my love, shh.’ Rosa held her tightly, smoothing strands of hair from her wet cheeks.

But Maya could not be quiet. She submitted to her desperation, swept along in its torrent, the enormity of it all. She thought of her shiny black tap shoes in Brno, of her school, her puppy Antonín. Omi. All were gone. She gulped for air. She could not see a future, she could not imagine anything beyond the barbed wire and stinking mud. How could she have thought a show would make a difference? How could a few minutes of a dance wash away the misery of all she had lost?

‘*Liebchen*, my precious daughter, this is your chance.’ Rosa’s whisper was warm in her ear. ‘I want you to dance, my darling.’ She stroked Maya’s back firmly and gently, the same strokes Maya had known since she was a baby. ‘I want you to share, to create – to *live*.’

‘Not here, not here,’ Maya murmured, over and over.

‘Dance, my Maya, dance. Dance for your whole life.’

The storm passed, billowing away in her mother's soft words. She relaxed a little, leaned into the safety of Rosa's arms, and allowed herself to be soothed. Exhaustion overcame her. Slowly, their heartbeats and breathing melded into one, mother and child, until, finally, mercifully, they both drifted into an oblivious sleep.

Maya's throat was tight and sore when she opened her eyes a few hours later, but her body felt calm. She extricated herself carefully from Rosa's grasp and quietly clambered down the wooden ladder and into the deserted Appellplatz. The camp was perfectly still, bathed in the light of a full moon. She breathed in deeply, relishing the cool, soothing air.

The Uncle Emil memory popped into her head again. This time, her childhood gramophone was playing a popular snatch of music, *Ich tanze mit dir in den Himmel hinein* ... I'm dancing with you into heaven. She heard the music as if it were playing in her ear: stringed instruments and flutes on a scratchy record, gentle waves of sound lapping around her. She felt her body start to sway; slowly, slowly. Her feet began to move in time. One, two, three ... one, two, three. She wrapped her arms around her thin waist in a caress, then opened them wide as she began to waltz in circles around the square. One, two, three. She sang the lilting song in a voice too tiny for others to hear, imagining herself dancing into the sky. The notes lifted her tenderly. She felt herself floating on the cool breeze, drifting through its soft eddies and waves, skimming the roofs of the dormitories, upwards towards the glittering stars of the cold night sky. The despair had gone. In its place, the graceful beating of her heart as she danced in the light of the moon.

11

The early Sunday afternoon air was still warm as the prisoners emerged from their dormitories into the Appellplatz. They came one by one, old and young, malnourished and sick, their eyes lifted from their feet and their steps a fraction lighter than they had been that morning.

Maya sat with the performers in the kitchen, hidden from the crowd, trying to tame her hair into a bun with a piece of string plucked off the dormitory floor. The air was buzzing with anticipation. Nobody had a costume, but each had found a splash of colour. Maya took a goose feather and tucked it firmly into her hair.

The square was filling up fast. Families and friends grouped together, chatting freely as if they were going to the Sunday matinee at the cinema in Prague. A group of Polish engineers was leaning against the wall of a dormitory at the back of the Appellplatz. Maya thought how strong and well fed they looked.

The master of ceremonies climbed the steps onto the stage and the audience fell silent. He had borrowed a clean jacket and fashioned a bow tie out of green leaves.

Maya moved towards the stage, her heart beating quickly and anticipation tingling in her fingertips. She did not know whether she could dance; her whole body was exhausted. She glanced down at the tap shoes, so elegant on her feet, and thought of all the times she had performed.

The faces of the crowd were expectant and hopeful. She checked the laces and felt the physical thrill of performance, the tremble of pleasure.

Erna grasped her hand and gave it a squeeze. 'Just perfect,' she whispered.

The master of ceremonies started with a joke. The audience was not sure whether to laugh. A hesitant ripple of appreciation ran through the crowd. There were no repercussions from the guards or Commandant. He told another, and this time the laughter was a little louder.

'Now, let the music begin.' He flung his arms wide. 'It is my pleasure to introduce our first performer ... Maya Schulze. A big round of applause for Maya!'

The Polish technician cranked the ancient gramophone and Strauss's first strident notes rang over the camp. Maya climbed the steps and took her position on the stage. Five hundred pairs of eyes snapped towards her. The notes of the prelude faded into silence and the *Radetzky March* began. She started to move.

Maya danced as she had never danced before. She felt separate from her body, as if her feet were not touching the wooden boards. She looked down as the tap shoes darted back and forth, the heels clicking and then the scuffed toes scraping the wooden boards, her skirt flying around her. She was Ginger Rogers, her face alight as she moved across the stage. Her hands soared through the air like graceful swans.

As she danced, a deep sense of peace overcame her; she felt warmth and light flow from her and settle on each member of the audience. Their deadened faces lit up. She willed them to live, felt her vitality wash over them with every sweep of her arm. Her dance went for less than five minutes, but it seemed to last for eternity.

When the final notes settled over the Appellplatz, the camp turned back to grey. Maya exhaled slowly, stepped forward, and took a deep bow.

The clapping started slowly, gingerly, eyes darting sideways towards the guards. But quickly it swelled and burst, a rapturous thunderclap of applause that sent the crows screaming from the top of the trees.

Maya glanced over her shoulder at Erna. Stay invisible, Franz had warned her. Now here she was, the eyes of the entire camp on her, every inmate and guard swept up in a tide of exuberance. Her cracked lips broke into a wide smile. She bowed again.

She could see Rosa and Franz, holding hands, smiling. At the other side of the square, the Commandant stood stiffly, his arms folded. But yes, she was sure there was a faint smile at the corners of his mouth. Some of the guards looked at her with raised eyebrows like class bullies at a school concert, pretending not to care, but some were clapping too. At the back of the Appellplatz, the group of Polish engineers laughed and cheered. One was staring at her intently. She met his gaze. Held it. Their eyes locked together high above the heads of the buzzing crowd.

Maya bowed again and stepped back into the shadows at the rear of the stage. A slight breeze chilled her bare arms, but she hardly felt it. Her heart was still beating to the rhythm of the music and her cheeks were flushed as she picked her way down the wooden steps.

The concert lasted for a little over an hour. Maya's dance was followed by a mime act, in which the artist had whitened his face with ash from the kitchen stove. He held the audience entranced as he moved, contorting his rubber body into a bird, a fish, a balloon. He wafted off the stage as if blown by a strong wind, making way for a small group of folk singers with a slightly off-key rendition of a popular Czech ballad.

One by one, the performers took the stage. There was a Charlie Chaplin impersonator followed by a haunting violin solo that had the audience wiping tears from their cheeks. Erna and Pavel sang a duet. Her voice was surprisingly strong and clear; they gazed into each other's eyes as the crowd watched, enraptured. The main act was a play in three parts. It began with a parody of the Appell and went on to gently ridicule the conditions in the camp. 'We present to you the highest quality dregs, made with Poland's finest potato peelings . . .' Maya glanced fearfully at the guards, but they were laughing too. The prisoners were really getting away with it. She allowed herself to laugh until her sides hurt.

And then the finale. All the performers gathered on the stage, holding hands and singing a song they had practised during the long days digging. It spoke of strength and humanity. 'Don't forget to be a *mensch*,' they sang. '*Denn wir tragen den Willen zum Leben im Blut* ... We all have the will to live in our veins, and faith, yes faith in our hearts!' The crowd went wild. They danced around the square, some alone, some in groups, their shattered nerves and the strain of the last few weeks forgotten for a few precious minutes.

When the concert was over, the prisoners slowly dispersed, humming, tapping tunes against their thighs with a glimmer of hope in their eyes. From somewhere, the sound of a harmonica buoyed the mood. The putrid stench of rotting horsemeat wafted from beyond the fence – tonight's dinner. No one seemed to mind.

Maya huddled with the performers as they hugged and kissed each other, talking over each other in their excitement. She had not seen this many people smile at once since she arrived at Sawin. All fears of reprisals from the Commandant were temporarily forgotten. They felt human again, strong, able to go on.

She glanced furtively towards the Polish engineer, still standing with his colleagues at the back of the square. He was tall and handsome, broad-shouldered. His dark blonde hair, thinning on top, was neatly combed and slicked against his elegant head. He looked gentle, intelligent. He patted his pockets, searching for a cigarette, then placed it between his lips, clapped a colleague on the back and gestured towards the crowd. He turned in her direction. Could he be coming to see her? He was not looking at her; perhaps he had not noticed her after all.

Something pulled deep in her chest, a surprising and overwhelming yearning for him to come to her.

Look at me, look at me.

He smiled with careless ease as he talked and joked.

Oh, look at me.

He was relaxed, confident, laughing with a friend. Then, yes, he was turning, he was looking directly at her, he was coming. He was coming.

He stopped in front of her. Her heart thumped and her cheeks still felt hot from the dance. She turned towards him shyly and smiled. He examined his fingernails then lifted his head. He smiled back. His kind eyes looked at her, right into her. She could not speak, she could barely move. The chatter and music in the Appellplatz blurred as they stood staring at each other, silent but conversing, human to human. She felt faint with the intensity of it.

He started to speak, fast, in Polish. A jumble of harsh vowels.

'I am Jan Novak.' That much she could grasp.

She smiled. 'I am Maya Schulze.'

Sydney, July 1995

Maya gazed out of the window. 'A handful of words, no more. It was the most profound communication of my life.' Her smile had become girlish. 'From that moment I was infatuated, and so was he.'

'Really?' Kate tried not to sound sceptical. 'It was that immediate? Boom-diddy-boom and you were both in love?' She thought of the men she had met in the bars in Asia; the beer-fuelled attraction, the inevitable disappointment.

'Of course not,' said Maya. 'It took time for us to get to know each other. I cannot say we were straight away in love. But how can I explain? We connected. It was . . . *graceful.*'

Lovely. Kate wrote the quote in her notebook.

'Do you think it was because of your situation? That you were grabbing at the human connection as a way to survive?'

Maya laughed. 'At that moment, on the day of the dance, there was nothing further from my mind. I was not thinking about surviving, I was thinking about dancing! But how can you explain what draws two people together? It was immediate and strong. It has never happened to me like that before or since.'

'But, hang on – he was a guard. He was a *Nazi*. He was part of the machine that was eliminating your people. How could you have even thought of being with him?'

Maya smiled. 'Oh no, he definitely was not a Nazi. Quite the opposite. He hated the Nazis. You must remember that Poland was occupied,' she went on. 'The Germans despised anyone who disagreed with their doctrine; they saw the Polish as inferior to themselves. Jan was trained as an engineer, and he was useful to them, but he was definitely *not* one of them.'

12

Chelm, May 1942

Jan climbed the stairs to the apartment three at a time. His heart was still pounding to the beat of the music. Her smile . . . oh, her smile! He pushed on the front door and burst into the hallway, then his stomach sank. His father was already home.

They had not seen eye to eye since Jan returned home from his engineering studies at university. At first they had argued every day – about the war, about politics, about the role of Poland in all of this. Now they agreed to disagree and sat mostly in icy silence.

The Poles had suffered under German rule for three years now, since the Nazi tanks rolled in and the Polish army rolled over – they literally gave up! – and all of their futures changed. While Jan spent his student years gently seething at the ignominy of his country's situation, his father had sought, and achieved, personal advancement. He rose from police inspector in Warsaw to chief of police in Chelm, bringing the entire family here, to the end of the world, to enforce Nazi law on the border of Ukraine.

Jan could not forgive him. His father was now a confirmed Nazi sympathiser, ignoring the hardships wrought by the Germans on his own people, supporting their sick philosophy despite the fact that, to his Nazi superiors, he was nothing more than a useless Pole.

How could his father not see how ridiculous he looked, in his smart uniform, clicking his heels?

Jan's mother bustled out of the kitchen and gave him a peck on the cheek. 'Your father is home,' she warned him softly. As if he didn't know. He could smell the smoke; sense his presence dominating the apartment.

Jan took a moment to compose himself then stepped into the living room. It was simply furnished but elegant, looking over the refined grey stone buildings of Chelm and not far from the main square. He had to admit that their father's new position had benefited the whole family. When they had arrived, Jan's sister, Danuta, had squealed in delight at the size of her bedroom and the view from her window. The army barracks were close – plenty of opportunity for Jan to pursue his boyhood dream of becoming an officer one day. There was a regular supply of delicious food and wine from Germany, an excellent bilingual school for Danuta and, of course, this job for Jan. His father had quickly organised for him to work as an engineering inspector on a major new irrigation project. Not bad for an engineering student.

But, still, the rumours. Even those Poles with their heads in the sand, those who professed never to read the newspapers or concern themselves with politics, knew the Nazis were creating mass movements of people all over the country. In Warsaw, you couldn't take a tram from one side of the city to the other without passing through the Jewish ghetto. There were massive camps being built for political dissenters, gypsies, homosexuals and, of course, Jews. What was going on inside, no one really knew. Why were the Poles not fighting back?

'Come in, sit down.' His father was trying to be civil, but, to Jan's ear, his words sounded harsh and boorish. 'Tell me, how are the channels coming along?'

Mr Novak seemed inordinately interested in the daily progress of these damned channels. The Nazis were building a network to drain the swamp and make the land arable. Germany was already running out of food, and the plan was to cultivate the entire area of eastern Poland as a breadbasket to feed their people.

Jan had been genuinely impressed the first time he saw the plans. A vast swathe of marshy ground criss-crossed by neat lines. It was one hell of a feat of engineering. But very labour-intensive. His boss had shrugged when Jan had ventured this opinion. 'Labour is free,' he'd said. 'It will all be done with Jewish labour.'

Jan had been a little taken aback the first time he saw the labourers – of course he had. Who wouldn't? Their eyes were hollow. They looked ... defeated. Something about their passivity irked him. They just did what they were told, like farm animals. But their conditions seemed to be tolerable. Today they had even been laughing and dancing, for God's sake.

He thought again about that girl. Her dance, how they had all watched her body become fluid, like mercury, moving to the wildly incongruous notes of the *Radetzky March*. Her fair hair; her amazing smile. It was the first time he had really looked at any of them; to his shame, it was the first time he had really thought of them as human at all.

'The channels are making progress, sir,' he replied. 'We're ahead of schedule.'

His father nodded in approval and drew deeply on his pipe. The conversation was over.

⌒

Jan arrived early the next day at the little cottage he was renting in Sawin, just a few streets away from the camp. Billeting there during the week saved him the seventeen-kilometre daily bicycle ride from Chelm, and, of course, it provided some distance from his father. It was in this house that he kept his radio, well-hidden at the back of the cupboard. At night he would close the curtains and tune in to the BBC for news of the outside world. Listening to – even possessing – a radio was punishable by death. But he was careful, he would not get caught. The act itself was a symbol of his resistance.

He pulled on his uniform quickly and smoothed his hair in his little mirror. He had not stopped thinking about that girl all night. Maya, that's right. She'd said her name was Maya.

He looked for her as he stood with his colleagues in the Appellplatz, waiting for their orders for the day. She was easy to spot; her light hair shone in the sunshine among a sea of brown and black. She moved easily and gracefully, holding the hand of an older woman – her mother? – as they filed to collect their shovels. A professional dancer, perhaps?

Something unfamiliar had happened to him as he watched her perform. He had seen the humanity in her eyes. There was something about her. The vitality of her dance, yes, the way her body moved. But also a calmness that gave him hope. Unlike the girlfriends he had known before, those silly, giggling girls with their lipstick and elaborate hairstyles, with Maya he had felt a connection, a deep cord that would not let him go.

He had to talk to her again. But how? Consorting with a Jew was a serious crime; that had been made very clear to him on his first day at the camp. Yet, to be honest, the SS were seldom here. For much of the time, the camp was controlled by Jan's superior, the chief engineer, Czyprinski, a Pole and a decent man. He would often invite Jan to share a vodka at the end of the day; he seemed genuinely interested in Jan's perspective on the building works. Jan could trust him. The only others in authority were the police – not the officers under his father's command, but the Polish Jewish police. For some reason the Nazis thought they would make more efficient captors. They were as terrified of the Commandant as everyone else.

Still, to meet Maya again meant taking a terrible risk. He would have to bring her somewhere secret, away from the eyes that were everywhere in the camp, ready to betray one of their own for a few extra rations. But where? He thought of the farmers he had met. Was it safe to ask one of them? There was one Polish woman, in particular, with whom he had a good relationship. He would often share with her the German delicacies that his father brought home from work. Could that farmer's wife be trusted? She was kind and gentle. And she had seemed interested in his personal life. He would ask her. He had a whole *wurst* he could give her in return for her silence.

He gazed over the fields, over the hunched backs of the labourers, row after row of grey mounds as far as he could see. Where was Maya?

Yes, it was a risk, but he was willing to take it – just to see her smile again.

13

Maya bent forward, stamping on the earth to harden it before she plunged in the spade. She wiped the sweat from her forehead and dug again. The damp dirt smelled fresh. It was teeming with tiny creatures, ants and worms; alive. The drainage channels were taking shape, stretching behind her, a satisfying progression. When she stood up to ease her aching back, she could see the heads of the prisoners bobbing up and down along the neat lines.

The guards were lazy in the unseasonal heat. Some sat with their shirtsleeves rolled up and their sticks at their side. There was little need for force these days. They moved automatically, prisoners and guards, well-rehearsed in the daily routine. In the distance, she could see the Polish technicians. Franz was talking to them; they were bending over a large piece of paper that shone white in the sun. She tried to make out Jan, the shape of his shoulders and his slim waist, but he was not there. The memory of their meeting danced in her chest.

She sensed him before she saw him: a quickening of her heart, the hairs standing up on her arms. He had broken away from the group and was walking along the trenches, stopping to talk occasionally, squatting to point and instruct. The light caught his hair as he ran his fingers through. He smiled and walked towards her. His hands were large and clean.

He spoke to her in Polish. At first, she could not hear him over the rushing in her ears. She lowered her eyes, an automatic response to authority. But his words were gentle; they floated through the air, soothing, forming a shape. She looked up at his lips. He was saying something about lunch. He nodded towards the woods, pointed at his watch and signalled one o'clock. He looked at her steadily; she met his gaze. A conversation with their eyes.

Then he was gone. His square shoulders, his strong arms. He was the first man who had ever asked her to lunch. What did he want? Could he really be interested in her? *Her?* With mud up to her ankles and callouses on her hands? Could she dare to believe it was possible? She watched him as he made his way along the trench, her eyes wide and cheeks flushed, her heart singing.

⌒

At one o'clock, the whistle blew for lunch. It meant little to the prisoners; the meal for them was nothing more than a scrap of black bread saved from breakfast, maybe a hunk of cheese bartered from the farmers and swiftly hidden in their pockets. But it was time to rest, to climb out of the half-dug trenches, rub their tired feet and breathe deeply in the sun. Maya clambered over the dirt towards the edge of the marsh, as if she were going to relieve herself behind the trees. She looked left and right. The others were sitting in groups; no one was looking her way. Rosa was chatting to a friend and drawing circles in the dust with a skinny finger. She had not noticed her.

Maya walked quickly towards the trees. There was a crackle of gunfire beyond the wood; it had become as normal to her as birdsong, but today it brought with it a new kind of dread. Was this an elaborate ruse to lure her to her death? Or – worse – perhaps there would be a group of them there, young Polish guards laughing as they ripped at her clothes. Rosa had warned her of this possibility often enough.

She thought of his eyes, locked on hers. The connection between them. Surely he had felt it too? She had not imagined it. It was worth the risk. Even if he was going to hurt her, it was better to find out and feel alive than to do nothing at all.

Still, her heart thumped with dread as she reached the trees, treading cautiously over the leaves and twigs, pushing low-hanging tendrils to the side with hands that she realised were trembling.

'*Cześć*.' He stepped towards her. 'Hello.' Dappled greens and golds of woodland sunshine reflected on his face.

Maya nodded. A blush prickled behind her ears.

He smiled at her. She did not speak, unsure what to say. He grinned in embarrassment. '*Chodź ze mną proszę.*' He held his hand towards her. 'Please, come with me.'

His hand felt warm in hers. Her heart pounded.

He led her along a narrow path between the trees. She became calmer as they walked, her hand secure in his firm grasp. A large black fly settled on the back of his jacket; she watched it swaying along with the movement of his shoulders, his head ducking beneath the branches. They did not speak.

Soon they came to a stream. Where was he taking her? He jumped down the bank and beckoned to her to follow. She looked around; there were no groups of jeering guards here. She thought of the prisoners, just a few hundred metres away in the fields, their one bowl of water a day. It was worth trusting him, if only for a drink.

She grabbed his hand as she slithered down the bank, steadying herself against his strength. He pointed at her dirty shoes and she obediently pulled them off, then laughed with sheer joy as she stepped into the cool current. The force of the clear water caressed her ankles and the backs of her aching legs. She cupped her hands and splashed her face and neck, gasping at the freshness. A soft symphony murmured around them, the sound of the roiling, trickling water and the rasping of frogs, the coo of a pigeon above their heads. Jan took her hand and held it to his lips. She giggled, suddenly dizzy, not quite believing this was happening.

When they had dried off, he led her further down the path, deeper into the trees towards a farmhouse. Wood was stacked high against a whitewashed wall and chickens scratched in the yard. Jan knocked gently at the door and pushed it open with the assured manner of someone who had done so many times. '*Moja przyjaciółka*,' he said. It sounded similar to the word 'friend', *přítel*, in Czech. Maya followed him into the kitchen. Her fear had subsided now; it was as if she had always known him, as if he had always been here in the trees, her entire life waiting for him.

Her eyes adjusted to the smoky gloom of the farm kitchen. A short woman was standing at the stove, stirring something in an enamel pot. The smell of onions and parsnips was intoxicating. She smiled warmly at Maya and invited her to sit at a rough, wooden table. Maya sat on the bench and folded her hands in her lap. Jan took a seat opposite her, smiling encouragingly. Suddenly she felt very shy. The farm woman chattered in Polish and Jan nodded and smiled, but he did not take his eyes off Maya. The woman ladled large, steaming bowlfuls of soup. White bean soup, Maya's favourite. For a second time, she gasped with pleasure. It was so unreal. The farmer's wife took a freshly baked loaf out of the oven and held it against her thigh as she sliced off hunks. Maya ate greedily; Jan threw back his head and laughed.

When she had finished, Jan glanced at his wristwatch and started to pull on his boots. A baby wailed from a bedroom. There were children here? The risk to all of them was immense – passing food to a prisoner was, she knew, a serious offence. The only Poles she had seen, apart from the engineers and the officious Jewish police, were the farmers who ignored her on the daily trek to the swamp. And now this woman had cooked her soup! The farmer's wife pressed the rest of the still-warm loaf into Maya's hands and kissed her on both cheeks. The kindness filled her more than the food.

A far-off whistle blasted from the edge of the forest. Jan brushed Maya's cheek with his finger, smiled at her warmly, and motioned for her to take a different path back to the working party.

∾

That evening, Maya slipped most of her evening rations into Erna's bowl, and shared the bread she had smuggled back to camp with her parents. She lay awake long into the night, her belly still full, the taste of the delicious white bean soup lingering in her mouth. A thousand thoughts played over in her mind.

He had kissed her hand. A guard had kissed her hand. He was kind and he had given her food. What did it mean?

She rolled over on the hard wood and thought of him. She closed her eyes and found herself in the stream again, Jan smiling at her. She imagined they were dancing and looking into each other's eyes.

At last, with the frogs and the water still playing their music in her ears, she slipped away to dream of possibilities.

14

Kate greeted Maya with a kiss on the cheek, as she would her grand-mother. Maya's skin felt soft, like velvet. A delicious smell wafted from the kitchen. 'I have made you my favourite – white bean soup! Although with Australian ingredients it never tastes quite as I remember it from those days in Poland.'

They sat at Maya's cluttered table by the window. Kate kept her notebook close. It was in these moments, prompted by smell or taste or music, that Maya would often recall her most vivid memories.

'Soon he started to bring me food every day,' Maya began. 'We would sit by the stream or in the cool clearing and he would watch me while I ate, stroking my ankle. I would tuck half of the provisions into my pocket to smuggle back to the camp for my parents or Erna.'

Kate was imagining the scene. 'But wasn't it terribly dangerous – for both of you?'

'Oh yes, I was risking a beating, or even my life. He was too. Every good deed, every kindness offered to a Jew by a Polish person was punishable by death. But we were falling in love! I do not remember thinking much about the danger.'

'One thing I still don't understand is why you trusted him. How did you know he wouldn't betray you?'

95

Maya helped herself to another ladleful of soup, then spooned it into her mouth slowly.

'Maya?' Kate was not sure whether she had heard – or had she already forgotten the question?

'You know,' Maya said at last, 'in all my life, I have never thought about that. From the moment we came together, there was no question. We were simply two young people who needed to be together, regardless of the darkness around us. We never spoke about it, but since those first moments I believed he was my destiny.'

Kate wrote fast, underlining as she went. 'But why him? What was so special about *him*?'

Maya laid down her spoon and nodded a welcome to the memories. 'I was living in hell, and he let in the light.'

Sawin, May 1942

At first, their love was no more than a collection of stolen moments. Their eyes would meet as Maya filed to work, or Jan would smile at her as he peered down at her from the lip of the trench. She got to know his presence: the way he held his shoulders, the crunch of his boots on the earth, his silhouette against the sun. When it was safe, he would beckon her to leave the swamp and meet him in the woods. He would press a loaf of bread or a hunk of cheese into her hand and she would return to work after a few minutes, flushed, refusing to look her mother in the eye.

Jan was polite and courteous – but he was still a guard. Maya dared not question his intentions or resist his requests to follow him. She could not risk angering him; he might still betray her. Nor did she tell anyone of their frequent rendezvous in the woods. Rosa and Franz would have been appalled their daughter was consorting with a guard. Instead, she buried her secret deep in her chest. It was bright and sparkling, precious, a treasure that she unwrapped and examined at night as she lay next to Rosa in their bunk. As she turned it over, its glow radiated from her stomach to her fingers and curled her toes in the straw.

How could love exist in a place like this? It was sharp as a knife and as hot as a flame. It was danger. It was hope. It was glorious.

She sat one lunchtime with her feet in the stream and felt a familiar tingling in her stomach as his footsteps approached. Today they would have more time; Czyprinski had called a temporary halt on the digging while they waited for some heavy machinery to arrive from Lublin, and the prisoners were free to sit in the sunshine for the rest of the afternoon.

Jan sat down behind her, smiled, and pressed the back of her hand to his lips. '*Jesteś piękna*,' he said softly, gazing into her eyes. She shook her head, not grasping his meaning. He pointed to her face, then vaguely around him at the trees. He pulled her hand towards him and placed it over his heart. Was he telling her she was beautiful? She smiled; though she did not understand his words, it did not matter. She felt his meaning deeply.

A wren darted in and out of the branches over their heads. '*Ptak*,' he pointed. Ah, that she understood! It sounded close to the Czech *pták* – bird. She made flapping motions with her hands; he laughed and nodded. He looked around. '*Woda*,' he said, pointing at the stream. '*Voda*!' Maya exclaimed. 'Water!'

At last, they were using words to communicate. She wanted more, to find a way of understanding his thoughts and fears. Surely to learn Polish could not be too hard? New languages had always come easily to her; as well as her mother tongue, German, she spoke Czech, and was nearly fluent in French and English. Besides, Polish was a Slavic language too. From a distance it even sounded like the language of her homeland, as if the Sawin townspeople were speaking Czech with a lisp. She would learn – and then she could ask him the reason for his kindness to her.

'*Uč mě*,' she said. 'Teach me.' He nodded enthusiastically. He understood.

'*Lubię cię* . . . I like you.' He laughed shyly.

'*Lubię cię* . . .' she repeated. She felt herself blush. He clapped his hands.

When their words ran out, he handed her a parcel of food and she threw her arms around him in a hug. He held onto her tightly, for a few moments too long, as if he did not want to let her go.

15

My darling Jan

You were patient with me then, spending our precious minutes together teaching me to speak. I learned quickly, I had so much to say. Remember when you told me that you loved me? I pretended not to understand, but I did! And of course, my darling, I already loved you too by then. Perhaps I already understood that our time together would be short. There was no time to wait; I wanted you, I craved you. It was the knowledge of your existence that got me through each hour.

More than fifty years have passed, and I feel again like I did that summer. Young and fresh. Alive.

Do you remember too, my love, as I have remembered? Do you relive those days, wherever you are?

Sawin, June 1942

Jan's mother knocked softly on his front door. Eufrozyna Novak was generally an inexpressive woman, but her eyes shone as she handed her son a basket of food. 'There is some wine sent to your father straight from Berlin,' she said, lifting the cloth. 'And some jam too. Are you sure you're eating enough?'

'Don't worry about me, Mama,' Jan said, and laughed. He leaned down to kiss her on the cheek and showed her to a seat at his sparse table.

Mrs Novak removed her gloves and looked at her son. 'You look happy,' she said.

'I am.' Jan turned his back to fill the kettle. She knew him better than anyone. Could she somehow see written on his face this dangerous – this wonderful – game that he was playing?

'Your father sends his greetings.'

'Oh, I'm sure he does.' Jan could not hide the contempt in his voice. 'He must be ecstatic that his own son is playing such an important role in solving the Jewish question.'

'Please, Jan.' Mrs Novak shook her head. 'Your father is a good man. He loves his family. He loves you. The decisions made by the Reich are not his decisions. He's just doing his job.'

'But Mama, do you see how they live? We direct them to work all day long with no food, in all weather. Some are so thin they're having trouble lifting their spades. Their feet are literally rotting in the trenches. It's not right.'

Jan's mind snapped to Maya, the twist of her waist as she shovelled the earth into the wheelbarrow. He felt his passion for her shimmer like an aura around him as his mother searched his eyes. Surely she must see it too?

'My son, your concern is admirable. I'm proud of you. But I hope you're not allowing yourself to become involved? You must keep a distance. You must be professional.'

Just yesterday, Maya had pulled him to his feet and held his hand. She had wanted to teach him how to dance. Still dancing, despite her suffering! She had begun with a simple tap move. He had followed, his large boots kicking up dust. Their first dance. His heart had nearly exploded with happiness, the impossible lightness of her spirit.

In any other world, his parents would have loved her – she was so full of life and vitality. He could imagine her pirouetting to his father's large gramophone collection; they were both lovers of music. If she had been a Polish girl, his mother would have already been making plans for the wedding.

But, no, it could not happen. She was a Jew. His father was chief of police. He had to be sensible. The consequences of him, Jan Novak, his father's son, being caught with Maya could not be contemplated. He was putting his whole family in danger, let alone Maya and her parents.

He thought of her smile. God, he loved her smile.

'Mother, don't worry. I won't get involved.' He flashed the boyish grin he knew she loved, and poured her a cup of tea.

Not even one hour later, he resigned himself to the fact that he had no choice but to get involved with Maya. He found himself wandering over to the camp at dusk, hoping for a glimpse of her. He yearned to touch her. He would not harm her or demand anything from her physically. To do so would be like crushing a butterfly, or defacing a work of art. But to be near her, that was all he needed. Just to have her look at him.

He saw her at a bench with her friends, a young Czech couple. The man looked thin and drawn; he must be sharing his food with his wife. How pointless – did he not realise that his life depended on remaining strong for work? Jan stopped himself. They were human too. He would have done the same for Maya, if he had been born one of them.

He sauntered through the square, taking the long route to increase the chances that Maya would see him. The other young woman noticed him first; he saw her nudge Maya with her elbow and glance in his direction. Maya looked up. He felt a stab of joy, a moment of pure pleasure, as her eyes met his.

She touched her friend on the arm then stood and walked slowly towards the latrines. She did not look at him, but he knew where she was heading. There was a space behind the building where they had met before. It should be safe there. He forced himself to wait, then slowly followed in Maya's direction, making sure no one was watching.

She greeted him shyly, her cheeks flushing. Happiness surged through him at her obvious pleasure in seeing him. He grabbed her hand and pulled her towards him. She felt small and yielding in his arms, his body strong and masculine against hers. He could feel the life in her. He could hold her for ever.

They stood in a wordless embrace for what seemed like hours, though in reality little more than a minute ticked by. The birds sang themselves into a frenzy in the trees and the setting sun lit up the sky.

'*Szybko!*' A man's voice barked an order, too close for comfort. Maya stiffened. Jan pulled her closer, as if shielding her with his body. He peered around the corner of the wall and saw a Polish guard turn his back as a prisoner scurried towards the kitchen on some errand. Jan signalled with his hand that Maya should wait, then nodded when he could see it was safe for her to go. He watched, hardly breathing, as she darted away into the luminous light of the dusk, the last rays of the sun tinging the ends of her blonde hair with pink.

❦

The next day, the Commandant's face was dark. 'Too slow, too slow,' he muttered. A cloud of unease settled over both engineers and prisoners as they watched him disappear from the swamp.

At the evening Appell, he ordered the prisoners to stand in their straight lines for more than two hours. He sat, motionless, on an upholstered chair in front of them and watched them with steely eyes. At first, the heat was uncomfortable. But then, as the sun lowered behind the trees and their cooling sweat turned to chill, they began to shiver. Their thin soup simmered and bubbled in the cauldron, untouched. There was no sound other than the crows calling in circles above the trees as the day faded into dusk. The Commandant did not move; his eyes did not waver.

Jan stood with the other engineers and the Polish guards behind the Commandant. They, too, were in disgrace, but, out of Ondyt's line of sight, they were at least able to shuffle their feet or lean on a wall. Jan watched Maya intently as she shifted her weight from one foot to the other, trying to find relief. She must not be the first to fall. Her mother stood to her right. She was swaying slightly from side to side like a stalk in the breeze. Maya edged imperceptibly closer to Rosa, ready to prop her up if she fainted.

Hundreds of prisoners stood with their heads bowed. There were easily enough of them to overwhelm the Commandant and the guards, if they had the energy, if the will had not seeped out of them. For the first time, Jan understood a little of their impotence. He stood like a schoolboy in trouble, his eyes downcast and his hands limp at his sides.

Suddenly there was a dull thud and someone hit the ground. It was the moment the Commandant had been waiting for. He stood up sharply and gestured towards the lump of the body at their feet. They all looked; it was impossible not to. It was Jaroslav, an accountant in his early fifties. The prisoners had been worried about him for weeks – he was so thin, so ill. Somehow, each day he found the strength to march and dig, but it was only a matter of time before the cancer and the starvation overcame him and he could not.

He opened his eyes as the Polish Jewish guards grabbed him by the armpits and dragged him to the front of the crowd. They laid him limp at the Commandant's feet. He curled into a ball, his skeletal arms automatically shielding his head. He looked up, not with fear but, worse, with resignation. Jan's stomach clenched with the inevitability of what was going to happen. Collectively, the prisoners visibly relaxed in the knowledge that the Commandant's attention was no longer on the crowd; that today, at least, it would not be one of them. Jan saw Rosa grab Maya's hand.

'*Schweinehunde*,' the Commandant addressed the prisoners, his eyes on Jaroslav. 'Jewish pigs, see what will happen to those of you who are lazy.'

His kicks sounded hard at first, low and dull, then wet and fleshy. Maya had closed her eyes, but Jan forced himself to look. Across the Appellplatz, five hundred prisoners stood with their eyes averted as the Commandant kicked the life out of the prisoner. *Whump, whump, whump.* The crack of teeth, the grunt of his breaths.

At last, mercifully, the sound stopped. Silence. Jan could hear his own breaths rasp in and out. There was a scuffle as they removed the body, the quick scrape of brush strokes in the dirt as someone swept over the blood. The Commandant started to address the crowd.

Jan did not listen. He allowed himself to look at Maya. There she was, standing still and stiff. Little more than three weeks had passed since they had met, and his heart already swelled at the sight of her. How quickly, stupidly, he had fallen for her. She was a Jew, a prisoner, standing there facing death like the rest of them.

He watched as Ondyt strutted between the rows of cowed prisoners. His stomach clenched as the Commandant stopped in front of Maya. He was *touching* her! He was running his gloved hand over her shoulder and now . . . no! . . . over her breasts.

Jan could see Maya's mother, how her chin was trembling as she looked steadfastly at the ground. But Maya was standing strong and tall. As if she could sense Jan, she lifted her head and looked straight at him.

He had never despised himself more. Why was he not saving her? Why was he not running forward, grabbing the rifle from the Commandant's hands and setting them all free? Instead, he stood, like the others, watching passively. 'I cannot help you,' he told her with his eyes. 'There is nothing I can do.'

Maya held his gaze until the Commandant kicked her foot with his boot and continued down the line. And somehow, in their shared impotence, Jan wanted her more.

16

Kate sat rapidly tapping her pen on her desk. Her brain was racing, fuelled by several coffees. She was meant to be finalising her piece on the opening of a Greek community centre in the western suburbs, but her mind turned once again to Commandant Ondyt. It was proving harder than she had expected to locate a Polish engineer from the Second World War, but perhaps Ondyt was the key.

She was eager to find Jan now. But it had been over a month, and none of the leads she had followed up so far had borne fruit. She was still meeting with Maya every week. She was letting the memories come naturally rather than pushing her for information; they were both finding discussions about the camp harrowing. Sometimes Maya would stop talking and gaze through the window. Then she would change the subject – 'Oh, look at that light on the leaves, isn't it beautiful?' – before standing and heading to the kitchen for tea and cakes.

Avenues of investigation occupied Kate's thoughts all day and most of the night. She had called the Polish embassy. A brisk lady had answered the phone. It was outside their scope to track down missing persons.

'He's not missing as such. He was a war hero. It's for a feature I'm writing.'

'You must try the State Archives.'

She looked, for the thousandth time, at the pile of Maya's pictures and documents laid out on the desk in front of her. She picked up a photograph. It showed a large crowd standing in a square, with buildings that looked like wooden barracks along two sides. The people were wearing suits and dresses, normal city clothes of the time rather than the striped pyjamas that most people associated with the Holocaust. 'You have to understand,' Maya had said to her, 'we were professionals and business owners. We loved the theatre and opera. Before we came to the camp, we were somebody. There, we became nobody.'

That was the first problem – the camp in Sawin had not been a death camp. It was one of thousands of labour camps in which the Nazis had used the stronger Jews as slave workers until they were too weak to continue. Then they had transported them to nearby Sobibór or Majdanek for extermination. Maya told her it was quite easy for them to walk out of the camp in Sawin. 'But, really, where would we go? We did not speak Polish, we had no papers. We thought it was better to do what the government told us.'

Kate ran her finger over the map of Poland stuck to the partition next to her desk, marked with sticky notes and drawing pins. Sawin was right against the border with Ukraine, with Sobibór a fingernail's distance to the north. Sobibór had been razed to the ground as the Allies approached. No clues or records there, let alone evidence of a makeshift camp of wooden barracks in the middle of a Polish village.

'Bastards,' Kate muttered to herself under her breath. No one looked round. Swearing was a common occurrence in the newsroom.

The small passport-sized portrait of Jan gazed up at her from the detritus on her desk. He was wearing the uniform of a Polish guard. That was the second problem. Jan wasn't a Nazi. If he had been, there might have been records from the trials or collected by the Simon Wiesenthal Centre in Los Angeles, where teams of people spent their days tracking down war criminals to bring them to account. But Jan was an ordinary Pole, one of hundreds of thousands caught up by the German invasion.

The third problem was that Jan Novak was apparently an incredibly common name in Poland. There were hundreds listed in the databases Kate had managed to access, but there was no way of telling which, if any, was him. 'Your job is not easy,' the historian at the Jewish Museum in Sydney had told her. 'Anyone who collaborated with the Germans was tried after the war. He was probably sentenced to death. Or maybe he changed his name and escaped.'

Apart from the letters, the only other evidence that Jan had existed was another photograph, a small, grey image of a group of men and women standing together in some sort of trench. Their feet were in the water pooled at the bottom, and they were smiling at the camera. Jan stood to one side, holding a cigarette and squinting at the sun. Maya, looking much older than her sixteen years, was in the middle with her trousers rolled up above the muck. They looked normal and – dare she say it – quite happy? Their smiles unsettled her.

She could not give up. She quickly wrote letters to the State Archives in Warsaw, and, for good measure, to Yad Vashem in Israel and the United States Holocaust Memorial Museum in Washington. She doubted they would have heard of Jan, but perhaps they could at least send her some background on the camp and Commandant Ondyt.

By the time she had finished, it was late afternoon and the newsroom was speeding into an expectant frenzy. Kate put the finishing touches on her story, then shut down her computer and retraced her well-worn steps to the pub. She joined her colleagues there regularly now. She felt she was becoming one of the crowd.

As usual, she found herself steering the conversation to Maya's story. The other journalists were doubtful.

'You reckon her relationship with this bloke would survive all this time?' Eleanor, the education reporter, took a swig of beer and rolled her eyes.

'Yeah, he woulda had his way with her and forgotten all about her,' said Jackson.

'I almost don't care. I just really want to help her find him.' They had not seen how Maya's face lit up when she discussed Jan. Even if Maya *had* romanticised their relationship over the years, perhaps that was how she needed to remember it.

Claire, a journalist from SBS TV, leaned over from the next table and tapped Kate on the shoulder. 'I couldn't help but overhear. I'm going to Poland next week to research a project about Polish war criminals in Sydney. I'll be going to the State Archives – want me to check him out?'

Bingo! Kate scrawled Jan's name and some identifying details on the back of a beer mat and bought Claire a drink.

⌒

Two weeks later, Kate pulled an envelope out of her bag and handed it to Maya. 'I got this yesterday, from the Holocaust Museum in Washington. There's a whole file about Commandant Ondyt. It's in Polish, but they've sent a translation, too.'

Maya glanced at the paper with disinterest.

'Here, let me read it for you,' said Kate. It was her first documentary proof of the war crimes Maya had been describing. The thrill of it ran through her wrists from the paper in her hand.

The Main Commission for Investigating German Crimes in Poland
To the council of Chelm
In execution of the ordinance of the council in Chelm, on February 15, 1946, we report the following:

In the local commune of Sawin, a concentration camp for Jewish people was established from 1940 to 1943.

Teodor Ondyt, aged 55, from the Reich, was the camp Commandant. He committed the crime of murdering Jewish people.

Maya said nothing.

'Can you tell me more about him?'

Maya thought for a moment. She was silent.

'Maya?'

'He was ... *staccato*,' Maya said quietly at last. 'Abrupt, harsh and cold, like the metal of his gun. He became quite obsessed with me. I was terrified of him.'

'Did he ... do anything to you?' She regretted pushing Maya. Suddenly her story seemed very real; it was the first time Kate had really considered that this woman in front of her had actually lived through these experiences, that they were a part of who she was.

'Not physically.' Maya shut her eyes. 'He did not hurt me physically, though he threatened to many times. Yet he was responsible for the loss of everything I knew and loved. For that, I will always remember him as the devil.'

Sawin, June 1942

Maya quickly realised that the most terrifying thing about Commandant Ondyt was his unpredictability. Some days, the prisoners would barely see him; on others he would strut around all day with his rifle on his shoulder like a third arm pointing at the sky. He would often call Maya to him and make her stand by his side as he barked orders at the Polish guards. It made her feel useless and exposed.

He visited the swamp, kicking clods of earth behind him as he strode above the lines of workers in the trenches. He would call an Appell at strange times of the day or night, dragging the prisoners to attention and leaving them in the square for hours on end. They knew not to raise their eyes. Sometimes, the standing would become too much. Some would faint, others would list precariously, those around them backing off slightly to distance themselves, as if the weakness would somehow infect them. The Commandant would emerge with his twisted smirk and humourless eyes. '*Stramm! Stramm!* Stand up straight!' Those who could not were selected to stand to one side. Later, the rumble of cartwheels would cut through the evening air and the group would be bundled aboard. 'You are going to a recuperation centre,' the Polish guards told them. 'Leave your possessions here. You don't need them. You can get them when you return.' It was easier to believe that was true.

～

Four weeks after the concert, the Commandant summoned Maya to his house at the edge of the camp. Rosa was aghast. 'No, no, I will not let you go alone,' she cried, but they knew Maya had no choice.

She left the dormitory just before eight. The Polish policeman at the gate waved her through. He was clearly expecting her. His face was expressionless, though she was sure there was a shadow of unease around his eyes. She walked resolutely to the Commandant's front door and knocked timidly. Her hands were damp and she wiped them on her skirt as she waited for him to answer.

He opened the door quickly. Her stomach lurched to find herself standing so close to him. He was still wearing his uniform, but he had removed his hat. His grey hair was thinning on top; it made him look smaller and more inconsequential than he did in the camp.

'*Kommen*,' he ordered quietly, and let her inside.

His house was small but tastefully furnished, with upholstered chairs and a mahogany table. He told her to sit. She felt dirty and dishevelled as she perched on the edge of a seat with her back straight and her hands clasped to stop them trembling. The sickly smell of his cologne filled the room; his rifle stood against the wall.

'Tea?' The Commandant laid out two cups and saucers. She was not sure whether she would be able to drink, but she was thirsty and she dreaded the consequences if she said no. She nodded silently.

He sat opposite her, looking her up and down. The methodical ticking of a clock filled the silence. Should she start a conversation? She had seen people beaten for less.

He took a sip and placed the cup carefully back on the saucer. 'You are a dancer?' he said at last. She nodded again.

'Stand up.'

She placed her cup and saucer on a side table. She could not control her hands and a few drops spilled. She rose slowly.

'Show me.'

What did he mean? What should she show him? She hesitated, her heart pounding in the stillness of the room.

He stood too, his eyes fixed on her, then picked up his chair and placed it at the edge of the room. He pushed the table aside, leaving a small space in front of her.

'Dance for me, Maya. I want you to dance for me.'

It was a command, but there was a hint of pathos at the edges of his voice. She still did not move.

'Dance!' This time he barked the order. Adrenaline shot through her as she realised what he wanted.

'Is there music?' Her voice was dry and cracked.

His face darkened. She had said the wrong thing. He lifted his hand to strike her, and in that fraction of a second she felt her feet lift her up onto her toes. Instinctively, her hands formed themselves into *port de bras* and she spun in a pirouette away from him. He lowered his hand. She spun again, then again and again, pirouette after pirouette, her eyes fixed on the Commandant to prevent the dizziness. Her toes screamed in pain, but she ignored them; she felt a surge of light as she whirled on the spot and the chairs and table blurred around her.

The Commandant clapped his hands gleefully. He sat on his chair at the edge of the room with his knees spread wide.

Maya stopped spinning; for a moment she was motionless. There was no music, just the clock. The ticking grew louder and then she could hear, in her head, the thread of a melody from Swan Lake, playing to the rhythm of the clock. The music grew from somewhere far beyond the fear. Her body started to move fluidly, turning the orderly beats of the ticking into something soft and slow.

The Commandant watched her, entranced. Minutes passed as she filled the small space with swans' wings. She reached for the sky and sank to the ground. She knew she was dancing for her life, but she sensed too that she was not without power as he gazed with wet lips at her moving body.

The hands on the clock moved slowly; the Commandant did not stir. She had been dancing for half an hour. The evening light had faded, and the room was almost dark. She sensed rather than saw his eyes glinting in the shadows.

She was tiring. The lack of food and the relentless labour were taking their toll. Her arms were heavy and her steps became less graceful. She could no longer see the Commandant, but she could feel the heat of his desire. While she danced, she was safe. To stop would be suicide.

Another half an hour passed. It was completely dark now.

A match struck and lamplight filled the room. He stood and held his hand in a signal to halt. Her breath came in shallow pants; he was breathing heavily, too.

'Go now.'

She hesitated, hardly daring to believe that she was free to leave. But this was her chance. She walked quickly to the door and fumbled with the latch as she felt him loom behind her. The door opened and the cool night air hit her cheek.

'Good evening, Maya,' he said, politely. He stood and watched her, leaning his shoulder against the door jamb, as she half ran, half stumbled, back to the camp.

〜

The next day, Maya refused to look at Jan as he beckoned her to join him in the woods. He returned, hurt, to his colleagues at the far side of the field. Kaminski, an engineer not much older than Jan, poked him in the ribs. 'She's dancing for someone else now . . .'

So they'd guessed. Of course they had. Jan sucked on his cigarette, ignoring his colleagues' lewd jibes. They would not betray him, and, even if they did, his father had some power at least. But Maya? The risk was so great for her now. Whether she was lured by the food or a genuine desire to see him, he did not know. But it had to stop.

Yet how could it stop? He thought of her smile, her hair. He craved her. When he was with her, he felt peaceful. Without her, his rage turned his stomach sour.

Then he saw her move, a flash of blonde hair disappearing behind the trees. He threw his cigarette onto the ground and shoved Kaminski on the shoulder. 'And you know about dancing?' he joked, turning his back on the sniggering engineers as he slipped into the woods and made his way circuitously to the stream. He saw her as she descended carefully down the bank and stooped to cup cool water in her hands. She let it run down her arms, poured water over her head and behind her neck. Then she immersed her whole body in the stream and gasped as she came up for air.

She saw him. To his shame, he realised that she was crying. He slithered into the stream to join her and took her in his arms, feeling her thin shoulders bend to him, feeling strong. 'The Commandant,' she whispered.

'What did he do?' In just a few weeks her Polish had already improved; they could manage this simple conversation.

'Nothing. I am fine. But I am scared.'

He stroked her hair. All he wanted to do now, at this moment, was protect her.

'I will keep you safe,' he whispered, his lips brushing her ear. She did not seem to understand the words. He pulled away and looked her in the eyes, wanting her to know. 'Maya, I am here.'

17

My darling Jan

I cannot tell you how pleasant it is to have the company of this young lady. She is bright and kind. She knows just what to ask, she prompts at the right time to bring up the memories, to take me back to you. She helps me to make sense of it all.

And I give in return. I have learned many things in my life. I have so much to tell her, so many things to guide her through.

I tell her she should get out and have fun, but she looks away. There's a story there, I think. I know the look of suffering. She may not understand, but of course the feeling will pass. She has youth and life. She doesn't realise what that means.

I sometimes daydream that she is our daughter, yours and mine. Is this what it would have been like – to be a mother?

Sydney, August 1995

The wind was howling but it was sunny and bright. That was what was different about winter in Sydney. Even during the colder months, the endless sky was usually high and blazing blue. Kate's heart lifted. Eleanor, the education reporter, had asked her out to brunch. Hallelujah! A group of them were meeting at a café on Oxford Street.

Kate was early. She ordered a smoothie – such a delightful and unexpected Australian food staple – and armed herself with the newspaper while she waited for them to arrive.

'Hey, how *are* ya?' Dan Greene, a state parliament reporter, slid into the bench opposite her. She had only met him once, after work at the pub, and she was surprised he remembered who she was. His eyes crinkled at the edges and in his hands he held a newly purchased novel. She felt herself blush. He was so attractive.

Eleanor and her friend from university, Lou, joined them, and the four of them chatted easily about the day's news as they sipped their strong coffee. The conversation was interesting, even though Kate did not fully understand the detail of the political intrigues they were discussing. Compared to the events in Asia that she was used to covering, Australian state politics seemed trivial, like the local council meetings in the village hall that she had reported on during her time at her first local paper in the UK.

When talk turned to Maya, they listened closely and asked questions.

'Mate, sounds like you're onto a cracker there.' Dan smiled at her.

'The problem is, I'm not sure I'm ever going to be able to find this engineer.' Kate's great project had become something of a good-natured joke in the office. People would peer over her shoulder at the papers and photographs littering her desk. She was making some progress, but she was no closer to actually finding Jan. She had not heard back from Claire, the SBS journalist; perhaps nothing of use had turned up at the Polish State Archives.

'You know what?' said Dan. 'There's a lot of interest in the Holocaust right now. It hasn't slowed up since *Schindler's List* came out. Steven Spielberg's funding the survivors to record video testimonies. Why don't you think of these interviews with Maya as though you're recording her testimony? That's what we journalists do, right? We record history.'

She could have sworn she felt his foot brushing hers.

Eleanor was excited. 'I think you've got something there, even if you don't find the boyfriend. When have you ever read an in-depth account of what it's like to have survived the Holocaust?'

'There's been loads of accounts,' said Kate despondently.

'No, I don't mean an account of what happened – I mean a proper investigation into how someone can live a whole life after going through something like that. How do you carry on, day after day, knowing what the world can do to you? That's the direction I'd be taking, if it was my story.'

When she left them, Kate wandered through the weekend markets. She passed stalls laden with hippie hemp clothes and silver jewellery. She glanced at her watch. Nearly time to go to Maya's house. A bouquet of bright orange gerberas caught her eye. It was Maya's birthday next week; she would be seventy.

Kate lingered at a food stall, trying to find something to take for their afternoon meeting. Maya loved cake; she would shave thin slices off with her fork and chew them slowly, savouring every morsel until she had finished, then dabbing at the plate with her finger to pick up the crumbs and put them on her tongue, one by one. Kate chose a slice of lemon cake and a box of chocolates, German *Katzenzungen* – cats' tongues – with a picture of kittens on the front.

She arrived at Maya's house promptly at three.

'I brought these for you,' Kate said, handing over the flowers and the treats.

'Oh yes!' Maya exclaimed in delight, holding out the chocolates. 'These are my favourite! And in time for my birthday too. How did you know?'

Sawin, August 1942

It was Maya's seventeenth birthday. She woke early and lay still, her hands resting on her hollow stomach, staring at the cobwebs on the wooden ceiling above her head. The smell from the bakery was overwhelming today. She thought of poppyseed cake, crumbly and warm from the oven. What she would have given for a bite.

She had imagined that for her seventeenth birthday she might be taken to a concert or the opera, then out to dinner in one of Brno's elegant restaurants. She would order a delicious meal, eat it carefully so as not to drip gravy on the white tablecloth, maybe even sip some wine. Perhaps she would be allowed to bring a friend with her.

She held her rough hands in front of her eyes and examined their scratches and broken nails. Her fingers looked old. She thought of them tying the ribbons of her ballet shoes, just a few months ago. The war had not seemed real then. It was something that worried the adults, but she had trusted in them to provide, to protect her. She remembered her outrage when Hitler started to disrupt her everyday activities in Brno. When they had received the orders to leave, her main concern had been who would look after her puppy. She thought of him now, nuzzling the tickly space behind her ear, his smell of mud and wet grass. She smiled as she remembered his silky back and his meaty breath hot in her nostrils as she kissed his nose.

This was her first birthday without Omi. Where was her grand-mother now?

Rosa stirred and sat up, pulling strands of straw out of her hair. She opened her arms wide and embraced Maya. 'I have a present for you.'

She reached beneath the neat pile of clothes stacked at the end of their bunk and retrieved an aluminium bowl, not theirs, clean and unscratched. Somehow, Rosa had procured semolina and milk. Maya shuddered at what her mother must have risked for that. Rosa had cooked them together with some precious butter and sugar and left the mixture to harden overnight. A birthday cake! It was decorated with seventeen cats' tongue chocolates, arranged in a pretty circle around the edge of the bowl.

'Happy birthday, my darling.' Rosa laughed at Maya's delight. It had been so long since Maya had seen her mother laugh. It lit up her face.

The noise woke the other women. 'Happy birthday, happy birthday!' Different voices from different bunks. A breath of warm air wafted through the crack in the window.

Maya took one of the chocolates and licked it, savouring the sensa-tion. It was luxurious, smooth and precious. She nibbled a corner then placed it back on the cake, covered the bowl with her jacket and laid it back at the end of the bed as gently as if it were a newborn baby. She would share it with the other women after work, though she cut out a piece for Jan. She did not ask Rosa how she had obtained the ingredients.

The whistle sounded and Maya climbed down the ladder quickly. Somehow the sun seemed a little brighter as she pulled on her shoes and headed to the Appellplatz. She thought of her future self, watching her now, on her seventeenth birthday, through memories. It was not the seventeenth birthday she had planned, but at least she had chocolate. Oh, chocolate! She could get through today – any day – if she had chocolate.

Maya wiped the sweat from her forehead with a dirty hand. She could see Jan in the distance. As if he sensed her gaze, he looked up and smiled. He nodded towards the trees. Her heart leaped. Yes, on her birthday she would see him.

They had been meeting secretly for more than three months now. They came together at every opportunity, though often their rendez-vous consisted of no more than a brush of their hands as he passed the dinner queue, or a rapid embrace in the shadows when they knew no one could see. He was always a gentleman, but the way he looked at her made her heart constrict. She craved the feel of his arms around her; the illicit thrill of his touch was always tinged with pain that it might be the last time.

She found him sitting with his back against a tree stump, absent-mindedly chewing a blade of grass, his head tipped back and the sun on his face. He had flung his jacket over a branch. It hung there, stiffly starched. His polished boots were neatly placed beneath the tree, his trousers rolled above his ankles. One hand lay across his chest and in the other he was holding a fistful of socks, unfurled and ready to be pulled swiftly over his white feet. But, for now, his large toes were luxu-riating in the cool grass. His eyes were closed and a smile twitched on his sleepy lips. Maya noticed how delicate they were.

'Hello.' Her mouth was dry; her greeting came out as little more than a croak, but it made him jump. He stood quickly, slightly unsteady for a brief moment, before he turned to look at her. Her face burned under the intensity of his eyes. She did not know what to say.

'For you.' She pulled the slice of birthday cake from her pocket and handed it to him. It was the first time she had had something to give him.

His face lit up. '*Pyszne,*' he said, taking a bite and smacking his lips to illustrate the meaning of the word. 'Delicious.'

'My mother made it,' said Maya, speaking carefully in Polish. 'She is very clever.'

He smiled and gestured to the grass. 'Sit down. What are we celebrating?' After four months in Poland and Jan's careful lessons, she could converse more easily now.

'Today is my birthday. I am seventeen!'

His face lit up. 'Well, then you must have a feast.' He handed her a package of food, more than she could fit in her pocket. 'Let us have some lunch.'

He watched her while she ate and rubbed her back softly. Her body tingled with electricity under his hand.

'So, you are seventeen now,' he said when she had finished. He pulled her to her feet. 'Miss Maya, may I have the honour of a dance?'

She smiled. She had tried to teach him some steps, but he was no dancer. 'I would be honoured, sir.'

He wrapped his arm around her waist, and they set off in an awkward waltz. Maya giggled. 'No, no, like this!' He tried again but crushed her foot with his rough boot.

They stepped away from each other. He laughed; she began to laugh, too. Everything suddenly seemed ridiculous. It felt good to laugh, it had been so long. Soon she could not stop herself. She felt euphoric, dizzy. She bent over as her body was wracked with spasms. She could hardly breathe.

They both suddenly stopped. They stared at each other. Neither of them moved.

His mouth opened to say something, but no words came. Her nerves tingled with anticipation.

Then he strode towards her. He grabbed her shoulders and his soft lips found hers. Her first kiss. How strange to taste another person's mouth. It was sweet, like fresh grass. He cupped her face in his hands and she ran her fingers through his hair.

They pulled apart, panting quickly. They found each other's eyes. Then they kissed again, and again and again. Their bodies pressed together, their hands urgently clutching each other. She could feel the strength of his heart beating beneath his shirt, the slight catch in his breath as he held her.

In the distance, the whistle blew. He looked at her and smoothed her hair. His eyes were shining.

'Come here,' he said, pulling her to him and kissing her again, before at last they tore themselves away from each other and Maya turned back towards the swamp.

18

My darling Jan

Kate wants to clean my house. 'Is it dirty?' I asked her today. She looked embarrassed. 'I'm happy to just run the hoover over it and clean the bathroom.' Her funny English words. Luckily, I am a translator, and I knew what she meant.

In truth, I am glad of the help. I am not as agile as I was – and, of course, I have to remember what needs to be done. The cleaner the house, the better. I have not been able to stand dirt since the war. It seems I have spent most of the last five decades cleaning, washing, scrubbing. But it still sticks to me, the smell.

In some ways, I never left the camp. There has never been a day when I did not think about it. Sometimes it is near, sometimes far away. Sometimes it causes a physical pain in my gut. Mostly, it is like a violin weeping, a single drawn-out note, taut like a wire.

But today, things are better. My carpet and my bathroom are sparkling clean. As I sit here writing to you, with fresh sheets on my bed and the smell of disinfectant in the air, I wonder, Jan, whether in fact I imagined it all.

Sawin, September 1942

A rumble of trucks brought a new group of prisoners to the camp. Maya was resting outside her dormitory, leaning her head back against the wooden wall. The new arrivals were dressed in black; the men had large hats and locks of hair dangling down the sides of their faces. They were talking loudly in Polish, sounding optimistic; they seemed quite well fed. 'Orthodox Jews,' said Franz, nodding in their direction. Maya had never seen an Orthodox Jew before. In Brno, the Jews looked like everyone else.

The new arrivals stood by themselves in the dinner queue, devout and organised, well behaved. Maya caught the eye of a girl about her age who was standing quietly with her parents, looking around her to try to make sense of her new surroundings. Maya smiled in welcome. 'My name is Rachel,' the girl said in Polish when they came together with their bowls of soup in their hands. Her black eyes glittered out of her sharp little face.

They found each other again the next day. Rachel was eighteen, just one year older than Maya, shy and polite. She seemed relieved to have found someone to talk to. They had come from Terezín, she said. She did not know where they were going.

Maya showed her how to carry the spade to ease the bite on her shoulder. They giggled as Rachel tried to march in time. 'Like this,' Maya told her, grabbing her hand. At dinner they sat with Erna and Pavel and chatted like old friends. Rachel told them what was happening in Poland. Most Jews were now living in ghettos, she said. Food was scarce, but they made do.

'Life's really not so bad here,' Erna said, encouragingly. 'We have each other.' She squeezed Pavel's hand.

No, life was not really so bad. Not this evening, as they sat together in the September twilight, secretly sharing the food that Jan had smuggled to Maya earlier that day. She smiled at the thought of him.

Rachel looked beyond Maya to her parents at the opposite side of the Appellplatz. 'It's so long since I had a friend my age. I'm so glad to have met you.'

꒰

The Polish Jews were moved on in the middle of the night. Rachel hid under a bed so she could stay. The next day, she marched with Maya, bowing her head low so as not to be seen. 'I wanted to stay with you,' she whispered. 'I heard my father talking. He was afraid.' It was raining softly, covering their clothes and faces in a damp film.

The Commandant arrived mid-morning. They heard him before they saw him. His shouting echoed over the swamp, sending the birds shrieking in alarm. His rifle was slung over his shoulder as always, and he stopped to peer into each trench. He was clearly looking for someone. He was coming closer. Rachel's eyes were wide with panic.

Beyond the field, a Polish farmer waited patiently with his cart and horse. Maya knew what that meant. He had come here to transport the latest group to Sobibór. She thought of the train station, her first experience on Polish soil. What were they taking them back there for? The farmer was biting on a stick and his horse stamped its foot, impatient, as raindrops dripped off its eyelashes.

The Commandant strode past them. Maya watched over the top of the trench as his boots marched above her head. What small feet he had. He was walking away from them, towards the next trench. She dared to smile at Rachel. He had not noticed her.

No one was digging now. The prisoners stood quietly, unable to move, waiting for something to happen. The soft pattering of the rain quickened; trickles ran down their necks. Rachel crouched down, trying to hide behind the men's knees, her head bowed and her hands clutching her ankles.

The Commandant turned suddenly. He walked quickly back towards them. His boots appeared again above the trench.

'You!' he shouted. He squatted down, pointing at Rachel. 'Why are you here? You should have gone with your family.' She did not move, frozen in her little ball.

'Get out, get out!' His voice rose quickly into a scream; his rifle was in his hands. Maya realised she was shaking. Rachel looked up at her, questioning. Maya nodded.

'Well?' His face was centimetres from Rachel's as she clambered out of the trench. Maya noticed how tiny she was, barely as tall as the Commandant's shoulder, no larger than a child. 'Explain yourself.'

'I'm not feeling very well. I have my period.' Her voice was surprisingly strident. 'I thought it would be better to stay in Sawin.' It was the sort of excuse that might have worked on her mother when she wanted to stay home from school.

He narrowed his eyes. Nodded sharply. 'Go.'

She turned to walk back to the trench. She was looking Maya straight in the eye, trying to calm her terror. No one else moved. Even the trees seemed to stand still, watching, holding their breath.

A single shot cracked out and Rachel stopped walking. She stood completely still, but did not fall. Had he missed her? Rachel's eyes found Maya's. She looked confused, shocked. Maya opened her mouth to speak, but her breath caught as Rachel folded slowly forwards. Her eyes held Maya's until they did not, until, in no more than a breath, the briefest fraction of a second, their light went out.

Maya's knees buckled. She had never watched someone die before. She saw now how quickly life could be extinguished. A shout, a gunshot, a whisper and then nothingness. She could not stand, she was going to faint. She watched in horror as Rachel's body twitched into stillness, her clothes slowly turning dark in the drizzling rain.

'See!' the Commandant yelled, gesturing grandly with his arms. 'This is what happens to anyone who disobeys my orders.'

He turned Rachel over with his foot. Her mouth was twisted and a thin trickle of blood ran down her chin and into the mud. 'I will not be disobeyed!' he screamed, kicking the body viciously, suddenly overcome with rage. He lifted his rifle and fired again. At the far edge of the swamp, the horse screamed in pain.

At last, the Commandant lowered his rifle and wiped spittle from his chin. He turned to leave, then rounded on them again. He strode towards Maya and bent to look straight at her, almost pleadingly.

Then he pulled himself upright. 'What are you looking at? Work, work!' he yelled, and was gone.

Maya stifled a sob. How was this happening? How were they allowing it? Why was God allowing it?

Later that evening, a group of men loaded Rachel's body onto a cart as the rest of the prisoners queued for their soup. The horse stamped impatiently as Franz, white-faced, stopped to talk to the farmer.

'He says she will be buried in the Jewish cemetery,' he whispered to Rosa as they sat at their dinner. 'But those who are alive, he takes them to Sobibór, Majdanek or Treblinka. There are big camps there, maybe a few thousand people in each one.' Franz shook his head. 'He has taken twelve carts already. But he has never seen anyone come out.' He looked defeated.

Maya stared at the thin soup in her bowl. What was the point? What was the point of any of this now?

19

It was impossible to meet in the woods now. Jan caught her eye as they marched to the swamp the next day. They did not need to speak.

A few days later, she was walking by the kitchen when he grabbed her arm and pressed a piece of paper into her hand. He had written clearly so she could understand the Polish. 'Come up the ladder at eleven.' She knew what he meant. There was a ladder behind the stoves in the kitchen leading to a hay loft where the wood was stored. She understood the risk.

Sleep was impossible that night. She held Rosa tightly, trying to steady her breathing as she rehearsed in her head the terrible journey she was about to take. Yet there was no question of staying in her bed. Her desire for Jan ran through her veins like fire.

When the sighs had died down and soft snores punctuated the night, she gently disengaged herself from her mother's arms and climbed down from her bunk. There was a sliver of a crystal moon, but the clouds hung low in the sky and the Appellplatz was dark. The words of a prayer silently repeated: 'God, give me strength and courage.'

Once, when no one was looking, she had sneaked out of Omi's house. It had been a night similar to this, though the city lights had shone yellow in the distance. She had gently prised the window open and climbed out onto the roof – right there, onto the cold tiles! – and had gulped with the thrill of her audacity. She could hear the adults inside, laughing and talking. She had scrambled towards the edge, peered over at the cobbles two stories below, then slowly, slowly, clambered down the drainpipe. She was in full view of the street, in her school dress with the ribbons still in her hair, but no one had stopped. She remembered the relief as she set her bare foot on the pavement. The daring of it! But there had been nowhere to go, and it was far too hard to climb back up again, so she had had to knock on the door and surprise them all. Maya smiled now at the memory.

Just be bold, and no one will see.

She walked quickly towards the latrines. There was a risk she might be discovered, but if anyone asked, she had an excuse for being outside. A chilly gust of wind caught her cheek and she shivered involuntarily. She walked around to the front of the latrine building and pushed on the door. Two women were sitting there like hens laying eggs. Maya joined them, just another prisoner, holding her secret close.

When she was sure no one was around, she slipped out again and past the latrines, much more slowly now, crouching low in the darkest shadows of the building until she reached the fence. A strong hand grabbed her arm and pulled her around the corner. Jan smothered her face in kisses before leading her towards the kitchen and up the ladder. The night settled back in on itself and no one knew they were there.

The loft was pitch black and the wood smelled sweet. The darkness made their passion seem more intense, more possible. She lifted her hands and their fingertips met.

Was that a snatch of music she heard, or was she imagining it? Maya felt the urge to move her feet, slowly at first, rhythmically swaying. As her eyes adjusted to the dark, she could make out Jan's face, staring at her in the gloom. His eyes were wide with awe, with excitement. She pulled away and circled him, her senses ringing with the sense of him, breathing heavily. Not a hundred metres away, the Commandant lay sleeping in his bed. If they were caught, they would be shot. But for this moment, here in the loft, she was alive, with him.

Then he was kissing her, his lips urgently searching hers. She felt her body respond. She relaxed against him, her arms around his waist as he held her face firmly to his. She wanted every part of him, to submit completely to him and the safety he represented. He pulled her onto the hard floor, caressing her, his body heavy on top of her. He kissed her eyes and her hair. Tears coursed down her cheeks as she drank in the comfort she craved. Between kisses, he sang to her softly and stroked her cheek. *If I leave, do not cry. Behold, the world is full of beauty . . .*

Sydney, September 1995

Maya was singing – a lilting, melancholy song in Polish. It was about beauty in the world, she said.

It was late, but Kate did not care. Maya's words were flowing freely. They were getting to the heart of it now.

'We grew closer and closer every day,' Maya said. 'He was so tender. He touched me gently. We cuddled. We grew more and more infatuated with each other. The more dangerous it became, the more we needed to be together. I risked everything, again and again, just to be with him.'

'Weren't you worried you'd get pregnant?' asked Kate. It was something she probably would not have asked without her pen and notepad in hand – but, she thought, a question that had to be asked.

'Oh no,' said Maya, twisting her diamond bracelet around her wrist. 'Oh no, no. He was a gentleman. We cuddled and kissed, we were tender with each other, maybe obsessed with each other. But we never had intercourse – it just was not worth the risk of having a baby.' She lowered her voice. 'But plenty of people in the camp did, you know. Many people found a way, even though it was forbidden. Sex is the opposite of death, after all.'

Another evening alone, Kate thought as she walked out into the night; another weekend without human touch. She remembered how she had felt about Peter at the start. That need to be held. But she could not have imagined risking her life for him. He certainly had not needed her.

She stepped down from the bus, but instead of heading home she found herself wandering back down Oxford Street towards Darling Harbour. A couple walked past hand in hand, smug in their togetherness. They were laughing, as if highlighting her solitude. She felt a surge of loneliness. She was used to watching television alone, eating alone, shopping alone. Mostly she could ignore the lack of someone to greet her as she opened the door, or to notice when she wept. Yet, on days like today, when Maya talked of love, Kate felt that to go home alone was almost unbearable.

She needed a drink, to surround herself with people and laughter. She headed for a tourist bar, where she could hide in the crowd.

Rising chatter welcomed her like open arms as she walked through the door. She ordered a white wine and drank it quickly.

She was about to order another when she sensed a presence, a tingling on the back of her neck. She turned around. A young man was walking towards her, a lopsided smile on his face, a beer in his hand and hope in his eyes. He was good-looking and confident. His name was Tomas – a German! – in town for a telecommunications conference. He smiled at her with even, white teeth and sat down. His neatly pressed shirtsleeves were rolled up with just a little too much precision, exposing strong brown wrists. The bleached hairs suggested a recent holiday on a tropical beach or a windswept yacht. An expensive watch hung on his wrist and his shoes were freshly polished. He was already very drunk.

He waved to the barman and ordered in heavily-accented English, 'Two more!' Kate smelled a whiff of his cologne. What harm could there be in sharing a drink with him?

Tomas's intentions quickly became clear. Kate thought of the faded pictures of the guards on her desk at work. It was only a matter of chance, what place and time you were born. How would the war have suited this young man? Would he have been a Jan, in love and appalled?

Or, more likely, would he have been like so many German guards, young men following orders, thinking about their girlfriends as they meticulously itemised the time and method of each Jew's death?

Kate finished her second glass. Yes, please, she would love another.

When their conversation faltered, they listened to the music, drinking in unison as Seal's *Kiss from a Rose* filled the bar. Tomas tapped his feet, his movements over-exaggerated, compensating, hopeful. Kate gazed at the smattering of hairs escaping from his shirt collar, imagined undoing the buttons. As her misty inebriation grew, her eyes traced the solid line of his thigh, and she rubbed her toe against his calf. Words were irrelevant now.

Later, lying in the soft green light of her bedroom, she tasted bile and alcohol as he pulled her to him. To be wanted, oh, to be wanted by a man. The power of her craving surprised them both.

That night she drifted uncomfortably on a wild sea of dreams, buffeted by waves of anxiety and nausea, until she woke the next morning, parched, her make-up smeared across her face. He was gone. She rose stiffly, her head swimming, and felt her way to the bathroom. She drank straight from the tap and peered up at her reflection, just visible in the early morning light. Her hair was wild and the start of a bruise was swelling on her neck. She could smell him all over her. She touched her fingers to her lips.

For the first time in – how long? – she laughed out loud.

20

Sydney, September 1995

Kate visited Maya again the following day to pick up where they had left off. Shame stung her cheeks and her head was pounding. The faint aroma of Tomas's expensive cologne still clung to her hair, making her queasy. A one-night stand? What had she been thinking? She felt disappointed in herself, more alone than ever.

Maya looked at her with knowing eyes. 'Whatever you have done, I do not care,' she said at last.

Kate looked away, but Maya grabbed her wrist. 'Do not have regrets. Nothing is ever completely bad, there are always positives and new possibilities.'

Kate nodded half-heartedly.

'Oh cheer up, my dear.' Maya smiled her lovely smile. 'There is no shame in having fun. Every day, you must try to look for happiness. Find beauty, take every experience you can. Go – grab your life. It is in making that choice, to keep living and loving, that you will find your courage.'

Sawin, September 1942

The late summer sun was warm on their backs and beads of sweat prickled Jan's upper lip. The entire workforce was slow today, under the weight of the lazy heat. The Polish guards and engineers were relaxing too, stalks of sweet grass in their mouths and bees buzzing around their heads.

Jan wandered towards the trench where he could see Maya arching her back. His colleague Kaminski had come with him, a camera in a leather case swinging on his shoulder. Maya looked up and smiled. Jan felt his heart skip, and hoped he was not blushing. 'Good day, Miss Maya,' he called down politely. He sat down on the side of the trench with his feet hanging over the edge. 'It's too hot for work today. Come here and talk to us.'

Maya glanced around anxiously. Kaminski nodded. 'It's an order.' he smiled.

She climbed out of the trench and sat next to Jan on the bank, in the shade of a stone bridge above a trickle of water in the bottom of the channel. The camp, just a march away, seemed as if it were in another world. Today seemed . . . normal.

Kaminski beckoned to Erna, who was digging a few metres away. She scrambled towards them and they sat side by side, their toes squidging in the cool mud. Kaminski unfastened the camera case and put the viewfinder to his eye. 'My father brought it for me from Warsaw,' he said as he showed Jan the viewfinder. 'Stand there – more in the shade, the sun is too bright.' Maya and Erna smiled broadly for the photograph; Jan lit a cigarette and held it in the corner of his mouth, narrowing his eyes at the camera like a film star. Erna teased him, her bold familiarity surprising all of them. He threw the cigarette into the water and laughed. No one would have guessed they were engineers and prisoners. They were just a group of normal young people, playing with a new camera.

They were interrupted by a commotion in the channel behind them. A man was shouting above the sound of thudding splashes and the hollow bellowing of a cow. They clambered up the bank to see what was happening. A Polish farmer was on the edge of the channel, his arms waving wildly as his cow strained and pulled to free herself from the mud below. The water was up to her haunches and her eyes were wide and white with fear. A crowd of prisoners gathered around, laughing. The madder the farmer grew with the cow, the more buoyant their spirits became.

The Commandant strode towards the ditch and the laughter stopped.

'What are you doing, pigs? Who told you to stop working?' Jan and Kaminski leaped to their feet; Jan watched as Maya instinctively leaned back into him, to find there was no one there. Erna had dropped to the ground and was crawling on her hands and knees back to the trench. Maya stood exposed and alone by the stone bridge, but the Commandant was not looking at her. He walked directly towards the farmer and pointed his rifle at his chest.

The cow was tiring. She made a final lunge through the mud, her hooves slipping on the steep embankment, and called again for help with a deep *moo*. The Commandant swivelled his rifle and shot her between the eyes. The crows flew out of the trees and screamed as the crack echoed through the swamp.

The Commandant's eyes were wild with rage, his scalp bright red beneath his hair. He turned to the farmer, screaming at him, garbled words that Jan could not decipher above the pounding blood in his ears. How *dare* he? How dare this German monster abuse a Pole like this?

The Commandant threw his rifle impetuously onto the hard ground and grabbed a wooden fence post with his black-gloved hand. He laid into the farmer, beating him again and again on his back and legs until the farmer's cries grew weak and faded to silence.

⌒

Jan lay on his bed, trying to order his thoughts. That man was insane; all the Germans were. He thought of Maya, lying on her hard wooden bunk not five minutes' walk through the village from his own bed. There had to be some way of seeing her more safely, away from the camp and the pervasive risk of being discovered.

It was late in the evening by the time he had a plan. He walked quickly to the camp, drawing his cigarette smoke deep into his lungs as he watched Maya's dormitory door. At last she came through and headed towards the latrines. He grabbed her hand as she rounded the corner and pulled her close into their nook behind the building. They clung to each other by a shovel and a broom resting against the wall. The stench of faeces wafted from the ground.

'*Maryska,* my little Maya, I have thought of a way that we can spend more time together. It is just too dangerous to meet in the camp now. It is better to be outside the perimeter, where no one would think to look. I'll dig a hole under the fence. Look there, just there, it's the perfect place.'

The barbed wire extended a metre and a half from where they stood and ran behind the latrine building. It was out of the view of the guards, obscured by the wall inside the camp and a row of chestnut trees beyond the fence. No one ever ventured there. If a guard should happen to walk behind the latrine – which was highly unlikely – it would be possible for Maya to squeeze through the gap and exit the other side of the building, appearing as if she had come from the latrine itself.

'Is it not too dangerous?' she whispered.

It was dangerous, of course – Jan knew he was risking his life for this. But that was the point, really. It brought sharp edges to their love, somehow made it real.

Jan ran his hand through her hair and pulled away from her. He grabbed the shovel, looked left and right, then quickly threw it over the fence. It landed with a dull thud on the grass beyond. He pointed to the fence and then at his watch, pointing to his house and motioning two o'clock.

There was a bang behind them and they froze, hearts thumping in the shadows, but it was just someone entering the latrine. They held each other and shook with soft laughter as the woman finished her business. When it was safe, they quickly kissed each other goodbye and Jan watched her as she disappeared into the night.

⌒

She arrived at his door just after two in the morning, following the route he had pointed out to her. The gentle, mellow light of his single lamp shone around her as he opened the door; she was looking around frantically, terrified. Jan pulled her towards him, closed the door, then wrapped her in his arms, kissing her eyes and neck as she started to sob. 'Shh, shh my darling. You're safe, you're safe, I have you. I love you, I love you. I will not leave you.'

When she had calmed down, he made her coffee, real coffee, and offered her bread with cheese and gherkins. He put his hand on her knee as she ate, the tears still streaking her face. He was taken aback by her beauty, even as she sniffed and wiped her nose on her sleeve. He felt as though he would do anything – *anything* – to take away her sorrow and see her face light up again.

'Here's another loaf for your parents. You must all stay strong.' He wished he could do more – for all of them. He was sharing with them any spare food he could spirit away from home, but their need was so great. He imagined the Commandant's boots thumping into Maya's stomach if she were caught. A loaf of bread brought danger enough. Really, what else could he do?

She did not take her eyes off the food in front of her, steadily bringing each mouthful to her lips then chewing and swallowing quickly, as if the meal would disappear at any moment. He allowed himself to imagine her here permanently, in his home, eating food with him.

As soon as she had finished, he stood and pulled her by the hand onto the bed. He lay down next to her, caressing her, his body pressing against hers. He kissed her urgently, more roughly than he meant to. She turned her face towards the whitewashed wall and screwed her eyes shut as his breaths grew quick and hot. He pulled her towards him and felt her resist. Her tears swelled again and she let out an involuntary sob.

He stopped. Looked down at her face. She was so young, so frail. Just a girl. He thought of his sister.

Her tear trickled onto the pillow and he knew, in that moment he really knew, that he loved her.

'Do not be afraid, Maya, I don't want to hurt you. I don't want anything from you.' He kissed her lightly on the mouth and held her tightly. 'Let me just hold you. Come, Maya, let's just hold each other.'

Together their breathing slowed and they lay, not moving, melting into the heat of each other's bodies as their fear dissolved.

21

Sawin, September 1942

At the end of September, an indistinct hum descended over the camp. Flies buzzed in the heat from first light until sundown. Black, busy flies, covering the food and the beds in a cloak of irritating noise.

The smell by the latrines was unbearable. The choking stench of excrement, mixed with the smell of Maya's own sweat, overwhelmed her as she sat there. Perspiration trickled down her back and she tasted bitter vomit on her tongue as she pressed her rough shirt to her nose. The air was thick with heat.

A new word was being whispered in the camp now. *Fleckfieber* – typhus. The long nights were filled with muffled moaning and stifled sobs, and every morning a cart arrived in the Appellplatz to remove a new pile of bodies.

Maya counted the remaining prisoners on her fingers. At least a third of their original number had disappeared. Selections were held nearly every day; those who were not chosen were expected to work. Every morning, they pulled themselves out of bed and forced themselves to eat a crust of bread and take a sip of water before they filed out of the camp to the fields. Mosquitoes pricked their ankles as they walked and peppered their dry skin with bleeding welts.

Maya turned over in her bed, burying one ear in the limp straw and clamping a hot hand over the other to stifle the sound of throaty retching. The noise was animal, unrestrained. Her stomach twisted as she listened to the pitter patter splash of vomit hitting a metal bowl. A sharp cheesy smell filled the dormitory.

Was her mother going to survive? Rosa was so weak now. Last night, she had clung to Maya as they slept, trembling with vivid dreams. Maya had stroked her back and felt the cold sweat soak through her thin clothes. Then the sickness came. Rosa vomited three times straight, and when Maya brought her a cup of water, she vomited again. 'I'll go and fetch Dr Wutzke,' Maya whispered. He was the closest they had to a physician, a psychiatrist from Prague who was attempting to manage the ailments of nearly 500 prisoners without facilities or medications. Rosa lay back on her pillow, white and listless. 'I'll be fine darling, don't worry. You go to work, let me just rest a while and I'll feel better. Shush now, don't worry.'

'Let's hope it's dysentery, not typhus,' Franz muttered when Maya rushed to find him in the morning. 'Hide her when the Appell comes.' She watched her stepfather as he quickened his pace to join a group of men up ahead. He was animated as he conversed with the chief engineer. They had struck up a good relationship; the engineers sometimes came to Franz for advice, and it won him some freedoms.

That evening, he brought chicken soup in a pot, carrying it slowly so as not to spill it. It was still warm. Maya breathed in the aroma and her mouth watered. She clambered into the bunk and lifted Rosa's head, spooning hunks of chicken and carrot into her mouth. Afterwards, Rosa said she felt stronger. Franz embraced Maya tightly. 'Ah, my grandmother was right. There is no greater power than that of chicken soup!'

But the next morning, Rosa tossed and moaned. Maya lifted her mother's head and tried to coax a sip of water past her lips. She dampened the cuff of her sweater and gently mopped Rosa's forehead. What else could she do? She cleaned away what she could of the excrement in the straw and pulled a jacket over Rosa's bony shoulders. Rosa was shivering uncontrollably now. 'Pull this over your head if anyone comes,' Maya whispered. 'I'll be back as quickly as I can.'

She climbed down the wooden ladder and joined the other women. Her mother would not be alone in the dormitory. At least three other people were attempting to hide themselves in their bedding, pretending to sleep, pretending to be a pile of clothes, so sick they no longer cared whether anyone came.

Jan was in the Appellplatz. Maya felt unsteady on her feet, dizzy, when she straightened her back at Appell. A tight knot of worry twisted in her chest. She ran a dusty hand over her forehead and counted the seconds. The sun was already warm as Jan waved the inmates forward and out of the gate. Maya set her eyes on the ground. The usual rush of excitement at seeing him was replaced now with gnawing anxiety. She was helpless.

∽

The fields shimmered in the heat. The prisoners dug and scraped half-heartedly, splintering the hard ground into tiny shards of dirt. The guards found shelter from the oppressive sun under the trees and barely noticed the progress of the work.

Jan saw her beckon him to the woods. She knew how dangerous this was – why was she risking it? But he could see the urgency in her eyes; he followed as she melted into the trees.

He found her quickly and pulled her towards him, but she stiffened. He stepped back, surprised, and searched her eyes for an explanation.

'My mother is sick. I think it's the typhus.'

Jan shook his head, glanced at the ground. He knew this was serious. Everyone in the area was talking about the outbreak of typhus; there were calls to close the camp and exterminate the vermin to prevent the disease from spreading further among the locals. There was a doctor in the next village who had stocked up on medicine, but it was too risky for Jan to venture there. If he was going to help, he would have to make his excuses and find a way to go back to Chelm, quickly, before Rosa's condition worsened.

'I will help you,' he said, tilting Maya's chin up with his finger so she could see that he meant what he said. 'I'll find some medicine. Let's put off our meeting tonight. I'll bring whatever you need tomorrow.'

'Yes, that will be good. Thank you, thank you.' Maya wiped her nose. 'I can't survive in here without my mother. She is everything to me.'

'Trust me, I will do what I can.' He was not sure whether it was possible, but he would find a way. At last, a way of really showing her that he could protect her.

In the distance, they could hear the prisoners stumbling to their feet, coughing and yawning as they pulled themselves upright to head back into the trenches. Maya scrambled up the slippery bank and joined the group.

$\backsim$

Jan was impatient to leave as he escorted the prisoners back into camp in the soft evening light. The humming of the flies had abated. The Germans were not stupid. The latrines had been cleaned and the fetid ground was freshly swept. A small group of prisoners stood in the corner of the Appellplatz, their eyes downcast and their clothes stained. The unfortunate cleaners. He scanned the faces quickly for Rosa and exhaled with relief when he saw she was not among them.

Something had changed. There was a tingle of anticipation in the air, an uncertain knowledge that something new and terrible was about to happen. Everyone stood still in the square, paralysed, waiting. Jan heard the distant rumbling of a truck. It was getting louder.

'Attention!' The guards lined up, calling the prisoners into their rows. They moved quickly, shuffling tired feet and clasping aching hands politely in front of them, each one silently praying that they would escape notice.

The birds had started singing to the dusk in the trees beyond the camp. The Commandant marched out of his quarters and stood in front of the assembled crowd. He puffed out his chest and cleared his throat. None of the prisoners looked up at him. It was a dangerous strategy. Fail to respond to his demands and they could be beaten around the head. But catch his eye, and they could be dead.

'Good evening, Jews,' he began. His harsh tone cut the gentle evening air. 'We understand some of you have been sick. Sickness cannot be tolerated. We have decided to remove those of you who are ill. We have prepared special quarters for you. You will be cared for until you are strong enough to return here and work for us again. This will protect those of you who have not yet contracted the fever. This is in your best interests. It shows how much we care for you, our workers.'

Once the Commandant had strutted back to his house, Jan sauntered towards the horse and cart and clapped the Polish driver on the shoulder.

'Got a cigarette?'

The farmer felt in his pocket, then resentfully handed the pack to Jan.

'Which hospital are you taking them to?' asked Jan, trying to sound as nonchalant as possible. 'Actually, I was hoping to get hold of some medicine myself, just in case. Perhaps I can grab a lift with you, if you have room?'

The man spat on the ground. 'It's not a hospital I'm taking them to.'

'What do you mean?'

'We are not going to Chelm, we are going north. To Sobibór.'

Jan stiffened, immediately aware that he was in uniform. He nodded at the farmer. 'Well, keep up the good work.' It was not until he was well out of sight of the camp that he allowed himself to run for his bicycle and set off on the road to Chelm.

22

Sydney, September 1995

'Did you honestly believe them, that they were taking the sick prisoners to a hospital?' asked Kate.

'Oh yes, when you are told the same lies for months on end you believe them. Maybe we did not really want to hear the truth.'

'But you must have noticed those people left and didn't come back. What did you think was happening?'

Maya shrugged. 'Our life had become a matter of surviving each day. We could not think about the big picture. Oh, we sometimes hoped that the partisans in the woods would come to liberate us. We listened to their gunfire day and night and hoped for a miracle. But of course, it never came.'

'How did you do it? How did you keep going, day after day?'

'I never allowed myself to lose hope.' Maya placed her hand over her heart. 'It is always possible to believe in a better tomorrow.'

Sawin, September 1942

Maya shut her eyes. A woman behind her had started to sob; the Commandant had walked into the distance and the sick were being lifted into the cart. Every centimetre of her body wanted to run to Rosa, to check whether she was still hiding in her bed, but she forced herself to move quietly, calmly. She knew better than to give anything away.

She waited until the prisoner next to her peeled away from the row and walked steadily, serenely, towards the dormitory.

The jacket was still on the bed. Rosa's foot stuck out of the end; she was sleeping. Maya clambered up next to her mother and prayed to God that he would provide. '*Ribonoh Shel Olam*,' she whispered. 'Master of the Universe, if you help my mother survive, I will dedicate the rest of my life to you. Amen.'

Later that evening, Erna crept into the dormitory. She climbed up the wooden steps and shook Maya's feet to wake her. 'Maya, come.'

Maya followed her outside and around the corner into the shadow of the building. Pavel was waiting for them. He kissed her quietly on both cheeks.

'I've made a connection with one of the farmers from the village. He has been helping us – an egg here or there, a piece of bread. It's why we're still strong. Today I asked him for help with the *Fleckfieber*. He is willing to bring medicine, but it will cost us. Do you have anything we could give to him?'

Maya thought of her mother's jewellery, which they had distributed among the non-Jewish neighbours in Brno. Franz had already bartered most of what they had brought with them, sewn into the collars of their winter jackets. It had kept them alive, but she had nothing left to give. She had not yet heard from Jan, and the situation was urgent. Tomorrow her mother could be gone.

'Wait here.' She slipped back into the dormitory and climbed up to the bunk. She looked at Rosa's hand, shrunken and bony, the knuckles sticking out and fingernails rough and dirty. She remembered studying those fingernails as a small child on her mother's lap. She had known every indentation and curve: the shape of the thumbnail, large and wide; the tiny half-moon at the base of the little finger. There was still a groove in Rosa's ring finger, where her wedding ring had been rapidly twisted off, hidden in a pocket and then carefully squeezed into a gap in the wooden boards. Maya searched for it now. There it was, a tiny mound of gold wedged between the wood. It was stuck tight. She worried it with her finger, back and forth, and eventually worked it loose. She held it up to the light streaming in from the moon. Her mother had worn this ring for six years. Just six years. She and Franz were still so young, only forty-two.

Erna and Pavel were waiting for her behind the dormitory. Maya's heart swelled at the thought of them. Her dear friends. Just to stand there for ten minutes was a risk, and they were doing that for her.

'Will this be enough?' She handed the ring to Pavel. 'It's solid gold. It's all we have.'

'Yes, I think it will be enough.' He squeezed her arm. 'Go back to bed, Maya. I will do what I can. Erna will come to find you when I have medicine.'

There was nothing else she could do. She now had two men searching for medicine for Rosa, one a guard and one a Jew. Still, the worry ate at her as she climbed back into bed and lay awake through the hours of the night.

⁓

The Commandant was ferocious the next morning. So many prisoners were sick with typhus now, more than half had been too weak to attempt the walk to the swamp. He looked at them through slitted eyes as he left them standing for more than an hour in the warming sun.

'This insubordination is not to be tolerated!' he shouted. 'Too many of you missed work yesterday, pretending to be sick in your beds. May I remind you that you are here to do the business of the Third Reich. You may not stay in the dormitories. You think I don't know where you are? Those who do not come to work today, I will shoot in the stomach.'

It was a regular game; they knew it well by now. The Commandant strutted from row to row, prodding prisoners in the stomach with his rifle. 'Du . . . Du . . .' He was coming closer. Maya fixed her eyes on the ground, not wanting to give the slightest hint that she had noticed him.

The neck of the rifle hit her in the solar plexus. 'Du.' The Commandant paused, eying her up and down. His eyes rested on her breasts, for a second, making her stomach clench. 'Yes, you too, Maya.' He had taken to using her name.

A rush of rage. She raised her chin, looked him directly in the eye. There was no spark of human connection.

'Tell me, how is your mother today?'

She realised how dry her mouth was. She swallowed and grasped her trousers tightly with sweaty palms, trying not to display any emotion. The slightest stumble, the tiniest quiver of fear, could spell the end for Rosa. She rolled her tongue around her mouth, trying to summon up some saliva to enable her to talk.

'She is well, Herr Commandant.'

She studied his boots, shiny and polished. The reflection of his leering face was distorted in the gleaming toes. Her hatred for him sloshed and simmered in her gut. She pushed it down, keeping her face still.

'That's good to hear, Maya. Will we being seeing you dance again soon?'

The thought of dancing for him made her want to vomit all over his shiny boots. Ha, how would he like that? She could feel her mouth twitch and breathed in sharply through her nose. Surely she was not going to smile?

Breathe, breathe.

'I would be honoured, Herr Commandant.'

He extended his finger, gloved in black leather despite the heat, and stroked her chin and the line of her hair.

'Good, good. Join the group.'

He turned away quickly. Was it the heat, or could she see him blushing?

She joined the other selected prisoners. They were twelve young, strong girls. They waited in the sun while the others filed through the gate and along the dusty road to the swamp. Erna was with her, gentle Erna. Whatever his plan for them, she could survive if her friend was there. They stood close, their shoulders touching, until the Polish Jewish police herded them onto the truck and they clung to the rusty bars to steady themselves as they pulled away from the camp.

23

My darling Jan

How did we survive those miseries? How do I survive them still?

Over time, the things I witnessed have gradually lost their begin-
ning and their end. They have become a part of me, a physical imprint
that has grown and aged with my body, settling over the years into my
cells. There was no need to write them down, to recall each one specifically,
for to do so would have given them strength. I have survived the years
not by forgetting, but by smothering the bad with good, with meaning.

But now my memories are slipping away, I find myself desperate not
to let them go. The things I remember hold all that was dear to me, the
people I loved.

They needed to be written. Everything. Time is running out.

Chelm, September 1942

The journey was not long, no more than half an hour through pleasant
meadows and woodlands. Maya had half expected to see the welcome
sign at Sobibór looming at the end of the track, but instead they pulled
into Chelm, a small town with a busy market square and attractive buildings. People bustled about their normal day; children were laughing.
It was a world away from the camp.

Their destination was the German barracks. There were soldiers
everywhere, their uniforms starched and their stiff collars digging into

their necks. Some of them were young, no more than a year or two older than Maya. She was suddenly painfully aware of her dirty clothes and unkempt hair. She knew she must smell; even in the heat of the summer, there was only ever one bowl of water each day for washing and drinking.

They were shown to a dormitory – a proper, neat, army dormitory, with twelve white beds and clean sheets. Maya and Erna sat down hesitantly, hoping the lice they carried would not spread too far onto the blankets. They looked at each other with wide eyes. This was too good to be true. Later they were given a proper meal, with meat and potatoes.

'I think we didn't realise it, but the Commandant beat us to death and we've arrived in heaven!' whispered Erna as they ate.

After lunch, they were taken to a large shed next to the barracks. An earthy smell wafted out when the guard opened the door. It was brimming full of potatoes. 'We have brought you here to sort these,' the guard barked. 'Half of them are mouldy, half are fine to eat. Put the mouldy ones in this cart and the others over there.'

It was easy work, much easier than digging in the trenches. They sorted through the huge mound throughout the afternoon, chattering and giggling with the energy of a real meal in their stomachs. Maya prayed silently in gratitude, though she was still uneasy at the thought of Rosa. Had Jan or Pavel brought medicine? She wondered where the wedding ring was now, and pushed the thought away.

The next day was the same: a comfortable night's sleep, a good breakfast, and easy work. Maya hardly dared to believe it. She sat on the ground, surrounded by mounds of potatoes, daydreaming about Jan. Her mind wandered to their meeting, the sound of the stream and the smell of his kisses. What if she had not been sent to Sawin? What if he had not taken an interest in engineering and been conscripted to help the Nazis build their drainage channels? She could not imagine how she would have survived this long without him. The sun felt hot on her chest. She undid the top button of her blouse, then the two buttons below, baring her skin and lifting her face to the warm rays.

As if she had imagined him to life, there he was. Jan's face peered over the top of the potatoes. 'Is this how you behave on the Third Reich's time?' he said harshly, but he was smiling. Maya laughed, pulled her blouse together and stood up quickly. There were too many people about, too many Germans, to think of touching each other. But she held his eye as she did up the buttons and smoothed her hair. He summoned her with his forefinger.

'She's safe,' he whispered when she was near enough to hear. 'Don't worry, I brought her the medicine. She's safe.'

He turned away. She watched the back of his neck, pink in the heat of the sun, wondering how it was possible that the others had not noticed there was an angel walking among them, pretending to be a man.

That evening, Maya curled together with Erna on a single bed, whispering in the dark. It had been so long since they had slept alone that an army trestle seemed too vast for a single body through the night.

'Who were you talking to this afternoon?' asked Erna.

Maya was silent. She could make out the shape of her friend in the dark, but she could not read her face. She trusted her, of course. She knew about the bartering, about Pavel's tricks and deals, but hers was a secret so dangerous that she had dared not utter it to anyone.

'I was talking to Jan. I know him. We're ... friends.'

Erna's body stiffened for a second; the girl in the next bed snored softly.

Maya thought of those who had died, of their lost opportunities, the thousands of secrets they would never share, the loves they would never have. Now was the moment to confide, to make it real.

She hesitated. It was so dangerous. Her confession would bind Erna to her fate, too.

'We're in love. I see him all the time. He's good to me.'

She could not see Erna's expression, but her friend hugged her tightly, an unspoken reassurance. 'It's what I suspected,' Erna whispered.

'We all see how you look at each other. But you must take care, Maya. Do not let others find out.'

They lay still for a few minutes, then Erna whispered, 'I have a confession too.' There was a silence, as if she were deciding whether it was safe to share. 'Of course you can't tell anyone, not yet. Pavel and I have also found ways to be together. Many of the married couples are doing the same. Maya, I haven't had a period for five months now.'

'Don't worry,' Maya whispered. 'It's the lack of food, Mother told me. Lots of the girls haven't bled for months.'

'I don't think so.' Erna pulled Maya's hand to her belly, rounded and smooth under her coarse clothes. Her breath caught in what sounded like a sob. 'I've known for a while and now I'm sure of it. I'm pregnant.'

24

Sydney, October 1995

Kate felt sick and her breasts were sore. She tried to ignore the nausea as she clutched Maya's hand tightly. The dance hall was full of couples, middle-aged people laughing and joking, though there was no one who had potential as a friend. Other than Maya, of course. 'Do not be nervous!' Maya laughed as she squeezed Kate's hand. 'You will enjoy it. Everyone can salsa dance!'

Kate laid her bag on a chair in a corner and looked around. The instructor strutted into the middle of the hall and clapped his hands. He was wearing tight black trousers and his shirt was undone nearly to his navel. Who dressed like that in real life? Kate felt as if she'd stumbled onto the set of *Strictly Ballroom*; she was the only person standing there in work pants and a sweater, with the wrong shoes.

The couples obediently stopped talking and gathered themselves into a circle around the instructor. Maya motioned to her to find a place. 'Come, I will stand next to you.'

The instructor demonstrated the first simple move. It was nothing more than a step front and back, but with some sort of fluid hip movement that Kate had no hope of emulating. He clapped his hands again, his eyes sparkling. 'Now – you try.'

Maya grabbed Kate's right hand and held her firmly in place with an arm around her back. 'Forward and back, like this.' Kate was stiff and awkward. Maya laughed. 'Relax, relax!'

Kate tried again. It was impossible. The simple steps were just the beginning; the instructor was adding new movements much too quickly and the others were already prancing in pairs across the dance floor. Her feet would not move in time and her cheeks burned with self-consciousness. The voice in her head sneered. 'Two left feet! You've always been so *clumsy*, Kate.'

After a few minutes, she turned to Maya and shook her head. 'You know what? I'm going to head off.'

Maya looked at her in surprise.

'So soon? You don't enjoy it?'

'I just don't think dancing's for me. Sorry.'

'Just wait a few more minutes. Let us see.' Maya placed her hands back on Kate's hips. 'Shut your eyes. Listen.'

Kate reluctantly did as she was told. Maya started to sway, moving Kate's hips from side to side in time with the beat.

'Just listen to the music. That's right. Side to side, back and front.'

Maya's hands guided her hips gently.

'In Sawin, I managed to dance with no music. When the war was over, I thought there could never be music again. But then I realised it was the opposite. Music was the answer.'

Kate found herself moving in some sort of rhythm. She opened her eyes. No one was watching; no one was laughing.

'Think of the sunlight,' Maya went on, looking her in the eye. 'Think of the waves on the beach. Think of the opportunities, Kate.'

She let go. Kate relaxed into the movement. She realised she was doing it by herself, no longer so afraid, moving in time with the music.

Chelm, September 1942

Jan was surprised to discover the Jewish girls had some freedom to move around the town as they pleased. The Germans knew they could not escape; they had no papers and their foreign accents held them captive as effectively as barbed wire or guns.

He lent Maya some clothes he had borrowed from his sister, Danuta, so that she could pass as a local. He could not believe how easy it was. With Maya wearing a fashionable sweater and skirt, and with her fair hair, they could walk through the back streets holding hands, giddy with the audacity of it, a Pole and a Jewish girl together in plain sight.

'Let's dance!' Maya pulled his arm around her waist and guided him to the sound of a Polish folk dance that was being played by a group of violinists in a sunny park. She was whimsical and light today; he had not seen her like this for months. Perhaps it was the food, or maybe the knowledge that her mother's health was improving, but for these brief minutes she seemed to have forgotten that she was still a prisoner and he a guard. He laughed, too, lifting her feet off the ground as he spun her around. Was this how they could be, one day?

When they were tired, they sat in the shade of a chestnut tree and shared a slice of cake. He wiped the sugar from his mouth with the back of his hand and lay on his back, looking up at the light shining through the leaves.

'What will you do, after the war?' he asked. She looked at him and smiled. He realised how easy their communication was now.

'I will be a dancer! People will come from all around to watch me!' She raised her arms above her head into fifth position then let them float to her waist, buoyed on currents of air.

'And where will I be?'

'You will be right there in the audience!' She giggled. 'You will be a successful army officer. You will meet me after the show and kiss me. Like this.' She leaned towards him; he tasted the cake on her lips.

He wished it could be true. Could he make it true? Perhaps, perhaps. A future without her in it was no future at all.

'I love you *Maryska*,' he declared. She smiled, but he was deadly serious. 'I want to marry you. Then you can be safe. I'll introduce you to Danuta first, then my mother. Papa – he might be a little difficult. But in time he'll grow to love you too.' He had not summoned the courage to tell her what his father did for a living. How could he tell her something like that?

Maya laughed. She thought he was joking. 'And how many children shall we have?'

'Two children. I would like two.'

'Let's make it three!' She kissed his forehead.

Jan tried not to think of the carts laden with sick prisoners, headed for Sobibór.

'I cannot imagine a future without you. Will we be together, Maya? Please tell me we'll be together.'

'Of course, my love, we'll always be together,' she said lightly, eyeing the remains of the cake, missing his meaning. He looked away without smiling.

They made their way to the outskirts of town. He glanced around warily as they walked, his arm protectively around her shoulder. They were far away from his parents' apartment, but it would only take a neighbour or a friend of his sister to surprise them. He could not shake a sense of hopelessness, even as he felt her graceful movements beneath his arm. At any moment he faced the possibility that she would be nothing more than a memory, a brief imprint on his world.

They came to a photographer's studio. 'Let's remember this day,' he said, pushing the door open to a tinkling bell. Maya giggled and poked him as the old photographer fussed with a massive, old-fashioned camera. He positioned them next to a pot plant and drape, adjusting their clothes and repeatedly checking the shot. They stood clasping each other in a tight embrace until the flash ignited. Maya gasped in delight, and colourful stars and shapes exploded behind Jan's eyes.

꙳

Satisfied that Maya was reasonably safe and well-fed in Chelm, Jan left to spend a week with his university friend Jakub, in Warsaw. 'You will be all right, you have Erna,' he said, as tears welled in her eyes when he told her of his plans to leave. But he felt sick in his stomach as the train pulled away and the distance between them grew. In so many ways, her survival depended on him now.

The condition of his home city shocked him; the Nazi deprivations were affecting everybody, but many of his classmates were deeply concerned about the Jews. Since July, the German SS had been conducting mass deportations from the ghetto to Treblinka, which was, Jakub told him in a lowered voice, a killing centre.

'I saw it myself,' Jakub whispered. 'They had a row of men, women and children against a wall with their hands in the air. They shot them with machine guns . . . tat tat tat tat . . .'

'What do you mean, they're killing them?' Jan asked, stunned. 'I understood they needed a Jewish workforce for the munitions factories. What would be the sense in killing them?'

Jakub nodded. 'It's true, Jan. When was the last time you were in Lublin? They're cremating bodies in ovens there; people are walking through the smoke haze on their way home from work.'

'Bodies? What do you mean? How many are you talking about?'

'It's not just random shootings anymore,' Jakub said. 'There's talk of gas. They're using gas on them. It's murder on an industrial scale.'

Jan felt dizzy. He had been so swept up in his meetings with Maya that he had not allowed himself to really think about her inevitable future beyond the immediacy of keeping her fed and safe from the Commandant. Now his complicity throbbed in his gullet.

'How do you know all this?' he asked in a strangled voice.

Jakub looked him square in the eye. 'We have intelligence.'

'We? What do you mean, Jakub?'

His friend paused. 'AK,' he whispered.

The *Armia Krajowa*, the Polish home army. Jan had heard about the organisation on his clandestine radio – everybody had – but to hear the words from his friend's mouth made his heart leap.

He looked at Jakub. He was more like a brother, really, but Jan was still flattered to be trusted with this information. To even speak those words was courting death.

Jakub did not drop his gaze. 'Jan, are you with us?'

Jan nodded.

'You know what it means. It's dangerous.'

'I don't care. We have to do something about this sickness. I'll help in any way I can.'

'So be it.' Jakub handed Jan a piece of paper with an address scrawled in pencil. 'Learn this address then destroy the paper. We'll see you there at eight.'

Jan found the meeting room without difficulty and sat down next to a handful of young men. They looked excited and hopeful, thrilled with the responsibility.

The commander addressed them quickly. He was little more than a boy himself, but he was serious and precise. The AK was busy recruiting young people from across the country, he said. Some were to be sent for training in Britain and then parachuted back into Poland to support the resistance against the Nazis. 'You all can play a part. Whether it's disrupting their supplies or spreading propaganda – all of it counts to help us defeat our oppressors.'

After the meeting, Jakub introduced him to an older man sitting behind a table at the back of the room. Jan approached and held out his hand.

'I'm Jan Novak, and willing to be at your service,' he said.

'And what service can you provide, Jan Novak?' The older man did not lift his eyes from the papers on the table in front of him.

'I am with the *Wasserwirtschafts Inspektion*, working in the Lublin district.'

The man shuffled the papers. 'We've recently established an active unit in Chelm. If you give me your details, I'll have one of them make contact.'

'Ah, I live in Chelm.' Jan fiddled with his collar. 'In fact, my father is chief of police there.'

The man's eyes snapped up.

'I can bring you details of their irrigation projects,' Jan went on.

The man stood. 'Wait here.' He left the room and returned a minute later with two more men. He did not proffer their names.

'This is the boy,' he said to his comrades, nodding in Jan's direction. 'I think that, once we run a full security check on him, he could be extremely valuable to us.'

'I'd be happy to fight,' said Jan. 'Perhaps I can join the partisans in the woods, if that would help? We hear them every day. I could drop off weapons and ammunition for them. And I've had some basic military training.'

'Oh no.' The first man put his fists on the table and looked squarely at Jan. 'We don't need you to fight, young man. We need you at home, talking to your father.'

25

Maya and Erna returned to the camp on a chilly October afternoon. Woody mounds of leaves, shrivelled and crisp, lined the road out of Chelm. There was frost on the wooden fence posts and the cows' breaths dripped in strands from their steaming nostrils as the truck rattled past fields that smelled of rotting straw. Maya hugged her arms around herself and set her eyes on the horizon.

The girls were stronger and better fed than they had been the last time they drove along this road. Their shoulders no longer ached from heavy manual labour, the blisters on their feet had healed and they were rested from nights spent under woollen blankets. Still, they had jumped up and down in delight when they had received their orders to return to Sawin. Maya was desperate to see her parents, and, while she would not have the freedom of her weekend walks in Chelm with Jan, at least she would see him every day. Erna was yearning for Pavel. He did not know about her pregnancy, and now her belly was large and round. It was difficult to conceal it beneath her work clothes; she had become clever at positioning herself behind piles of potatoes whenever the Germans were close. Maya smiled at her now. Her friend looked pale and sick as they bumped along the rutted road. Maya would find Dr Wutzke as soon as she could. He would help Erna through her pregnancy; they would manage this somehow.

163

They smelled the camp before they saw it. The acrid stench of human excreta. No wonder the Germans thought they were dirty, the Jews, swilling around like pigs in their own filth.

The truck pulled to a halt in the empty Appellplatz. The prisoners must be away at work in the swamp. A few Polish guards were sitting around the square, but the Commandant was not there. The girls climbed down with sure, quick steps, and made their way straight to the dormitory, like travellers returning after a long trip overseas. Rosa's few belongings were neatly stacked at the end of a bunk. She was still alive.

The girls' bags were full of bread, jam and cheese, anything they could lay their hands on to hide among their belongings when they received their departure orders. They shared a small loaf and hid the rest in the straw. Maya looked at Erna, eating for her baby too, and wondered, after all, whether it would be possible for her friend to survive on the meagre rations in the camp.

The afternoon wore on. The wind became bitter as a watery sunset turned the puddles to steel. At last, in the distance, they made out the shuffling of weary feet. Maya jumped up, straining to see through the twilight as the prisoners filed back into the camp.

Their numbers had diminished considerably. Once there had been ten lines of fifty people at the evening Appell; now Maya could count only six. The prisoners looked shrunken and withered, hunched forward in dejection. Their muddy clothes, the same ones they had worn for more than six months now, hung limply off their thin bodies; not working clothes, but city clothes, unsuited to the looming harshness of a Polish winter.

Maya spotted Rosa. How thin she was! Her skin was pale and taut, stretched over her cheekbones, dry like paper. The corners of her mouth turned down, but her face broke into a smile when she spotted Maya. Franz was nowhere to be seen.

After Appell, they flew into each other's arms. Maya let her mother's comfort seep through her skin. They held each other for a long time, mother and child, though Maya felt like the adult, large and strong against Rosa's tiny, shrunken body.

'Thank goodness you're here, my love, my Maya. Thank goodness.'

'Are you better now, Mutti? I tried so hard to find medicine for you. I even sold your wedding ring. Have you recovered?'

Rosa nodded. Her face was blank. She started to say something, thought better of it, then sighed and took Maya's two hands in hers.

'My darling, I have something to tell you.' Her eyes were dark and heavy as she looked at Maya. 'The typhus took Franz. He is dead.'

⌒

The world shifted. Franz was dead. How her mother had loved him; how he had made her laugh. What had he experienced while Maya was in Chelm eating real food and sleeping on a soft mattress? She did not cry. Too many had already died for that. But the ramifications of his death loomed large. There would be no one to maintain their relationship with the engineers; no one to help smuggle extra food into the camp. Providing for Rosa was now Maya's sole responsibility. And what about when this was over? Who would care for them then? She held her mother tight, thankful to be together, terrified of ever letting her go.

The camp was colder and darker than she remembered it. After work, she pulled off her sodden socks and hung them from the ceiling, watching her toes turn white as she heated them by the stove. She sat with Erna at dinner, chasing a few grains of barley in the bottom of her bowl. The rations had not improved. She finished the watery liquid and tipped the solids into Erna's bowl. 'You need this more than I do.' Erna ate them quickly. She instinctively ran a hand over her belly. It was only a matter of time until she was discovered.

Pavel was distracted and fearful when he joined them. His cheeks were hollow, and his hair was turning grey. 'The Commandant is out of control,' he growled. 'He beats someone every day, and every day we wait for it to be us. We're not working fast enough for him, the channels must be dug more quickly.' He grimaced. Maya noticed he was missing a tooth. 'And the typhus. So many have died. We don't know where the bodies are buried.'

Erna said nothing. 'Now this.' He glanced at her belly. 'My child to be born into this.' He banged his bowl on the table, making them jump.

That night, Maya slipped out of bed and made her way through the icy blackness to the hole beneath the fence. But Jan's house was dark and empty; she scurried back to her mother's warmth in the bunk.

The water in the trenches was freezing cold the next day. The prisoners stood with numb feet for hours; Maya's toes felt large and swollen, the skin ready to split. Her heart jumped when she spotted Jan, a cigarette in his soft lips, the collar of his warm woollen coat pulled high around his ears. But he did not look at her. The prisoners huddled for warmth under the trees, rubbing their chapped hands, their chests tight and sore in the cold air. But Maya's cheeks burned red. She followed him with her eyes.

Why did he not look at her? She thought of their last outing in Chelm. He had told her that he loved her, that he wanted to have children with her. She had laughed; should she not have laughed?

He cast his cigarette on the damp ground.

Look at me, look at me ... But he turned his back and walked away. It was as if he was deliberately ignoring her. Her chest constricted with despair, but she did not cry. She had no tears left.

Over the next few days, sheer survival became her main priority. It was so cold now, and the rations so meagre, that when she woke up each morning the end of the day seemed like an impossible dream. Her feet were quickly red and bleeding from the trench, and the skin peeled away as she removed her wet socks every evening with trembling fingers. Every part of her felt numb. It would be easier to stop, to lie down in the icy water and give up. A bullet would be a welcome release.

Jan continued to ignore her. She tried to catch his eye in vain, but he would not look in her direction. She squirmed with misery at night in bed, turning over and over in her head why he had abandoned her.

Without his rations, she doubted whether she and Rosa would make it through the month. Maya pulled her mother more tightly to her as she sobbed softly into the straw, until they both fell into a fitful sleep. Maya dreamed of Jan running his fingernail along her inner thigh. She woke briefly, hot longing beating in her stomach, then slipped back into sleep. In her dream, she saw Franz at the bottom of the trench. His body was cold and twisted, sticking out of the hard, Polish ground. The water rose, covering her knees, rising to her thighs, washing around her groin. But it was not cold; it was warm water, blessedly warm, running over her legs and bringing feeling back to her feet.

'What in heaven's name?' It was Mrs Meyer, in the bunk below. Her voice was high and indignant. 'What on earth – is that *piss*?'

Maya buried her face in Rosa's armpit, mortally embarrassed, as the urine quickly turned cold against her skin.

26

Sydney, October 1995

'Do you ever, even for a minute, forget what happened to you?' Kate asked.

'Oh no, of course not,' said Maya. 'I can never forget what happened to me. It has always been a part of who I am. But, you know, good came of it too.'

'What do you mean?'

Maya pulled back the lace curtain.

'Look at all those people out there, going about their lives. Everywhere they are waking up, washing, embracing, arguing. Children are playing and cars crawling along the road. It is an ordinary day. No one is thinking about their certain death. But the day I discovered I would die, it was in some ways a blessing. It put everything into focus.'

'But you still thought you were going to die. How was that good?'

Maya smiled her radiant smile. 'Look at the sunshine, Kate. Since that day, I have come to realise that no day is ordinary. Every day is a good day.'

Sawin, October 1942

It was impossible for Jan to face Maya now. Now he knew with certainty what the Nazis were planning, that Maya was never meant to survive. None of them were. Three weeks ago, they had been walking in Chelm,

169

whispering in each other's ears. He had pledged his love for her. Now he knew he could not have her – would never have her. How could he keep this information from her – but, then, how could he tell her? He could not bear to even look at her.

As the sun set, he stamped his way back to his cottage and shut the door. He stoked the fire to warm the room. His quarters were small, at least, and would heat quickly. He drew the curtains and allowed himself to inspect his clandestine radio. It was as he had left it. His fingertips tingled with the responsibility of what he was going to do.

Mr Novak had been delighted at his son's renewed interest in the war effort once he returned from Warsaw. 'So how are the Germans going to transport this grain I'm helping them to grow?' Jan had asked nonchalantly over dinner. His mother caught his eye, but said nothing. By the end of the evening, once the brandy was flowing, he was poring over a map with his father. Now he had the names and locations of at least two bridges and a supply depot that would be useful to the AK in their push to disrupt Nazi infrastructure throughout Poland.

But it was a dangerous balance to maintain. He strongly disagreed with his father about many things, but of course he would not want his family to suffer because of his actions. Even his father deserved better than to be betrayed by a son. And then there was Maya. They were risking their lives every time they saw each other, here in Sawin. He knew that if his radio were found, if his father's colleagues implicated him in the flow of information to the resistance, he would be shot against a wall. Who would miss him more? His sister or Maya?

He poured a shot of vodka, drank it in one gulp, then poured another. It helped.

By eleven, he was impatient. He glanced at his watch every few minutes. It was still too early to radio the information through to London. He drummed his fingers on the table. He could not sit still.

He was startled by a soft knocking at the door. It was Maya's knock. His heart leaped with fear and anger. It was still early, pitch dark but far too dangerous for her to have scrambled under the fence and walked through the village. Did she not care? She was putting them both in danger.

He opened the door quickly and pulled her inside. 'It's too early, Maya. You could have been caught.'

She stood with her back against the wall, panting, as he peered through a crack in the curtains to check no one had seen. They seemed to be safe, for now. Her eyes followed him as he moved around the room, agitated and angry.

'*Dlaczego nie bryzyzendlesh* . . . Why didn't you come?' she said at last.

'*Dlaczego nie* przyszedłeś.' He corrected her Polish, without thinking, holding her at arm's length.

She held her chin high but her eyes pricked with tears. 'I've waited for you,' she said. 'Every moment since I returned from Chelm I've waited. I was worried about you.'

He could not look her in the eye. Then he realised that his tears were welling too. He heard his father's voice in his head: 'Men do not cry.' But it felt good. She wrapped her arms around him and he buried his wet face in her neck as he started to sob.

When he could talk, he pulled a chair close to the stove and handed her some bread and salami. She quickly put half into her pocket and held his hand as he sat down. He needed to tell her. He needed – what? Absolution? He just needed her.

'Maya, there's something you must know. All this time I haven't told you, but how can I not tell you now? Sawin is just one of many camps on this side of the Bug River. They're draining a huge area of marsh so they can cultivate it. The workers are all Jews.' He lowered his eyes. 'I don't know how to tell you this. None of you are expected to live. They give you just enough food to exist so you can dig. If you are strong, you can dig a little longer, and if you are weak, you will die sooner.'

Maya's eyes were wide. She swallowed.

'There's worse,' Jan continued. 'There are three large camps near here. Sobibór, Majdanek and Treblinka. That's where they're killing the sick prisoners.'

Again, he could not look at her. He felt her hand tremble in his. For a moment, he thought she might collapse.

'How long have you known about this?' Her voice was small.

His head hung. All along he had not acknowledged it to himself, had not wanted to believe the horror, but, deep down, he had known. His knuckles were white as he clasped her hand.

Maya pulled away. She ran to the bathroom and vomited. When her heaving had subsided into gulps and sobs, he pulled her to him. 'I'm sorry, I'm so sorry,' he whispered.

'How?' she stammered at last, pulling away from him. He did not reply.

'Maya, we need to get you out.'

Her body was rigid; she stared silently at her hands but said nothing.

'Maya? Do you hear what I'm saying to you? It's too dangerous for you here. The only way out is to escape.'

'But what about my mother? What about Erna and Pavel? I couldn't leave them.' Her tears started again. 'I can't believe it. It can't be true.'

Later they lay together, silently holding each other, both of their faces wet with tears. The truth seemed to be finally seeping through. She was calm, staring at the ceiling, obviously considering what it meant. 'I'll help you,' Jan told her. 'I'll keep you and your family strong. I'll bring you more food. Then we'll get you out.'

'Thank you, thank you, thank you,' she whispered, over and over, as they felt the warmth of their bodies against each other, breathing in and out.

～

Maya could find no words. For six months they had been told the transportations were to a rehabilitation centre. They had wanted to believe the lie, to live with some hope that, if the work and the deprivation became too much, they would be cared for as human beings. But everything was different now. She was going to die here. The knowledge did not scare her; it made her furious.

Angry tears spilled down her nose and onto her dress, streaking her smooth cheeks with silver. She had lost her childhood. She thought of herself last year, knowing with certainty that she would grow up, fall in love, marry and become a mother. Her childhood dreams were like friends to her, images of herself becoming a famous dancer on the stage, maybe travelling and seeing the world. Even when she arrived here at the camp, it never entered her mind that she might not survive. Her life was uncomfortable and terrifying, but she believed there would be an end. All the prisoners did. This experience was contained, a bubble of horror, something they had to endure with closed eyes.

Now her future veered towards a different path. She thought about death, what it meant. Soon there would be a world without her in it. The trees and the grass would go on. There would still be birds in the sky, music on the wind. But she would not be part of it. Death was more than ceasing to exist. It was the end of possibility.

She looked at the other women in the dormitory. The living dead. In some ways, it would be easier. If they were dead, they would not need to keep surviving. The struggle was so exhausting.

She thought about the Commandant. His leering, lingering stares took a new meaning now. She was nothing to him. A plaything. A corpse.

Then she thought of Jan. Something about him had changed. She had seen it in his half-closed eyelids, the eyes sliding strangely beneath them, left and right. The smell of alcohol on his breath. The new heaviness about him, as if his feet were weighted. This evening, everything had been different.

Had he known they were all going to die all along? And not told her? Could she trust him now?

But then, Jan was risking his life too, for her. She had no choice but to believe him. For him, she would strive to stay alive.

How could she tell the others? Her mother was barely coping. She was alone and afraid without Franz; her thin body shivered through the night. And Erna? Erna who would soon be unable to walk the few kilometres to the swamp, the life kicking inside of her.

She would tell Pavel. Pavel would make things right. He had connections on the outside.

He merely shrugged when she confided her terrible secret the next day. 'I know.' She looked up at him in surprise. Others already knew?

'There are transports leaving every week from the camps all around this area,' he said grimly. 'At first the Polish thought it was chaotic and insane, but it's organised. They're systematically killing people, Maya. They're exterminating us.'

Maya's eyes were wide with shock. 'Systematic?'

'Don't worry. You're strong; Erna and I are strong. They take only the weak ones. The trenches aren't finished yet. They still need us.' He put his arm around her shoulder. Solid, like an older brother. 'Cheer up, chicken, it's going to be all right.'

She did not speak of it again.

That night, she dreamed she was back in the classroom in Brno, pirouetting and leaping. She was Giselle, graceful and strong. Her classmates were gathered around her, laughing, while her heart broke.

27

My darling Jan

I think I would like to die soon. Oh, don't be shocked. It's not that bad.
Death has been my companion since right back then. The only difference
is that now I can plan a little.

In my imagination, death has always been bright white. A sigh and
then the light. Nothing to be worried about. Welcome, in fact. A chance to see
them again, Mother and Franz and Omi. But back then, it terrified me so.

In those days, in the camp, it was so arbitrary. It could be a case of
where you were standing, how you looked at the ground – all these things
made the difference between living and ceasing to live. And then you told
me the truth, and it really didn't matter anymore.

Sawin, December 1942

Dirty patches of snow littered the ground the day that Erna's labour
pangs began. Maya found her in the latrine block, wide-eyed and pale.
'I think the baby's coming. I've been awake with pains most of the night.'
Her voice was an urgent whisper. 'Can you get a message to Pavel?'

They had rehearsed this day. Pavel had worked out a way to hide
her – in the wood loft above the kitchen, where Maya and Jan had
met those months ago. It was unthinkably dangerous. Erna was slow
and heavy, unsteady as she climbed the wooden ladder. But there was
nothing else they could do. It was there she would have the baby,

175

a cloth between her teeth to keep her from crying out. Jan had warned the Polish guards; bribes had been paid that should buy their silence for a few days at least. But when the Commandant returned – well, what would happen then, no one could contemplate.

Maya peered across the Appellplatz towards the Commandant's house. The windows were dark. No one had seen him for days, yet his presence hung in the air. She looked at Erna's taut, round belly and imagined the Commandant poking it with his rifle. This was uncharted territory. Labour and a baby? It was hard to see how they would keep these things concealed.

It was best not to draw attention to Erna. Maya left her friend where she had found her and walked quickly through the Appellplatz. A male acquaintance was kicking dirt in a corner with his threadbare shoe. 'Tell him it's time,' Maya whispered and turned back quickly for the safety of the dormitory.

Appell was easier without the Commandant. The chief engineer, Czyprinski, was in charge. He commanded them with a pointed pen, not a rifle, a sheaf of papers billowing in the biting wind as he held them in his gloved hand. He greeted Maya by name as he passed along the rows of prisoners. She smiled back, carefully, avoiding his eye. The Polish guards were starting to take liberties in the Commandant's absence; the threat of their grabbing hands and smothering mouths haunted the girls as they walked at night. But Czyprinski spoke to her respectfully before he continued to count the prisoners quickly and organise them into groups for the day's work. There would be no beatings today.

Pavel was absent, but he was not the only one. Even with the diminished numbers, Maya could tell at a glance that others were missing. Many were sick, shivering in their beds, overcome with the cold and lack of sustenance. Just yesterday, Rosa had refused to get up, turning her back to Maya and shutting her eyes. 'I cannot, I simply cannot,' she had whimpered, like a schoolchild. Maya pulled her mother upright and cajoled her down the ladder. She knew what it meant to stay in bed. She had seen the prisoners who lay staring at the wooden slats above their head for hours on end, gradually soaking the straw with despair. They were giving up.

She thought of Erna throughout the day as she rammed her shovel into the hard earth. It clanged metallically and bounced back at her. Her shoulders ached and the frozen water made her toes swell until her entire legs went numb. But the digging kept her warm and she could see Jan in the distance. He made it possible to keep going.

It was nearly dark by the time they arrived at the camp. Rosa gave her a knowing look. Everyone in the camp knew what was going on. 'Here,' Rosa said when they entered the dormitory. 'Take the rest of my water – she will need it now.' She smiled at her daughter. 'And bring her some food. I do not need to know where you get it, Maya. But thank God that you do.'

Maya hugged her mother and, when it was safe, peeled away from the other prisoners towards the back of the kitchen.

Pavel greeted her in the loft, closing the wooden trapdoor quickly behind her. She could just make out Erna in the dim lamplight, a dark mound in the corner, barely moving. Even in the gloom Maya could see the concern on Pavel's face. 'It's lasting so long,' he said. 'The pains are every three or four minutes. It's been like this for hours. We need help.'

'What can I do?'

'There's a midwife who lives close to here – she's in the next village. It's about ten kilometres to the west. It was too dangerous to contact her before. We were hoping we wouldn't need her. But Erna is getting weaker and weaker and we have no choice. Maya, I know you leave the camp at night. You need to go now, bring the midwife here. Don't let anyone see you. Go quickly now, please.'

'Of course, of course,' Maya whispered. She embraced Pavel hurriedly and clambered down the ladder, her quick breaths catching in her throat. Should she ask Jan for help? Maybe he could borrow a car; it would be quicker. But why risk his life too? She could do it, it was not too far. She knew where to go. If she half walked, half ran, she could be there within two hours.

The first heavy drops of rain hit her face as she emerged from her hole under the fence. Good, it was less likely that people would be on the road. A distant gunshot from the woods made her jump, but she was not afraid. Let the partisans come now if they wanted. They could give her a lift. She circled back around the camp, easily concealing herself in the black shadows as the rain picked up to a steady downpour and melted the remnants of snow. Her clothes clung to her skin; she found the road and started to jog, giddy with adrenaline, her battered boots splashing through puddles and melting ice.

The village of Staszyce was further than she expected. She had no sense of the time when she stopped for breath at the outskirts and tried to orient herself in the night. A few dark houses lined the road; the only sound was the swelling wind and the forceful beating of the rain on the dirt. Pavel had described the house, its battered door and three bushes in the front garden, but this he had heard third-hand. Even Pavel, with all his dealings and connections, had not had the freedom to come here. Thoughts of the death camps flickered in her mind in shards of black and white. She had no idea what reception she would get. Still, her Polish was passable now; Jan had taught her well. She walked between the tiny houses and settled on the one that best matched Pavel's description. She knocked, quietly at first, as if the Commandant were lurking behind the bushes that lined the front path. Then louder, insistently.

An elderly woman answered the door. Light and warmth spilled out of the farmhouse kitchen behind her. She looked at Maya in surprise then grabbed her by the arm and pulled her inside. Maya did not know the Polish word for 'midwife', so instead blurted out the words she could remember. 'My friend, Sawin, baby, come quickly!' The woman looked confused, then alarmed as the realisation dawned that Maya had come from the camp. Her twisted hands flickered in the lamplight as she pulled the curtains together. She pointed Maya to a seat by the fire, pulled on a heavy overcoat and limped out into the pouring night.

Maya sat and watched the rainwater evaporate off her clothes in coiling strands of steam as the minutes dragged past. Her mind wandered. She thought of Jan, of her mother. She thought of Franz, of the cold rain buffeting the earth where his body lay. Then, with a rush of wind, the door opened and the old lady returned with a younger woman, holding a bag. '*Przyjdź szybko*, come quickly!' The younger woman motioned to Maya and they hurried out together, heads bent low against the storm. There was a cart and horse outside. Maya clambered aboard. In the light of the open door, she met the old woman's eyes, strangely young and eager, full of compassion. Another Pole willing to risk her life for a Jew. 'Thank you, thank you,' she murmured as the cart pulled away along the muddy road back to Sawin.

⌒

The midwife hesitated as they approached Sawin. The harsh beams of the searchlights fractured against the solid sheet of rain; the dirt had disintegrated into myriad potholes full of water that would freeze by morning. The camp was calm and quiet; there were still no lights in the Commandant's house. Maya muttered a silent prayer as she pulled back the barbed wire to let the midwife through. Her jacket snagged and Maya set her free, her hands trembling with cold. If the midwife was surprised at the existence of this camp with its hundreds of slave labourers, she did not show it.

The pounding of the rain masked their footsteps as they hurried towards the kitchen building. Maya looked for the guards; the bright tip of a burning cigarette showed her they were sheltering in a doorway. She and the midwife would not be seen. 'Quickly,' she whispered, beckoning the midwife towards the ladder. 'Be quiet, please be quiet.'

They arrived in the loft to the sound of Erna's soft moans. Pavel's relief at their arrival filled the room. The midwife hoisted herself to the top of the ladder and got to work, swift and efficient. She palpated Erna's belly, hesitated, then felt again. 'Ah,' she turned to Pavel with a smile. 'Two. There are two babies.'

Maya caught Pavel's face in the lamplight. A flash of joy and pride mixed with terror. How could they possibly keep two babies quiet?

She left them then, knowing she had a full day's work ahead in the freezing rain with no sleep. But her steps were a little lighter as she made her way back to her bed and hung up her sodden clothes, the first twinge of dawn lighting her way.

⌒

The next evening, Pavel was back in his usual place in line at Appell. It was still raining, but more softly now. The pattering of raindrops on the tiles of the dormitory roofs muffled all other sound; God must have finally remembered them. Maya followed Pavel at dinner, soup bowl in hand, to visit her friend. She found Erna propped up against the straw in the loft, one baby clasped in her arms and the other wrapped in a towel asleep on her outstretched legs. Her face was puffy and streaked, but she was smiling. 'Two little boys!' she whispered. 'They're my miracles. They're meant to be here.'

She handed a warm bundle to Maya in exchange for the soup, which she gulped hungrily. The baby squirmed and snuffled in Maya's arms. A shock of black hair plastered his head and his tiny fingers flexed and curled, moving in time to an unheard melody. He woke and locked his gaze on her. She watched him, spellbound, this faultless baby boy with his perfect eyelashes and fingernails, his eyes endless and infinite. She stroked his head with her forefinger. Her hand seemed obscenely large and rough against his soft pink skin. Suddenly it did not matter, none of it mattered, not the camp, not the hunger or the rain. All of it was forgotten as she held this new, beating life in her arms.

28

Kate shifted in her seat. She was having a quick lunch with Eleanor at the little sandwich shop behind the newspaper office. The gentle warmth of the sun on their backs made her nauseous. Her period was late. Her belly was taut beneath her trousers and her breasts were tingling. She could not remember taking precautions during her drunken encounter with Tomas. There was no doubt about it now. She was pregnant.

She had no idea what she was going to do.

'I know a place,' Eleanor said in a low voice. 'You need to have a doctor make the case that the pregnancy risks your physical or mental health, and they'll do it for you. Loads of women I know have had abortions. They all go there.'

'Thanks, Eleanor.' Kate wiped her mouth with a serviette, its edges stained purple with beetroot. 'But I'm really not sure an abortion is what I want.'

The baby already felt real to her; she was overwhelmed with the need to protect it. She felt that somehow it connected her to all the other women in the world who, at that moment, were also feeling the first pangs of new life deep inside.

'Have you told anyone?'

'Who would I tell?' Kate thought of Maya. What would she say? The conversation she would have to have with her mother didn't bear thinking about.

'Inevitable question – but dare I ask who the father is?'

Kate shrugged. 'You don't know him. He's definitely not in the picture.' She didn't even know his surname.

'What about your family in the UK? Can they support you?'

'Not really. I can't imagine what Mum would do if I turned up pregnant. No, I think I'm going to try to do it on my own. I can get maternity leave from the paper, right? How much do you reckon a nanny would cost?'

Eleanor laughed. 'As if that's something I would know! My sister has kids, I'll ask her. How far along are you?'

Kate calculated quickly. 'A couple of months, I suppose. I've been pretty sure about it for a week or so.'

'Well then, you've got time. Don't make any rash decisions.' Eleanor took a last bite of her sandwich and scrunched the paper bag into a ball. 'Bloody hell, Young, you're a bit of a dark horse, aren't you? Are you good with babies?' She gave Kate a playful punch on the arm.

'Never even held one!' They both laughed.

Eleanor stood up. 'I need to dash, I've got a press conference in the city in half an hour. But listen, mate –' she smiled at Kate '– don't worry, I've got your back.'

⌒

The next day, at Maya's house, Kate wanted to know more about Erna. 'I just can't imagine what it was like for her, giving birth in a situation like that.'

'Oh, it was difficult, of course,' said Maya. 'But it was *life*! Remember, we lived with the knowledge that at any moment we could die – we could be shot or beaten to death. We knew how fleeting life could be and we valued every second of it, no matter how hard it was.'

'Tell me about the babies. How did they make you *feel*?'

Maya thought for a moment. 'There is no better way of experiencing the power of the universe than to gaze into a newborn baby's eyes.' Her eyes glistened with the memory. 'When I looked at that little boy . . . I don't know. I connected with eternity.'

Sawin, December 1942

It did not take long for news of the babies' arrival to spread through the camp. Keeping them safe quickly became a full-time operation. The women took turns to sit with Erna through the night, walking around the loft with the babies, shushing them quiet through the stillness. Each family surrendered a little food at each meal; the prisoners' eyes darted to and fro as they sat shivering at breakfast or dinner, their knowing looks and unspoken arrangements uniting them in resistance.

After two days, Jan pulled Maya behind the latrine building. He pressed half a loaf of bread and a can of milk into her hands. 'For the new mother. I'll bring you more. Every day I'll bring you food.'

'Do the guards know?'

He smiled. 'I've taken care of it. While the Commandant is away, they're reasonably safe. Just keep them hidden as well as you can.'

She gasped at his kindness. He had taken so many risks for her and her family, and now for her friends too? Oh, how she loved him. She kissed his hands in gratitude before she left to take the precious sustenance to Erna.

Later, Maya sat with Rosa as she unpicked her small sweater from home, passing precious wool for Maya to wrap around her fingers into crooked skeins. Rosa sang a melancholy Yiddish lullaby while she worked. '*Shlof zhe mir shoyn yankele mayn sheyner . . .*' Sleep, sleep, Yankele, my handsome son, close your little black eyes . . .' Mrs Meyer sighed softly. She was knitting with needles made of sticks, her thick fingers moving with surprising agility and her tongue flicking along her bottom lip. Mrs Kolman joined the song. She was also knitting; a tiny blue jacket poked from beneath the straw by her hip and the sleeve of a second emerged stitch by stitch. 'Sleep then, my little one, my clever one . . .' the women sang, buoyed by the unexpected harmony of their voices. Maya thought of home. 'Sleep while you are still in your cradle by my side, it will cost your mother many tears to make a man of you . . .'

When the sweater had disappeared, Maya kissed her mother on the forehead and slipped out into the icy Appellplatz. She darted behind the kitchen, looked around her for a long minute to make sure she had not been observed, then quickly clambered up the ladder to the loft. The straw smelled damp and the little family sat in darkness. Erna was asleep, her deep, regular breaths billowing as a white mist in the cold, her hand resting on her baby's chest as he lay swaddled in a jacket beside her. Pavel sat next to her, his back against the wooden wall, with the other baby nuzzled into his neck. He patted his son's back rhythmically, 'Shh, shh, shh.' The baby mewled and squirmed. Pavel grinned a thank you as Maya handed him the milk and bread.

'Here, can you take these?' He pointed to a pile of soiled cloths in the corner. He reached forward to grab Maya's wrist as she stooped to gather them, and pulled her closer, looking into her eyes. 'Thank you, my friend,' he whispered, quietly, so as not to disturb the babies. 'Thank you.'

⌒

When the twins were two weeks old, the sun came out and a sliver of warmth brightened the glistening trees. Maya could not believe their good fortune. Two whole weeks and still no sign of the Commandant. Two whole weeks of life.

After the Appell, Czyprinski called a group of girls to follow him, including Maya. They marched behind him to the far edge of the village, in the opposite direction to the swamp. They came to a row of shabby white houses, with jagged holes in the roofs and mouse droppings strewn on the floor. 'The Third Reich has requisitioned these buildings and is repurposing them to accommodate more technicians,' Czyprinski announced in slow, steady Polish. 'We need you to clean the bricks.'

He handed out small wooden hammers and assigned each girl to a house. Maya clambered over the overgrown garden and pushed on the creaking wooden door. It was dark and cold inside. At the back she found a tower of bricks, thrown haphazardly into the icy mud. Her job was to knock the mortar off and then stack them neatly against the wall of the house.

The work was easy and Maya started to relax. Each brick was unique. One edge was whitewashed, but the other sides were rough and grey. There were different textures and patterns, white lines and scratches, or tendrils of green moss clinging to life against the hard clay. She examined each one, feeling its roughness in her hands. The weak sun shone against the white of the houses and warmed her face. She blinked in the brightness and thought of the twins. They had never seen the sun before. She could not wait to go back to the camp and cuddle them.

Towards lunchtime, she saw Jan striding purposefully up the garden path. He looked more relaxed than she had seen him for weeks. Their relationship had taken on a new, desperate intensity since Maya had discovered the prisoners' certain fate, and when they came together they clung to each other as if each moment could be their last. But somehow, the inevitability of the situation also freed them to take more risks. Maya would rather die having held Jan than live for a few weeks longer without his embrace.

He smiled at her. His top button was undone, and she watched his Adam's apple glide up and down his delicate neck as he swallowed.

'No one's around,' he said. 'Come to my house. I think it's safe.' There were no guards in the street; she could hear the other girls steadily working. Maya carefully placed the hammer on the top of her neat pile of bricks and darted in the direction of the main village. Within a few minutes she had made it to Jan's house. She knocked softly on his front door and slipped inside.

He held her tightly for a moment then kissed her gently. 'How are things in the camp? I have my ears open. I've paid off the guards who take the Appell, and none of the others suspect, as far as I can tell.'

'Perhaps at last God is helping us,' said Maya. 'Erna is recovering her strength, thanks to the food you're giving us. We're just trying to plan for when she's missed at work. We'll have to take turns to look after the babies.'

Jan shook his head. 'They won't be able to keep them in the camp when the Commandant returns. If he suspects anything, you will all suffer. I'm making enquiries. There must be a family who's willing to keep them safe on the outside.'

'Oh Jan, thank you. Thank you so much.' Maya wrapped her arms around his neck and allowed herself to trust that he would succeed. In time they moved to the bed. They lay fully clothed, legs entwined. Maya shut her eyes, bathing in his warmth. Her mind wandered to babies, the babies she might one day have with Jan. She pictured herself, clean and healthy, wearing a new blue dress, standing in their kitchen as Jan arrived home from work, hung his hat on the stand and kissed her, their children quietly playing at their feet. She saw him sitting in the front row as she danced on stage, felt the warmth of the footlights, heard the gentle music.

Jan's breathing had slowed. His foot twitched slightly; he was falling asleep. The moment stretched around her, endless, perfect. She stroked his back.

How fragile life was. How quickly it could change. How wonderful it could be.

Ten minutes passed. Suddenly, the air was cracked apart by urgent knocking on the front door. Jan leaped to his feet, but Maya sat motionless on the bed, frozen. A familiar shout turned her stomach to ice. It was the Commandant.

'*Raus, raus!* Get out! I know you're in there. Get out, you pigs, get out!'

Jan looked at her, aghast. There was nothing they could do. The house was just a small room, really, with a few sticks of furniture and the bed. There was no way of escaping, nowhere to hide. Maya stood up. Jan touched her on the shoulder, looked into her eyes for the briefest moment, then breathed deeply and opened the door.

The Commandant's gun was in Maya's face. 'Get out now,' he hissed. 'I'll shoot you in the stomach. I'll put you on the shit wagon and take you to the cemetery.'

Maya felt dizzy, unsure whether her feet would carry her through the door. The Commandant put his face next to hers. A high-pitched cacophony of cruel, spiteful words fell around her like poison rain. 'You pig! You bitch! Your day has come. Move, quick, quick! Hurry up, you whore!'

She walked slowly into the street. The Commandant's face was a blur – all she could see was the tip of his rifle, black metal, small and round, an endless black hole pointing directly between her eyes. It was the only thing that looked real.

Slowly, slowly. She made it as far as the pavement. He jabbed the rifle between her shoulder blades; it would bruise by tomorrow. Would she make it to tomorrow? 'Walk,' he ordered. She set off along the narrow street, holding her head high and struggling to quell her nausea. Jan walked with them, a few inches higher than her on the pavement. Together, the trio made their way through the village, passing people who stopped to stare, then through the village square, past the bakery. All the time, the frigid tip of the gun pressed into her back. Every step one more second of life.

They marched through the gates of the camp and into the Appell-platz. The Commandant exploded at Jan. '*Geh mir aus den Augen* . . . Get out of my sight.' Jan disappeared; from the corner of her eye Maya saw him running at full speed towards Czyprinski's office. It was just her and the Commandant. She could feel his hot breath at the back of her neck.

'Stand here and wait for the shit wagon. I'll shoot you dead. I'll shoot you in the stomach.'

She stood, stiff and cold. Nothing happened. There was no sound. After about five minutes, she started to wonder whether the Commandant was still there. She held her head low, staring at the ground. It was too dangerous to look. After half an hour she was certain he must have gone. Small groups of prisoners had started to assemble in the Appellplatz. She had often been among them, trying not to watch a punishment, assaulted by the horror, but at the same time deeply relieved it was not her. Her feet were getting sore from standing in one place, and it was freezing. The sun disappeared and clouds raced across the grey sky.

Someone must have alerted Rosa. She stood with the prisoners, looking as if she might collapse. Mrs Kolman supported her. Jan was nowhere in sight. Where was he? Had he abandoned her here?

An hour passed. Maybe more. She could tell by the dusk that it was dinnertime, but no dinner was served. She thought she could hear a baby crying, but maybe it was the crows, wheeling in wide circles above the trees, black against the fading light. Behind her she could hear raised voices, perhaps Czyprinski's, definitely the Commandant's. She could not hear what they were saying. She knew they were deciding her fate.

At last, the Commandant reappeared. He marched towards her, his face cold and efficient. This was it. She looked at her mother and smiled, trying to convey her love with her eyes. Who would bring food to Rosa now, to help her survive another day?

The Commandant stopped in front of Maya, his gun in its usual position, slung over his shoulder. She swallowed hard, keeping her face still. He extended his black glove and grabbed her chin roughly, forcing her head to an awkward angle, almost snapping her neck. He held her there for a few seconds then let her go and shoved her shoulder, sending her flying backwards onto the ground.

'One more time, and you're both dead.' Quietly, factually. And he was gone.

Maya sat in the mud, trying to summon the strength to stand. Something was not right. Why had the Commandant not shot her, or at least sent her away on a cart? There would be a punishment, she was sure. There always was. The fear of it forced her breath from her body, and she could barely walk as Rosa led her back to the dormitory.

Later that night, Maya was woken by a scream. At first, she thought it was her own, but then, as sleep fell away, she realised it was coming from outside. Loud and incessant. And then it stopped. Maya curled into Rosa like a little child. After the events of today, it was not safe to investigate.

The next morning, Rosa came back from the latrines with tears running down her face.

'The Commandant found the twins,' she sobbed. 'He drowned them in a bucket.'

29

My darling Jan

These interviews are stirring my memories like tadpoles in a pond. They surround me and nip at my toes. How could I have ignored them for all these years?

Recounting my story reminds me of the enormity of what we lived through. There were so many losses, Jan. What was it all for? It is impossible to comprehend.

I can hear the cries to this day. The twins. Alive and real, even though they are dead.

Sydney, October 1995

'Oh, those little babies.' Maya was sobbing. She wrung her hands in distress. 'Those perfect little boys, fresh and new in the loft. The icy bucket. I can't bear it. It is not fair that I survived when they did not.'

'I can't believe one human being could do that to another.' Kate's heart was thumping with the shock of what Maya had just told her.

'Oh, humans are capable of dreadful deeds.'

'But still, how could he have done it?'

'It happened because he hated the Jews. It was hate, pure and simple. You do not know what it is to be hated like that, Kate. Hated so much that we were to be removed from this Earth.' Maya covered her eyes with her hands and wept.

'I think we should take a break,' Kate said, moving to sit next to Maya and putting an arm around her. She regretted pushing her so far. In her focus on gathering details for the story, she had not considered the type of memories that might surface, and what that would do to her friend.

She heard her mother's voice in her head, a little gentler now. 'Come on, then,' she said, giving Maya's arm a squeeze. 'Let's have a nice cup of tea.'

Sawin, December 1942

Maya ran through the camp, but she could not find Erna or Pavel. She searched in the loft and behind the dormitories. Had the Commandant meted out the ultimate punishment on them too? Her panic rose until she spotted Erna alone by the perimeter fence. She was crouching in a heap on the ground with her head in her hands. Maya touched her gently on the shoulder. When Erna looked up, there were fresh scratch marks on her grey face.

'Come, let's get you back inside.' Maya pulled on Erna's arm; her hands were blue.

'They're gone . . .'

'I know, I know. Come, it's bitter out here. You should come inside with me.'

Erna did not seem able to move. Her eyes were wide and vacant, as if she did not see. Maya gripped Erna's arm and finally managed to help her to her feet. She took her hand and started to guide her towards the dormitory; Erna stumbled. She could barely walk.

The whistle blew; it was already time for work. There was no time to collect Erna's warm clothes; they would have to join their line in the Appellplatz. Maya could see Pavel at the other side of the square. He nodded towards her, a silent thank you, but something about him was unsettling. He looked almost . . . relieved.

Maya dug harder than ever all morning. It was the only way she could assuage her fury, and today she needed to fill Erna's wheelbarrow as well as Rosa's and her own. Erna stood without shoes in the freezing water of the trench, barely moving. By lunchtime there were two dark circles on her dress where the milk had leaked. The women folded her in their arms and kissed her forehead. There was nothing else they could do.

It was bitterly cold after work. The prisoners huddled around the makeshift stove in the dormitory, rubbing their feet and blowing on their fingers for a moment of warmth. Icy gusts swept through the cracked windows, rattling the panes, and the women stuffed straw inside their clothes for extra insulation.

Maya was hungry. She had not seen Jan since the incident with the Commandant. Had he been punished? Sent away? Worse? Her fear for him melded with desperation at her own situation. She and Rosa could not carry on without him; it was impossible to survive the winter conditions on the camp rations. It was so cold she did not know whether either of them would make it through the night.

'Erna will sleep with us,' Rosa announced. It was a good idea. The warmth of their bodies would keep them alive. It was still early evening when they helped each other into the bunk, the three of them squeezed tightly together, legs and arms wrapped around each other.

Maya awoke in the night with numb feet and fingers; Erna's eyes were open and she was staring at the boards above their head. 'Just one more day – you can keep going for one more day,' Maya whispered to her friend. 'You must do it for them.'

⌒

The next morning was Christmas Eve. Maya awoke to dismayed gasps billowing in clouds of steam from the women's mouths. The stove was dark. Mrs Meyer's feet, unbooted, stuck out of the end of the bed, strangely grey and blotchy.

'Don't look, Maya. Quickly, follow me,' Rosa ordered. 'Mrs Meyer died in the night. It was too cold for her.'

Maya glimpsed the old lady's gaping eyes and bent fingers, frigid against the wood, as her mother hurried her and Erna outside to the breakfast queue. Already one of the women had helped herself to Mrs Meyer's shawl; she wrapped it around her neck as she waited in the icy wind.

Maya concentrated on her bread and coffee. She tried to comprehend what was happening, but she could feel nothing. The twins and Mrs Meyer. Omi and Franz. There were too many now, the losses too great to fathom. Please, please, not Jan as well.

'At least there's one less person to feed and keep warm,' she said, for something to say.

Her mother looked at her in shock. 'Never speak like that, Maya. Mrs Meyer was our friend, our neighbour from home. She did not deserve to die like that.'

Maya shrugged. They were all going to die anyway; what did it matter how?

Rosa softened. 'Never forget that you're human, *Mayalein* – never. Do not let them take that from you.'

Maya looked away, ashamed. She could see the Commandant at the far end of the Appellplatz, barking orders at a group of men. Their backs were to her; their heads hung low. One of them turned and she realised with a shock that it was Jan. His body was stooped and deflated; she barely recognised him. He was still in disgrace, then – but he was alive. The relief surged through her. Mrs Meyer's life for Jan's. A trade with God.

What had she become?

One more day. Just keep going. One more day.

⌒

Later, when they returned from the swamp, a large Christmas tree had been erected in the square. Jan was still there, with his head hanging low. Beneath the tree was what looked like a heap of old clothes. Surely they weren't going to distribute warm clothes for Christmas? It seemed too good to be true.

The Commandant blew his whistle and the prisoners assembled in their lines. There was a lilt in his voice; he was enjoying himself. He announced that there was too much insubordination. This was the cost. He waved his hand at Jan, who walked slowly to the pile of clothes and pulled them back. Maya gasped in horror. Underneath lay the corpses of Mrs Meyer and two other prisoners, with dark blood starting to congeal around their fresh bullet wounds.

The Commandant spread his arms wide in a grand gesture. '*Frohe Weihnachten, Juden*. Happy Christmas, Jews.' He laughed out loud and turned towards his house.

⌒

Jan's despair swelled as if it would burst from his chest as the Commandant strutted away. His hands were shaking. He could not bear to think of what had happened only two hours earlier.

The gun had felt heavy and cold in his hands. '*Schießen!*' the Commandant had barked. 'Shoot! I order you to shoot!'

For a moment Jan had entertained the wild idea of turning the gun on the Commandant. He had offered as much to the AK, after all. But he had been too weak. He had stood, aiming the gun, watching the prisoners shiver as they fixed their eyes on the ground. He could not do it. He could feel the Commandant behind him and braced himself to be beaten, or worse. But then two shots rang out and the prisoners fell to the ground. The Commandant slung his rifle over his shoulder again and sneered at Jan. 'Make no mistake – they are dead because of you.'

The smell of beetroot soup and pierogi wafted over the Appellplatz and a plume of men's laughter rang out from the Commandant's house. The bodies were barely cold and already the guards were settling in for their Christmas Eve feast.

Jan found Maya in the crowd. 'Meet me in our place in thirty minutes,' he whispered as he walked past her. He did not care about the danger. Let them shoot him if they wanted. He could not be part of this anymore.

When it was time, they crouched together behind the latrine. He uncovered a plate piled high with steaming food that he had spirited away when the cook had turned her back. She was there now, in the kitchen on the other side of the square, counting the dishes again in confusion. Jan carefully tipped the food into Maya's empty bowl and scraped the dregs.

'Eat this alone, *Kochanie*, my darling. Take care, no one must know we're still seeing each other,' he whispered.

'What did you do? How are we both still alive?'

He squeezed her shoulder quickly but looked away in shame. 'Nothing will change. I won't stop seeing you. I'll still provide for you. I'm willing to risk everything for you. Go now.'

They slipped away in opposite directions, and he walked quickly back towards the Commandant's house. Light shone through the window into the grey camp outside. He would not be able to eat; the food would stick in his throat.

Through the window he could see his colleagues, puffing on cigars and raising vodka to their lips.

And there he was. His father, slapping the Commandant on the back.

30

My darling Jan

I have been dreaming again, here in my chair. It was a lovely dream, though mother was frightened. We were not in the camp; we were in my little bed in the loft in Prague. My father must have been dead already and there was a ruckus outside the window.

In my dream I was scared, but at the same time I was thrilled. My mother had come to me for refuge. No one would hurt her while I was there to protect her. Together we were safe, in each other's arms. I was in heaven. I started to pray: please, please, never let this end.

The smell of my mother, her perfume and her soft hair. I could feel her breasts beneath her dress. The thump of her heartbeat quietened as the rampage subsided. I nuzzled my face into her neck.

My mother. My earliest memory; my deepest love.

Chelm, January 1943

Jan's father summoned him to his office in the first days of the new year. Jan had been waiting for this moment. Without his father's intervention, both he and Maya would have been dead by now. A series of rapid phone calls from Czyprinski's office, a pleading with the Commandant, and a deal had been made. How his father had persuaded the Commandant to spare them, he did not know.

His father had said nothing to him since. There had been a whole week of silent disapproval. Jan could barely breathe; he longed for the holiday to be over and to return to work at the camp.

Mr Novak's office was stark and orderly. A photograph of the Führer hung on the wall.

'Sit.' Jan's father motioned to a chair at the other side of his desk. He slowly removed his glasses and laid them carefully on the polished wood. Jan's blood rushed in his ears.

'You know she will not survive?' Mr Novak said at last. 'They are calling it the *Endlösung* – the final solution to the Jewish question. For the last year it's been German policy to bring Europe's Jews to Poland and . . . dispose of them here.'

Jan swallowed. Of course, he knew. He said nothing.

'There's no question of you consorting with a Jew.' Mr Novak shook his head and rubbed his eyes. 'I will not hear of it, Jan.'

Jan nodded.

'If it happens again, I'll have no choice but to act.' Mr Novak's face was deathly serious. 'Do you understand what I mean? For God's sake, boy, you're risking all of our lives.'

'I understand.'

'I'm serious, Jan. It will never happen again. She's a Jew. She's dead already. Your life isn't worth it.' Mr Novak stood and showed his son the door. 'Now go.'

Anger and resentment burned in Jan's chest as he left the building. He had to act urgently, there was no choice now. The only possible way to have a future with Maya was to get her out.

He knew there was a steady stream of young Polish women being taken to Germany to work as labourers. Some were being forced, but others chose to go because they had heard conditions were better there than at home. With their Slavic background, they were considered by the Germans to be the lowest of the low, almost subhuman. But at least there was food and shelter, which for many Poles were becoming increasingly precarious now.

Could he somehow organise for Maya join them? There were two things that gave him hope. First, Maya did not look like a Jew. With her blonde hair and in the right clothes, she could easily pass as a local. They had managed it often enough walking hand in hand through the streets of Chelm. Second, she had a remarkable ability to speak different languages. While Poles would pick up her accent, in a foreign country he was sure the Germans would believe she was Polish.

It would mean sending her to Germany, right into the belly of the enemy. But it was perfect, actually. No one there would suspect. She would be safe; she would have work and enough food. After the war – and he was confident that would not be too long – he would come and find her. They would escape together and leave these dark days behind.

She would need an identity document. But that should not be a barrier. The AK were creating false papers all the time. He would go and organise it right now.

He glanced up at the dark January clouds reflected in the window of his father's office. He had no doubt that, if they were caught again, his father would have him arrested. If Maya disappeared, so did the danger. He would not tell Maya, not yet. Best not to get her hopes up. But the more he thought about it, the more he realised it could work.

He shoved his hands deep in his pockets against the cold, strode into the street with a lift in his step, and started to plan.

31

Sawin, February 1943

Winter's true ferocity did not bite until February that year. Black clouds hung over the camp, swollen and heavy with snow. There were no more than fifty prisoners left. Every morning they were bullied and beaten to work, dizzy with malnutrition and fever, their toes aching with cold. When the snow came, they stood in frozen channels, their bare feet instantly raw and red as they stepped through the ice, the pain of their blisters now more intense even than the pain of their hunger. But the irrigation system was developing fast, a miracle of engineering, really, built by their stiff, blue hands. There was a push to get it finished. They said it was so the fields could be planted for spring. Everyone knew it was because the workers would all soon be dead.

Rosa was quiet as they collected their breakfast. The servings of black bread were smaller now, but the heat of the warm coffee was enough to sustain them for a few hours. Maya was worried about her mother. She did not speak much these days; she was losing strength moment by moment.

The Commandant had been away since Christmas. While he was gone, Jan brought extra rations every day. Maya carried them, carefully wrapped, heavy weights banging in her pocket, hoping they would provide enough energy to enable her mother to withstand the cold. Sometimes Rosa would stare at the food, not understanding, too exhausted even to chew or swallow. Despite the extra rations, she was losing weight.

After breakfast, Maya took her mother's thin hand in hers and guided her back to the dormitory. It felt as if she were leading a child. She removed her ski jacket and wrapped it around her mother's shoulders as the other women lit the stove and blew on the embers to fan the flame. They sat on upturned boxes to share the warmth.

As always, they cheered themselves with stories of their past lives, of holidays at Lake Como, of dinners at fine restaurants in Prague, of parties and falling in love. They allowed themselves to cry a little, and to laugh. While they could laugh, they were still human.

Erna joined them. She had spent the morning with Pavel, but she often sought the company of the women in Maya's dormitory. There were dark circles under her eyes, but her strength was slowly returning. Rosa sat in silence, examining her fingernails in the weak light. They had once been long and elegant as her fingers intertwined with Franz's larger hands. Now, she bit them into shape and scraped them clean with a splinter of wood broken from the dormitory floor. Maya held the women's attention, trying to raise their spirits by recounting an incident from a ski trip to Austria. She had been eight at the time, and had fallen face first into the snow; it had taken them some time to dig her out. She warmed to her story and its memory of a different time and place.

Rosa threw her head back and laughed. It was the first time she had laughed in months. Light from the stove glowed on her face.

The door flung open with a gasp of icy air. The Commandant strode into the dormitory. He had returned. His face was dark, an expression they knew well.

'*Du*,' he pointed his rifle at Mrs Kolman. She sat there, motionless. The wind whistled through the open door and lifted the corner of her scarf.

'*Du und du. Raus.* You and you. Get out.'

He pointed at each woman in turn. They knew what it meant. Behind him, at the gate beyond the Appellplatz, they could see a cart and horse. Steam snorted from its nostrils.

He pointed at Rosa.

Time slowed. Maya could not breathe. She looked at the Commandant, looked him straight in the eye as if the power of her gaze could change his mind. The dormitory's wooden bunks swirled around her. He was saying something, but she could not make out the words.

'Maya?' He rose up to his full height, but his voice was quiet. 'Would you like to go with your mother?' It sounded as if he were speaking from a great distance.

For a moment she thought she was in a dream, fiercely afraid but rooted to the spot. She could not move, could not speak.

He was giving her a choice. If she went with her mother, they both would die. But how could she let her go alone?

'Did you hear me, Maya?'

The decision was incomprehensible, impossible. She looked away from the Commandant and found her mother's eyes. Neither moved. It was as if they were suspended, immobile in the terrible moment. They both knew this was the end.

Rosa opened her mouth to speak, but Maya heard her own voice. The words flew from her mouth like a flock of birds at a gunshot.

'No, no, I don't want to go.' She watched herself lift her hands protectively in front of her.

The Commandant smirked.

Rosa rose slowly, smoothed her skirt and headed for the door. She did not take any belongings with her. She knew there was no need.

Maya still could not move. She watched as her mother paused for a second and smiled.

'Be strong, Maya. You're going to live,' she said, then turned and made her way towards the gate.

She did not look back again.

Maya realised at last that she could move. The world had slowed around her, the air was thick. She could see her mother in the distance, hesitating as she stepped onto the cart, reaching her hands up for support as they hauled her onto the rough wooden tray. Maya wanted to call out but there were no words. The farmer spat and lifted the horse's head from the grass. Maya stumbled forward. She could feel the eyes of the camp on her. The Commandant watched her with a smile playing on his lips. She started running, running towards the gate. The cart jolted and pulled away, its load swaying and bobbing, the prisoners holding onto each other for support as it gathered momentum. It was too late. She reached the fence and watched the cart round a bend in the road. Rosa was gone.

Jan appeared from somewhere; Erna was there too. Unseen hands transported her back to the dormitory, somehow helped her up the ladder, removed her shoes and covered her in her ski jacket. She felt tears wet on her cheeks. She was drowning, struggling for air. Rosa's sweater hung at the end of the bunk, still holding the shape of her.

Without her mother, the world took on a different structure, its boundaries shifting and unstable. Rosa was her beginning, her first human touch, all that was real. She was stability, an unseen comfort, a strong hand holding hers as they walked quickly along the street. Her mother had taught her to brush her teeth and plait her hair. It was her voice, her gentle instructions, that guided Maya's actions every day. 'This is how you fold a skirt – see, you smooth the pleats like this.' It was impossible to comprehend that the world could continue without her mother in it.

Less than an hour had passed. Already, Maya could not remember Rosa's face.

She covered her eyes with her cold fingers. The Commandant had given her a choice. *'No, no, I don't want to go.'* Her betrayal screamed over and over inside her head. She looked around the dormitory, its cluttered wooden beds, the prisoners' ragged clothes hanging from the ceiling. For what had she stayed?

Now, she was completely alone.

Sydney, October 1995

'I never found out where they took my mother.' Maya looked at Kate with tears in her eyes. 'It could have been the death camps in Majdanek or Sobibór. She could have died in a field. It has been my worst nightmare my whole life. Since that day I have tried to imagine her, how she looked as she walked away, that last time she saw me.' She gazed at the diamond bracelet on her wrist. 'This is the only thing I have of her.'

'I can't imagine what it must have been like for you.' Kate's hands had wandered to her belly. The bond between mother and child already felt strong.

'I could have gone with her.' A tear dropped into Maya's lap. 'But I made a choice. I chose not to go, and she died alone.'

'You were only seventeen.' Kate took her hand.

Maya nodded, but she was not listening.

'I made a choice,' she repeated.

'You chose life,' said Kate.

For a long time, Maya said nothing. She spoke at last, slowly, searching for the right words.

'You must not think it was the end of me. In a way it was the beginning. After my mother was gone, I was no longer afraid. There could not be a greater loss. Even to lose my life was not so great. That day I survived the most intense pain, and somehow it freed me to live with more courage. That is what made me strong.'

32

Sawin, March 1943

The evening whistle blew. Maya knew she had to move, but she could not. People scurried around, making their way to the Appellplatz for dinner. She would be beaten if she did not obey the whistle. She did not care.

It blew again, more urgently. Something shifted and she sat up. She was late. She could not feel her limbs, but her body moved by itself, carrying her down the ladder, finding the floor below. She watched herself with disinterest as she opened the door and walked into the icy yard.

There was more food than usual for dinner. So few prisoners were left now. Erna sat next to her but they did not talk. Erna understood.

The next day, the sun was shining and the cold had eased. For a second when Maya awoke, just for a second, she forgot. But then she turned her head to see the straw next to her empty and cold. Rosa was gone. The world rang with emptiness.

She could not eat. Automatically, she slipped her portion of black bread into her pocket. Jan would bring her food, there would be more for her now. She forced herself to join the line for work, numb and sick, and allowed herself for the first time to imagine what it would be like to give up. But her body was still strong as her feet carried her along, and the blood beat warm in her ears.

Rosa was everywhere and nowhere. The road, the fields, the ditch echoed with the absence of her. The crows wheeling in the sky called her name, the trees in the distance were darker, more dangerous now. '*No, no, I don't want to go.*'

❧

All morning, Maya dug and dug, feeling nothing but the pull of her muscles and the sweat prickling her neck. Around her, the others worked too. But everything was different.

At lunchtime, Jan beckoned her into the woods. It was a long time since they had taken this risk, but now she ran to him like a small child. He held her tightly and at last she was able to cry, gulping sobs muffled in his jacket so they would not be heard. She looked up at his face and, to her surprise, he was crying too.

Finally, he pulled away and indicated for her to sit. He spoke urgently. She struggled to comprehend.

'*Kochana moja*, my darling Maryska, we're running out of time. We need to get you out.'

His words started to take shape. She wiped a muddy hand across her face and tried to concentrate.

'I have a plan, Maya. You're still strong, you're young. Your Polish is getting better every day. I've spoken to my connections in Chelm. They're finding documents for you. I can't tell you more about this, but you must trust me.'

She nodded.

'I'll find a way to hide you. When we have the documents, we can get you out of Poland. The key is for you to speak Polish. You will *be* Polish. Do you follow, Maya?'

Was he really taking this risk for her? For a daughter who did not go with her mother? He could be tortured or hanged, shot or sent to a death camp. She did not understand.

He stroked her hand. 'Look at me, Maya.'

She saw in his eyes it was real.

'I've been working on this plan for a long time, but we can't wait any longer.' In her heart, she felt a tiny beat of fear – or was it hope?

'We need to hurry,' said Jan. 'They're taking prisoners to Sobibór every day. There's no time to lose.'

Chelm, May 1943

Danuta knocked softly on Jan's bedroom door. 'May I come in?'

She tiptoed into the room and sat on his bed. They automatically assumed the same positions they had done as children, he by the pillow, she at the foot of the bed, leaving the expanse of blankets between them for a game of soldiers or cards. He noticed for the first time how mature she looked, with her hair bound in a scarf to hide the hairpins and her dressing gown pulled tight across her chest.

'I overheard them talking this evening,' Danuta whispered, glancing over her shoulder to check they were alone. 'Papa said he had news from Berlin. They're going to close all the labour camps in this area and dispose of the inmates. He told Mama not to mention it to us, least of all to you. But I thought you should know.'

Jan had suspected this already – there were so few prisoners left now that the closure of the camp was inevitable – but to hear that explicit orders had already arrived from Germany shocked him deeply. It was more than six weeks since he had asked his comrade in the AK to enquire about false identity papers for Maya, but there had been no further developments. Now he realised the true urgency of the situation. She could be taken at any moment.

'Did Papa mention when this is going to happen?'

'No, he didn't give a date. If it's any consolation, he didn't sound happy about it.'

Jan snorted.

Danuta pressed on. 'Why did he say not to tell you? I don't understand, you work there. I would have thought you'd need to know.'

He shrugged. 'Jan, are you still in love with that girl?'

Jan looked at his sister. He had revealed the romance to her in a fit of exuberance last year, during those precious weeks when he and Maya could see each other more freely in Chelm. She had kept his secret well, he had to give her that. But the stakes were so high now. Could he trust her? He nodded.

'Then we must get her out,' said Danuta. He recognised her tone of voice; she was planning an adventure.

'It is not that simple, Danuta.'

'Oh shush.' She laughed. 'We can do it. I know we can. Just like we saved that kitten when a man threw it in the river. Do you remember? Or the time you fought that boy because he pulled the legs off a fly? I'm sure there's a way; we just need to make a plan. I'll help.'

She leaned forward and, for the first time since they were children, slipped her hand into her brother's and gave it a squeeze.

⌒

When Mr Novak left for work the next day, Jan sat with Danuta in the kitchen while his mother washed the dishes.

'Mama?' said Danuta.

'What do you want now?' Mrs Novak said with a smile.

'We have something to tell you.' Danuta cleared her throat. 'Jan is still in love with that Jewish girl.'

Mrs Novak slowly placed the dishcloth on the counter and looked at them, aghast. 'Oh no, Jan. Surely that's not true? I thought that had come to an end after . . . the incident?'

Jan thought of the prisoners flying backwards, the smoke rising from the Commandant's rifle. It had been his fault. How many more lives was he going to risk?

'Mama . . .' he began.

'No, no. Jan, you must stop it immediately, it's not safe.'

'You don't see what I see.' There was an unexpected shrillness in his voice. 'Every day they're tortured or killed. It's not human. They're taking them by cart to Sobibór or Majdanek, and you know very well what happens to them there. A few weeks ago they took her mother.'

Mrs Novak put her hand over her mouth. Her eyes turned to Danuta then back to Jan.

'Mama . . .' Jan wiped his arm across his eyes. 'Please, please understand. She's only seventeen, and she's completely alone in there.'

'But there's nothing you can do, my son. It's against the law to help a Jew. What if your father found out?'

'I can't sit here and do nothing.'

Mrs Novak did not speak for a few seconds. She seemed to be thinking, weighing up the possibilities. 'That poor woman,' she said. 'There's nothing stronger than the bond between mother and child. How must she have felt as they took her away?'

'Mama, it's dreadful. You can't imagine. We have to help them.'

'What do you mean, Jan? What can we do?'

'We have to get her out.' Jan felt his eyes stinging, anger exploding in his chest. 'Please understand. I have to do this. It's the right thing to do.'

Mrs Novak shook her head and left the room. Danuta shrugged. 'Well, I at least will help you,' she whispered so her mother could not hear. 'Just let me know what to do.'

They turned in surprise as Mrs Novak walked back into the kitchen. Her face was white as she sat down, looked at each of her children, then leaned in and took both of their hands in hers. She spoke in a low voice, as if Mr Novak could hear her all the way from his office.

'You're a good man, my son. I'm proud of you, and I'll help you. We can't save them all . . . but we can save one.'

33

Kate glanced at the clocks on the wall of the newsroom. It was morning in Poland; she had tracked down a historian who lived in Sawin and he was waiting for her call. She trotted back to her desk. She was grateful to be at work. It took her mind off her situation. She had half-heartedly written down the details of the abortion clinic that Eleanor had given her, but had not followed through. She had no idea what she was going to do.

The historian answered the phone after two rings. His English was precise but his accent so heavy that she could barely follow him through the crackling phone line. 'Yes, we have some records here,' he said, raising his voice to help her understand. 'The Germans were very accurate record keepers, you know.'

She heard him move away from the phone and talk quickly in Polish to someone else in the room. 'I am here with a Mr Wójcik.' He spelled out the man's name for her. 'He lived in Sawin during the war. He says he remembers the Czech girls. They were very clean. But they all died, no one survived.'

'Well, at least one of them survived.' Kate was forced to speak so loudly that a couple of journalists' heads turned in her direction across the newsroom.

There was a muffled pause as the historian covered the mouthpiece with his hand. 'No, no. He does not think so.' He was almost shouting.

213

'He says he remembers; he was standing in front of his house and he saw a Ukrainian guard walking with people behind him. They looked dirty and they were walking slowly. They were limping, they looked very hungry. One of them waved at him and Mr Wójcik asked him where he was going. He said, "They are taking us to the fire, they are taking us to Sobibór."'

'And what date was this, please?'

Another silence. 'It was the summertime, 1943.' Around the time of Maya's escape.

Kate now had a timeline and a list of serious human rights abuses committed by Ondyt. She had discovered that he was considered one of the most brutal SS commandants in the area; he had stood trial in Poland, but after that the trail ran cold.

She was no nearer to finding out what had happened to Jan.

Sawin, June 1943

The Ukrainian Special Services arrived in June. Their uniforms were black and there was a skull and crossbones on their caps. They were tall and strong, with shaved heads and thick necks. Their language was harsh and uncouth and they never smiled. Their job was to liquidate the camp.

It was more than a year since Maya had arrived in Sawin. Only a few prisoners remained now; most were close to death. Their stomachs were distended with hunger or sickness, their eyes dark and hollow. They all knew the end was coming. The smells emanating from the kitchen nauseated them; they felt by turn too hot or too cold, and every voice raised in anger sent adrenaline coursing through their bodies. At night they twisted and moaned in uneasy sleep. The death camps beckoned, inevitable, an end to their suffering.

The drainage system was close to completion, and the prisoners were of no use there now. In the swamp, the wheat already blossomed and thrived. Each evening, the prisoners gave thanks that they had survived another day. Each morning, they awoke wondering whether it would be their last.

The Ukrainians were less organised than the Germans in their mission to wipe out the last of the Jews, but they were brutally effective. Every morning, there were selections in the Appellplatz, the number of prisoners sent to Sobibór limited only by space on the cart. The Commandant came and went, busy and officious. When he was gone, the prisoners were unsure what to do, where the boundaries lay.

Maya and Erna helped in the kitchen; there was little other work for them to do, and it meant they could grab an extra potato or some barley. It was mid-morning and the girls sat in the sun waiting for the water to boil. Two German guards and a handful of Polish engineers were leaning against the wall.

'Would you like a cigarette?' a German offered. Erna nodded and walked over to them.

'My name is Hans,' he said shyly.

'My name is Erna.'

They were soon talking and smiling, united in their unease at the Ukrainian guards stalking around as if they owned the camp.

'You don't look like a Jewish girl,' Hans said to Erna.

He licked his lips and glanced at the other guards. One of them slapped him on the back.

'Ah, beautiful girl, beautiful girl . . .' Hans leered. He readjusted his crotch.

Erna smiled back and flicked her hair. Maya pulled her by the hand. 'Come on, let's go back inside.' But Erna did not seem to care.

Within a week, Erna had disappeared. Maya lay alone in her bunk, hugging herself as her panic mounted. Where was she? She had not been on any of the transports. Had she been shot? Surely someone would have told Maya? The suspense heightened her senses. She could hear the Ukrainians' drunken swearing, their voices billowing above the camp as the prisoners tried to sleep, outbursts of laughter scaring the nesting birds from the trees.

The bunk felt large and empty. She felt the thinness of her body beneath her ragged clothes. But she was still strong. She was young. While the others had long ago relinquished their dreams of a different future, she would not give up. She could not. She thought of Jan, and it gave her a spark of strength.

Jan, too, was afraid of the Ukrainians. They belittled the technicians, fixing their eyes on them with icy suspicion as they walked from trench to trench. He winked reassuringly at Maya whenever he had the chance, but she could see that he was nervous.

It was too dangerous to see him now. The Ukrainians had almost immediately found their hole under the fence. Now they patrolled each night with large dogs, sniffing trails through the shadows, snarling and snapping whenever they saw movement.

Still the papers had not come.

Maya pulled herself out of bed and descended the ladder. Jan would have left her extra rations in the usual place near the kitchen. She was risking her life to retrieve them, but it did not seem to matter. Now Rosa was gone, nothing really mattered anymore. Her feet moved automatically, pulling her towards the food.

As she darted from the dormitory, she could hear Ukrainian whispers behind every corner. She shut her eyes and pictured herself with Jan, hand in hand in a meadow full of summer flowers.

The cloth bag was there, as expected. She slipped back to the dormitory and opened it in the dark. There was bread and cheese, but also a letter folded into a tiny square. A peal of laughter rang out from the Ukrainians' quarters as they jostled and pushed each other like drunken teenagers. She pushed the square of paper deep into her pocket and crept out again towards the latrine. No one was there. A weak lantern flickered yellow light against the wall. She unfurled the note and read it quickly.

Come quickly, tonight. There will be a ladder by your window. I will meet you at my house at three am.

She tore the paper into tiny pieces and threw them into the stinking hole.

⌒

Only two dormitories were operating now. The twenty remaining men slept in one of the original wooden barracks, while the eighteen women had been moved to a brick house on the boundary of the camp, right across the street from the bakery. Its smells haunted them day and night. Maya's bunk was third from the door, next to a creaky window that looked out over a quiet street. At first a cruel draft had blown through the gaps in the glass, but lately the evenings were warmer and Maya loved to watch the fluctuating life of the village below. She returned to her bunk quietly now, taking off her shoes as she entered the dormitory and placing them at the end of her bed. She pulled on her warm trousers and filled her pockets with her remaining possessions – her mother's scarf and her own watch from Brno. It was still working. Twelve forty-three am.

She lay back on the straw and looked out of the window. The ladder was there. How had Jan managed to carry a ladder, in full view? The street was deserted and dark and a cool mist hung in the air, turning the distant village lamps into concentric circles of hazy light. A cat melted into an alley. She looked at her watch again. Twelve forty-five.

The Ukrainian guards normally checked on the prisoners each night between two and half past, then again at four. The timing was critical. At three they would likely be sleeping, snoring away the alcohol until it was time to wake again. She must not fall asleep, though she was exhausted. She occupied herself by telling herself a happy story of moving to a different country, far away from here, of a life filled with laughter, new friends, a baby girl. She could not picture the ending.

Sometime after two, the heavy door latch scraped and a beam of light shone into the room. The Ukrainians' torches were large and heavy, black. The guard moved from bed to bed, taking his time, aiming the bright arc along the women's bodies. Maya could smell the vodka on him.

He reached her bunk. She watched as red flowers of light burst through her closed eyelids, sending colours swimming and exploding. She concentrated on breathing slowly, relaxing her eyelids so they did not twitch and betray her. The torch did not move off her face. He was not just checking her, he was watching her. She wondered whether he could see her racing pulse beating in her neck. She needed to swallow, but people do not swallow while asleep. She steadied her tongue. The light moved, but it was too early to relax. She forced a sigh and rolled over, turning her back to him. She heard his lazy footsteps move to the next bed.

It went quiet. She opened her eyes a fraction, then slowly, hesitantly turned her head to survey the room. Yes, he was gone. He would take about ten minutes to reach his hut; she would give him twenty, just to be sure. She was wide awake now. She concentrated on the ceiling, following each groove and knot in the wood above her head, fixing it in her mind. She did not intend to see it again.

She checked her watch in the weak light from the window. It was time. But she hesitated; danger fizzed around her.

'You can do it, Maya. Do it now.' A voice in her head. It sounded like her mother's.

Steadily and quietly, she sat up in bed and pulled on her shoes. She had practised opening the window many times during the day. She knew how it slid on its tracks, the point where it stuck; knew that to minimise the sound she must open it quickly. Without hesitating again, she grasped the latch and pushed. A tiny creak heralded a rush of cold air. No one stirred.

Quickly, she pulled herself onto the sill and looked down. The ladder was about a metre below. She turned herself onto her belly and found a rung with her foot. She was on the ladder. She gave the window a shove to close it and swiftly clambered down, rung by rung, panting with fear. She was in the street.

This was the most dangerous part of her journey. The Ukrainians' quarters were at the end of the street. She had to pass them to make her way to Jan's house; there was no other way. She hoped they would be asleep, but she knew that if one of them looked out of the window, her life would be over.

Slowly, slowly, she inched along the wall, keeping to the shadows. She could feel the mist wetting her hair and skin. She reached the Ukrainians' window. Crouching low, almost on all fours, she silently crept past. There was no noise from within.

She was past. She stood up quickly and ran around the corner and down the street to Jan's front door. His window was dark. She knocked quietly, and realised she was shivering.

The door opened and there he was. There was no time to embrace, and he did not welcome her in. He grabbed her hand wordlessly, and led her back down the street towards the bakery, just across from the camp. He was moving so fast that Maya had to run every few steps to keep up with him. She was out of breath and dizzy, but his hand was warm. The camp was so close she could smell a guard's cigarette smoke. The patrol must have begun.

Jan led her to a back alley behind the bakery and motioned for her to wait. He was gone for a few minutes, no more. She stood alone in the quiet street, her breath leaving her chest in quick rasps. When he returned, he was shining a tiny torch, covered with his hand at first, to guide her way.

Behind the building they came to a courtyard. It was very dark, but in the weak torchlight she could make out a trapdoor at the foot of the bakery wall. He pointed inside. They descended together, Jan holding her hand to guide her. They were in a cellar; the air was cold on her skin and she could see nothing in the dark. He handed her the torch and she held it as he opened another, tiny door at the foot of the far wall, leading to a space beneath the shop front. Jan motioned to her to enter. She crept through, feeling the way with her hands. It was too dangerous to speak, but he leaned inside and kissed her quickly on the cheek before pushing her gently on the back to urge her inside. She heard the thud as the door shut then a loud rasp as he pulled some item of furniture in front of it. She was trapped inside.

She felt around her with her hands in the darkness. The dirt floor was cold. When she tentatively tried to stand, she found she could not. She was in a hole; there was no room to be upright. She felt in front of her again and her hands touched a soft, warm body. She gasped.

'Maya?' It was a voice she recognised. Oh, a beautiful voice. 'Don't worry, Maya, be quiet. It's just us here, we'll make room for you.'

Somehow, Erna and Pavel were in the hole too.

⌒

Jan slipped back to his house a little after four. There was no point trying to sleep; he would need to go back to work soon.

His panic had subsided into determination. He had kept her strong and healthy, and he had taught her to speak passable Polish. But there was a gaping hole in his plans – her false identity documents had not yet arrived. Maya's escape would be noticed within the hour; extra SS were already arriving following the disappearance of her friends Erna and Pavel. She could not stay in this area of Poland, but to travel anywhere required papers. The Nazis' love of documentation had kept the Jewish prisoners more effectively imprisoned than the guards ever could.

He should have acted sooner. He cursed under his breath. There had been days, weeks sometimes, when the Commandant was absent. He should have got her out then; if only he had been braver. Now the Ukrainian guards had arrived, and death stalked in the shadows.

Where were those papers? He'd told his AK contact that it was urgent, but Maya was not the only Jewish person for whom time was running out. Without those papers, he had to keep her hidden. There was no other choice.

He felt suddenly exhausted. His forehead was hot but his feet were cold and aching. He poured himself a cup of coffee as the first birdsong twittered from the trees. Not long now, and they would start the Appell. The first place the Commandant would come looking was his house. They would find nothing here; he had already buried his radio, just in case. But fear fluttered in his stomach.

He put his head in his hands and thought of Maya's smile. Would his plan end in death, or in a meadow filled with flowers?

ᴄ∽

Maya could tell it was morning only by the noise above their heads. They were directly underneath the bakery. Distant footsteps thudded behind the counter and the oven door creaked heavily; she listened to the clatter of metal trays as the baker took out the loaves. A shaft of dim light made its way into the hole through a crack in a floorboard above, but it was very dark. Maya rubbed her eyes, sore after a few hours of fitful sleep sitting up, and tried to make out her surroundings.

The hole was no more than a metre and a half square. In this space the three of them sat – they could not stand, and there was no room to lie down. The walls were musty with dark moss and the dirt beneath their legs smelled of mould. Maya stretched her legs as best she could. Pavel flicked on a small torch; when her eyes focused, she could see in its weak light that they were sharing their accommodation with scores of spiders, large and small, clinging to the roof and scurrying along crevices in the walls. There was no food or toilet; no water.

It must have been very early, barely dawn. Erna put a finger to her lips and gestured for Maya to be quiet. She pointed above their heads and then towards the far wall, the direction of the camp. She clasped her hands around her knees. Pavel's arm was around her shoulders. They seemed smaller, childlike. The closeness of their warm bodies calmed Maya. Thank goodness they were here.

Suddenly, there was a commotion from the direction of the camp. The Commandant's voice rang through the morning air, shrill and furious. Maya was surprised how close it sounded. '*Maya ist weg!*' he screamed. 'Maya is gone! I will shoot her dead!' She imagined him swaggering around, red in the face, gun at the ready, hoping to find her behind every barrel or doorway. Who would be the target of his wrath today? Guilt sat heavily on her shoulders, and she covered her ears with her hands.

Before long she could hear urgent footsteps in the shop above. The air became stifling as she tried not to cough. The bakery floor was just centimetres above their heads. Heavy boots stamped into the cellar, but there was no sound of furniture being moved. She exhaled slowly, concentrating on being silent. The fugitives in the hole grasped each other's hands, blind as moles, listening and praying. Maya mouthed the words she remembered from her childhood. 'May it be Your will, God of our fathers, that You should lead us in peace and direct our steps in peace . . .'

At last, all was quiet. Maya strained to look at her watch but she could not make out the numbers. Pavel put his hand to his lips, signalling silence.

They sat there the whole day. Over the hours, she stopped flinching at every muffled sound from the bakery. As she relaxed, boredom became the main enemy. Time stretched in front of her, each minute no easier than the last. In the dark there was no reference point by which to mark the day, no change in light and shadow, no singing of the birds or settling of the afternoon into night. Maya's joy at escaping the camp blackened into despair, pressing at her chest, threatening to explode if she could not get out into the fresh air.

The minutes and hours seemed unending. But, at last, Pavel spoke in a normal voice. 'So, Maya, what a pleasure it is to have you here!'

He flicked on the torch. His face was inches from hers; she could see his youthful stubble growing in little black dots on his chin.

'How long have you been here?' she asked. 'I was looking for Erna all day. I cannot believe that you are both outside the camp!'

'It's been two days already,' said Erna. She told Maya her story quickly. After their meeting by the kitchen, the German, Hans, had quickly made his intentions clear. 'I'm married—' Erna had begun, but then thought better of it. If he heard, he did not show it. Anyway, a Jewish husband who was facing certain death did not seem to count. Every day since then he had found her, brought her small gifts of food. She started to encourage him. When he pulled her to him and felt between her legs, she thought only of Pavel, of the opportunity. Three days ago, he had offered to get her out of the camp. 'Only if my husband can come too,' she had replied, brazen. Hans was furious, and they realised they did not have a minute to lose.

After nightfall, they had clambered over the barbed wire, snagging Pavel's leg badly, and limped towards the trees. How the dogs or the Ukrainians had missed them, they did not know, and their luck continued when Jan found them, terrified but together, and brought them to the cellar.

So here they were. All they had brought was a toothbrush and their Swiss army penknife, their only remaining possessions, hidden in their bags from home.

'Who can blame him for taking a fancy to this beautiful lady?' Pavel asked grimly. The light was too dim for Maya to see his eyes.

Jan arrived late that night. They heard a scraping sound, then the door opened, and he helped Maya to climb through silently. She saw that the entrance to the hole had been obscured by a heavy desk. She shuddered. What if no one had come to pull it away?

Jan peered out of the cellar into the courtyard outside to check that it was clear then led them outside. There was a toilet there, food and water. He embraced Maya as Erna and then Pavel relieved themselves. '*Kocham cię, moja Maryska.* I love you, my Maryska,' he whispered.

She took a hunk of bread from him with trembling hands. It was so long since she had last eaten, she could barely stand. He sat beside her and stroked her knee while she ate.

'This is a huge risk,' she said finally, holding his arm tightly. 'They're looking for all three of us now. The camp is just over there. You're risking your life for us.'

He shrugged.

'There's no other way,' he whispered. 'There's still no sign of the papers. Stay strong, my Maya. I will not abandon you.'

When it was time for him to leave, she held his words tightly in her chest as she clambered back into the black hole.

34

Sawin, June 1943

Time and space lost their meaning. They heard dull sounds around them, but it was impossible to gauge their distance. A dog barking, an engine revving. Was it in the street outside, an early warning of their imminent discovery? Sometimes the clang of the bakery door sounded close and sharp, and Maya could sense the customers browsing the shelves, coupons in hand, oblivious to the starving prisoners not five metres from where they stood. She missed the sound of birdsong.

They slipped into a rhythm, each of the three in their own corner, working together to stretch their legs or arch their backs to ease their cramps. They got to know the sounds and movements of each other's bodies, the smells, the tiny trickling noises of digestion and the comfort of their gentle breathing. Maya could tell from a brush against her toe whether it was Erna or Pavel. She was thin and soft; his bones jutted from beneath his trousers, tied up with string, but there was a solidity about him, a sense of safety. He tried to keep their spirits up, whispering flippant jokes whenever it was safe, sometimes shaking with silent laughter.

Jan brought them food and water. Each night he looked more strained and pale. There was no comforting news; he was avoiding the camp as much as possible, volunteering to oversee the digging in the fields and then quickly slipping home at the end of Appell. Later

225

they slept, one always staying awake to prod the others in case they snored. The baker and his family had no idea they were there; any sound would be fatal. As she closed her eyes, Maya could not imagine the vastness of the world outside.

After what must have been about a week, Erna made a decision. It was too dangerous for them all to be here, in this hole. If they were discovered, then all three would be lost. No, it was better that she and Pavel take their chances. Jan had brought them up to the court-yard to eat. Erna looked towards her husband, crouching by the wall as he quickly devoured a chunk of bread. 'He's my husband. I will either live with him or die with him.' For the first time since the death of her babies, she looked at peace. 'I love him,' she said. 'There's no other choice.'

'Wait for a few days, at least,' Maya whispered.

'No, my mind's made up. Hans knows we've escaped. The risk that he'll find us all is too great. I trust in God. I'm ready to go.'

She walked resolutely to the trapdoor, descended into the cellar and re-emerged with the penknife, holding it firmly as if it would protect her. 'Come, my love,' she gestured to Pavel. 'It's time.'

Before Jan and Maya could stop them, they walked out of the courtyard. Jan hugged Maya tightly, then signalled that it was time for him to go.

She did not remember to cry until she had climbed back into the hole, alone.

꙾

She awoke suddenly to the sound of gunshots. Or perhaps it was the clatter of a dropped cake tin above her head. She could feel dust falling on her face and the dank smell of mildew tickled her nose.

Now Erna and Pavel had left, the hole was her only companion, its boundaries and geography as intimate to her as a living thing. If she put her head in one corner and her feet in another, she only had to bend her knees a little and she could lie down flat. She moved around during the day – this corner at lunchtime, this bump in the afternoon. She stared, unseeing, into the gloom. She imagined herself as one of the spiders, choreographing a dance in the shape of an intricate web, singing soundlessly to the cadences of the floor. There was no other way of passing the time.

Erna had left her the little torch. Maya flicked it on and off, for company. Sometimes she shone it close to the walls, examining their minute specks. They were crafted from the rough, grey stone foundations of the bakery. She got to know their lines and crevices, ran her fingers along the mortar and imagined she was tracing her route to freedom.

She thought about Erna and Pavel. The sense of them still lingered, their presence suspended in the dust. They had no papers and no money. They had trusted that they would survive through the sheer force of their will. She imagined them standing against a wall, their hands behind their heads.

Jan brought her no news of them, but he looked worried and drawn and avoided her eyes. Panic twisted her stomach as he pulled the desk back in front of the door, locking her inside. Her chest constricted, and she felt she might burst in her craving for cool, fresh air. What if something happened to Jan? What if the Commandant discovered him, sent him away, killed him? Then he would not come. Then she would die in here.

She thought of Uncle Emil. When she was little, he had brought her a pigeon egg, tiny and smooth, a precious thing that she had taken in her hand once he unfurled the cloth. 'Hold it against the light,' he had whispered. Inside, suspended in its translucent yellow cushion, she had seen a tangle of red blood vessels, a quick heartbeat at the centre. She felt like that bird now: a pulsing life encased in stone.

The hole was so dark. She found herself shaking, even though it was warm under the bakery. It took every ounce of her will not to shout, to scream through the floorboards, 'I am here!'

The next night, she knew she could not take it any longer. Jan arrived with cheese and egg sandwiches. She grabbed the parcel and took a bite, chewing slowly, letting the taste linger. She swallowed and looked up at him as he stood guard by the gate.

'I can't do it,' she said simply. 'Jan, I'd rather die than stay in this hole.'

'Maryska, there's no other option,' he said softly. He knelt down by her side and put his arm around her. 'I still don't have the papers. They're coming – they will come, I'm sure of it. But for now, this is the safest place.'

Tears stung her eyes and one spilled over onto her cheek. She could not stop them. Before long she was sobbing, deep, racking sobs, begging him, holding his trouser leg, pleading. 'I cannot, I cannot.'

Jan looked around nervously. It was the dead of night. 'Be quiet, my love, they'll hear you.' Her sobs swelled large and forceful, as loud as cats.

'I'll get you out,' he said quickly. 'Maya, be quiet! The baker's family is asleep upstairs. Just one more night, my love, and tomorrow I'll move you. Just give me one more day to make a plan.'

She nodded wordlessly, took another bite of her sandwich and tried to swallow while her sobs subsided. 'Promise me, promise you will come for me,' she whispered. She divided the remainder of the sandwich into portions for the next day and slowly, unwillingly, clambered through first one trapdoor then the other, back into the hole.

The next night, he brought her a bundle of clothes. She was to dress as a Polish farm girl. He would join her on the outskirts of Chelm; it would take her three or four hours to walk there.

'You have to understand the danger you are in, Maya.' He was unusually stern. 'You will be outside with no papers. If you're stopped, you will be arrested.' She understood. Her downfall would be his, too.

She nodded.

'It's too dangerous to travel at night – the partisans are very active now. I won't put the desk over the door, so you'll be free to go. Leave early, at first light, and stick to the woods away from the road. I will be waiting for you.'

He kissed her and helped her back into the hole for the last time.

Sydney, October 1995

'What happened to Erna and Pavel?' asked Kate. 'Did you meet each other again?'

'I never heard from either of them again.' Maya shrugged her shoulders. 'I feel very strongly that they would have survived. But remember, there was really no way of contacting anyone after the war. All this time, I have had no contact at all with anyone I knew before I came to Australia. I had to start again, completely from the beginning.'

'Well, wouldn't it be fantastic if we could track them down? I'll see what I can find out.'

Later that evening, Kate rang the Polish historian back. 'I hear there were a number of escapes from the camp. I'm wondering whether you can help me find two more people, while you're looking at the records?'

'No, no,' the historian barked over the phone. 'No one escaped and survived.'

'But according to Maya's testimony, there was a young couple. Their names were Erna and Pavel Horwitz. Erna had given birth to twins in the camp and then they escaped.'

She could hear the historian pause above the crackling of the long-distance line.

'Oh yes, I know that story. It's something that many people here remember. There were twins in the camp and the Commandant drowned them. After that, people's perceptions changed. A lot of families started to help the Jews on the inside when they heard about it.'

'But do you know what happened to the couple?' Kate pressed.

'Let me look . . .' She could hear him shuffling papers. After a few minutes he returned to the phone. 'Ah yes, I have it. You're correct, it's recorded in the Commandant's trial after the war. There *was* a couple that escaped, but they were captured a few days later.'

It was Erna and Pavel, it had to be. Surely no other couples had escaped the camp?

'And what happened?'

The historian paused. 'I am sorry to tell you this. The Commandant beat the woman to death.'

35

Sawin, June 1943

The weak light from the little torch flickered as Maya tried to make out the time. Its battery was nearly spent. It should be dawn now, but she could not tell. She pulled on her shoes and tentatively pushed open the small door, which, for the first time, was not obscured by the heavy desk. She climbed out quickly, tiptoed through the cellar then up the ladder. Light flooded in as she opened the trapdoor. The courtyard was bathed in pink as she emerged into the cool air.

She had pulled on the peasant clothes before she went to sleep. The shoes were ill-fitting and the skirt was too large, but with Rosa's scarf over her hair she could pass for a local farm girl. She yawned and looked around her. The courtyard looked smaller in the light, more normal. Its rickety gate opened directly onto the street that ran along the edge of the camp. The only safe way to exit was through the bakery itself.

She gingerly opened the back door of the bakery and walked through to the shop. Though it was still before opening time, and the shelves were empty, the smell of bread greeted her warmly as she tiptoed through, over the cleanly swept floor, towards the front door. There was a bell above it to alert the baker to new customers. She paused for a second, unsure what to do, then, with a flash of inspiration, she wound the scarf around the clapper and slowly, slowly pulled the door towards her. She slipped through. There was no way to retrieve the scarf; she

231

hoped its discovery would not place the baker and his family in any more danger.

The street outside was empty. Behind the bakery, the wall of the camp loomed large and terrifying. She could see the window from which she had made her escape. The ladder was no longer there. The few prisoners inside would be eating their breakfast soon, but she could hear no noise. From the street, the camp appeared still and calm. What did the villagers imagine was going on inside?

A brown cat leaped silently onto the road at her feet. Its loud purring followed her as she jogged around the corner and darted towards the road out of the village, leaving the camp and Sawin behind her.

She had barely walked a kilometre when she heard the distant rumbling of an engine approaching along the dusty road. She threw herself into the deep grass edging the field to her right, slithering on her belly beneath dripping fronds. The tip of her nose brushed cold, damp soil. Its earthy smell reassured her, reminded her of something in her childhood, of lying on the grass and gazing at the individual blades shining emerald against the sun, the white petals of the daisies looming large in front of her eyes.

For the first time since she had stepped out of the hole, she realised she was free.

The hum of the engine grew into a roar. She dared to look through the thick stems of grass as the vehicle approached. It was a German car. Two SS guards sat stiffly in the front. One of them was rubbing his eyes. She plunged her face back into the earth, shielding her head with her hand.

Silence settled. Nothing stirred. The field was quiet and real, and finches were chattering in the corn. She lifted her head again and brushed leafy debris from her cheek, then slowly pulled herself onto her knees and hesitantly stood up, crouching low, scanning the road for any sign of life. Her watch showed it was six o'clock. She needed to get moving; it was a seventeen-kilometre walk to Chelm, and Jan was waiting.

She weighed up her options. It was not safe to be seen by anyone, not even the locals, no matter how friendly they might seem. Her Polish was reasonable by now, but she still had an accent. It would not take them long to realise who she was. No, the only option was to make it to the dense wood, about two kilometres in the distance.

This time she walked for about ten minutes, quickly, her eyes fixed on the trees, before she heard another engine. It turned off up ahead. She picked up her pace. Her shoes were already pinching her feet, but the green leaves were closer now, waving in the breeze. She started to pant as the road inclined towards the wood. She ignored her breathlessness and ploughed on, looking behind her every few seconds, her Polish farm skirt swishing in front of her legs with every step.

Finally, she reached the shadows of the wood. She darted deep into the trees and allowed herself to rest for a moment. She could not see the road – she was safe – but there was no clearly defined path and it was difficult to judge the direction in which she needed to walk. She waited for her breathing to slow then started off again, daring every few minutes to walk back towards the road to check her bearings. It was slow going. She could feel the heat of the rising sun through the leaves high above her head.

She did not rest until mid-morning. She was tired and hungry, and her tongue felt swollen with thirst. She came to a clearing in the trees, a small grassy expanse ringed with firs. She sat down, took the shoes off her aching feet, and inspected the blisters blooming at her heels. She had no idea how far she had come, or how far she had to go.

The grass was soft as she lay down to rest. Above her, the sky was blue and endless. She dug her nails into the solid earth, as if she were about to let go and fall through the sky, her arms spread wide and the wind gushing past her face. Small white clouds skimmed past and she followed them with her eyes, imagining herself flying with them towards a brighter future.

By lunchtime, the trees started to thin and she could see the road clearly to her left. She was nearing Chelm. There were cars and a bus; a farmer plodded along, large boots stamping the beat of his heavy gait, his shoulders hunched and the smell of his cigarette filling up the fresh air. She stooped low as she came to the edge of the wood and scanned the sunny cornfields to orient herself. She could see two figures in the distance. Was that them?

Slowly, keeping below the level of the corn, she crept towards the town. Red poppies and bright blue cornflowers marked her path through the field. Yes, it was them! She could tell by the way one of the figures moved that it was Jan. He was leaning on a fence, talking to a smaller figure beside him. His sister, Danuta.

At last they saw her. He nodded in her direction. She was close enough now to sense his anxiety; the relaxation in his posture was a little too forced, his hand pushed low in his pocket as he tapped his fingers against his thigh. He signalled to her to get down as an army truck juddered along the road. She knelt in the corn and waited for it to pass.

The corn rustled and parted, and Danuta appeared. She was standing tall, making a show of hitching her skirts and crouching down to relieve herself. She was younger than Jan, maybe eighteen, and she shared his fine features and blonde hair. When she smiled, her eyes were kind. Maya smiled back. Her heart was beating fast.

Danuta was carrying a small bundle under her arm. As she stood and pretended to pull up her undergarments, she dropped it at Maya's feet. Then she quickly turned and walked back purposefully towards her brother.

Maya unwrapped the bundle, worrying at the string with shaking hands. Inside was a pair of elegant court shoes wrapped in a blue silk dress. It was smooth and cool against her rough fingers. There was a hairbrush, a water bottle and a face cloth. Still crouching in the corn, she drank thirstily and then wet the cloth and wiped the grime as best she could from her face. She brushed her hair and scraped the broken knots from the bristles, watching them fly away on the breeze. Then she pulled off her Polish farm clothes and secreted them deep in the stiff stalks. 'Thank you for protecting me,' she whispered to the clothes, childlike, and wriggled her arms into the dress. It slipped over her slim, shining body like a soft new skin and fell towards her knees. It was cinched at the waist and cut low at the neck, accentuating her breasts and the curve of her clavicle. She smoothed her hair instinctively as she stood up above the corn, squeezed her feet into the shoes that were too small, and smiled at Jan. He stared back at her, mesmerised, as she walked towards him, no longer a Jewish prisoner but an elegant woman, emerging from a cornfield.

⌒

They had discussed the plan in depth. 'They may be watching me,' Jan told her, shrugging his shoulders. It was too risky to appear to be together, so they would follow separate paths and watch each other closely. If one noticed danger, they would send a warning, a series of coughs.

Jan set off first, taking the road to the left with Maya following about twenty metres behind him. Danuta walked along a parallel street. Maya glimpsed her from time to time through the connecting alley-ways, walking with her head down and her arms clasped at the elbows, holding herself tightly as if on a winter's day. It was a weekday and most people were at work; the cobbled streets were empty. Maya held her head high and tried to walk with confidence. She caught her reflection in a shop window. So thin, but also so alive.

Her eyes were fixed on Jan's back. His hands swung at his sides, more relaxed as they made progress. He stopped to light a cigarette and she stopped too, studying a row of hats in a milliner's window. It was all so normal. A man in a suit walked past on the opposite side of the street. She moved her face away from him, her nose nearly touching the glass. He was gone. Jan moved forward again.

Her shoes were starting to pinch, forming new blisters over those that had developed during her long walk. She did not care. Her ears strained for the sound of a cough, but none came. After a while, Jan picked up his pace. He veered to the right and stopped her with a slight gesture of his right hand. He pushed open a black door and entered a building, followed a minute later by Danuta. Maya leaned against a wall, trying not to look.

No one had noticed her. She looked left and right, scanning dark alleyways and closed doors. The street was quiet. Quickly, she walked towards the door, left ajar by Danuta, and pushed. It was heavy; she needed some strength to open it enough to slip inside. She found herself in a cold and gloomy stairwell. She shut the door quietly behind her and started to ascend, putting her weight on her toes to prevent the clack of her heels on the stairs. She kept climbing, dizzy, her heart pumping and her legs screaming with fatigue, to the third floor, as instructed. Jan opened the door and pulled her inside.

ᅟᅟᅟᅟᅟᅟᅟᅟᅟᅟᅟᅟᅟᅟᅟᅟ⌒ᅟᅟᅟᅟᅟᅟᅟᅟᅟᅟᅟᅟᅟᅟᅟ

She found herself in a living room, full of light, comfortable and elegant. She hesitated as her eyes adjusted. A large window looked over the roofs of Chelm below; a vase of flowers had been put on a side table and the cushions were freshly plumped. A mahogany dresser stood across one corner of the room. It was neatly stacked with blue crockery and covered with photographs; Jan as a little boy, Danuta with a puppy. A wedding scene from the twenties, a handsome man and his young bride. There were two large, upholstered sofas, on one of which Danuta had thrown herself, the back of her hand to her forehead as she recounted the terror and excitement of the last half hour to someone in another room.

The kitchen door opened and the delicious smell of coffee wafted out. A middle-aged woman stepped out, wiping her hands on her apron, a wide smile on her lipstick-tinted lips. Her dark hair was drawn back into a fashionable French roll, with a grey streak at her brow. She wore a dark skirt and a cream silk blouse.

'Maya,' said Jan, 'May I introduce you to my mother?'

Mrs Novak reached both her hands towards Maya, who sank to her knees and kissed them. She looked up. The woman had Jan's eyes.

'Thank you, thank you,' Maya murmured, over and over. She could not think what else to do; this family was risking so much.

'Now, now,' Jan's mother said, embarrassed, pulling Maya to her feet and putting her arm around her. 'I've just made some coffee. Would you like some?'

Maya started to relax as she sipped, the strong, bitter drink burning her tongue and radiating heat through her chest. She sat in a corner of one of the sofas, legs crossed, politely holding an ornate cup and saucer on her lap, in her blue silk dress and fashionable shoes. She was trembling inside at the unreality of it all; aware of her animal smell here in this lovely living room.

They made small talk, mostly about the price of food, Danuta interjecting from time to time, asking questions, teasing her brother. He was on edge still, his eyes darting to the front door. 'Enough, Danuta,' he said at last. 'Maya's tired. You can ask your questions another time. Please, show her the bathroom.'

For the first time in a year, Maya washed with warm water. She scrubbed her nails and the back of her neck, wrung out the cloth and watched the grimy traces of the camp bubble away down the plughole. She could hear Jan laughing from the living room.

After lunch, they sat around a small table in the kitchen. Jan's mother became serious.

'I need you to understand,' said Mrs Novak, speaking slowly and clearly so that Maya could follow the Polish. 'Under no circumstances can my husband discover that you're here. He must have no idea – no idea at all. He's at work until about six every day, so once he leaves in the morning you're free to move around the apartment. But from five, and all weekend, you must hide.'

Maya nodded. Please, not a cellar.

'Come, let me show you,' Jan said brightly. He led her back into the living room and carefully pulled back the large dresser that stood diagonally across the corner of the room. Behind it, in the triangular space where the two walls met, was a mattress, carefully made up with ironed sheets and feather pillows. A neatly folded set of pyjamas had been placed at the end of the bed and there was a teddy bear on the pillow. 'I thought of that!' Danuta laughed. 'It was Jan's when he was a little boy. I thought you could cuddle it while we're all in the room pretending we don't know you're there!' She jumped around, excited and happy.

Maya was suddenly overcome with exhaustion. She promised Jan's mother that she would do whatever was required, then politely asked if she could go to bed, right now. She climbed behind the dresser and waited for Jan to scrape it back into place, the cups and saucers tinkling as he did so. With leaden limbs, she changed out of the silk dress and into the pyjamas, lay her head on the soft pillow and almost immediately fell asleep. She dreamed she was dancing, but no one could see.

36

My darling Jan

The smell of coffee. I did not notice it at first, but it is winding its way to me where I sit on my bed. Kate is making me a coffee.

It has roused in me a long-forgotten yearning, a rush of excitement. A hand holding out the steaming drink, the warmth burning my throat, giving me strength.

It is hard for me to decipher what is real. This disease is making everything seem so . . . imagined. These days I cannot remember whether I have experienced something or just thought it. My whole life seems to be swirling in eddies somewhere at the top of my head, images coming and going in a white sea.

But the smell of coffee reminds me there is something important to remember. There is a memory floating above me, just out of reach. It shimmers at the edges; I can see its colours. People are moving around it like shadows, but I cannot grasp their substance. It is warm and pleasant, somewhere I want to be.

I feel myself curled next to a warm body, safe, a clean feather eiderdown resting over my feet and coffee bubbling on the stove. I turn over, luxuriating in the sense of comfort, the soft breathing, in and out. Each minute stretches before me, precious. But I know this time will end and we will be separated again.

I nestle closer, weaving my small hand through the larger fingers, shutting my eyes and wishing, wishing I could stay here forever.

Now the memory has become large and real. And I realise it is not you next to me.

No. The coffee has brought me to my mother.

Chelm, July 1943

Maya came to know his steps outside the door, the sound as he turned the latch, the rustling as he took off his coat and placed his newspaper on the hall table. Jan's father was a man of consistent habits. He returned regularly at six o'clock in the evening, embraced his wife and daughter and shook his son's hand. The moment she heard him, Maya would feel the need to clear her throat. She counted his steps as he walked around the room, gauging when he had disappeared into the bathroom or kitchen, praying for a snatch of music on the radio to mask the noises she could not prevent her body from making. His normal seat on the sofa was no more than two metres from her mattress behind the dresser, where she curled up tight, her face pressed into her knees, managing her breathing.

Every evening, he would wash his hands and face then settle to listen to the radio until it was time for dinner. His voice was deep and obtrusive, dominating the muffled conversation from the dining room. They talked mainly of the German war effort. She listened for the spikes of Jan's passionate interjections above the scraping of forks on plates, the thud of chairs on the woollen rug.

After dinner, Mr Novak would crank the gramophone and music would fill the living room, notes rolling and tumbling around her shoulders behind the dresser. His favourite was Wagner. It was not to Maya's taste; she found it overindulgent, perhaps reflecting his day at work, the decisions he had made. Some evenings, when he was in a more reflective mood, the soft chords of Chopin or Brahms poured from the gramophone like warm water. She would bathe in them, stretching out her legs and arching her back. There were popular songs, too, 'Rebeka' and 'Dobranoc, Kochanie', which made him chuckle while she tapped her fingers silently on the mattress.

The weekend was the worst. The family was different when he was home, the air heavier, their tones more muted. Mr Novak did not stray far from the living room. He sat thumbing his newspaper or reading a book, while Maya read too, silently turning the pages of a Polish novel, praying she would not sneeze or cough. The Saturday hours stretched long and grey until he left for his early evening stroll and Jan let her out to visit the bathroom and quickly devour a meal.

On the second Sunday, the Novaks had company. Jan looked drawn and worried as he ushered her back behind the dresser in the early morning. 'He's invited the SS here. They're coming to our house,' he whispered. 'This weekend, of all weekends. You must be very quiet. I don't know how long they'll stay.'

The family arose early. Maya listened to the clattering of pans and dishes from the kitchen and the apartment was soon filled with the sweet onion smell of stew. She clenched her muscles to try to prevent her belly from rumbling. It was a long time since she had eaten red meat. Mrs Novak must have saved her rations for weeks to provide this feast for the Germans.

They arrived promptly at eight o'clock. The pitch of Mrs Novak's voice was higher than normal as she led them into the living room. Maya lay her cheek on the floor and peered out through the tiny gap under the dresser, her view obscured by dust and spiders' webs. She could make out three pairs of shiny German boots. They were planted steadfastly in the middle of the room and the feet inside them rocked slightly forward and back as their occupants shook hands. Mr Novak was trying to talk to the guests in German. His choice of words made him sound inferior; his accent was too soft, implying weakness.

She could hear Jan and Danuta whispering to each other from the back of the room. 'Please, meet my son.' Mr Novak's voice was obsequious, almost pleading. Maya's stomach clenched as she saw Jan's feet move into the room, heard his halting German greeting in words that did not sound like him. Mr Novak was boasting about Jan's work in Sawin, how the irrigation project was nearly done, the fields now fertile. She felt sick as she heard Jan laying a map on the table and imagined his finger extended, describing the work. There was a muttering of approval. No mention of the hundreds of Jewish prisoners who had made those irrigation ditches; who had paid for this grand German plan with their lives.

The group moved into the dining room and Maya changed her position. She found herself smiling. The absurdity of it! A roomful of SS and her, here, behind the dresser. She thought of Franz and his knowing nod the day they were brought to Poland from Czechoslovakia. We're better than them, he had let her know. She suddenly felt strong.

After a long hour, she heard the scrape of the door and the Germans re-entered the living room. They were chattering freely now. They were drunk and their slurred words were crude. Either they were alone, or they were sure the Novak family could not understand. 'Like a toad . . .' one of them was saying. 'Pathetic,' another snorted, then burped loudly. 'These Poles, so obedient, they'll do anything.' She felt a surge of compassion for Mr Novak. She imagined him in the kitchen, overseeing the preparation of coffee, hurrying his wife to make sure it was right.

When the Germans were gone, she heard Mr Novak slump heavily onto the sofa, then the fizz of the match at the end of his pipe. There was the click of the needle on the record, then dusty scratches amplified through the room. The first notes of *Die Moldau* by Smetana tumbled from the gramophone. He sighed and shifted in his seat. Mrs Novak called 'Goodnight', but he did not answer. Maya closed her eyes and let the music take her with him. It swelled and grew inside, giving her hope. She thanked him for the music, for the safety of the space behind the dresser. Most of all, she thanked him for his son, who was a good man.

She imagined herself with Mr Novak, floating up above the elegant room towards the stars, head of police and Jew hand in hand as the violins and cellos bathed them in gentle light. She wished she could dance, for him.

37

Chelm, July 1943

Maya stayed in the apartment for the whole of the next week. Having taken leave from work, Jan sat in the dining room with his family, wondering how it was possible that his father did not sense her presence from the next room. He felt the apartment glow with her; the danger and the thrill of her proximity.

Mr Novak was in a bad mood. He spooned his soup into his mouth aggressively; a tiny morsel of carrot stuck to his greying moustache. Jan watched it with mounting irritation. His father had shaved this morning, as every morning, carefully trimming his moustache into the exact style made popular by Hitler. Even his father's moustache was trying too hard.

'Jan.' He sprang to attention as his father barked his name. 'Did you hear what I said? We're getting close. Our intelligence is good. Soon we'll uncover this network of *Vaterlandsverräter.*' Now he was even using the German word for 'traitors'.

'That's good news indeed, Father. I didn't realise the home army was active in this area.'

Mr Novak looked up at him quickly. He frowned, his eyes searching Jan's face. 'Everyone knows—'

Mrs Novak interrupted him with a loud cough and dropped her spoon with a clatter. 'Jan, please will you bring me a glass of water from the kitchen?'

243

By the time he returned, talk had moved on to Danuta's day. But Jan's mother caught his eye.

'Jan, it's becoming too dangerous,' she whispered urgently after Mr Novak had retired to bed. 'She could betray us all.'

'She'll never betray us. It's more likely that Danuta will let something slip. She's so stupid sometimes.'

'Listen to me, Jan. I support you and will do what I can to help. But you told me she'd only be here for a few days.'

Jan's heart was beating fast. He still did not have the papers. 'I understand, Mama. I'll do what I can, tomorrow.'

He knew Mrs Novak was right. Maya had to move on.

⌒

The next day, he approached his AK commander. They stood casually in the shadow of a doorway. Jan drew on his cigarette and looked in the other direction, as if it were a coincidence that they both happened to have their backs to the same door at the same time.

'I think my father may suspect something.' He swallowed.

The commander did not seem surprised. He took his own pack of cigarettes from his pocket and motioned to Jan that he needed a light. 'Go to Krakowska Street,' he whispered as Jan leaned in with the match.

Jan nodded. It was where the AK provisions were distributed – ironically, a stone's throw from his father's office and the dreaded Security Police detention centre. More than once, Jan had spotted his father climbing the steps, his polished boots glinting as he hurried to a meeting with his Nazi overlords.

But today, thankfully, the street was quiet. Jan looked left and right then darted into an alley and knocked on the door, two short and then three very rapid knocks, the sequence he had been told. The door opened a few centimetres and a rough arm pulled him through.

Somehow, his arrival was already expected. A man with dark stubble nodded towards a back room, without speaking. Inside it was very dark. The window had been blocked out with a blanket and a small bulb provided the only light. A cupboard and a wooden table were the only furniture. The man unlocked a drawer and retrieved a revolver, which he pressed into Jan's hand, then reached towards the back of the cupboard for a cardboard box. He set it on the table and opened it; it was full of pills. He carefully counted out four of them in his rough hands and folded them in a square of brown paper, which he secured carefully with string.

'There's enough in there for you and for her. It goes without saying – if you're caught, neither of you must live to talk.'

Jan nodded, his heart thumping.

'And the papers? I can't move her without the papers.'

The man sighed and glanced at his watch. 'You're not the only one waiting for papers. The counterfeiters are working as fast as they can.'

Jan opened his mouth to speak, but the man turned his back, replaced the box in the cupboard and locked the door. 'I'll see what I can do. Now go, and make sure you're not seen.'

◯—

The following Saturday, summer sunshine shone in slanting beams through the open window and the sounds of the street below floated into the living room. Mrs Novak had persuaded her husband to go away with her for a few days. 'You're tired, my love,' she urged. 'Jan will watch Danuta, there's no need to worry.' How strange to think of people going away, still.

Maya sat with her back in the corner between the two walls, her feet stretched out in front of her. She quietly closed the book on her lap and ran her finger over the staring glass eyes of the teddy bear, imagining Jan as a child. She could hear Jan's mother and sister in the bedroom, talking softly, wooden drawers scraping open and closed.

Later, when Jan's parents had gone, Danuta gave her a bagful of clothes. She had sorted them into greys and browns, inconspicuous and sensible. The apartment felt spacious and luxurious as they sat together on Danuta's bed, with Maya trying on sweaters and shoes. Maya's mind flicked to Erna, to the nights they had spent clutching each other for warmth, the babies, the secrets. Where was she now? She imagined Erna and Pavel in the woods, holding each other close.

'Mama says this blouse brings out the colour of my eyes, but I don't like the way it sits against my neck. Please take it.' Danuta was still a child, really, though she was more than a year older than Maya. She looked like Jan, yet knew so much less about the world.

The front door opened loudly and they froze. Danuta held the blouse suspended in the air, her mouth open, but it was only Jan. 'Good news!' he called. He burst into the bedroom with a large manila envelope in his outstretched hand and lowered his voice. 'I have the identity papers!'

It had been months, so long that Maya could not remember a time when she was not waiting for the papers. They had become no more than words, an abstract idea that she had never really believed could be real. Jan carefully pulled a document out of the envelope and handed it to her. He had used the photograph of her taken months ago when they had slipped into the studio on a weekend off from sorting potatoes in Chelm. Her hair was dishevelled, and she looked gaunt and afraid – someone that she did not recognise.

He sat next to her on the bed and put his hand on her knee. Danuta was trying not to watch his fingers as they stroked Maya's leg. Maya looked into Jan's eyes. They both knew what the papers meant.

'You are free,' he whispered, and kissed her hair. Her throat was swelling; she could not talk. She nodded, tried to smile.

Danuta clapped her hands together and sprang off the bed. 'I'm so glad Jan brought you,' she said. 'Nothing exciting ever happens around here.'

On Monday morning, Jan took Maya to collect her travel documents. He had dispatched Danuta first, but the official had demanded that Maya present herself in person. She would need to leave the apartment.

Dressed in Danuta's clothes, with a hat tilted low over her forehead, she stepped with Jan into the sunny street. Her false identity document had been folded and placed carefully into a borrowed handbag that she carried over her shoulder. She clutched it to her tightly, its precious contents burning through the leather and warming her gloved hand. Jan linked his arm through hers and she lifted her chin as they set off down the street.

The Polish–German labour exchange was not far. They reached the looming grey building and walked in silence to the first floor. A group of Poles was sitting on stiff wooden benches in a reception room. They shuffled their feet and sighed occasionally with the air of people who have been kept waiting for some time. The room smelled of musty paper and ink. From time to time, there was the loud thud of a stamp from behind a row of windows.

Jan walked directly to one of the kiosks and looked the official squarely in the eye. Maya held back, behind his left shoulder. There was a disgruntled ruffle behind them, indignant whispers. They had jumped the queue. She stared at her feet, hoping it had not drawn unnecessary attention to them.

'Identity papers?' The official looked past Jan to Maya. She lifted the handbag off her shoulder. Her hands were shaking and it seemed to take an age to loosen the clasp. She handed him the document.

He looked at her over his round spectacles. 'What's your name?'

They had practised this, over and over, she and Danuta, bending her tongue to get the Polish intonation right. 'Maria Szulc.'

He nodded and smiled reassuringly. He took out a sheaf of pale yellow forms and began to fill in the top sheet of paper with a black fountain pen. She watched as the ink slowly traced the rounded letters of her assumed name. When he had finished, he reached for a second form. He did not look at Maya or Jan again until, with a flourish, he stamped both forms with the Nazi eagle and handed them across the counter.

'Thank you.' Jan nodded, again looking the official in the eye, then took Maya's hand and led her quickly out of the office and back into the fresh air.

When they returned to the apartment, Maya looked at the forms. Below the stamp the official had written the date: 15-7-1943. The date of her second escape. The date that spelled the end of her time with Jan.

'Don't worry, my love. This is our plan, remember?' Jan held her chin in his finger and thumb. 'You will find work on a farm – we know how much you love potatoes!' She thought of her time in Chelm, sorting through the unending pile of mouldy vegetables, as he playfully tousled her hair.

'The war's turning,' he went on. 'We'll beat the Nazis, I'm sure of it now. Go to Germany, hide there in plain sight, and when all of this is over we'll find a new home, together, far away.'

'Where shall we go?' She leaned into him, trusting and safe.

'As far away as possible. I don't know – maybe Argentina? America? Australia, with the kangaroos?'

She allowed herself to laugh. It was so far away, so impossible. She shut her eyes as he kissed her neck.

⌒

The next day, they packed Danuta's discarded clothes into a little suitcase; Maya buried a pair of shoes, some toiletries and photographs among the neatly folded skirts and sweaters, and clicked the lid shut. Jan slipped a snapshot of himself into her pocket. 'In case this suitcase also becomes German property!' he joked.

The train would depart at midday. The minutes felt heavy as they sat on the sofa, trying to read a magazine, their eyes straying to the clock on the mantlepiece and willing the time to slow. Jan felt nervous and distracted, walking from room to room, pulling back the lace curtain to check the street, patting his pocket.

He heard Danuta's muffled giggles from her bedroom. If Maya were caught, his sister and mother must not be implicated. He had already put them in so much danger.

Finally, he called Maya.

'My beloved,' he began. It sounded formal and old fashioned – but how else to broach a subject like this? 'Take this.' He handed her the brown paper packet. She unwrapped the pills and looked at him, not understanding.

'Cyanide.' Jan lowered his eyes. 'You know I love you and I want you to live. I would happily give my life for you. But if you're captured and tortured, if you can't bear it any longer, this poison will give you an escape. Your body may die but your soul will live for ever.'

He took the pills from her and placed them inside a blue velvet pouch that had belonged to Danuta as a child, keeping two for himself. He pulled the white ribbons that closed the pouch, then tied their ends securely in a bow before hanging it around Maya's neck. Maya did not speak. She looked at him with complete trust, moving her hair out of the way to allow him to fasten the knot.

And then it was time to go.

Maya hugged Danuta and Mrs Novak, then Jan led her onto the echoing stairwell outside the door. A tear spilled from her eye and picked up pace as it ran over her cheek. She licked it away from her top lip. Jan lifted the suitcase in one hand and held her arm tightly with the other. 'Stop crying,' he hissed through his teeth. 'Don't attract attention.'

The streets below the apartment were busy. The lace curtains on the third floor above their heads fluttered gently in the breeze. Behind them, the innocuous window behind which Maya had hidden for more than two weeks. Danuta and Mrs Novak were there still. Were they breathing a sigh of relief, now the danger had gone?

They set off, pretending to be normal. Maya's high heels tapped on the cobbles and Jan could see the swell of the little cyanide pouch beneath her blouse. They walked quickly, even though they had allowed ample time to reach the station. He imagined he could hear the hiss of the train already. He tried not to think about the danger, for these were their last moments together, the last time he would guide her with his strong arms and feel the comfort of her next to him.

In just a few minutes, they would be apart. For how long, it was impossible to say.

~

They had just rounded a bend in the road when Maya saw him. She did not recognise him at first. He was dressed in civilian clothes, in a tweed suit and polished shoes, and he was carrying a newspaper under his arm. He was walking slowly, uncharacteristically calm and nonchalant. For a second, just a split second, she was struck by how insignificant he looked without his rifle, just a little man in a grey suit. And then fear jolted from her stomach and into her mouth.

The Commandant halted, looking in their direction from the other side of the street. Behind him, she could see her reflection in the shining windows of a hardware shop. Everything slowed down. All she could hear was the sound of her breathing. She swung away from him to hide her face, but her eye had caught his. His cold stare enveloped her and obscured the sun.

'Run!' Jan pulled her by the arm into an alley. She tripped and almost fell. The smell of urine wafted from the cobbles as she staggered, never letting go of his hand, watching the little suitcase swing and bang against his legs as he pulled her forwards.

They turned a corner to the left. There was a wooden gate. Jan rattled it; it was unlocked. They pushed through into the small backyard of a café. Maya could hear the clink of coffee cups and the hum of custom-ers talking inside. Jan pushed her towards the fence, covering her with his body as if they were in a passionate embrace. She could feel his heart pounding through his suit.

They waited. Nothing happened. Five minutes passed, and then another five. 'Do you think it's safe?' she whispered eventually. Her train would be leaving soon; to stay in Chelm was now unthinkable.

'Wait here.' He slowly prised the gate open a few centimetres and peered into the alleyway. He waited, then stuck his head out, looked left and right, and beckoned to her. Terrified, she followed him back into the world.

They retraced their steps carefully to the main street. They could not see the Commandant. They were no more than a hundred metres from the station, but to get there they had to cross a large, open square. It was full of people. A musician was playing the violin and colourful flowers danced in pots outside the cafés around the edges of the square. Maya hesitated, her hand on the small, hard train ticket in her pocket. She bent a corner of it with her fingernail, her tiny pass to a new life. Her train was already boarding.

Jan smiled at her. They did not speak. Both understood. They had come this far; there was no other choice than to walk with confidence towards Maya's freedom.

By the time they reached the station, the train's whistle was cutting discordantly through the noise and commotion of a hundred people saying their goodbyes. There was less than a minute to go before departure. Steam rose in great white clouds from the engine and it was easy to lose themselves in the crowd. The Commandant could be anywhere; every turned back, every hat could be him. Maya anticipated the shock of a gunshot between her shoulder blades. Why was he not here? Had he not recognised her?

She thought about the cyanide. It felt strangely comforting as it banged against her chest. But she knew she would never take it.

Jan pulled her, half trotting, behind him as he strode the length of the platform to the far end of the train. The crowd was thinner here. Poppies poked out of the long grass by the siding beyond the platform. The sun beat down on the tracks and Maya realised how warm she was in her woollen coat. The whistle blew again.

He pushed her against the fence at the edge of the station, his body completely obscuring her from the crowd. He held her tightly in an embrace; she could feel both their hearts thumping in unison beneath their clothes. The last whistle. She could hear the brakes releasing and the carriage start to move. Jan cupped her chin in his hands and kissed her fiercely. His lips were demanding and desperate, the kiss more of an urgent lament than a sign of affection. Maya tried to respond, but her eyes were on the train. It was definitely moving. In her panic, she did not even shut her eyes.

'*Kocham cię; do zobaczenia.* I love you. Till we meet again,' he whispered as he released her. The words caught in his throat.

She pulled away from him, lurching towards the open door. He grabbed the suitcase and threw it onto the train as she leaped up the steep steps. The door shut with a bang.

She turned to say goodbye, but he was already gone.

Sydney, November 1995

'I have never forgotten that moment,' said Maya. 'I turned and he was gone. In my heart I bade him farewell. I thought we would meet soon. But of course I never did see him again.'

'So you were totally alone, sitting on a train pretending to be Polish, heading into the unknown. You must have been terrified.'

'You know, I somehow felt that God was watching over me.' Maya smiled. 'I remember I sat there, grateful for the angels, grateful for Mrs Novak and Danuta, and of course grateful for my Jan. As we pulled away from the station in Chelm, I started praying and it calmed my breath a little. I realised I was going to be all right.'

'And what happened next?'

'The train took me to Lublin, where I went to an assembly point for Polish slave girls. It was very dangerous for me. We had to sleep in a large school hall and I could not risk speaking to anybody, as they would recognise my Czech accent. So I just tried to make myself invisible on a top bunk. And then the next day we set off on a cattle train for Germany.'

Kate's hand fluttered to the little half-German baby in her belly. 'And what then?'

But Maya had closed her eyes and her head was nodding forwards. That was enough for today. As Kate bent to kiss her cheek, carefully so as not to wake her, she realised Maya's lips were moving. '*Sh'ma Yisrael.* Hear, O Israel: the Lord is our God, the Lord is One.'

Later that evening, Kate dialled the long number for England. 'Mum?' There was a pause on the line; Kate imagined her mother settling into the stiff-backed chair by the telephone, wiping invisible dust from the table with a quick sweep of her hand, removing her clip-on pearl earring.

'Mum, I have something to tell you.' Kate swallowed. 'I think I'm pregnant.'

Another silent second ticked by. The dappled leaves behind the window; her mother's Wedgewood collection on the sill.

'Oh. I see.' The heaviness in her mother's voice made Kate instinctively curl her legs towards her chest, small like a child. Her mother sighed. 'And what are you going to do about it, darling?'

'I don't know. I only just worked it out.'

'And can I ask about the father?'

Kate shut her eyes to block out the blurred memory of Tomas. 'He's not around any more.'

There was a pause as her mother stood to shut the door. When she returned, her voice was lower, conspiratorial.

'Let me handle your father. He won't be happy. He's so old-fashioned. You just worry about taking care of it. You *can* get abortions over there, can't you?'

Kate smiled despite herself at her mother's impression of the world beyond Surrey's borders. 'Mum, I haven't decided yet.'

Another pause. 'A baby is a big thing to take on, Kate, with all your gallivanting about the world. You'd have to come home.'

What a thought. Leaden skies; stifling propriety. Kate would feel as if she had failed if she packed it all in now. She sniffed. Her mother must have thought she was crying.

'It's all right, darling. These things happen. Just take care of it.'

Kate hung up. What was she going to do? The baby was already real;
she could sense its presence in every breath she took, in every mouthful
of food she swallowed. Its little life blazed inside her. She thought of
Maya, clinging to life, never letting go of hope.

Life. Her baby had life. To destroy it seemed as unimaginable as to
destroy herself.

38

Maya did not move from her corner of the carriage for several hours. She rested her chin on her bent knees and hugged her ankles, feeling the cyanide pouch soft against her skin as the cattle train rattled towards the west.

She was with ten Polish women, some of them as young as she, all of them growing increasingly scared as they came closer to Germany. They sat on the dirty floor in darkness as the train lumbered through the Polish countryside. Maya put her eye to a chink in the wood and saw sunny fields and trees rushing past.

She listened to the conversation. Ukrainian vigilantes had been roaming the fields around Chelm, killing farmers and abusing the women. It was not safe to live alone, not with the men away and the fighting getting so close. The women nodded in agreement. In the town itself, food was becoming scarce. There was work in Germany, good work in the factories. At least they would have food and safety, there in the land of their oppressors. Really, did they have any other choice? They looked tired and defeated.

Maya did not join the conversation. When she shifted to relieve her aching back, she accidentally caught a young woman's eye. She smiled. The woman held out a thin arm, offering a butter biscuit. Maya refused, miming that she felt nauseous and could not talk. It seemed to work.

255

In the late afternoon, the cattle train juddered to a halt with the high-pitched squeal of metal on metal. 'This must be the border,' a middle-aged woman grumbled, arching her back to stretch. There was a clanking and banging of bolts being drawn, and the heavy door rolled open. Two young soldiers of the Wehrmacht peered into the dim interior. Dogs barked in the distance; it felt like her arrival at Sobibór, a lifetime ago. But these Germans were not here to kill; they were simply keeping order, guarding the train. In the distance, she could see bees buzzing around white flowers in the apple trees, and warm sun streamed through the open door.

The engine stilled to silence and the steam dissipated from the platform. They must be stopping here for a while. Maya shifted towards the door and let her legs dangle into the fresh air, squinting in the sun. The middle-aged woman leaned her shoulder against the opposite side of the doorway and lit a cigarette. She was not smiling.

A German soldier made his way slowly along the platform towards them. He was young and relaxed, with his rifle casually banging against his shoulder as he walked. As he came within earshot, the woman jerked her thumb towards Maya. '*Jude,*' she said loudly.

Jude. The months and hours of endurance, her love, her grief, her escape – all plummeted together like lead into a single word.

Jew. Pig. Dead.

This second, no more than a heartbeat, no longer than the hundreds of thousands of other seconds that had brought her here, to this train doorway, on this station in east Germany – was this the second her journey came to its end?

Maya watched herself as if from outside her body, her shapely legs dangling out of the door, her Polish clothes crumpled with the journey and her brown eyes looking directly at the German soldier. She smiled. Her beautiful smile.

He smiled back.

Maya grabbed her suitcase and hopped down onto the platform. She put on a Polish accent and asked in German for the way to the bathroom. When she returned, she walked quickly to another carriage at the far end of the train. No one looked up as she entered. She sat on her hands to calm their trembling and prayed that the woman would not come to seek her out. But she saw her toss her cigarette onto the tracks; the smoke curled towards the sky as the engine juddered back to life and sped her on her journey to the heart of Germany.

Sydney, November 1995

'I remember the first thing I noticed about Germany after I arrived was that there was no barbed wire,' said Maya. 'I was no longer a Jew; I was a Polish farm girl. There were people everywhere – thousands and thousands of them, from Russia and Poland, Hungary, Croatia. They were from countries all over Europe, all of the vanquished nations, people coming to Germany for work because staying at home was not an option.'

'Did that Polish woman find you again?'

'No, God must have been on my side. That woman was scared too. I forgave her straight away. I was too concerned with speaking my best Polish.'

Kate could not imagine how frightened Maya must have been. A Czech Jewish teenager, whose life depended on people thinking she was Polish.

'And people never suspected anything because of your accent?'

'Oh, I told them I came from a small village on the Polish–Czech border,' Maya said. 'I was sent to work on a farm in Westphalia. The husband was away fighting with the German army, and his wife was trying to manage the children and the farm by herself. I had to learn to milk a cow! It was dangerous trying to pass as Polish, yes, but they were kind enough. No one questioned where I was from.'

Kate looked up from her notepad. She realised Maya was crying. She reached out and took her friend's hand, as she had so many times before, when the memories became too much.

'I was all alone. When I hurt my hand and it became infected, the farmer's wife took me to the hospital at a local convent. She left me there. I remember –' Maya swallowed a sob '– it was the first time I really understood that my mother was gone. I felt so unwell and there was no one who cared about me, other than Jan.'

'And did you have contact with him during all that time?'

'Yes, we wrote to each other every day. The Germans maintained a very efficient postal service, you know. And then ...' Maya trailed off. 'And then ... that's when I got the letter.'

Kate knew which letter Maya meant – the one she had shown her the first time they met. She pulled the envelope from her folder and handed it to Maya, who held it to her heart.

May 1944

Maryska, my love, my dearest

This may be my last letter. The Germans have suffered heavy losses and Chelm will soon be conquered by the Red Army. The Russians have already crossed the River Bug and I can hear the bombardment in the distance. It seems the Third Reich is over, the time is near.

My darling Maya, you must wait for me where you are. For now you are safe at the convent. We do not know what will happen. Soon there will be no mail, no travel, no order. But I will come for you. I promise I will come. Believe in this.

Dance for me, sing for me. Stay strong, my love. This is our final test. I love you.

For ever

Jan

'We had already been apart a whole year, I knew I could wait a little longer. I decided to do what he said, to stay strong. For as long as it took until we could be together again.'

When Kate arrived home, the light on her answering machine was flashing. It was Claire, her colleague from SBS TV, asking her to return her call. Kate stood bolt upright. She had forgotten about Claire and her trip to Poland to search the archives.

'I've got something for you.' Claire said when she answered the phone. Maya could hear the pleasure in her voice. 'Here in my hand I'm holding a record of a Jan Novak who's a retired officer of the Polish army. It's all in Polish, but I have the translations. I can send them over tomorrow.'

Kate stared at the phone in disbelief.

'He was stationed at Chelm and Gdansk, and now he lives in a city called Lublin. It's in the east of Poland, maybe an hour or so from Chelm and the area you've been researching.'

Oh my God. It had to be him.

'I didn't get the chance to visit there, but I found a great fixer in Warsaw who did some hunting for me.'

'And?' Kate forgot her nausea in her excitement.

'Have you got a pen?' said Claire triumphantly. 'Because here's the family's address.'

39

My darling Jan

She says we have found you. I can hardly believe it! A letter – a real letter, rather than these constant ramblings of mine – is on its way to Poland as we speak.

And for the first time in this search, I find myself afraid.

Will I recognise you? Will you stand there with your blue eyes and delicate nose, smiling your broad smile? Will those cheeks that shone red with the cold now be wrinkled and worn? Will you limp and stoop?

You and I spent such a short time together really, not even two years. I am not sure whether we are still the same people we were back then. When I think of those days, it is as if I am watching a different Maya, hardly me.

I have remembered it all with such sentimentality, like a dream. Now it will again be real. We supported each other through life and death, you risked your life so many times for mine. But I have no knowledge of what happened to you after that. You probably married, had children and grandchildren. I know there is a chance you forgot me.

Jan, will you remember me?

Soon I will find this out, my darling. The time has nearly come.

Sydney, November 1995

Kate felt another wave of nausea. She left Maya to visit the bathroom. She was not sure she could continue the interview today.

Maya seemed to understand. When Kate came back, she handed her a cup of peppermint tea. 'Sit, eat something,' she muttered as she plumped a cushion for her. For a second, Kate felt like a little girl, waiting for her mother to bustle in with a thermometer.

'I'm okay, I think. Let's carry on.'

'No, no, not now.' Maya smiled at her sweetly. 'Kate, you have done your job. You have found Jan. We just wait now. He will write back to us, I am sure. But now it is your time to talk. Tell me, what is wrong?'

'I feel a little sick, that's all.'

Maya nodded, but said nothing, waiting for Kate to speak. Kate lowered her eyes. 'Maya, I've made a terrible mistake. I think I'm going to have a baby.'

Maya smiled. 'Oh, I could see that.' There was no judgement; no desire for further information.

'I don't know what to do.' Kate spoke in a small voice. She could not see how she could make this work, on her own in Sydney, on a young journalist's salary.

'Well, you must love your baby!' Maya's face lit up. 'I never wanted children of my own. I have seen the children of my friends, the burden they carry, the responsibility of replacing everything that their parents lost. They grow up believing the world to be a dangerous place. Sometimes they buckle under the weight of proving it was all worthwhile. But you are young, Kate. You have nothing to fear.' She clapped her hands together. 'And of course – you have me.'

Westphalia, Germany, July 1945

Maya looked at herself in the mirror. She was nineteen now, but a woman twice that age stared back at her. Her face was blotchy and her eyes dark and sunken. Narrow, dry lips; mouth set and hard. Her hair was cropped short in a boyish style. She combed it through with her fingers, red and cracked from the laundry, trying to fashion it into a softer shape, then leaned closer and peered at her reflection, her nose nearly touching the glass, staring directly into her large brown eyes. They were empty.

For more than a year she had hidden here, like a mouse surrounded by snakes. She mostly worked in the hospital laundry, dragging heavy sheets stained with blood and excrement across the cold stone floor and hauling them into a massive vat of boiling water. The work was heavy and hot, her days shrouded in steam, but it was better than the camp in Sawin. The nuns were kind. They never asked where she came from. They believed she was Maria, a Polish farm girl. She had never had to tell them who she really was. A Jew. *Jude*. Perhaps they understood it was better not to ask.

But the strain of pretence weighed heavily on her. Every moment, every day, she watched her words, carefully mangling her educated German into the broken syllables of a Polish Catholic girl trying to speak a foreign language. The first mass was the worst. She knelt in the hard wooden pew, her eyes darting right and left as she tried not to let them see she was copying, mimicking the movements of their whispering lips and gentle hands. At times, now, she almost believed her own pretence.

She looked through the little window of her room at the top of the convent tower. Outside, a shimmer of dawn promised to illuminate the night sky. The grey pine forest beyond the fields was deathly quiet, anticipating the new day. Soon the sun would be up and the *ratter-tatter* of German guns would echo in the distance, drowning out the birdsong. But for now, just for a few minutes, she could remember what the world was like when it was still.

She had not heard from Jan for many months. She made herself believe it was the postal service; that he was busy fighting with the AK.

He would come for her. He was coming. Now. Soon.

She pulled on her jacket. Her finger ran over the letter 'P' stitched onto the lapel: Polish worker. She thought of the blue coat she had brought from home in Brno, the Star of David stitched in the same position. She had kept her secret well.

The pre-dawn air was damp and cool. It was impossible to see her feet on the dark, narrow stairs as she descended towards the laundry, running a hand along the smooth wall to guide her way. It was a Sunday, but still there was washing to be done. Last night, as every night, Allied planes had flown over Welver, high in the sky like defecating birds. When the sirens sounded, she had rushed to the ward to help the nuns convey the injured patients to a bunker underneath the hospital. It was a slow process. Many of them were young, just boys really, the broken remnants of Hitler's youth, waging a losing war. She felt a glimmer of pity. They were German too, but they were not to blame.

Bombs were falling every day now. When the bombardment started, she had climbed onto the roof with one of the nuns, carrying a pot of red paint and a paintbrush precariously up an ancient ladder. Maya had painted a large red cross across the grey tiles. It had taken all morning. The hospital still had not been hit, and now she was almost used to the drone of the *Tiefflieger*, the planes flying low, the anticipation before the thud and plume of smoke from the town. The nuns shook their heads and prayed for deliverance from beneath their stiff cornettes, the starched white cloth folding away from their faces like angels' wings. But Maya secretly welcomed the bombs. When the walls shook and shavings of plaster fell from the ceiling, she would run back to her eyrie and gaze out of the window, willing the Allies to come, to end the war. Only that would bring Jan back to her.

She reached the laundry and quickly set to work. She stoked the fire under a copper vat and waited for the water to boil. Once it was hot, she hauled bloody sheets from a huge tub where they had soaked overnight and lugged them, streaming pink water, into the boiling cauldron. She could hear singing from the chapel, the sweet lifting of women's voices. This morning the sound made her stomach clench, and her hand trembled a little as she wiped the sweat from her forehead.

Today she was going to confess. Mother Superior had invited her because of her devotion, observing how Maya sat in the chapel alone, sometimes for hours. She went there every day, seeking out the solitude, the smell of the wax and the flickering candles. She would gaze at the Virgin Mary, her namesake, and share the sorrow in her eyes. She prayed to the trees and the woods and the birds outside the window – please, please, let this end. To be invited to confess was a sign of the nuns' trust and respect, a forbidden privilege for a slave labourer. How could she decline?

She stumbled over a broom as she moved around the steamy room and made herself sit down, be calm. She knew what to do. Yes, she could do it. It was just a matter of getting it right.

She thought back to before the war, to her real life, when Omi and her mother had sent her to take lessons from the Catholic priest in Brno. Maya thought of her twelve-year-old self, how bored she had been as the old priest intoned and prayed. She strained to remember those lessons now, his gestures and calm words, and knew they might save her life.

When it was time to go, she wiped her chapped hands and made her way through the chilly stone corridors to the chapel. She yearned to tell her heavy secret to the unseen Father behind the screen. The burden of concealing her true identity hung from her like lead, the guilt that she was not who these kind nuns thought she was. She imagined herself entering the confessional, finally speaking in normal German, letting her words flood out, saying that she was Maya, a Jew, here in their midst. Sister Oberta hurried past her in the corridor, smiling, as if she could see through to her soul.

Maya turned into the chapel and sat on a cold wooden pew, waiting for her turn. She clasped her hands in her lap and silently rehearsed what she would say. She thought of the other women who had sat here on this hard seat, waiting to confess their desires and jealousies. 'Hear, Oh Israel, the Lord is our God.' The ancient words popped into her head and she felt her throat constrict. She had never practised her own religion, but the *Shema* spoke to her now, the prayer of her people.

The large chapel door burst open with a rush of air. '*Schnell*, Maria! Come quickly, we need your help!' It was Sister Magdalene, dragging a massive white sheet. For a moment, Maya thought there must be a problem with the laundry. The nun was talking quickly. '*Die Alliierten sind da!*' she exclaimed. 'The Allies have arrived! Quickly, help me carry this sheet to your room.'

Maya slumped under the weight as they wrestled the sheet up the wooden stairs to the attic. Sister Magdalene pulled a skein of string from the depths of her deep black pocket and together they tied it to each corner of the sheet, then, with difficulty, suspended it from the windowsill.

Outside, Maya could see people running around like ants from a nest kicked open by a boot. A small group of German soldiers stood to one side of the yard. They seemed lost and unsure what to do. Most of them looked no more than fifteen years old.

'They're coming from all directions!' Sister Magdalene cried. Nuns poured out of the doors and into the courtyard, dropping to their knees and crossing themselves. Maya turned to Sister Magdalene, who was also kneeling. She gestured to Maya to join her. '*Holy Mary, pray for us . . .*'

Without thinking, Maya recited the words, repeating the Catholic prayer over and over as her war ended outside the window.

40

Maya turned twenty the month that atom bombs fell on Japan and the war exploded into peace. That evening, she celebrated alone, sitting on her creaking metal bed and thinking of the birthdays she had had before. Franz, Omi, Erna and Pavel, her mother – all gone. She had not realised how deeply she felt their absence. There was still no word from Jan. She yearned for him, to be held by him. It was impossible to imagine a life without him.

She started to cry, quietly and controlled at first, silent sobs shaking her shoulders. 'I am completely, utterly alone,' she said aloud. 'There is no one, not one person, who cares.'

For the first time since she had left her childhood home in Brno, she allowed herself to wail – a birthday present to herself. The intensity of the sound shocked her for a moment. It came from deep inside, surprisingly high-pitched, hardly human. She wailed for Jan and for the future with him she knew she would not have. She threw herself on the bed, pounded her heels against the wooden wall, furious, wild. She wailed for them all, the people who had gone, for their suffering and their ferocious endurance. She wailed for her mother and for the fact she could not remember her gentle face. But most of all, she wailed for herself – for the injustice that, after all of this, she was facing the horror of still being alive when they were not.

After a few minutes, she caught her breath and realised she was bored with crying. She wiped her sleeve across her eyes, blew her nose and sat down at the small wooden desk in the corner. She smoothed a sheet of writing paper and took out her pen. How many times had she written to his parents' house in Chelm? She had received nothing in reply. This would be the last letter to which she would attach a return address.

'I have looked for you, my love,' she wrote. 'I have contacted the Red Cross in Soest, but they say there is no communication with Poland. Now I have the opportunity to leave. You gave me my life, and now I must take it. Please understand I do this for you. I believe and trust that you will find me, as you promised. I will always love you.'

She licked the envelope and pressed her lips in a kiss against the seal. Then she reached for a form in her bag. Her emigration papers. The form was thin and it rustled as she flattened it out on the desk in front of her. She started to fill it in, carefully and neatly.

After a few minutes she hesitated, her pen in mid-air. She had to state her preferred destination. She thought of her Czech homeland, full of ghosts. Poland, cold and grey, a place of danger and despair. She thought of trees and sunshine. Of great, blue, open skies, of space and freedom.

She thought of the globe in Omi's front room. How as a child she had traced her fingers across the coloured countries as it spun. She thought of a country that was as far away as possible from Europe. A country where she and Jan had once imagined themselves with the kangaroos.

'Australia,' she wrote, and smiled.

Sydney, December 1995

Maya phoned Kate in excitement. 'A letter has arrived. From Poland. Come here, we will open it together.'

'No, open it now! What does it say?' Kate could not contain her impatience. At last! The story would have a conclusion.

There was a pause on the end of the line as Maya read. Then a sigh. 'Would you like me to translate?'

'Yes! Quickly! Have we found him?'

Maya translated every word.

Lublin, December 1995

Dear Maya,

Thank you for your letter to me. I was very surprised to hear from you after all these years. I remember you very well. Both my mother and brother were very fond of you, in the short time that we knew you.

I am afraid to tell you that my brother Jan died in the Warsaw uprising sometime in September or October 1944. We do not know exactly when he died or the manner of his death. His body was never returned to us and we did not hear from him again. We assume they disposed of the corpse along with those of many thousands of other people who died in Warsaw at that time.

I am very sorry to hear that you are unwell and I wish you all the best. Please accept the love and warmth of the Novak family.

Yours sincerely

Danuta Kowalski (nee Novak)

'Oh Maya, I'm so sorry.' Kate imagined her story fluttering away out of the window.

Maya sighed. The phone crackled in the silence. At last she spoke.

'Oh no, do not believe that.' Her voice was bright. 'Because Jan is alive.'

41

My darling Jan

Of course I have always known there was a chance you were dead. I am not stupid; far from it. Do you think through my career at the High Court, through those years of travelling and my laughter-filled life, that I did not acknowledge the possibility? Oh, I understand the world and what it can do.

At first I was detached. When existence was still a matter of life and death, I accepted the loss of you day after day until it became normal. I had to keep going, never give up. I learned to look for beauty around me.

Afterwards, it was as if it had happened to someone else. I watched Maya and Jan as if through water. I did not allow myself to feel, not really. It was the only way.

It was easier to forget when I came to Australia. The sea, the sun. The beautiful young people, so sure of their invincibility. Like Kate now, learning to dance. She is so . . . vital.

You see, I am still surviving, Jan. I survive every second of every day. The wounds will never heal, but I have learned how to endure them.

As a teenager I chose life. I wanted to survive. And all these years I have done so because of you.

So it really does not matter to me whether you are alive or dead. I can feel you still. You might as well be in the next room.

You are my reason why.

Sydney, December 1995

The summer day clung to the Sydney streets like a wet sheet, steaming up windows and trickling down the sides of glasses. Kate opened the front door to a crescendo of cicadas. Their metallic noise beat down on her head like little hammers.

She was not long out of bed, the cover still musty with last night's sweat as she had tossed and turned, the fan bathing her toes in strokes of cool air. Her decision had swooped around her head for hours; the thought of it made her want to cry.

She retrieved the newspaper from the doorstep and made herself a black tea to calm her nausea. A portrait of Maya was on the front page of the Saturday magazine. Inside, they had devoted 3000 words to Kate's story. Not her intended news story of the grand reunion between Maya and Jan, but a good story, nonetheless. The editor had rung her personally after Kate had filed. It was one of the most beautifully written features he had ever read, he'd said.

Last night, her new friends had joined her in the pub. They were officially celebrating the end of her mammoth and ultimately unsuccessful investigation, but it felt more like a farewell. 'Now perhaps we'll finally get a story on the government's new multiculturalism agenda,' Jackson had joked. Dan had arrived, and held her gaze longer than was necessary as he toasted her with a beer. Eleanor had covered for her when she refused alcohol, and steadfastly refused to judge her when they spoke quickly in the bathroom. If it hadn't been for her situation, Kate realised, she would have finally had a social life to look forward to.

She flicked through the magazine pages to find the story. Her eyes lingered for a second on her by-line before she skimmed the familiar words, printed and real, here in black and white. They were Maya's words. It was her story, not Kate's.

She put down the magazine and sipped her tea. Next to it on the coffee table lay her most recent bank statement. She had scanned it many times; the figures had not changed. Without an income, she simply would not be able to care for a baby. Eleanor had promised her support, but what did that mean, in a practical sense? None of her new friends knew anything about taking care of a child. If she became a single mother here, she really would have to do it on her own.

Her hand wandered to her belly, taut and bloated, and she imagined the tiny heartbeat within. *I'll look after you*, she promised silently. It was all that mattered.

She stood quickly and picked up a cardboard box; she might as well start packing. She swept into it her papers and the six full notepads that contained Maya's testimony, now transcribed and sent to the Jewish Museum. She would take them with her. She found Peter's letter, still on the mantlepiece under a stack of old papers and magazines. She ran her finger over his familiar black handwriting. It was her last piece of him. 'His loss.' She shrugged as she tore it up and threw it in the bin.

She would book the ticket on Monday. There really was no choice. She was going back to England.

∼

Maya had wanted to meet her by the sea. As Kate's bus rounded the bend to Bondi, she gasped at the depth of the blue where the ocean met the sky. Girls in bikinis lay on the bright sand; surfers veered across the edge of the relentless waves, shooting sparkling spray into the air.

She alighted and saw Maya waiting for her on the grass. She was walking in circles with her arms clasped behind her back, as if searching for something on the ground. As Kate grew closer, she could see Maya's lips moving slightly as she seemed to play out a conversation in her mind.

'Look at the colours!' Maya exclaimed when she noticed Kate, gesturing towards the sand and sky.

They embraced, as they always did now, and sat on a bench. Seagulls swooped overhead and a pigeon strutted at their feet, pecking at crumbs. Kate flattened the Saturday magazine onto Maya's lap and pointed to the pictures. Jan looked up at them, still staring uncomfortably at the camera; still smoking with friends in the ditch in Sawin.

'You did a good job. It is what I needed to say.' Maya put down the magazine when she had finished and gazed at the sea. 'Now, we can concentrate on getting to know each other more. I will buy you a season pass to the Australian Ballet.'

'Maya.' Kate was not sure she'd be able to find the words. 'I have something to tell you. I can't manage it here on my own, on a junior journalist's salary. I'm going to have to go back to my parents' house in England. I told them last night and they weren't happy, but I think they'll come around. It's their grandchild, after all.'

Maya turned to her and smiled. Her beautiful smile.

Kate felt her throat catch. 'I'm so sorry to leave you,' she said.

'Oh now, now. To know you has already been a gift,' Maya said gently. 'Oh! Look!'

A small plane was crawling across the sky, leaving dissipating plumes of white skywriting against the blue. It neared the zenith and Kate realised it was drawing a love heart.

'How extraordinary!' Maya laughed. 'Do not be sad. Go and love your little baby. And know that I will always, always be all right. How can I explain? They took everything from me but my choice to love my life, whatever shape it takes. And that is the choice I made long ago.'

Kate's chin wobbled. Maya took her hand.

'Look at me, Kate. Here, with you, today, on this beautiful grass by the ocean, I am alive.'

42

My darling Jan

This is my first letter to you since I left Europe. I do not have your address, my love. I will keep it safe until we see each other again.

First, I must tell you that I am married. Yes! It happened quickly, I admit. It was just one more chapter in my escape.

I met Edward in the distribution office in Westphalia. He stamped my emigration papers and then asked me out to dinner. He is a Jewish academic and joined the British army; he landed in Normandy on D-Day. He studied at Oxford and writes me letters in the style of the Romantics. He told me that, as his wife, I could come with him to England. I knew I could not stay in Europe. Communism had arrived in the Czech Republic and Poland. I could not live under another 'ism'. I did not hesitate to accept his proposal.

We married in a registry office in north London and settled into a little flat in Golders Green. The ability to find joy returned slowly to me. For the longest time, I looked at a flower or a brightly coloured bird with no emotion. But then, gradually, these things ignited a spark in me again. Edward took me to hear Yehudi Menuhin play at the Albert Hall. It was as the music washed over me that I realised, for the first time, that the Nazis were fading into the past.

Together we travelled to the Czech Republic to look for my family, but none of them had survived. My cousins, my aunts, my Uncle Emil – all gone. We visited Omi's apartment and I could not stand its emptiness. But I was thrilled to discover our neighbour, Mrs Černý, was still there. She did not recognise me at first. But guess what? My mother had left her most valuable jewellery in Mrs Černý's care when we left. The old lady still had it – a solitaire diamond ring, a delicate diamond and pearl brooch, a diamond bracelet and a string of pearls. It was enough riches for Edward and me to plan a comfortable future. I sold some of the pieces, but I kept the diamond bracelet. I shall never take it off.

We arrived in Sydney in 1949. This city is truly beautiful, Jan. I woke at dawn as the SS Toscana sailed into Sydney Harbour, the steam rising above the lapping dark blue water. I could not believe the brightness of the sun after London's rain. There were whole rows of salami hanging from the ceiling in the David Jones food hall! So much food, when Europe still has so little.

We were supported by Jewish Care and found a little bedsit in Paddington. I was delighted to discover there was a sizeable Jewish community already living in Sydney's eastern suburbs. But despite my fluent English, I have not been able to find the words to discuss my experiences with them. How do you explain what it is for your whole life to be wiped out? One day, I bought a loaf of bread and saw the shopkeeper's shoulders shrug. 'We suffered too,' he muttered. Some of them are worried our arrival from Europe will stoke anti-Semitism in Australia. Others simply do not believe me. Oh, the arrogant naivety of people who have never experienced fear.

Yet, Jan, with this sense of otherness comes strength. I have important skills now, an acute sense of who to trust, a heightened perception of people's goodness or badness.

I have made a decision to see the good. In time, I will heal.

Sydney, December 1999

Kate opened the front door to a rush of heat. Empty cardboard boxes and discarded tinsel littered the front porch, the detritus of a sweaty Christmas – the last of the millennium. Her heart lifted towards the endless blue Sydney sky as she navigated the stroller through the gate and set off up the hill.

It was too hot, and Kate was too tired, to work today. She was the mother of a three year-old now, but Stella still was not sleeping through. At last Kate had given in, carried her into bed and sought a restless sleep curled around her daughter's warm, writhing body. From five in the morning they had sat together in the living room, watching the Teletubbies as the first light brightened the curtains and the birds started to sing. She had cancelled her interviews today and they were going to the beach, mother and daughter, to enjoy the sunshine.

Stella's feet bounced up and down in front of her as the stroller rattled over the uneven pavement. Sometimes, Kate thought she could glimpse Tomas in her daughter's laugh, but, to be honest, she did not have a clear memory of how he looked.

The week after the story about Maya was published, the editor of the weekend magazine had called Kate at work. 'A position has become available. We'd love to take on a strong writer like you.'

Kate had gone to meet her. The job was perfect. No more fleeting news stories, but the chance to get her teeth into real investigations, and to hone her writing skills. Plus it meant a substantial pay rise.

'There's a problem – I'm going to need maternity leave,' Kate had said.

'We really are very keen for you to join us,' the editor had replied. 'We'd be happy for you to work from home for as long as you need to.'

The baby came into the world on a crisp, sunny day in June. Kate had been floored by the passion with which she loved her daughter; it had a primal ferocity that overwhelmed her. Birthing a child connected her somehow to all the women who had gone before – Rosa; Erna, in a wood loft; her own mother. She had held the warm bundle tightly and marvelled at her tiny, perfect nose and mouth. This was her greatest achievement. It was why she was alive.

The day after Stella was born, Maya had visited them in hospital. She held the baby in her arms and whispered to her in German as Stella

gazed back intently into her eyes. The two of them had been insepara-
ble since. Maya was the only person, other than Kate, who could calm
Stella's screaming in those early days. Stella would melt into her, her ear
to Maya's heart, and shut her eyes as Maya sang gentle Jewish lullabies.
Maya had visited nearly every day to help during the first few months;
Kate could not have done it without her.

Now it was becoming harder for Maya to navigate the journey from
the north shore to Darlinghurst; there had definitely been a deteriora-
tion this year. Kate visited her as often as she could, but she was worried.

The hill was steep, and her face was red by the time they reached
Oxford Street and set off past the still-closed shops towards the bus
stop. Kate caught her reflection in the window. Hair tied back, no
make-up, clothes thrown on in the few seconds available to her while
Stella was preoccupied. A momentary spark of elation at seeing herself
in the window as a mother was, as always, tinged with disappointment
that she was doing this alone.

Her parents' silent fury with her had not abated. They had agreed
to help her financially – living in Sydney was far from cheap – but
they had shown little interest in their granddaughter. Her mother had
once sent a birthday card and a wrapped wooden rattle, but it was for a
child far younger than Stella. Kate phoned dutifully to give her mother
updates on Stella's progress, but the calls were clearly a chore for both of
them. It was months since she had spoken to her father. Maya seemed
more like family now than they did.

Once they reached the beach, Kate unbuckled Stella from the
stroller. There were screaming toddlers everywhere, running at full pelt
across the sand, laughing and crying, squealing with delight or wailing
in outrage. The mothers were in groups, talking and talking, pausing
only to draw breath or to peer down the back of their children's nappies.
They smiled at Kate. She was one of them.

She sat alone and opened the paper while Stella played, glancing up
frequently to check her daughter was safe. Kate felt it was important
to keep up with current affairs – though, in reality, nothing seemed to

matter anymore outside the world she had built with Stella. She was secure in a circle of good friends now, which had expanded beyond her single work colleagues in ways she could not have predicted. Having a baby had brought her into the embrace of the working mothers in the office, who held her up with supportive hands and endless cups of tea. Their conversation veered from politics to their husbands' habits; endless details of sleep or toileting; laughter and raucous accounts of pub visits back in the days, long ago, before they had children.

Stella made her way towards her across the beach. She patted her hands on Kate's thighs. Clumps of wet sand stuck to Kate's shorts and fell onto the towel. She pulled a wet wipe out of her bag from amid a jumble of juice bottles, nappies and screwed-up tissues, and firmly wiped the sand and snot from her daughter's face. Stella's thin blonde hair bounced around her head in soft curls, blowing away from her face in the breeze. She smiled at Kate with straight little teeth. Her features were as familiar to Kate as her own. Every eyelash and blemish, the shape of her mouth, the slant of her nose – Kate loved them all.

∽

Maya stepped out of the shower, towelled her hair dry and glanced down at her naked body. It looked as if it were sinking into itself, the skin on her once-strong legs now sagging like old elastic and her stomach creased with wrinkles. Her breasts hung low like pendulous papayas. She laughed at herself. Who would have thought she would one day grow to be this old? She squeezed a dab of toothpaste onto her toothbrush and set to work inside her mouth. Funny, how she could mark out her whole life through the daily brushing of teeth. Every morning, every evening. Brush the left side first, then the right – a sequence taught to her by her cousin Irena during her first year of dentistry in Prague. Upper front and back. Then the bottom. Brush each facet of the tooth, do not forget the back of the molars. Spit, rinse and brush again. Every morning and every evening, all these years, though now more awkwardly, with arthritic hands. Their toothbrushes had not lasted long in the camp. In the end, they had just used sticks and water, or a finger, trying to scrape off the worst. Her teeth had survived, somehow, though they were now yellow and cracked. Her gums had never recovered. She spat and ran her tongue around her mouth.

She walked back to the bedroom and saw with surprise that her clothes were laid out on the bed. Had she already done that, before she went to the bathroom? The limp blouse and skirt looked strange, she could not be sure they were hers. She picked them up and held them to her cheek. Yes, they were hers all right. She laid them back down and felt at a loss – how to put them on?

How boring it was, to be at the mercy of her deteriorating mind. It made her feel pointless, this slow descent into chaos. She had trouble distinguishing day from night now; one hour faded into the next – she could no longer tell them apart. It was as if time had become a rushing river that was sweeping her along. She would sometimes grab onto branches or sticks and slow for a moment, a second of clarity, then away she would rush again while everything blurred. She could not judge the speed of an oncoming car, or remember how to turn on the stove. She felt as if she were sinking in quicksand.

It took her several attempts to line up her buttons correctly. How small her achievements were these days.

A framed photograph of Kate and Stella smiled at her from the dressing table. She remembered how much she loved that little girl. The happiness of feeling a beating heart beneath another's skin.

Finally dressed, Maya felt her way along the wall of the hallway. She could not trust her feet to guide her anymore, and the hall opened before her like a dark tunnel. She sighed with relief when she reached the bright living room. The mantle clock ticked heavily into the quiet. Its regularity calmed her.

A lifetime of possessions covered every surface and wall. Masks from Africa and prints from India. Moroccan lanterns and colourful scarves; on every windowsill pots filled with plants, reaching towards the light. The familiarities of her life, though she felt increasingly removed from them. It was as if they were memories of someone else, someone stronger.

Her past gnawed inside her like a living organism, but her whole life she had tried not to let it influence the present. Since her arrival in Sydney, she had been driven to learn, to eke the most out of every experience, to do the opposite of what people expected of her. She had exercised every day, pushing her body to the limits of its capabilities. And then there had been music – always music. How she had danced and sung.

It was a path that Edward had not been able to follow. He could not stand the disbelief in Sydneysiders' eyes, let alone their pity. He never learned to stifle the trauma as Maya had done and, as the years went on, it tinged every part of his life. While Maya strove for happiness, he slumped into depression. Then came the drinking. She made up her mind that enough was enough and closed the door behind her for the last time. She was alone with nothing again, but this time she knew she could manage by herself.

Maya ran her hand across the glass of a photograph on the mantlepiece. It showed her second husband, Izsak. He was Hungarian, fifteen years older than her, a teacher who had shared her love of music. She had curled on his lap as they listened to Tchaikovsky above the sound of the waves in their little cottage on Sydney's northern beaches. He had showed her the world; had held her hand as they climbed down the banks of the Ganges and felt cool water rush past their thighs, heady with the smell of incense and yellow flowers. Until that moment it had been hard to maintain her faith in God, but in India she found a glimpse of peace.

They had separated as good friends after ten years, and she had set off around the world alone. Travelling as a single woman in the 1970s was terrifying, but it also gave her a sense of total freedom. No one knew who she was, where she was going or from where she had come. She was just a speck in the universe, watching in awe as it unfolded around her.

How vivid those memories were.

The clock was still ticking. Maya sat on the sofa in front of a silent television. A picture of Glen smiled at her from the top of the set. The husband who had stuck. They had married in their fifties and had enjoyed fifteen good years together. He had discouraged her from looking back, from even talking about the camp. He thought the memories would be too painful. It had annoyed her at first, and she thought for a while she would have to leave. Yet he had held her tightly when she tossed and moaned in the night, when she could not escape the memories.

She remembered with a jolt now that he was dead. How could she have forgotten something like that, even for a moment? But, then, she had always known he would die. They always did.

She pulled a blanket over her knees, despite the December heat. She was still Maya; she was still happy. She did not know whether she had fulfilled her purpose, but she had certainly tried.

'I did it, didn't I?' she said, and realised, as always, that she was talking to Jan.

43

Sydney, December 1999

Stella was asleep when they arrived at the geriatric clinic. Kate gently unfastened the car restraint and lifted her daughter into the stroller. Stella was heavy with sleep, a thread of snot streaked across her cheek.

They passed through sliding doors to the brightly lit lobby. Kate had been here for the newspaper before, but never on personal business. There were elderly people everywhere. Last time they had just been a crowd of obstacles as she rushed to see the person she had come to interview. Now she realised each of them had their own story.

She found the specialist's rooms and they waited. Stella woke up and started to chatter. She toddled around the room, knocking magazines onto the floor and refusing to be pacified by the muted daytime television on the wall. Kate was relieved when the doctor finally called her in.

'Hugh Hanley.' He extended his hand in welcome. 'What can I do for you?' He was grey-haired and kindly. Probably not much younger than the patients he treated.

'I'm here to see you about my friend,' said Kate. 'She's a patient of yours, Maya Schulze-Johnson. I'm worried about her.'

'Your friend?' He scanned the notes in the file on his desk.

'Yes, she has no surviving family. There's really no one to look out for her other than me.' She glanced at Stella, who was trying to climb

283

onto the doctor's examination bed. 'I'm doing what I can, but she's definitely declining and I feel like she needs more dedicated care than I can give.' She offered Stella a biscuit, which the little girl held aloft like a prize.

The doctor looked sympathetic. 'Look, I can only discuss her medical details with the next of kin. Does she have a guardianship arrangement in place? If not, I'd suggest that's something you should think about organising as soon as possible. But I can talk to you in general terms. What's the issue?'

'She's been managing well on the whole, but she's often quite confused. She gets really anxious sometimes, like when someone knocks on the door or if she's feeling hungry. She's repeating herself all the time and she doesn't seem to know what time of day it is. I'm not sure she's eating properly, either.'

'These are all things we see a lot,' said Dr Hanley. 'The path into dementia can be especially difficult for people who've experienced trauma.'

Kate nodded. 'And she seems to be seeing things. It's as if she's hallucinating. She's actually frightened, especially in the evening. She lives on her own and I'm worried about leaving her.'

Dr Hanley wrote in the file then looked up at Kate. 'She'll have compartmentalised her memories when she was well, but now, with the dementia, her defence mechanisms have stopped working. I've seen it often with Holocaust survivors. I once worked with a gentleman who flatly refused to take a shower – it was too triggering for him. And another lady started hoarding food. They'd find it in her pockets every day.'

'You mean she's reliving what happened to her? How awful.' Kate thought about the camp. Maya had spent her entire life looking forwards, burying the memories.

'We can't tell. Sometimes Holocaust survivors with dementia relive the entire experience. Or they can forget it completely. But even without dementia, we know that the survivors tend to suffer nightmares and fear of abandonment as they age.'

'What can I do to help her?'

'That's the problem.' Dr Hanley smiled at her. 'If she's afraid, she'll be finding it hard to trust. What she needs is a family, an environment to make her feel secure and reduce her social isolation. I'd suggest sorting out the legal stuff and getting her on the waiting list for a nursing home.'

Kate thought of her own grandmother, surrounded by the shouts of grotesque old people. The smell of the home.

'I was wondering whether there's something we can give her? Some sort of medication, to calm her down?'

'To be honest, there's not a lot we can do medically. This is more a question for social services. But I'll contact the GP and perhaps you can bring her back to see me.' He must have seen the urgency on Kate's face. 'I'll see if I can fit her in before New Year's. Now, you'd better take your little girl home before she completely wrecks my rooms.'

Dr Michael Robinson
General Practitioner
St Leonards
RE: Mrs Maria Schulze-Johnson, D.O.B. 25/08/1925
Dear Dr Robinson
I reviewed the case of your patient Mrs Schulze-Johnson today. Her memory has clearly deteriorated and she is finding it increasingly difficult to manage alone.

Her companion reported that Mrs Schulze-Johnson is very restless in the evenings, but there did not appear to be overt depressive or psychotic symptoms.

I suggested that Mrs Schulze-Johnson might like to try zopiclone to calm her in the evening and ensure a good night's sleep.

I discharge Mrs Schulze-Johnson back to your care. If she should develop any further behavioural or psychological symptoms of dementia, please refer her back to me.
Dr Hugh Hanley
Geriatrician

44

Sydney, December 1999

It was one day before the end of the millennium, and Stella and Kate were caught in the rain. Grey clouds pounded together, and the first squall spattered against the windowpanes. In seconds, fat raindrops were bouncing off the front path; rivulets of water teemed over twigs and rocks. The sky went black, and sparks of distant lightening lit the sky. Stella laughed out loud, holding her face upwards with her mouth open wide.

Kate's fingers shook as she tried to unlock the front door, but not from the storm. She had taken Maya to see the GP. It had not gone well. Maya had looked horrified when he closed the door, and was too distracted to answer his questions. Kate thought he would call social services right there and then, but he had just prescribed her a sedative and told Kate to keep in touch.

Stella laughed as Kate pulled off her sodden T-shirt and leggings. Kate undid her little shoes – Stella's first proper sandals – and wrapped her in the largest towel she could find in her disorganised linen cupboard. Thunder ripped the sky and she held Stella close.

Her tears came then; they dripped onto the towel as she cuddled her daughter. Self-pity and guilt, a million thoughts of what Maya had been through – but, more than that, the cold fear of what the future might hold.

She had Stella to think of now. She knew how dementia progressed – the carers often fared worse than the patients. The stress. The responsibility of it.

'Pull yourself together, Kate,' her mother's voice whispered in her ear.

With her free hand, she grabbed a tissue from her bag and blew her nose. There was only one person she wanted to talk to. She reached for the phone and dialled Maya's number.

The answering machine answered as usual in the voice of Maya's late husband. Kate waited for the husky message to finish before the beep.

'Hi, Maya, it's Kate. Give me a call. Just remember you need to put a nine in front of my number now, it's different to what you've got written in your book. Okay, talk soon.'

The mantlepiece above the empty fireplace – where once had sat Peter's now long-forgotten letter – was crammed with photos of Stella. One of them, taken by a photographer friend from the newspaper, showed Kate and her daughter looking at each other, laughing. Stella was reaching out to pat Kate's ear, her thin hair slightly matted at the back from the pillow.

It was all right. She had Stella. Perfect Stella.

Kate kissed her daughter's nose, then turned on the television for a moment's peace while she went to the kitchen to pour herself a glass of wine.

∽

Maya heard the phone ringing like distant bells from the convent chapel. The sound had no connection to her life. At last, her husband Glen answered the phone and she could get back to what she was doing.

She was busy staring at the blank wall above the television. It was rustling like a living creature in the luminous grey twilight, the shapes of the wallpaper swirling and merging wildly in and out. The furniture around her was moving too, the muted shapes of chairs and sideboard shifting suddenly in the dark and making her jump. It was all very disorientating.

The rain buffeted the trees outside. It hammered on the ground like the static soundtrack of an old movie. Maya rubbed her upper arms, as if to warm herself.

She could see them clearly now, the people she loved; their shapes took form in the churning wallpaper. She was mesmerised. Yes, they were really there, all of them, dancing together in front of her. Omi cutting into a piece of cake and winking at her as Mrs Meyer chattered. Franz embracing Rosa. He smiled over her mother's shoulder as he rubbed her back. Erna and her babies, rocking gently. And Jan, of course, tall and strong.

The absence of those she loved called to her from every shadow of the room. White memories; skeletons with skin. They were flying around like dazed ghosts.

She caught a fragment of movement from the corner of her eye; it was her dog, Antonín! He was running to and fro, burying his nose in the earth, bottom up and tail wagging. She called out to him in delight, '*Herkommen!* Come here!'

The sound of her own voice shocked her, and the pictures stopped. What was happening to her? She remembered her doctor's words, so long ago, but perhaps this afternoon? 'It's not unusual for someone with dementia to see and hear things that aren't really there. No, they're not necessarily hallucinations, but it might make sense to take a little sedative in the evening to keep you calm. Do you need me to write it all down for you? Is there anyone who can help you manage at home?'

She thought of the cyanide pouch against her skin for those long months in Germany. Each morning never knowing whether this would be the day she would be discovered.

The tiny flicker of trauma that had never gone out exploded again into licking flames. The enormity of her losses – not just her family and her home, but the missed education, the toll on her body, the forfeiture of what could have been. She felt it physically. How could she have imagined a normal life, after all that?

And now this. Her dementia was bringing yet more loss – of dignity, of control. This was the greatest loss of all.

A white pill bottle lay on the table with its contents spilled out in an irregular line. She looked at the pale little spheres against the dark wood. Cyanide? She grappled to remember what they were for.

She picked up a glass, but it was empty. It was an effort to stand up, but she willed her legs to move. They felt heavy as she limped to the kitchen, but soon the blood started to flow and she enjoyed the movement.

Back at her chair, she sat down heavily and counted out the pills. '*Eins, zwei, drei* . . .' How many was she supposed to take? She lifted the first to her mouth and placed it on her tongue.

45

Sydney, December 1999

Maya awoke later, really cold now, shivering. Had she slept? It was pitch black and all she could hear was the roaring of the storm outside the window. She was in the black hole again; the earth was musty and damp. Where was the light?

'Help me,' she whispered, finally.

A shot of lightning momentarily lit up her surrounds; ah, she was in the living room. She rose from her chair and fumbled for the light switch, squinting as the shadows brightened to life.

There were pills on the table in front of her, and a glass half full of water. She felt that she had been here before, sitting in this chair, but it was long ago. She would be a good girl and have another pill.

Her fingers were stiff with cold. She twisted off her rings and put them on the table. She felt hungry – she could not remember when she last ate – but she was always hungry these days, in the camp. She longed for a piece of black bread and watery coffee, but she could not remember the way.

Jan was waiting for her. She brightened now. Yes, that was right, that was what she was doing. She had to get away from this hole, this cold, black hole, and walk to Jan. He had a blue silk dress waiting for her and would hold her tight.

Her yearning for him ran like electricity through her legs and she stood up quickly. Dizziness slapped her around the head. She swam through it, holding onto the back of the sofa – watch out for the barbed wire – as she made her way to the bedroom to find her shoes. But it was too dark.

She felt way her back to the living room again, afraid and cold, but less dizzy now. She would have to walk in bare feet. There was no time to lose – the Commandant could be here any time. He was waiting overhead, outside the door. He had never left, all these years, and now he was coming for her.

She watched her hand fumble with the door handle then open it to the howling wind. She stumbled through, leaving the door gaping wide with the shock of the rain. It was teeming down. She lifted her face to the sky and stood for a moment, fascinated by the raindrops glittering like tiny daggers in the light of the streetlamp as they fell. She pulled her cardigan more tightly around her shoulders and set off down the road. Rivulets of water rushed over her feet and brown leaves and cigarette butts hurtled towards the drains.

She had no sense of where to go, which way to turn, so she headed towards the next streetlamp, at the end of the road. Its hazy yellow light shone weakly through the rain as she walked, keeping to the shadows in case a passing car should see her. Her Polish was not good enough yet, she must talk to nobody. She was surprised how well her legs were working. Her heart pumped warm blood and she knew she was alive.

Beyond the lamp, she could see the inky outline of trees, rustling and bending in the storm. They would offer her protection now, as they always had. She must get to the trees. She stepped towards them, into the lighted area in the middle of the road, then stumbled back as a car veered towards her out of nowhere, bright headlights shining through the rain and wheels splashing a wave of water over her ankles. She landed heavily on the pavement. A sharp pain shot through her hip, but she pulled herself over onto her knees and, using a letterbox for support, stood up on shaky legs.

She knew how to ignore pain. She had lived with it inside her all her life. She kept going.

Her route became clearer once she had crossed the road. There was an opening in the fence and a grassy path led down a hill, down, down through the trees. The stones were sharp under her feet as she set out along the track. By the time the car had completed its U-turn and its headlights lit the street again, she had melted into the shadows of the bush.

‿

She was getting closer to Jan, she could feel it. Though the wind was blowing fiercely and her clothes were soaked, she hardly noticed the storm. It was as if she were walking through the woods on a summer's day, towards Chelm, where he was waiting. Her heart beat fast with anticipation. She had seen him only yesterday, but it seemed like years ago.

The track had become steep, quite treacherous in places, and it was slow going. Her feet were cut and she had lost a toenail on a large rock, but she did not care. She hitched her skirt around her waist and scrambled stiffly over boulders and moss, sliding down on her haunches, supporting herself with her hands. Her hip was sore. She rubbed it through the wet fabric that clung to her skin. It was just a scrape. She thought of their friend in the camp, Mrs Becker. She had fallen into a trench one day and broken her wrist, but no one had taken any notice. She had tried to keep on digging, digging, but soon she was taken away on a cart. No, she must not show any weakness. Her legs were moving fine; she must push on.

By the time she reached the bottom of the embankment, the thunder was further away and the rain was easing. She could make out weak, creamy moonlight around the edges of the clouds. They moved fast across the sky, racing, like her, towards Chelm. She would follow them now; they would lead the way.

There was water here, a river running along the bottom of the gully. The rocks were slippery as she walked into the shallows. It was not frozen, not the water of the trenches. It felt warm as it rushed and tumbled around her bleeding toes. Its music filled her with a feeling she had had before, of safety. Freedom.

Steep cliffs rose above her on either side of the embankment; she could make out the silver bark of towering gum trees in the moonlight. Above her, at the top of the ridge, red and blue lights were flashing, lighting up the trees. She sat down in the water and watched the branches swaying in the wind. They would protect her, they said. She had to get to Jan, but he would wait. It was time to rest now. She shut her eyes and let the water run over her.

$\backsim$

The sun rose the next morning on a world shocked into stillness by the excesses of the previous night's storm. The light glinted off the rain-drops that still clung to the leaves, and tiny swirls of steam lifted off the muddy ground as the December day heated up.

Kate was up before Stella, woken by the ringing of the phone. She stumbled into the living room, tripping over a doll, and saw the answering machine flashing red.

'This is Sergeant Dixon from Gordon police. Could you please call us back as soon as possible.'

Despite herself, her heart jumped with excitement. It was the journalist in her; something was happening. She pressed redial and he answered immediately.

'Ah, thanks for calling.' The sergeant sounded young and earnest. 'Do you know a Maria Schulze-Johnson, also known as Maya Schulze-Johnson?'

'Yes, she's a close friend of mine. Is everything okay?'

'When did you last speak to her?'

'We saw each other yesterday. I tried to call her last night, actually, but she didn't answer. What's going on?'

'We've had a call from a neighbour last night and we attended Mrs Schulze-Johnson's home this morning. We found your number on her answering machine. Do you have any idea where she might be?'

Icy fear clenched in Kate's stomach.

'Oh gosh, no, I have no idea. Sorry.'

'Well, please let us know if you hear from her.'

When she hung up, she felt suspended, unreal. Maya missing? It was unthinkable that something might have happened to her now, in Sydney, where she was supposed to be safe.

She called the police desk at the newspaper. Her colleague James answered, his voice thick with lack of sleep. 'We heard something last night about an elderly lady walking through the streets in Turramurra,' he told her. 'A driver thought he hit her, but by the time he'd got back to the scene she'd disappeared.'

Turramurra was Maya's suburb – it had to be her. Kate put down the phone and went to rouse Stella, but it rang again almost immediately. It was James. 'Yep, I reckon it's her,' he said. 'They've called in police search and rescue.'

Her hands were shaking as she pulled on Stella's shoes. The little girl squirmed and fidgeted, kicking against Kate's hands. 'Stella, hold still!' Kate snapped, more harshly than she had meant to. Her voice sounded distant and cracked.

A police car was parked at the other side of the street as she pulled up outside Maya's house. She unbuckled Stella from the car seat and carried her to join them. 'I'm her daughter,' she lied. 'What's the latest?'

'We reckon there's a possibility she's wandered into the bush,' the officer told her. 'Is there any reason she might have, that you know of? Has anything happened?'

'She has dementia,' Kate said. The police officers nodded and caught each other's eyes. Their radios bleeped and crackled at their hips.

A young officer emerged from the trees. 'Nah, I can't see anyone going down there. Seen how steep it is?'

Kate adjusted Stella's heavy body on her hip and set off down the path. Puddles of water swirled in the yellow-grey clay and stuck to her shoes. She quickly reached the edge of the embankment and saw what he meant – a steep drop fell beneath her, and she could see water glinting at the bottom, at least a hundred metres below. Currawongs called to each other from the tops of the trees. It was another world; wild Australian bush at the edge of suburbia. It could swallow you whole and no one in the street would ever know.

The buzz of a distant helicopter grew louder. The *thunk* of car doors being closed in the distance.

When Kate and Stella got back to the street, more police had arrived. An ambulance and police rescue were there too. Kate's stomach plunged. A few journalists were gathering, but she did not say hello. She caught sight of herself in a car window, looking strained and older somehow. Thinner. A different person. A person whose whole world rested on the fate of another.

She hefted Stella onto her hip and headed for home. There was nothing she could do.

Kate sat with Stella in the living room all day, waiting. Wiggles videos were on endless repeat, a jolly background as Kate's desperation mounted. Eventually, Stella tired and slept, her head buried in a cushion, snoring faintly in the heavy afternoon air. Kate checked the dial tone from time to time, then worried she had missed a call while the receiver had been to her ear.

It was four o'clock when the phone rang. She jumped up to answer it. It was Julia, another colleague from the newspaper, who had arrived for the afternoon shift. Kate pictured her sitting in the little glass office, the chatter and click of the police radio.

'The police have found Maya down by Cowan Creek,' Julia said quickly. 'She's alive. They're looking at winching her out. I'm on my way. Tell me what you know about her.'

Kate was on her feet, the telephone cord pulled to its full extension as she grabbed her car keys. How to describe Maya for a newspaper article? Her love and her losses, her strength, her spirit. All would be boiled down to a single paragraph – a few words to capture this woman whose life, she now realised, meant everything.

She looked out of the window at the glow of the afternoon sun. 'She's a survivor.'

⁓

Maya was sitting up in bed and sipping a steaming cup of tea by the time Kate arrived at the hospital. There was a drip in her arm and her face was bruised; a bandage covered an ankle that stuck out of the sheets. The sun reflected geometric shapes from the window onto the white and blue hospital blanket.

The rescue made the evening news. Kate watched the footage out of the corner of her eye as a nurse busied herself taking Maya's blood pressure. It showed a helicopter winching Maya, strapped to a stretcher and held by the burly arms of a paramedic, high over the rustling leaves of the canyon.

'Maria Schulze-Johnson is a seventy-five-year-old Holocaust survivor,' the newsreader intoned. 'More about her remarkable survival on *A Current Affair* tomorrow.'

'And who is this?' Maya's eyes lit up and her mouth opened wide with surprise when she saw Stella. As always, Kate imagined the teenager she must have been, seeing the hope and excitement beneath those long eyelashes.

'This is Stella, remember? Look at you, covered in bruises!'

Maya put down her cup on the hospital table, shaking slightly and spilling a few drops, but Kate resisted the urge to help her. Stella clambered onto the bed, nestling her face in Maya's armpit.

A large woman wearing grey trousers and a navy cardigan tapped Kate on the shoulder. 'Do you have a moment?' She was carrying a brown folder full of notes and there was a lanyard with her name around her neck: Judith Isles, Social Worker.

'It's remarkable. Apart from some bruising and dehydration, she's actually doing very well.' The social worker's voice was silky and reassuring. 'We're lucky it wasn't cold overnight. She was soaked through. They're treating her for hypothermia and shock, and she's had some medication to control the delirium. But she's going to be fine.'

Kate exhaled in relief. She watched as Stella crawled around the narrow bed, hoisting herself over Maya's knees. Maya was delighted, engrossed as a child with a kitten.

'Our main concern today is her safety,' the social worker went on. 'When something like this happens, we're always very wary about sending someone back to live alone. We need to draw up a plan for her future care. Does she have any family in Sydney?'

Stella had made it back to the top of the bed and was hugging Maya tightly, laughing and pecking at her neck with little kisses. Maya's eyes were distant now, fixed on a point on the wall, at peace. The muted television flickered with images of the New Year's Eve fireworks, the start of the new millennium. Across the Harbour Bridge shone a single stylised word: 'Eternity'.

For the first time in her life, Kate's path was clear. She turned to the social worker. 'What would it take for me to become her full-time carer?'

~

The next day, Kate dropped Stella with Eleanor. She hated leaving her, but she had a lot to do. She needed to concentrate.

She pulled up outside Maya's house and extracted the key from her purse, a precaution they had wisely taken after the fourth time Maya had misplaced her own.

It was musty and dark inside. Dishes were piled in the sink and a plant sat dry and dead on the windowsill. There was an undeniable waft of urine – from the carpet? – and an empty bottle of pills lay on its side on the coffee table. The answering machine was lit up with messages.

Kate decided to do the washing up to clear her head. She gathered the dirty cups, some of them with blooms of green mould spreading across the dregs. Letters and papers were strewn everywhere. She stacked them into a neat pile; she would have to find a cleaner to help.

Maya's journal caught Kate's eye. She knew it was wrong to look, but she could not stop herself. Still a journalist, then. It was written in Maya's increasingly shaky hand, in German. Kate tried to remember the words. Each page took the form of a letter. *My darling Jan ...* Hundreds of letters addressed to Jan, and never sent.

She flicked through the pages. Over the months, the letters grew shorter and Maya's handwriting more unintelligible as she found it harder to direct the pen. By the end she had just written a single sentence, over and over, in large, wobbly script, as if she were learning it as a child. *'Ich bin Maya. Ich bin ...'*

Tucked into the back of the journal was an envelope. The postmark was November 1945, and it had come from Poland. The coppery hand-writing had faded but when she held the letter to the light, Kate could just make out the name. Danuta Novak.

Kate was excited now. As far as she knew, correspondence with the Novak family had ceased much earlier. Jan's father had worked with the Nazis, after all; Kate had assumed it would be too dangerous for Danuta to write to Maya.

She quickly went next door, carrying the letter like a prize. The neighbour, who was Polish and also Jewish, had been a good friend to Maya over the years. She answered with a tea towel in her hands. 'Please, can you translate this for me?' Kate asked urgently. The old lady dried her hands and found her glasses.

My dear Maya

It is with great distress that I write to tell you my brother Jan is dead. He went with the Armia Krajowa to Warsaw, to liberate the city from the German occupation. He was there for nearly two months. Many people died there. Jan was just one of them. We have heard he fought bravely to the end.

You will always be in my thoughts.

Danuta.

'Oh my God.' Kate clasped her hand to her mouth. 'I don't believe it. She knew he was dead all along.'

46

Westphalia, Germany, November 1945

Maya received a letter from Poland at last. The nuns delivered it to the British army barracks where she was staying on a grey November morning. She held it in her hands and felt the blood drain from her face. Her plans to go to England with Edward were nearly finalised. Just a few weeks now; he said they would be there by Christmas. She imagined his expression when she told him she could not go, that Jan had found her at last. Her heart pounded in her chest.

Holding the letter carefully as if it might break, she made her way to her bedroom, and closed the door. She slowly tore one corner of the envelope and prised open the flap.

The letter was from Danuta. Why not Jan? It seemed to be written in his hand. She read it quickly. Though it was brief, she could not grasp its meaning.

Jan was dead? But the war had ended months ago. *Many people died there. Jan was just one of them.* She could not feel her body. Nothing seemed real.

She sat on the bed, reading and re-reading, looking for a hidden message or a shard of hope. But the letter was brutal and direct. There could be no misinterpretation. Jan was dead.

No, she did not believe it. She would not believe it. He was alive. They had made a pact to live together. He would not have betrayed her. The letter was not true. He was alive.

The room was cold and dark, and she realised she was shivering. She moved at last, lit the lamp and drew the curtains. 'I will stay strong, my darling Jan,' she said aloud. She did not cry.

Sydney, October 2002

Kate had placed Maya's chair amid the fallen blossoms of the jaca-randa tree. The flowers spread around her feet like a purple blanket and bees buzzed here and there in the sun that filtered through the young leaves. The silky notes of Mozart's Clarinet Concerto in A major floated through the garden from a CD player by the back door.

Stella sat next to her on the grass, her back hunched as she leaned over a book, her spindly legs crossed and a smear of dirt on her cheek. Maya stroked Stella's blonde hair out of her eyes and smiled.

Kate arrived from the kitchen carrying a cup of tea in each hand. 'Isn't it lovely out here today?'

Two years ago, they had pooled their money to buy the house together. It had been too hard to manage Maya in her own home. She would stand at the end of the hallway, clutching the wall as she felt her way with a tentative foot, frozen in horror at whatever gaping void she saw beyond her shoes. And Stella was growing too large and exuberant for Kate's tiny house in Darlinghurst. They found a cottage among the trees, close to a respite centre where Kate would drop Maya while Stella was at school. On the days it was impossible to venture into the office, Kate would sit in the sunny front room with her computer and her notepads, writing at speed to pay the bills.

Maya was much less confused now she was taking a raft of medications – 'They'll give her a couple of good years,' the doctor had said – but her gradual decline was unmistakable. She was growing thinner, though she ate with relish the food that was cut up for her and served on a plastic plate. She could no longer read a book or follow a movie; instead, she shadowed Kate around the kitchen as she cooked dinner and asked the same question over and over. Sometimes, she would search the house frantically with her empty handbag clutched in her hands, or pace around the living room as if looking for a way out. Stella would join in too, unsettled by Maya's agitation, and Kate would swallow bitter gulps of resentment as she finished her wine in the kitchen.

But here in the garden, with Mozart and Stella and spring flowers, Maya sat quietly and moved her hands as if dancing in time to the music.

Kate put down the tea and retrieved the diamond bracelet from her pocket. It had belonged to Rosa; it had survived so much longer than its owner. She had finally removed it from Maya's wrist to keep it safe; Maya had been taking it off frequently, and then losing it, along with her hearing aids and glasses. It was too valuable to risk it when Maya was not supervised.

'Here, shall we put this on?'

Maya looked up at her, beaming. She closed Kate's hand around the bracelet and squeezed. 'It is for you.'

'Oh no, Maya, I couldn't. It was your mother's. It's far too precious.'

But Maya was firm. 'In my life I have met heroes and I have seen strength,' she said. 'But the most important thing I have known is kindness. And you, Kate – you are kind.'

⌒

Dan arrived in the afternoon, rattling his car keys then shoving them deep into a pocket of his loose jeans, his kelpie trotting at his heels.

They had bumped into each other at the supermarket a couple of years earlier. Kate had heard he was in Indonesia and married, but he had been delighted to see her. 'Nah, it didn't work out,' he had said. 'Not Indonesia, and not the marriage.' He had looked at Stella, who was trying to pull Kate towards the confectionery aisle. 'Bloody hell, you've been busy,' he had said. 'Look, I haven't been back long. It's great to see a friendly face. Let's have a coffee if you can find the time.'

He had turned into a close friend, perhaps her closest. He would visit to watch Maya and Stella while Kate left the house to run errands. He was happy to grab some milk or change a lightbulb, or simply make a pot of tea for her and put away the shopping while she worked on a freelance story.

'How are things today?' His wavy hair was held back off his forehead with his sunglasses; his dark brown eyes caught Kate's.

'All calm at the moment.' He was the only other person who had seen Maya's evening restlessness.

Stella wrapped herself around his knees and he laughed as he tried to walk forward, taking tiny steps. His hands were gentle as he prised her away.

'Go. I'll manage things here while you take Maya to the museum.'

A visit to the Sydney Jewish Museum was their monthly ritual. Maya had at one time been a guide there for several years, taking groups of children and tourists from display to display, smiling sweetly and talking softly as she described the Holocaust and what it had meant for her family. Now, her thoughts were too scattered for her to act as a guide, but she still visited to sit with her friends, the survivors who understood.

Kate left Maya with them in the café and wandered to the uppermost level of the museum. It was cool and quiet; the distant sound of hushed talking reached her from below and footsteps echoed from the curved marble staircase in the lobby. Grainy black and white pictures of starving children stared out from the display cabinets that lined the walls. She stopped briefly to look into their eyes, noting their dead expressions. It was hard to believe they had once been happy, lively children.

On the top floor was a display of the Righteous Among the Nations. She skimmed the stories of the gentiles in Europe who had had helped the Jews to survive. Stories of heroism and compassion. Would she have done the same? She imagined Maya as a teenager. What would have happened were it not for Jan and his family? Without them, there would be no Maya.

She glanced at her watch. She would give Maya another half an hour. To pass the time, she browsed a row of thick folders and stopped at one labelled *Sobibór*. The word jumped out at her from the spine.

The folder was heavy, a green-bound compendium of horrors that had once taken place in that part of Poland. Kate looked over her shoulder, feeling guilty somehow, half expecting Maya to appear. But her curiosity was too strong, and she started to read.

After a few minutes, she stopped with a gasp. An article explained how Himmler had visited the camp to trial the use of Zyklon B gas to more efficiently exterminate the Jews. He had tested it on a group of one hundred teenage girls and had watched them through an observation window. Kate thought of him nodding in satisfaction after their deaths, his self-satisfied moustache taut on his upper lip, shaking hands with the camp commandant at a job well done before lunchtime. It had been in April 1942, the same month Maya had stepped off the train with her parents.

Kate shut the folder quickly. She felt prickly and sick; she suddenly yearned to hold Stella tight. She had to get out of there.

Maya had not quite finished her tea when Kate hurried into the café. She nodded at the other elderly men and women gathered around the table, neatly dressed for their day out. They beckoned her to join them. 'Eat something . . .'

Kate declined and hurried Maya to take her leave. Maya put a last morsel of cake into her mouth and passively allowed Kate to help her stand and wrap a scarf around her neck. 'Come on, Maya, we'll miss Stella,' Kate whispered. But the goodbyes took an age, each interaction leading to a new thread of conversation – more plans for next week, another question about an offspring's business or wedding. Finally, they made it through the café and into the foyer. She steered Maya through the people buying tickets and browsing the gift shop.

Maya stopped. 'Here we are, that's the exit.' Kate pulled on Maya's hand, but, despite her urgency, Maya would not shift. She stood in the middle of the crowd, her feet obstinately planted on the spot, staring ahead. If this had been Stella, Kate would have picked her up, kicking and protesting, and carried her to the car. Frustration beat inside her chest and she wondered what everyone would do if she screamed.

'Maya . . .' she pleaded. Maya's eyes were fixed on the milling visitors, her mouth slightly open as if in shock. Had something triggered one of her memories? They had been to this museum so many times, and this had never happened before. Kate rubbed Maya's arm, worried now.

A group of people moved away and she realised Maya was staring at one elderly gentleman in particular. He was chatting to the receptionist. His curly hair was grey and his back stooped. In one hand he held a coat and an umbrella; with the other he was adjusting the roll-neck of his knitted sweater. As he turned to leave, Maya stepped forward and grabbed his arm.

'Pavel?' Her face was alive, her eyes wide and alight. 'Pavel? It is me, Maya!'

47

Sydney, October 2002

They sat in the living room at home and drank tea while Pavel talked. His accent was thick, his voice strangled with age, but he had launched into his story almost as soon as he sat down. It flooded from him like a tide. Maya, Kate and Dan listened, spellbound, taken back to June 1943, when Pavel and Erna had escaped the hole; when he had held his wife's skinny hand and led her through the trees beyond Sawin.

'We were young, we were brave. We did not for one minute think we would not survive,' he said. 'What young person thinks they will die?

'We were caught the next day. They just took us back to the camp; no shooting, no beating. We went back to our bunks and carried on as usual. We thought the camp was finished, they did not care anymore who comes or goes.

'Then, after dinner, the Commandant arrived. I was strong by then, I had had food for a few days, I wanted to survive. I felt like punching him in the head!'

'You shoulda done.' Dan shifted Stella into a more comfortable position on his lap as he listened.

'That man, he always had his rifle on his shoulder.' Pavel smiled at Maya, who nodded. 'I thought, maybe I can rip it from him and take command. I can hold it on the guards while the others run through the open gate.'

He paused, grappling with the memory.

'The Commandant, he aimed that rifle at Erna's chest. He was not looking at her, he was looking at me. I was ready to jump. He pulled her by the arm to the front of the group. Roughly, like this.' He shook Maya's arm; she startled.

'Then he beat her. He rammed that rifle into her stomach and kicked her with his boots.'

Kate covered her mouth with her hand. She imagined the shiny black boots as they hit the soft fabric of Erna's dress. Dan quietly stood and carried Stella from the room.

'I could not move,' Pavel went on. 'It felt like I was dreaming. I did nothing.' He shook his head and reached for his tea. Maya was sitting close to him, her hand gently kneading the wool of his sweater like a cat. Her face did not move.

'If Erna was dead, I wanted to be dead also. But then I got more angry. That night I escaped again.' Pavel's mouth twisted with bitterness.

'I ran and ran. I found a farmhouse about five kilometres from Sawin and stayed in a barn there for two days. I did not eat. All I knew was that I had to get away.

'On the third day, I heard the Ukrainians and their dogs. They were looking for me. I hid behind a tractor and they did not find me. I ran to another house where I knew the farmer. I often brought him valuables and he gave me bread and eggs. Oh, he was shocked to see me! He shook his head and shut the door in my face.'

Pavel told them he had decided to return to the original barn, where he had been safe. The guards had already searched there, and he did not think they would come back. On the way, he needed to cross the road, and in the dusky light he did not see a guard sitting underneath a tree, a bottle of vodka propped against his thigh.

'By midnight, I was in Sobibór.'

'What was it like?' asked Kate.

'Oh, very, very bad.' Pavel was smiling but his eyes were cloudy. He turned back to Maya, as if Kate was not there. 'But from the moment

I arrived, I decided to survive. It was for my boys, and for Erna. But also, you know, it was for myself.'

The next day, he recognised a former schoolfriend from Prague. This man was a tailor, and he had been given the job of sorting and altering the fine clothes confiscated from the new arrivals at the camp. A spark of recognition was all it took. 'I am a tailor,' Pavel lied confidently to the SS officer who processed his arrival. 'I am a former colleague of Miroslav. I will help him with his work.'

For the next few weeks, he spent his days sifting through leather jackets and furs, woollen trousers and silk blouses. From time to time, when he was sure the guard was distracted, he would unpick a gold coin or a banknote sewn into a seam and deftly slip it into his pocket. It would buy him food from the network of contacts he quickly established at the perimeter of the camp.

'Conditions in Sobibór were much worse than in Sawin. They were killing many prisoners. But I never lost hope. I made contacts. I looked forward to sinking an axe into the guard's throat!'

By October, with the arrival of some experienced Jewish soldiers from the Red Army, they were ready to make their move. 'We killed more than ten of those bastards!' Pavel rubbed his hands together and turned to Kate. 'We threw the gates open and we ran outside. So many of us! I found my . . . what is the word? . . . I found my strength.'

From there his luck improved. This time he found a farmer who was willing to help him. For months he lived behind the farmhouse. He got to know the sounds of the forest and the animals; he found a nook in the shed where he could hide himself easily the moment he heard an unusual engine or knock on the door. In the end, the camp at Sobibór disappeared and the danger slowly dissipated. The family were kind to him and invited him for dinner, though he was never to be seen in the open. He stayed with them for nearly two years, until the end of the war.

'I could never forget the kindness of those people.' He turned to Kate and winked. 'You know I married a Polish girl? We live in

Warsaw now. I have two sons, six grandchildren. I never forget Erna, but still I have a beautiful life.'

'And so do I.' Maya was beaming at him. 'But Pavel, do you know what happened to Jan?'

Later, Kate stood on the deck with Dan, watching him smoke. The cigarette crackled and his face lit up orange with each drag. 'That was intense,' he said, flicking ash onto the grass below.

Stella was in bed and Maya and Pavel were still talking on the sofa. They had relaxed into German now. Maya laughed often, her face open and bright, as if she were a young woman.

Kate leaned back against the wood of the balustrade and folded her hands across her stomach. 'You know Jan's dead? All these years she's been yearning to find him, but I have proof that he died at the end of the war.'

Dan drew on his cigarette. 'I guess she needed the idea of him to survive. She learned how to survive, didn't she? Her whole life has basically been about surviving. It shaped her whole personality.'

'Oh no.' Pavel emerged from the living room, patting his pocket to find his tobacco. 'Maya is not like this because she survived – she survived because she is the wonderful person she is.'

Dan offered Pavel a light; Pavel cupped his hands around the flame, a moment of intimacy shared by smokers throughout time.

'I do not believe that I found her here in Sydney!' Pavel's crackling chuckle rumbled in his chest. 'I come here for two weeks on holiday, that is all, and here she is after all these years!'

'How do you think she's doing?' Kate asked. 'She isn't very well – her memory's getting worse.'

'She is no different.' Pavel waved his cigarette through the air. 'She is Maya.'

He coughed then leaned towards them and lowered his voice. 'I treated her very badly, very badly. She gave me a gold ring to buy medicine for her mother. I used it for food.' He wiped his eye with the back of his hand. 'We had to survive.'

Kate opened her mouth to reply, but there was nothing to say.

'After we left Maya, we did not know whether she lived or died. We left her in a hole, on her own. I tried to forget. Now at last I can help her.'

'Help her? How?'

Pavel coughed again, a deep, roiling cough, and stubbed his half-smoked cigarette into the ashtray.

'My brother-in-law Stanislaw is a high-ranking officer in the Polish army. He lives near Warsaw. I will ask him to find what happened to Jan.'

⌒

Two weeks later, Kate was preparing dinner while Maya watched Stella as she spun around to the happy yellow and red notes of a Wiggles DVD. Her arms were flung wide and her stubby fingers floated on waves of air. Sometimes she stopped, dizzy and unsteady on her legs, laughing as she stumbled and bumped into the furniture. Maya tapped the melody with her hands in her lap. She startled each time Stella fell, instinctively reaching forward to catch her, then settled back into the sofa as the music carried them off again.

Kate paused from chopping vegetables in the kitchen and watched them through the open door. She thought of the roads that had led them here, to this moment, this music. Here, in their living room, their pasts and their futures had melted away. They meant nothing now. An old lady and a child dancing to the Wiggles, living and breathing to their own choreography.

She dried her hands on a tea towel and thought how unexpected this all was. She thought of the newspaper, of the adrenaline of a breaking story. She did not miss it.

'Come on, darling, the postman's been. Let's go and see if there are any letters.' It was Stella's job to bring in the post. She loved the responsibility. Sometimes Kate sent letters to herself, just to be sure there would be something in the letterbox.

She watched by the front door as Stella trotted up the path and clumsily retrieved a handful of envelopes. She stopped on the way back to the house to examine a camellia blossom, the letters dangling from her hand. 'Come on, sweetie,' Kate said, but she did not feel impatient today.

There were six envelopes, most of them bills. But one was more interesting: a thick envelope addressed to Maya. The address was written in fountain pen, the letters round and ornate.

'This is for you.' Kate sat down next to Maya and put the envelope in her hand. Maya read the address slowly, running her finger along each line. 'This is for me,' she announced at last. Kate smiled.

Maya turned the envelope over and, with stiff fingers, opened the seal. She pulled out a handwritten letter and unfolded it. As she did so, a lifetime's photos of Jan fell into her lap.

48

My dear Maya

I cannot tell you how astonished I was today to receive a visit from a Mr Stanislaw Tatz, the brother-in-law of Pavel Horwitz. He bore a message for my husband, Jan Novak, all the way from Australia. After all these years, my family is delighted to find you at last. My husband spoke about you often. Your story is our family's story. The children know every step of your escape. My husband said his small part in it was the greatest act of his life.

May I tell you something of our family? I met Jan in 1955 in Warsaw. My father was a general in the army and Jan was his captain. I was in the national volleyball team and Jan used to come and watch me compete. He said he always liked sporty women! He lost touch with his family after the war, I never met them. He was pleased to become a part of my family and we had a comfortable and happy life in Warsaw.

We quickly had two sons. We were both in our thirties and did not want to wait. We loved skiing in the winter and boating in the summer. After Communism ended here in 1989, we could travel more in Europe. We went to Prague and Brno to see if we could find you, but we had no address and no documents.

Our sons are both married and we have three grandchildren. The eldest is named Maya – after you!

Maya, I have some sad news. Jan died of liver cancer nearly two years ago. We lost our shining light. My tears are still fresh as I write this to you. Just two years more and he could have spoken to you again.

I enclose some photographs of our family. You can see that Jan was handsome through his whole life. Can you see how similar our eldest son is to him? They have the same nose.

Thank you for contacting us, my dearest Maya. Please write back at this address. If you can make the long trip to visit us in Poland, we would love to welcome you.

Yours
Alicja Novak

Warsaw, August 2003

Kate, Maya and Stella arrived in Poland on a warm summer's morning. They stood placidly in the immigration line, tired and unsteady after their long flight from Australia. The Polish voices all around them sounded like lazy bees.

Alicja was waiting for them as they walked through customs at Okęcie Airport. Her white hair was tied loosely in a bun at her neck and her arms were open wide to embrace Maya. They held each other tightly for more than a minute as the crowd poured around them like a stream past a stone.

At last, Maya took a step back and slipped both hands into Alicja's. She gazed into her face, trying to make sense of it. 'It is wonderful to see you again,' she said, in English. She raised Alicja's hand to her lips and kissed it, then held it to her cheek.

A man with thinning hair and an aquiline nose stood at Alicja's shoulder. '*Mój syn*,' said Alicja, giddy with excitement. 'My son, Janek.' He was holding a massive bouquet of flowers and smiling broadly. 'Welcome to Poland,' he said, in English. 'My mother does not speak English. I will try to translate. You must be tired after your journey. Please, follow me.'

'Mummy,' whispered Stella, as they arrived at Janek's car, 'why did Maya say it was wonderful to see her again?'

'She's just a little confused after the flight.' Kate turned to Janek and said quietly, 'I don't think she realises that this is the first time she's met your mother.'

'And yet I have known *her* my whole life.' He smiled as he shut the boot.

∽

The Novak household was a forty-minute drive away. The outskirts of the city were not as Kate had imagined. Grey concrete Soviet-era buildings towered above their heads; row after row of lifeless balconies and zigzag staircases lined the gloomy streets. People stood in doorways, talking and laughing. Kate thought of the history, the collective denial of a nation during the Holocaust. Which of these people had turned their backs? Did any of them remember?

They pulled up at a small house with acacia trees in the garden and lace curtains in the windows. Maya stopped at the threshold, inhaling the cooking smells from the kitchen. Her eyes shone with tears.

Jan's presence hung in the living room. His impression was still visible in the seat of a battered leather armchair in the corner. There were books with pictures of warfare and aeroplanes on the spine; a model car on the mahogany desk.

Alicja bustled in and out of the kitchen, clanking pots and crockery as she set the table for lunch. She laid out plates piled with latkes and country cottage cheese, *twarożek*. Maya hummed a snatch of a long-forgotten melody. '*Jedz, jedz, jedz, Kochanie.* Eat, dearest, eat'. Alicja carefully placed a large tureen of steaming white bean soup at the centre of the table. 'My father told us how much you loved this,' Janek said to Maya.

Conversation flowed easily, despite the language barrier. Through Janek, they compared their attempts to find each other's families. Janek told them his father had tried to find Maya in the sixties; he had traced her to England, but he never imagined she would have travelled on to Australia.

After lunch, Maya settled in the garden with the sun warming her back and the heady fragrance of the acacia trees wafting over her. Stella played on the lawn with Alicja's youngest grandchild. They pulled handfuls of grass and threw them in the air. The blades fell around them like emerald snowflakes.

'This is where my father loved to be,' Janek said to Kate. He told her Jan would play hide-and-seek with his grandchildren among the trees, leaping out to shock them and sweeping them into his arms, nuzzling his nose into their sweaty necks. Sometimes he would lie on his back where they now sat, puffing on his pipe or staring through the leaves at the white clouds above. When it became clear that he was not going to survive the cancer, this is where he asked to be. They would bring his favourite armchair here, the radio and the newspaper. When he could no longer read, Janek sat at his feet and read it to him.

'What happened to him after Maya escaped from Poland?' Kate asked.

'He did not speak of that time,' said Janek, shaking his head. 'It was a painful part of his life. We know he fought with the resistance in Warsaw, but he did not like to discuss the ten years before he met my mother. There was always something sad in my father, even when he was laughing. We thought it was best not to talk about it.'

Alicja brought a stack of heavy photograph albums, sat down next to Maya and spread them open; the wax paper crackled as they turned the pages. Some of the loose photographs fell like black and white leaves around their feet – Jan with two little boys, sitting on a wooden fence with a tennis ball in his hand; an older Jan, balding, sitting in a restaurant surrounded by friends. Alicja on the volleyball court. A black and white photograph of her in a high-necked white lace wedding dress, Jan holding her by the arm. He was tall and stood stiffly, hair slicked back from his high forehead, handsome.

Alicja showed off the wedding photos, pointing out different members of the family, her parents, the bridesmaids. There were no Novaks among them.

Jan had always dreamed of being an officer in the Polish army, his son translated as his mother spoke softly. 'Here is a photo of him graduating from the officers' academy. See, it was under Russian command.' She pointed at the flag fluttering in grey and white above the building.

'He fought in Szczecin and Berlin, and by the time he was twenty-five he was a captain. The youngest ever.' Another photograph of Jan, proud and tall in his uniform.

'My father never found it easy to work for the Communists.' Janek turned to Kate and lowered his voice, as if his mother might suddenly learn to speak English. 'He was about to be promoted to general, but they discovered his links to the AK. His branch in the war was supported by the Polish government in London and the regime did not approve. So he was moved sideways. He became an engineering lecturer in Gdansk for a while. He never became a general.'

Alicja opened another album, this one further back in time, of Jan as a young man during the war. Maya was more animated now, peering at each photo with her eyes screwed up.

'Look, Kate, look!' she said at last, pointing at one of the photographs. Kate, pinned in place by Stella's weight on her lap, craned her neck to see. The photo showed Jan standing by the side of a trench, talking to two young women. They were leaning on their shovels and dark water covered their feet. There was a bridge behind them with a bicycle balanced against the railing. Jan held a cigarette between his lips like a film star, and he was smiling.

'Look, Kate,' said Maya, pointing. 'There is Maya.'

49

Sawin, August 2003

The sun shone through heavy clouds and illuminated the countryside with a luminous light, bright yellow against the grey, as Sawin came into view. The little village nestled amid sprawling fields, surrounded by dense black woods on either side. Maya longed to touch the trees, to feel the electricity running through their branches and smell the freshness. She put her hand to the window. Her skin looked old with its Australian sunspots, the swirling wrinkles on the knuckles.

She sat with Stella in the back of the car and listened to Polish words crackle from the radio. The speaker's intonation was different to that of her neighbour and the other Poles she knew in Australia. It was more resigned, beaten down. Recognition stirred somewhere deep inside her.

She felt as if she had always been here. Australia, the purple jacaranda trees and the clear light, seemed suddenly dreamlike and unreal. Like postcards from a different life, a film she had seen long ago. She could barely imagine herself in it.

Janek parked the car and they stepped out, stiff after the long drive. Maya breathed deeply. The air was heavy and humid. She was really back in Sawin. The smell of the street, the slant of the sunshine; there was no other place it could be.

Last time she was here, she had barely been functioning. To be seen by anyone could have resulted in death. The fear was still real, but now

319

she had a right to be here. No, more than that – she *needed* to be here. She had survived.

Kate was already taking photos. 'So where was the camp?' she asked.

Maya looked left and right. She was disoriented, like someone in a dream where everything has shifted slightly from how it should be. She remembered Sawin as being smaller, simpler. Now the streets wound here and there in all directions, and the landmarks were wrong.

She set off stiffly, past low, modern houses with coloured shutters and television antennae. Parked cars obscured most of the cracked pavement. There was no sign of the whitewashed farmhouses that she remembered.

She looked down at her feet, her sturdy sneakers taking one step at a time. The same feet that had walked these streets so often, though then her shoes had been full of holes and wet, always wet. How grateful she had been that Franz had insisted she bring her good leather shoes. After a few months, so many in the camp had gone barefoot. Her legs had once been strong, always carrying her forward, no matter how little she had eaten or how much her head had spun. Now, her breaths came quickly and her legs were reluctant, as if hands were pulling her back.

They came to the main square, a grassy park shaded by towering trees. The faint strains of Madonna's 'Holiday' wafted from the open window of a hairdresser's salon. Near the road sat a massive grey tank on top of a memorial stone. A white eagle insignia spread its wings from the turret and its gun pointed away into the thick branches of the trees. Janek translated the plaque. 'It's about the partisans who fought in the war.'

'Is there any mention of the Jews who died here?' asked Kate. Janek shook his head.

Maya ran her fingers over the cool metal of the gun, feeling the round smoothness of the barrel. 'But I *was* here. We all were,' she whispered.

They walked beyond the square and came to a bakery with an old, battered door. Maya stopped still, put the back of her hand to her forehead, and looked around her. 'There.' She pointed towards a field crossed with deep, muddy furrows. 'It was over there.'

The field was empty and completely quiet. They walked towards the fence; a remnant of barbed wire twisted around one of the posts. Maya examined it, pushing her thumb against one of the rusty barbs. It left an indent in her thin skin. It was not the same type of barbed wire they had used in the war.

An old man emerged from the house behind them. His hair was white and his front teeth were missing. Janek and Alicja chatted to him in Polish as he gestured expansively towards the field and the woods beyond. 'This is his land,' said Janek. 'He spent the war fighting at the front. He said there were a few labour camps in the area, but as far as he knows, no Jews ever came to Sawin.'

'*Dziękuję ci*. Thank you,' Alicja said softly as the man adjusted his corduroy trousers, spat into the street and turned his back.

Maya did not blame him. He was not the only one to deny what had happened. She gazed towards the fields, trying to picture where the Appellplatz once was. Not a trace remained. She brushed away a mosquito that was biting her arm. At last, yes, something that was real. Sawin's mosquitoes, at least, had not changed.

She stooped to pick up a handful of stones from the field where the camp once stood, and slipped them into the pocket of her cardigan.

They drove on to Sobibór, no more than twenty-five minutes away. Maya thought of the first march, those long hours through the fields to the camp. Then she had been terrified but, as they pulled up outside the little station, she felt anaesthetised. The world had gone on, regardless.

The death camp had been destroyed by the Nazis. Now there was nothing other than a huge, bare space and a grey wall. Birds were singing in the trees. Maya bent down and placed the stones on the ground, a mark of respect to her mother.

'Everything is gone,' she said. 'But I need to see it. I need to see with my own eyes what they did.'

'The camp at Majdanek is still standing, I believe,' said Janek. 'We can take you there. If you want?'

～

It was late afternoon when they drove through Lublin's grey streets and pulled into the car park at Majdanek. A hot August wind howled along the dusty path, whipping the gravel into eddies as they stepped out of the car. Kate slammed the door and turned to survey the sweeping field that had once housed the death camp. 'Oh,' she said under her breath. The size of it.

The camp was in a suburb of the city, a large green space edged with tall buildings, their lace curtains and coloured balconies looking directly over the site. 'The whole city must have known what was going on,' muttered Kate, but her words were swept away by the wind.

A straight, purposeful railway track stretched far into the distance with rows of wooden huts along each side. Behind them, tall grass swayed and bobbed and clouds darkened on the horizon. Most of the summer tourists had left for the day, but an English family walked ahead of them from the car park and along the path at the edge of the tracks. The teenagers' unwilling feet trudged loudly through the gravel; the girl kicked at tiny cornflowers by the side of the path with her dusty sandals. 'Hurry up, Bianca,' snapped the mother. 'The crematorium shuts at five.'

Kate took Stella by the hand and they walked together towards one of the wooden huts, slowly, as if entering a church. Inside was dark and still. The wooden walls smelled sweet in the heat, like a sauna. Chinks of sunshine shone through a few broken tiles in the roof and illuminated patches of dust on the dirt floor. A lawnmower revved in the distance.

'Mummy, look!' said Stella, running to the exhibit at the far end of the hut. There were piles of empty suitcases, bent and misshapen. Names and numbers were written on them in chalk, but they belonged to no one. In a cabinet was a display of enamel bowls, saucepans and plates, photographs and round spectacles. 'It's Mickey Mouse!' Stella pointed at a child's brooch.

The next hut was full from floor to ceiling with shoes. The smell of stale leather filled the room, like the back of a wardrobe on a steamy summer's day. They peered through the semi-darkness. There were men's and women's shoes, boots and fashionable pumps, some faded red, some with high heels. Stella's cheeks were flushed as she stood on tiptoe for a better view. 'Why did the Germans take their shoes, Mummy?'

Maya thought of her suitcase, lost on the station. She had considered bringing her tap shoes. What had she been thinking?

'Let's move on,' said Kate, pulling her gently by the arm.

Outside, the wind was growing stronger. It was slamming the sides of the huts and rattling the windows, gushing over their sweating arms like warm water.

When they arrived at the gas chambers, they left Stella outside with Alicja and Janek and walked together through heavy doors and into a cool concrete room with scratches on the walls. It was quiet, like a crypt. There was no one else there. They passed through dim chambers and echoing passageways to the shower room, where the ceiling was held up by black wooden beams and rows of shower heads jutted down in neat lines. There were two large concrete tubs in the corner, and, beyond, a store cupboard was stacked high with cans of Zyklon B. Above them was a little window, glazed and barred. From here, the SS could watch their victims as they died.

They came to the crematorium with its row of five ovens, gaping like black mouths against the red brick, stained with soot. The doors were flung open to reveal the industrial mechanism that fed the bodies inside, four at a time. A cart for carrying corpses stood in a corner.

Maya grabbed a handrail to steady herself. The heat prickled her ears and her heart banged heavily in her throat with familiar, nauseating disgust. She heard herself speaking, '*Hashem. May the martyred souls be redeemed.*' A prayer to a God that had not heard.

Memories pulled at her like impatient children. She could not stop them. Rosa holding a suitcase, her eyes fixed on the distance as she marched, grasping Maya's hand tightly. Franz, carrying Rosa's backpack as well as his own on the long walk to Sawin. A railway track strewn with bodies.

The grief that for so long had been a scar, examined daily, tore open into a gaping wound. The terrible, terrible fact that she was still alive, all these years, and they were dead. The loneliness of a world without them in it.

She heard the sound of her own moaning, a rising, ripping sound she did not recognise. Her sobs sounded high and childlike. Kate reached out to put an arm around her, but Maya turned and fled, her aching feet carrying her with unaccustomed speed through the corridors towards the light outside. She called out to the gushing wind. It swirled around her, a burning furnace. Through her howling she could hear distant footsteps on the gravel, *snunch, snunch*. They grew louder and louder. The marching of shoes, thousands of shoes.

Time was an ocean. It was pulling apart, opening up. She thought of Moses, of the faithful Jews following him through parted waves. Warm water was beckoning her, urging her to dive in. But she hesitated. At the far side she could see the shadowy shape of her mother, waving.

There was Kate, emerging from the open door, running towards her. Then the stony ground rushed up to meet her and the world went black.

⌒

Maya opened her eyes to see Kate, Janek and Alicja peering down at her. Stella was holding her hand, tears streaking her cheeks and strands of hair whipping her face in the hot wind.

'Oh, the heat.' Maya sat up slowly, brushing gravel from her elbow. Her lips were pale.

'Here, have a sip of water.' Kate offered her a plastic bottle. 'Do you think you can stand?' The empty camp stretched into the distance.

She turned to Janek. 'There's no way she's going to be able to walk back. Can you go and get some help?'

Kate, Stella and Maya sat together in the open field while they waited. The long grass bent against the wind, invisible fingers running across green velvet. A doe and her fawn hesitantly emerged from the trees.

Stella picked a cornflower and presented it to Maya. 'This will make you better.' Maya pulled her onto her lap. Together they examined the pointed blue petals and straight green stalk.

Stella flung her arms around Maya's neck. 'I *hate* the Germans!' Her chin was wobbling.

'Shh,' said Maya, realising she could smile again. 'If there had never been any Germans, I would not have had you, would I?' She settled Stella beside her, one arm around her, and turned the flower over in her other hand. It was already shrivelling in the heat, but beautiful despite its imminent death. 'When I was a girl,' she said, 'not that much older than you, I could not imagine the future, only an escape from the present. Now here I am, with you and this beautiful flower. It was worth it.' Her smile shone like the sun.

'Are you okay?' Kate asked.

Maya's breath caught in her throat. She felt the Jewish voices around her, calling from the leaves of the trees that stood tall and still in the distance, their roots still curling through the Polish soil. Her people were singing in the air. Their voices were clear and strong; they were here.

Now she understood, finally, why she had needed to survive. That the point of it was – had always been – to come back to Poland alive.

50

Lublin, August 2003

The next day, Danuta greeted them at her apartment door with open arms. She was small and thin, dressed in a tidy trouser suit with a brooch on her lapel. Her hair was freshly waved and her face alive with anticipation. Alicja rushed to her and kissed her sister-in-law on both cheeks. 'Oh, she looks like my father!' Janek exclaimed.

They settled in Danuta's crowded living room, which overlooked the old part of town. She took Maya's hand and asked her a question in Polish, but Maya's face was blank. Danuta tried again in English. 'Maya, do you remember me? I am Danuta. Danuta Novak.'

Maya smiled kindly but without emotion. She clearly could not place the elderly lady in front of her.

'Maya has good days and bad days,' Kate tried to explain as she helped Danuta with the coffee cups. 'Sometimes she's just as she was, funny and perceptive. But yesterday she had a shock, and it's as if she's in another world.'

'I understand,' said Danuta. 'I looked after my father for many years after my mother died. He had the disease also.' She looked out the window. 'My father, he did not go to a good place. He was always crying, again and again asking for Jan. All day he would look for him.'

'So your family really thought Jan was dead, all this time?'

'Of course. We did not question that it was true.' Danuta hesitated. 'We did not even know he fought in the Warsaw Uprising. We just heard from a colleague that he had been killed. Why would we not believe it? To think of all those times I went to Warsaw. It is only three hours from my home. I might have passed him in the street!'

'But didn't you ever go to look for him? To confirm that it was true?'

'Oh no. Thousands of people were dying every day. They just burned their bodies in the street. We accepted it. And do not forget who my father was.' A shadow of anger darkened Danuta's face. 'He sympathised with the Nazis until the end. We never told him that Jan was AK, and of course he never knew that we harboured a Jew in our living room! It would have split the family, and we could not let that happen, not with just the three of us left.'

Danuta's neck was blotchy with emotion. She rubbed it with her neat little hands.

'Jan never came back to see us. He did not write to me. For sixty years I lived with the grief of losing him. For all that time he was dead to us, and, you know, I wonder whether it was almost better to believe that than to know he deliberately abandoned his family.'

'The funny thing is, it's been the opposite for Maya,' said Kate. 'It was her hope of seeing Jan again that kept her going through most of her life. Even though she got your letter after the war telling her that Jan was dead.'

Danuta looked surprised and shook her head. 'I do not remember writing her a letter. How would I have known the address?'

'But I found the letter . . .'

Danuta shrugged. 'We all have different memories of that time.' She looked through the open door at Maya, sitting quietly with Alicja on the sofa. 'She won't remember, anyway. What is the point of worrying about it? Better to let her remember it the way she wants to.'

Warsaw, November 1945

Jan sat by the window in his tiny basement room and felt anger flicker like a flame in his stomach. His hands shook as he wrote. His stub of a pencil, found in his jacket pocket this morning as he had cowered in a doorway, slipped over the page. He scrunched the paper into a ball and banged his fist on the wall. The pain felt good.

The sun was falling, and the room was cold. He pulled his jacket over his shoulders and winced. His injuries had mostly healed, but they never let him relax. An awkward twist, a day without food, and the nagging aches would keep him awake at night, even now, all these months later. He lit a cigarette and let the smoke calm him. He had to think.

A group of boys ran past the window, silent like cats, on the hunt. Food was scarce. Due either to the rubble that still littered the streets of Warsaw or the utter helplessness of the populace, no one looked up from their feet as they walked any more. Beyond the square, the jagged remnants of buildings reached up into the gloomy sky like shards of glass.

He remembered how it had started, when he had finally realised there was no future in Chelm, with his family. The public executions had taken place in the main square; the comrades whom he had been furtively helping for months hung in the breeze while Chelm's citizens walked past trying not to look. His father was responsible. 'We successfully dealt with some traitors today,' he said over dinner that night. He had stared at Jan, seeking a reaction. 'No traitor will be spared.'

Jan had left a few days later to join the AK in Warsaw. It was time to fight back, to rid the capital of the Nazi scourge. He remembered their optimism as they passed around their weapons and tied their scarves around their necks. The first day he had found it thrilling, the gunfire and the explosions. It was hardly real; the cries and the shouts came to him as if from a great distance, as in a dream. His rifle had felt warm in his hands and his hatred of the Nazis had powered his body to extremes he never would have thought possible.

But the fight had gone on longer than they expected. The Nazis were too powerful; help never came. One by one, the buildings he had grown to know crumbled around him. There was loss after loss, every day, as his comrades were shot or arrested. Flames lit up the sky by night, flickering against their grimy faces as they ate hungrily, telling themselves things would get better.

After six weeks, he had started to doubt his resolve. He was tired and weak; rations were low and ammunition was running out. He was distracted and lost concentration; he did not hear the clink of the grenade. The next thing he remembered was waking here, in this tiny room, a blanket over his knees and grimy bandages wrapped around his arms and left leg. It had been eerily quiet outside; the bombardment had stopped. He had opened the door a crack and seen a mother and her child picking their way across the pavement.

His leg had been painful, but he could walk. It was cold outside. He could see a group of Nazi soldiers at the other side of the square. They were moving from door to door, bringing residents into the open air and standing them in a line, their hands on their heads. He had quickly retreated to the basement room and shut the door. No one need know he was here.

How many months had he been here, in this room? Now the war was over, and the Communists were in charge. His strength had returned and he had a decision to make. Maya was waiting for him, he believed that. He thought of her often, usually when he was tearing into a stolen morsel of bread or sipping thick soup brought to him by a boy whom he paid in cigarettes. Now he, too, had known hunger. He understood the way Maya ate, her eyes never leaving the food, even as she held his hand in hers and whispered her love for him. But she was in Germany. He would not go there to be among the people he hated. He could not.

He hoped beyond hope that Maya was alive. But there was no way he could bring her here, to Warsaw. The Poles' hatred of the Jews had not diminished. Those who had survived the Nazi executions, who had emerged, blinking, at the end of the war, scarcely believing they were alive, were now persecuted anew, even by Poles who had once sheltered them. The million acts of heroism, the humanity and kindnesses of the neighbours and friends who had assisted the Jews, were now held as dark secrets, remembered only fleetingly in the dark of the night. No one in Poland would admit to having helped a Jew now.

He thought of his mother's cooking, of Danuta, his bed. But he could not go home. He thought of his father and the anger welled again. His father, the Nazi sympathiser.

He held his head in his hands and dug his fingernails into his scalp.

He himself had stood in Sawin's trenches in his boots and woollen coat while the prisoners were barefoot in the icy mud. Had a part of him enjoyed it, the power and the superiority? He had risked his life for Maya because he loved her, attracted by her strength and determination to live. But he should have done more.

He thought of her smile, how it made him calm, the joy of holding her in his arms and forgetting the horror of the world around them. He remembered her dance, watching in awe as she flew across the makeshift stage, her free spirit.

Tears pricked his eyes. He had loved her for three years now. They had loved each other through the most inhumane conditions, and it had made them both stronger. He had planned to make her his wife – but he knew she could not come here, to live in fear again.

He had no choice but to give her up. It was the only way she could be free.

He picked up his pencil again and started to write. There was so much to say, but, in the end, he could say nothing at all.

My dear Maya
It is with great distress that I write to tell you my brother Jan is dead . . .

51

Warsaw, August 2003

Kate lay awake long into the night. The air was cool now, and Warsaw was quiet outside her window. Her ears strained for the sound of Maya wandering in the strange house, but all was still. She rolled over and saw that it was past two-thirty.

She had forgotten what it was like to struggle for sleep. It brought her back to eight years earlier, the time when she had first arrived in Sydney. The long nights, the loneliness, the self-criticism, the worry that her best was not good enough. Those feelings seemed inconsequential now, as if they had been felt by someone else. These days, the voice in her head was gentle and kind. It spoke of courage and possibility. It was Maya who had taught her this; her absolute conviction that there was good in the world. What if Maya had not survived? Kate's throat constricted at the thought. She silently thanked Jan and Danuta for their bravery, for bringing Maya to her.

She tiptoed into the garden, sat down in Jan's favourite spot under the tree, and dialled a familiar number on her mobile phone. Dan answered immediately.

'Hey you. How's it going?'

'Not too well. Maya got completely overwhelmed. I'm thinking it was too much for her to come here after so long. It's where she felt her deepest pain.'

'Yeah – but also where she felt her deepest love and gratitude,' Dan said.

'It's not what I expected. We went back to Sawin. There's nothing there. Nobody even seems to remember that there was a camp. It's as if it never happened.'

She could hear him breathe out as he sat down, ready for one of their long chats. 'It was a very long time ago,' he said.

'And you wouldn't believe Majdanek. It was massive, yet people ignored what was going on right under their noses. In some ways, I think they still do.'

'I know what you mean,' Dan said. 'I've seen it before, when I was reporting from South Africa, and I've seen it in Asia too – anywhere where people have done appalling things to each other. There's a general cognitive dissonance. People kind of know what's going on, but they don't want to know. And after all these years, I guess for most of them it's easier to just forget.'

'But it's not as though you can decide what's true and what isn't.' Kate thought of Maya, holding onto the hope of finding Jan even though she had a letter saying he was dead, and of Mrs Novak, grieving a son who was actually alive. She thought of how most did not want to remember, while Maya was unable to forget.

'There *is* truth,' she said slowly. 'We know there is. We're journalists. We owe it to Maya – to all of them – to keep on telling it.' She paused. 'I should have done more.'

'Hey.' She could hear the smile in Dan's voice. 'You've done great. You've become her family.'

Kate looked at her shadow, alone in the moonlight. She wished Dan was here to give her a hug. 'Dan?' she whispered. 'I miss you.'

He hesitated. 'Mate.' His voice was full of relief. 'I miss you too.'

After she hung up, Kate tiptoed back to the bedroom and kissed Stella gently on the forehead. She opened her laptop. The metallic blue light from the screen lit up her face as she composed the email she should have written years ago.

'Mum, I'm in Europe. I'm going to bring Stella over to the UK. It's time to meet your granddaughter.'

⌒

Early the next morning, Alicja took Maya by the arm and guided her along the street to a little white church. They did not talk. Maya held Alicja's sleeve tightly. The sun had come out after the rain and the fresh scent of grass lifted their spirits as they walked.

Inside, the warm smell of burning wax filled the nave and the morning light shafted through the windows. The walls and floor were white, almost dazzling in the sun. Alicja helped Maya to a pew and left her for a moment while she went to light a candle of her own.

Maya closed her eyes. They thought she did not understand, but this she knew. Jan did not die during the war. They had lived in the same world, breathed the same air, all those years. It had not been a question of belief. She had *known*.

Now he was close, closer than he had been for over sixty years. She knew him in every corner of his house, his smell, the feeling of him, like the undefinable presence that lingers when someone has just left a room. Her search for him had ended in gentle Alicja's arms.

She let go, allowing the river of memories to sweep her up. She floated on them, warm and relaxed in the light shining through her closed eyelids.

She made out the shape of her mother, a hazy grey shape, indistinct. She felt her now. Rosa was talking to her.

'*Mayalein, mein liebstes Maya,*' she said. She was young and beautiful. Her slim body was wrapped in a black lace dress and her chestnut hair fell softly around her shoulders. Her hands were outstretched, as if to embrace her. 'My little Maya, do not cry. There's been too much crying. Franz has gone, they all have gone. It is my turn now, you need to understand.'

Maya gasped, remembering. She was in the dormitory. The Commandant was there, pointing his rifle at Rosa as she rose slowly to her feet, her shoulders bent. Just now, she had been laughing.

'Oh, I know about Jan,' Rosa went on. 'He gave you hope. There was no better gift in a place like this. He was a good man.

'But, Maya, you must know that *my* hope came from you. Every day when you slipped back into bed, I pretended to sleep, holding you tight for warmth, loving you. Without you I could not have gone so far. You are my daughter, my love. You are everything to me.'

Tears ran freely down Maya's cheeks. But she was not sad. The simmering fire in her chest was dimming at last and new peace shone in its place.

'My darling, you had the choice to come with me. With everything I had, I needed you to stay, to survive. I experienced great joys and terrible hardships, but I knew what it was to live. But you, Maya, you were just seventeen. I wanted you to carry on, my lovely daughter – to live, to grow, to learn and love. Take life, Maya. Live, my *Mayalein*, go and live.'

Maya opened her eyes. Rosa was walking away now. The brightness of the church shone around her. She stopped and looked over her shoulder. Maya could see every contour of her familiar face, her smiling mouth, her dark eyes shining like stars. She knew every freckle and line. Her mother's face. It looked back at her, full of joy.

She felt the brush of Alicja's hand on her arm and realised she was sobbing out loud. Alicja rubbed her back. They sat for long time, silent together in the bright white church. At last, Alicja reached into her bag and found a tissue. She blotted her eyes and turned to Maya.

'I have told him you are here with me,' she whispered. 'Come now, my dear Maya, it is time to go.'

EPILOGUE

Care Review

Mrs Maria Schulze-Johnson, D.O.B. 25/08/1925

Mobility: Maya is immobile and her sitting balance is poor. She requires two carers for all moving and transfers.

Mental health: Advanced dementia and poor cognition. She may be anxious, calling out and talking to herself at times. Requires reassurance and support.

Physical health: Skin is dry and fragile. Pain patches and paracetamol suspension. Breathing normal, but can get wheezy at times.

Personal hygiene: Maya requires assistance of two staff to meet her personal care needs.

Social activities: While unable to participate in social activities, Maya likes to listen to music. She appears happy and comfortable.

My darling Jan

Today children are visiting. They fidget at the front of the room, running their fingers over their instruments. How old are they? They cannot be more than six or seven. Some will leave here deeply disturbed, that is to be expected. The dementia ward is nothing if not distasteful. Its drooling mouths and the waft of urine.

I sit in my recliner chair as I write to you. Well, not so much write as think. There is no difference now between thought and memory, dreams and speech. It is all the same thing. Thousands of images, snatches of moments. Pictures on the wall.

The boys are giggling. One shoves his neighbour. The girl behind pokes them both in the ribs. She has glasses and her hair is tied back with a bow. She is taking her duty seriously, and her recorder is at the ready.

On cue, the music starts. I watch the children through the blur of semi-closed eyelashes. The notes are discordant but strong, played with conviction.

My body is too weak to move along to the beat. I can no longer tell my hands what to do; they fly through the air or jerk from my lap, clawing at my face like little animals and making me jump. But still the notes carry me. They make today a good day.

My life is not so bad as it sounds. It is still a life, after all. And this is not the first time I have lost my privacy and freedom. Sometimes, when the carers manhandle me into the shower or flash their torches in the night, I find myself back in the dark hole, yearning for the light. But the urge to survive is still strong.

Words pop into my head unexpectedly, without origin or meaning. They hop away from me when I need them. There are words of many languages, Czech and English, French and Polish. But these days the German words are winning, their harsh sounds are crowding out the others. There is comfort in my mother tongue.

Ich bin. Ich bin.

When they wheel me back to my room, I concentrate on the trees shimmering outside the window. Strange, I thought they were gum trees, but now I see they are chestnuts. Mummy is here. A presence, a feeling. I can smell strudel from the other room. Warm raisins and apples. The smell of home.

I close my eyes.

'Maya . . .' It is Kate's soft voice. She is shaking me gently. Kate – the closest I ever had to a daughter. She is with a man who has wavy

dark hair, held back by his sunglasses. Stella too. She is growing big now, awkward and spindly. She clambers onto my lap like a small child.

'We've brought the wedding photos to show you,' says Kate, rummaging in her large bag for an envelope. What is she talking about? She pulls up the heavy vinyl visitor's chair next to me and lays a large photograph on the table. It shows Kate and the man, both flashing bright smiles into the camera. Stella is wearing a blue dress and her face is turned away to the side. There is an old lady in a wheelchair too. That must be Maya.

'I'll put this by the TV,' says Kate. She points to the writing underneath the photograph: Dan and Kate, October 2007.

There is something sparkling on Kate's wrist. The tiny, hard diamonds are as bright as wings. Immediately the memories fly up. I see my mother, sitting at the dining table, her chin supported on one delicate, white hand and the bracelet glinting in the candlelight. My toes curl with joy.

I grab Kate's hand.

'Thank you for coming, Mutti,' I whisper.

'Mutti will be here soon,' Kate replies. A tear runs silently down her cheek and drops onto the blanket.

The nurse speaks to them in a hushed voice. 'She's comfortable. She comes and goes, but at least she's comfortable.'

'C'mon, Stella,' says the man. Kate stands up. Her belly is large and round, like Erna's. Could it be twins? 'We'll leave you to it. I'll defrost that chicken for dinner.' He puts his arm around Kate's shoulder. She kisses him on the lips.

'Thanks, babe. I want to stay as long as I can.'

But Stella does not want to go. She snuggles into me, warm with the glow of life. I want to laugh but it comes out as a wheeze.

Kate leans in, whispering close to my face. 'Shh, shh. It's okay, darling. It's okay.' Her lips brush my ear.

I want to sit up, but I cannot. I have so many words still to say but I do not know how. Instead, I wrap my mouth around the most important words of all.

'I am,' I say. Kate nods. 'I am, I am, I am.'

Good, Kate seems to understand. I relax back as Stella tickles my arm with her forefinger. The warm sun streams through the window and lights up Stella's hair.

And there it is. My orchestra. It is playing the Radetzky March. The notes speak of joy and young love. Of yearning and fulfilment.

I smile.

I am.

Dancing towards the light.

MAYA'S DANCE

AUTHOR'S NOTE

This novel is a work of fiction. However, it is inspired by and closely based on the true account of Holocaust survivor Lucie Pollak-Langford.

I first heard Lucie's story while I was waiting for my daughter's ballet lesson to finish. One of the other mothers, Sonja, was visiting an elderly couple whom she had befriended years earlier, and she was worried that Lucie was showing early signs of dementia.

Sonja is a dance physiotherapist who met Lucie as a client. Over the years they had become extremely close friends – they had embraced each other's families, and Sonja had even become the legal guardian of Lucie and her husband, Peter.

'Lucie was in a labour camp during the Holocaust,' Sonja told me, as the strains of our daughters' ballet music wafted from the studio. 'One of the guards saw her dance and fell in love with her, and he got her out.'

From that moment, I have been consumed with Lucie's story. I accessed her documented experiences in her self-published book, *My Memoir*, and from several hours of oral testimony she recorded in the nineties as part of Stephen Spielberg's USC Shoah Foundation project. I also conducted extensive research, including from numerous survivor testimonies, interviews, and a trip to Auschwitz, Sawin, Sobibór and Majdanek in Poland.

The fundamentals of Lucie's story are the same as Maya's. She grew up in Brno, Czechoslovakia, and was transported to a labour camp in

Sawin via Terezín. She danced at a concert held in the camp and a Polish engineer, Jan Hensel, fell in love with her. Her mother, Irene, and stepfather, Felix, both perished before Jan helped Lucie to escape, hiding her underneath a bakery and then behind a cabinet in his parents' apartment in Chelm. She then lived for two years undercover in Germany as a Polish slave worker. Lucie was Sawin's only known survivor.

Kate's story and the way she finally locates Jan is fiction, although some of the people who help her and Maya along the way are based on real characters. In reality, Lucie searched for Jan throughout her life, but by the time she located him he had passed away from liver cancer that his family believed was caused by fallout from the Chernobyl nuclear disaster. At Lucie's instigation, Jan, his sister, Danuta, and his mother, Eufrozyna, were formally recognised as Righteous Among the Nations for their bravery in 1998.

I have changed Lucie's story in some significant ways. Lucie was just fifteen when she arrived in Sawin, and Jan was twenty-three when she met him. While perhaps it was more normal in the 1940s than it is today for a teenager to consort with an older man, the eight-year age difference does call into question Jan's motives for forming a relationship with a Jewish prisoner. Despite the obvious power imbalance, I firmly believe his intentions were honourable – he never took advantage of Lucie, and he went on to risk his own life, repeatedly, to save her and others. However, in my fictional rendering of the story I did not want this issue to distract from the narrative. So, after much thought, I accepted the advice of several readers to narrow the age gap.

It is impossible as a twenty-first century writer to properly convey the horror of what occurred in the labour camps in Poland, and I sincerely apologise to any survivors who may be offended by my inadequate attempts to do so. The Nazi atrocities described in the book are dramatised, but all of them reflect real life accounts. For example, the description of Christmas Eve is based on a true event that occurred on 24 December 1940 at Auschwitz-Birkenau, when the SS set up a Christmas tree, complete with electric lights, in the Appellplatz and placed beneath it the bodies of prisoners who had frozen to death as a 'present' for the living. The accounts of abuse of the Jewish prisoners and of local Polish villagers are based on Lucie's memoir and the trial records of Teodor Ondyt, the sadistic camp commandant whose name I have not changed. The shooting of Rachel is described in Lucie's book also.

The description of Sawin is loosely based on Lucie's account, though much of it is imagined. I visited Sawin in 2020 but could not find any remnant of the camp (or the bakery), although the little bridge over a drainage channel is still there. The stories of daily life in the camp are all based on fact. The food, the shoes, the slipping out of the camp at night, trading with Poles at the perimeter fence, and even the pancakes and birthday cake are all true. That prisoners in the Holocaust experienced starvation, exhaustion, typhus, random beatings and executions is well-known.

However, my geography of the camp, the village, the various houses and surrounding settlements is fiction, as are the descriptions of wartime Chelm and Warsaw. The details of the escape of prisoners from Sobibór based on recorded history, and the account of the Warsaw Uprising draws from the eyewitness account of Andrew Borowiec. Any inaccuracies are unintentional but inevitable.

Incredibly, it is true that the prisoners staged a cabaret in the camp in Sawin in 1942. Performances were not uncommon among inmates during the Holocaust – those in Terezín are well documented, and there was an orchestra in Auschwitz. I have borrowed the substance of the different acts I describe from several different accounts of concerts that were staged elsewhere. For example, some of my inspiration came from the musical *Prince Bettliegend*, written in Terezín and performed in 2017 at the University of Sydney. The song my prisoners sing, '*Denn wir tragen den Willen zum Leben im Blut*', was in reality a song written in 1938 by Fritz Löhner-Beda (lyrics) and Hermann Leopoldi (melody) in Buchenwald concentration camp. The mime act was inspired by an account of the life of Marcel Marceau.

Much of *Maya's Dance* is invented for dramatic effect. Erna and Pavel were real people, as were the twins, but I do not know whether they were related. Tragically, the twins who were born in the camp in Sawin suffered the same fate as those in the novel. Neither Erna nor Pavel survived. Maya's dash to the midwife is fiction, as is her private dance for the Commandant – although Lucie does describe meeting another camp commander who nearly blew her cover in Chelm. Jan's father was indeed chief of police at the time, but Jan's interactions with his family and the details of the AK activity in Warsaw and Chelm are all imagined.

I have made some omissions, too. In real life, there was another hero in Lucie's escape – a young German guard called Hans, who offered to help her because she did not look like a Jew. Distraught, Jan agreed to give her up to Hans so that she might survive. After a week in which she hid in Hans's room, trying to avoid his advances, Jan came to collect her and took her to the cellar. The Hans in *Maya's Dance* is a different character, and I would like to acknowledge here the important role the real Hans played in saving Lucie's life.

Finally, the account of Maya's life after the Holocaust is fiction. Lucie had three husbands, including Peter DeKlerk, to whom she was happily married for many years and who survives her. Peter told me that Lucie was the love of his life. While supportive of this project, he very sensibly asked me to change my protagonist's name for the novel. Lucie's favourite name had been Maria since her days in the convent, and that is why I chose Maya/Maria.

Due to the pandemic, I only got to meet Lucie once, in a residential facility near my home in northern Sydney. By then her dementia had advanced too far to hold a conversation, but she held my hand and squeezed it rhythmically as we spoke. I felt that she radiated calm and light.

Lucie died in 2021 with Sonja and Peter by her side. Like many Holocaust survivors, she wanted her story to be told. She was firm that she could not spend her life hating Germans; in fact, she believed that many of those she met during the war were good people. She never lost her strong will to survive, to put one foot in front of the other. She lived for the moment. She loved life. *Maya's Dance* is not a biography or Lucie's truth, it is Maya's story told through my eyes. But I have tried to stay true to the essence of Lucie's message. I hope I have done her justice.

ACKNOWLEDGEMENTS

Peter, I wish I had had the chance to know Lucie properly. Reading her memoir and listening to her testimony changed my life; I feel that she has taught me so much about the good in the world. You have been incredibly generous in allowing me to imagine some of Lucie's experiences in *Maya's Dance*, and in taking the time to talk to me about her. You will never know how much it has meant to me. Thank you.

Sonja, thank you for your friendship and your care for my family. Thank you for telling me about Lucie all those years ago, for introducing me to her family, for helping me to understand her world view, and for so patiently responding to all my texts and emails as the book took shape. I am truly, truly grateful.

I never realised how many people it would take to bring a book into the world. Thank you to the wonderful team at Simon & Schuster, especially Cass Di Bello, who instantly fell in love with Maya's story and whose recommendations brought the novel to life. Massive thanks also to Michelle Swainson and Rosie Outred for your efficiency and kindness in shepherding this demanding debut author through the publishing process, to Anna O'Grady for checking the Polish, to Fleur Hamilton and Gabby Oberman for your professionalism and support, and to Tricia Dearborn and Vanessa Pellatt for your sensitive editing and eagle eyes.

I am indebted to Pippa Masson at Curtis Brown, who pulled my story out of the submissions inbox. Do you realise what it's like to finally get an email saying, 'I have so enjoyed reading and am interested in talking further'? I am thrilled to have you in my corner. And huge thanks to the insanely talented Caitlan Cooper-Trent, who made the first structural suggestions that turned my muddled narrative into the novel I had always hoped it could be.

When I first decided to try my hand at fiction writing, I honestly had no idea where to start. Thank goodness I decided to sign up for the Faber Writing Academy's 'Writing a novel' course. It turned this old journo into a novelist. Kathryn Heyman, you are the most brilliant writer and entertaining teacher imaginable. James Bradley, your mentorship and guidance gave me so many lightbulb moments and kept me going from start to finish – thank you so much. Through Faber I met my darling Twinklings – Ali, Andrea, Carla, Jen, Judy, Kim, Liz and the indomitable Shona. I have simply loved sharing this writing journey with you. Thank you from the bottom of my heart for your wise suggestions about the text and your never-ending positivity.

Thank you, too, to the other readers of my early drafts – Ella (you are so clever), Karin (your turn next!), Marge (*every* writer needs a Marge), and especially my dear friend Andrea for her amazing ideas and advice, and for being possibly the only person in the world who would agree to speed with me through rural Poland in the middle of COVID to visit three Holocaust museums in three days. And for the emergency pierogi and vodka.

There are many people whom I would like to thank for their help with my research for *Maya's Dance*. I am deeply grateful to Tinny Lenthen and everyone at the Sydney Jewish Museum who gave their valuable time and insights. I am especially grateful to the Holocaust survivors who have shared their stories so eloquently, hoping it can never happen again. If only the world would listen. Thank you to Associate Professor Ian Maxwell of The University of Sydney for his insights into performance during the Holocaust, and to the amazing team at the United States Holocaust Memorial Museum, who have always so quickly and efficiently responded to my requests.

A key interview I did at the early stages of my research was with Zimra Segall of Jewish Care in Sydney, whose thoughtful descriptions of Holocaust survivors' experiences of dementia are woven throughout the book. I was privileged to gain further help from Montefiore, an aged care organisation that shared with me training resources on this subject. Thank you to Professor Susan Kurrle of The University of Sydney for taking the time out of her busy life to answer my questions about dementia management in the nineties. And thank you to the carers at Pax Hill Care Home in the UK, who looked after my own beautiful mother during her long years with advanced dementia. You treat your patients with such dignity and respect, and you have made me realise how all life, however fragile and impermanent, has value.

Thank you to Emma Slaytor and Marlena Stanhope, who helped me choose the music that forms the soundtrack to the novel, and for everyone who advised me on the German, Polish and Czech words: Lucie and Marie Rychetnik and her Polish-speaking neighbours, Daniel and Marie Davies (it was harder than I thought to describe how a Czech speaker might pronounce Polish!) as well as Jozefa Sobski, Danuta Szczypior and Maria Picknell.

I would also like to acknowledge the wonderful writers and researchers whose work has influenced this book: Viktor E Frankl and Eddie Jaku, of course, for describing their experiences and providing detailed insights into the psychology of those who lived through the Holocaust; Julia Baird and Leigh Sales, whose books helped me imagine how someone might find strength and beauty after trauma (Leigh, sorry I pinched one of your questions for my fictitious journalist!), and to writers Andrew Zielinski and Andrew Borowiec for their compelling accounts of wartime Poland.

There is also a host of people without whose support for me personally this book would not have been possible. Thank you to my business partner, Tim, and my colleagues Ainsley, Cindy and everyone at the

Prevention Centre for your help and encouragement. To my fellow book lovers Alison, Anna, Bev, Donna, Estelle, Fiona, Helen, Janice and Meredith – you have kept me reading over so many years; your critique of this book is really the only one that counts. And special thanks to Debbie, who has been so generous in putting words around loss and grief, many of which I have given to Maya.

Finally, I have the most supportive family imaginable. Thank you to the McCrindles and my extended family in the UK for always having my back. Dad, I have loved discussing writing with you, even if we disagree on the value of editors. Thank you for your writing genes. Pete, I could not have done this without your love and belief in me. Thank you for your unwavering optimism and for having exactly the reaction I hoped for the first time you read the book. Ella, Jamie and Katie – you are still my greatest achievements. I love you.

READING GROUP QUESTIONS

1. While Jan saved Maya's life, and she thought of him as one of the great loves of her life, there was a clear power imbalance in their relationship. Do you think it is ever acceptable for a guard to start a relationship with a prisoner?

2. Do you believe the two would have been romantically involved if they had met in different circumstances? Do you think they were really in love?

3. Besides her relationship with Jan, what else helped Maya endure the conditions in the camp and stay alive?

4. Do you have a passion for something the way Maya feels about dance? How does that make you feel?

5. Maya saw good in people and the world around her, even amid the most unimaginable horror of the Holocaust. What can she teach us about how we approach our own lives?

6. Maya's memory fails her later in life, yet she remembers much about her time in the camp. To what extent can we trust her recounting of it? How do you think trauma has impacted her memory?

7. What are your observations about Kate and Maya's relationship? Have you ever developed a special bond or trust with someone whose life experiences are very different from your own?

8. Many people risked their lives to help Maya. Do you think you would have helped a Jew, even if you knew it would put your family's life in danger?

9. What do you think is the role of fiction in respect of the Holocaust and other important historical events? How does fiction differ to first-hand accounts and historical records?

10. 'It was hate, pure and simple. You do not know what it is to be hated like that, Kate. Hated so much that we were to be removed from this Earth.' Discuss the degree of hate in the world today – and what can be done about it.

ABOUT THE AUTHOR

Helen Signy is an Australian writer who grew up in England – or, depending how she feels that day, an English writer who lives in Australia. She spent much of her youth travelling the world before becoming a print journalist in Asia and then in Sydney. Most of her writing these days involves science communications for academics, governments and not-for-profits, but she has never lost her passion for telling an amazing story. *Maya's Dance* is her first foray into fiction. Helen lives on the Northern Beaches in Sydney with her husband, Peter, and, at various times, her (nearly) grown-up children, Ella, Jamie and Katie.